RESCUING KAYE

Guardian Hostage Rescue Specialists: BRAVO Team

ELLIE MASTERS

JEM Publishing

Editor: Erin Toland

Proofreader: Roxane Leblanc

Published in the United States of America

JEM Publishing

This is a work of fiction. While reference might be made to actual historical events or existing locations, the names, characters, businesses, places, and incidents are either the product of the author's imagination or are used fictitiously, and any resemblance to actual persons, living or dead, business establishments, events, or locales is entirely coincidental.

ISBN: 978-1-952625-72-5

Dedication

*This book is dedicated to my one and only——my amazing and wonderful
husband.*
Without your care and support, my writing would not have made it this far.
You pushed me when I needed to be pushed.
You supported me when I felt discouraged.
You believed in me when I didn't believe in myself.
If it weren't for you, this book never would have come to life.

Also by Ellie Masters

The LIGHTER SIDE

Ellie Masters is the lighter side of the Jet & Ellie Masters writing duo! You will find Contemporary Romance, Military Romance, Romantic Suspense, Billionaire Romance, and Rock Star Romance in Ellie's Works.

YOU CAN FIND ELLIE'S BOOKS HERE:

ELLIEMASTERS.COM/BOOKS

Military Romance

Guardian Hostage Rescue Specialists

Rescuing Melissa

(Get a FREE copy of Rescuing Melissa

when you join Ellie's Newsletter)

Alpha Team

Rescuing Zoe

Rescuing Moira

Rescuing Eve

Rescuing Lily

Rescuing Jinx

Rescuing Maria

Bravo Team

Rescuing Angie

Rescuing Isabelle

Rescuing Carmen

Rescuing Rosalie

Rescuing Kaye

Cara's Protector

Rescuing Barbi

Military Romance

Guardian Personal Protection Specialists

Sybil's Protector

Lyra's Protector

The One I Want Series

(Small Town, Military Heroes)

By Jet & Ellie Masters

EACH BOOK IN THIS SERIES CAN BE READ AS A STANDALONE AND IS ABOUT A DIFFERENT COUPLE WITH AN HEA.

Saving Abby

Saving Ariel

Saving Brie

Saving Cate

Saving Dani

Saving Jen

Rockstar Romance

The Angel Fire Rock Romance Series

EACH BOOK IN THIS SERIES CAN BE READ AS A STANDALONE AND IS ABOUT A DIFFERENT COUPLE WITH AN HEA. IT IS RECOMMENDED THEY ARE READ IN ORDER.

Ashes to New (prequel)

Heart's Insanity (book 1)

Heart's Desire (book 2)

Heart's Collide (book 3)

Hearts Divided (book 4)

Hearts Entwined (book5)

Forest's FALL (book 6)

Hearts The Last Beat (book7)

Contemporary Romance

Firestorm

(Kristy Bromberg's Everyday Heroes World)

Billionaire Romance
Billionaire Boys Club

Hawke

Richard

Brody

Contemporary Romance

Cocky Captain

(Vi Keeland & Penelope Ward's Cocky Hero World)

Romantic Suspense

Each book is a standalone novel.

The Starling

~AND~

Science Fiction

Ellie Masters writing as L.A. Warren

Vendel Rising: a Science Fiction Serialized Novel

To My Readers

This book is a work of fiction. It does not exist in the real world and should not be construed as reality. As in most romantic fiction, I've taken liberties. I've compressed the romance into a sliver of time. I've allowed these characters to develop strong bonds of trust over a matter of days.

This does not happen in real life where you, my amazing readers, live. Take more time in your romance and learn who you're giving a piece of your heart to. I urge you to move with caution. Always protect yourself.

ONE

Kaye

———

My phone buzzes like a relentless swarm of angry bees; each text more aggressive than the last. Every word more cruel. More threatening.

Kaye, don't ignore me.

My ex-boyfriend, ex-lover, and ex-professor (don't judge) demands I respond, but I remain silent. Less than five seconds later, that demand turns ugly.

Dammit, answer me!

My hands curl into tight fists as his words seep into my soul like poison.

This isn't over until I say it's over.

Anger boils inside me, and there's something else lingering in the background. It's something I'm not ready to acknowledge.

You'll regret this. You'll regret leaving me.

Barbi, my best friend, notices the tense look on my face and comes over to where I sit on the couch. Taking the phone from my trembling hands, she swipes the screen and looks at the messages. A gasp of shock follows as she reads Scott's texts.

"You've got to block him." Her tone's firm. Her voice hard and unyielding. "He's trying to manipulate you and it's going too far. These are threats."

I retrieve my phone as another text buzzes in.

Darling, we need to talk about this.

The phone rings and I press cancel, declining the call.

You're acting like a child.

I clench my fingers around my phone and bite down, grinding my molars. I flop back on the couch and wonder.

Answer the damn phone.

Is he right?

Did I overreact?

Should we talk it out like Scott says?

Barbi gives me a stern look. "He's a lying, cheating, bastard, and this is going too far."

"He's just upset."

"Why do you keep defending him?"

"I don't know." I shrug, feeling defeated. "Maybe I should give him a chance to tell his side of the story?"

"What side would that be? That you caught him fucking Denise Hamilton in his office? It's not like his clothes spontaneously fell off and his dick slipped in that tramp's cunt. You saw what you saw. It happened. And he's trying to deny it. Worse. He's trying to blame you."

"But…" I place my phone in my lap and wring my hands as uncertainty about the whole horrible thing twists in my gut.

"No buts about it. You called things off. End of story."

My thoughts race in circles. I need to protect myself, but also keep my dreams alive. This is where the fear comes in.

"If I make him angry… If he gets Dean Alder to pull my spot, all my hard work goes up in smoke."

"If he dares to yank your spot in vet school, I'm going straight to his office and will feed him his balls. He doesn't have…"

"Don't."

"Why not?"

"Because he'll retaliate. You know how important this is to me."

"I don't know why you won't report him. Carmen and I will be right by your side." She spins around and drops onto the couch beside me. "He's sleeping with his students, you and Denise. Who knows how many others? That's a fireable offense. Let the university deal with it. If he retaliates…"

"He'll do it to spite me. To teach me a lesson." Barbi doesn't understand the power he holds over me. "All my dreams will go up in smoke."

"Then you find another veterinary school to attend."

I'm caught in a tug-of-war between being safe and taking a risk. If I say nothing, Scott wins. If I go back to him, who knows how long he'll be pulling my strings? If I report him, the chance I'll ruin my future is too much of a risk. I take in a shaky breath and let it out real slow.

Professor Scott Parker may hold my future in his hands, but I'm the one responsible for giving him that power in the first place. I was so eager to get into UC Davis's highly competitive veterinary program that I didn't stop his advances. I encouraged them, precisely because I knew he could help me.

I used him.

This is my fault. I'm the one to blame and now I'm paying the price for trying to take a shortcut. Scott seduced me with his power and dominance. He knew exactly what strings to pull to get me into his bed and keep me there. He also knew how desperate I was to get into vet school. I'm such an idiot.

"I did this to myself." I curl in on myself, angry and frustrated for getting myself into this mess. "I'm stuck between a rock and a hard place."

"But you don't have to get out of this by yourself. Carmen and I are here for you, and Rosalie will be too."

Rosalie is new to Barbi and me. New in that we've never met, but she grew up with Carmen, and the way Carmen talks about her childhood friend makes it feel as if we know Rosalie too. Now, Rosalie's moving in with us, and our little trio is becoming a quartet of sisters by choice.

Barbi's the optimist.

Carmen's the risk taker.

Rosalie is a survivor.

I'm the idiot.

Professor Scott Parker can crush my dreams in an instant. All it takes is one phone call to Dean Alder, head of Veterinary Medicine at UC Davis, who happens to be Scott's best friend, and I'm kicked out on my ass before I have a chance to begin.

Again, this is my fault.

Barbi wraps an arm around my shoulder and squeezes in reassurance. "You can do it, Kaye. I know you can. There's always another way."

"I just need to figure out how to handle this." I don't dare tell Barbi the best solution is to cave into Scott's demands.

"How about we start by blocking that asshole from your life?" Barbi's relentless. Like a mother bear protecting her own, she's not going to let this go.

But I can't let her fight my battles. This is my mess to fix.

"I'm not going to do that." I sit up straight and inject confidence into my words. No surprise, but I fail completely.

"Why not?"

"Because…"

"You're still hung up on him, aren't you?"

"I don't want to burn bridges I might need later. It's not just the scholarship. He can…"

My phone buzzes with another text. I grit my teeth, expecting another threatening text, but it's our bestie, Carmen. A profound feeling of relief rushes through me.

"They're ten minutes out." I squeal with excitement, eager to meet Rosalie. Carmen's told us so much about her that I feel like we're already the best of friends.

"Crap, they're early." Barbi glances at her watch.

"So?" I shrug because it doesn't matter.

Only Barbi is far more OCD than me.

"We haven't moved your things out of your room." She hops up from the couch and claps her hands. "Come on, your things won't pack themselves."

It's been only a couple of weeks since graduation, but it feels as if it's been a lifetime. The day Carmen, Barbi, and I graduated from UCSF, we were headed out for an amazing night on the town. Only, Carmen's father sent his goons to escort her home to Nicaragua. Which left Barbi and me to celebrate alone.

And boy, did we party.

We had a fabulous night.

Carmen, however, entered what can only be described as a living hell. Her father basically kidnapped her and held her hostage. He arranged a loveless marriage to a tyrant of a man, and Carmen had no way out.

At least until a group called the Guardian Hostage Rescue Specialists came into the picture. They were rescuing a woman named Isabelle LaCroix, and Carmen hijacked that rescue.

Suffice it to say, Carmen went back to her father. Which sounds bad. But she did it as part of a plan by the Guardians to free the women her father was trafficking. She acted as a cool, super-secret double agent. Part of that rescue, something she insisted on, included freeing her childhood friend, Rosalie.

Only things didn't go as planned.

Carmen spent the better half of a week beside herself with

worry over Rosalie's safety while the Guardians launched another rescue mission to get Rosalie back.

That was a few days ago.

Now Rosalie's moving in with us. She's finally here, and I couldn't be more excited.

The day Carmen called to tell us Rosalie was safe, a great weight lifted off my shoulders. I'm thrilled we're here for Carmen to not only celebrate her reunion with Rosalie but to welcome her into our little girl-gang.

But even with the great news, this thing with Scott hangs over me. I have to find a way to deal with my ex-boyfriend, and former professor, and the way he's trying to manipulate me. I take one last look at the phone before shutting it off, then slide it into my back pocket.

Barbi's right. I need to find another way to deal with Scott.

Somehow, I'll figure it out. Until then, I follow Barbi into what used to be my room and begin packing up my things.

Since I'm moving to UC Davis as soon as the fall semester begins, I don't technically need my room in our little townhouse. Barbi and I are going to share her room for the summer. Then, I'll move to a small studio apartment at Davis.

As for Rosalie, she literally has nothing. She escaped Nicaragua with nothing but the clothes on her back. We're hoping UCSF will accept her into their undergraduate program. Carmen says she knows people with pull who can make that happen. Which means Rosalie needs a place to stay. I'm happy to give her my room.

I guess we'll see.

In the meantime, Barbi and I rush around my room like two lunatics, throwing clothes in suitcases and cardboard boxes. We drag those from my room upstairs into Barbi's room downstairs. We make a total mess of things and are nowhere near done when Carmen's text comes in that they're almost here.

Barbi and I sprint down the stairs and fly out the front door to wait outside.

"Do you see them?" I lift on tiptoe, peering down the street.

"Do you think it's just the two of them?" She ignores my little dig. "Or do you think they brought some Guardian muscle to help?"

"Get your mind out of the gutter." I know exactly what's going through Barbi's head.

Over the past week, when Carmen was going out of her mind, worried about Rosalie, her new beau, Rafe, who is a Guardian, spent several nights with us. If the other Guardians look anything like him…

"Tell me you're not eager to lay eyes on one of those Guardians." Barbi jabs me in the ribs. "Sexy Navy SEALs? Hot as sin Hostage Rescue Specialists? Gorgeous Guardians? Lord, that word alone is enough to make a girl swoon. And you know they're all like Rafe. Tall, handsome, and packed with muscle upon muscle upon muscle."

"Dang, girl, you need to get laid." I shove her playfully.

"That's exactly what I'm thinking. I call dibs."

"Dibs?"

"That's what I said."

"On what exactly?"

"I'm getting me a Guardian."

"Sex on the brain. You've got sex on the brain."

"Well, unlike a certain someone who's been banging her professor for the last two years…" Barbi lifts two fingers to emphasize her point. "I've been solo for the better part of the year."

"Solo, yes, but you've been far from abstinent. Or do I need to remind you about graduation night?"

Her cheeks turn crimson and she pointedly turns away. We tore up the town grad night.

"We're not talking about grad night." Even though we're alone on the sidewalk, Barbi hushes her voice.

"Well, you can have any of the Guardians you want. I'm swearing off men for the time being. They're too much work."

"Foxes in the hen house!" Barbi shrieks, throwing her hands over her head and pointing down the block. "I see them."

Foxes in the hen house? I shake my head. Barbi comes up with some of the weirdest imagery.

My heart races and a chill rushes through me as a black SUV rolls through the intersection a block away. The engine growls like a wild beast, and every nerve in my body stands on end. It's like the car has a presence; a hum of power radiating from its dark body.

Or maybe that comes from the men inside.

And yes, there are men. Four Guardians. More than enough to go around.

When the SUV pulls up to the curb, all four doors pop open in unison, and four daunting figures step out. Somehow, they occupy the entirety of the space around them. Not just that. They search the streets for threats with deadly glares and hawk-like intensity.

The air around the men crackles with energy. The heat radiating from the hunky men oozes sex appeal. My gaze is drawn to the four Guardians standing tall and proud, their eyes glowing with an inner fire. Jaw-dropping, hot-as-sin, these men are a sight to behold.

As soon as Carmen and Rosalie emerge from the vehicle, Barbi and I rush to our friend and embrace her in a tight hug. Carmen squeezes us back; her relief a palpable thing.

"We're so glad you're home." My voice shakes with emotion.

"I'm glad to be home." Carmen pulls away and extends her hand to Rosalie. "Barbi, Kaye, I want you to meet Rosalie."

Rosalie steps close. Barbi and I throw our arms around her, welcoming her into our four-way hug of sisters-by-choice. Our happy tears form a river of love and affection between us. We're bathed in that moment as the four Guardians watch vigilantly for any signs of danger, ready and willing to defend us at a moment's notice.

The tearful reunion lingers until Carmen turns to me. "Barbi told me what happened with the professor." Her voice is heavy with sorrow for what this breakup means to me. "I'm so sorry things didn't work out."

I turn to Carmen and the words catch in my throat. I should say something—anything—but the name clinging to the edge of my tongue is the one person I can never mention in this house ever again.

I grasp Rosalie's hands and give a welcoming squeeze. "You are taking my room."

"Oh, no. I couldn't possibly. I can stay with Carmen."

"Nope. It's been decided. It's not totally cleared of my stuff, but I'm so happy to finally meet you." I swallow with a bit of a lump forming in the back of my throat.

What feels like a lifetime ago, this quaint little townhouse was mine. Now, it's changing hands. Welcoming Rosalie. It will no longer be mine; maybe never be mine again. Barbi and Carmen will stay. Their lives are here. I'm the one whose dreams pull me away.

Change isn't something I want, but it's inevitable. Like jumping off a cliff—there's no turning back. No matter how much it hurts. Nevertheless, it's something I must do. My heart's heavy leaving my friends, but I'm excited to be taking this next step toward my lifetime dream.

Movement out of the corner of my eye snags my attention. My gaze latches onto a strange figure slipping through the entrance of the drugstore on the corner. He's dressed in black, with a hood shielding his face.

I don't know who it is, but a chill slithers down my spine; like I've been plunged into an icy pool. It can't be Scott. He wouldn't sneak around like that. He's the kind of man who tackles things head on.

This weird reaction is nothing. I'm seeing threats only because the Guardians actively look for them, because that's what a Guardian does. That man ducking into the drugstore is just a man; a stranger I don't know.

He's not Scott.

Yet suddenly, my fear intensifies. What if it is? What if he's spying on me? Or looking for an opening to force me to talk with him? He'd do that. Confront me on the street, in public, where I won't be able to escape without making a scene.

Suddenly, Rosalie pulls me in for a hug. "You're too gracious offering your room. I feel bad that I'm making you move out of it."

I blink, trying to return to the conversation going on around me.

"Don't worry about it, and you're not making me move out." I give her a reassuring smile. "I'm going to be gone end of summer as it is. This is your home now, and it makes more sense than you sharing a room with Carmen until I leave." I turn toward Carmen and smirk. "Didn't know you were bringing the heat."

I'm about to have some fun with Barbi, but the moment my gaze lands on the driver, I'm struck dumb.

His sheer physical presence overwhelms me. Tremendously tall, his square-cut jaw and distinguished chin command attention. His eyes carry a wild intensity that pins me in place. He stands six-plus and his muscles ripple beneath his clothes, tense and poised for action. A wave of raw masculinity radiates off of him in pulses so strong I'm paralyzed by the intensity of it.

I can't tell if I'm attracted or repelled by the sheer strength of his presence. Which says a lot since dominant men attract me like flies to honey. Either way, I'm frozen in place like a mouse staring down the face of a lion.

When Carmen makes introductions, I swallow hard and the word "Hi" barely makes it out of my mouth. I extend my hand, feeling like I'm treading dangerously, inviting disaster, even though desire engulfs every cell in my body. This stranger stirs a latent heat I didn't realize was slumbering.

The moment our hands touch, heat spreads like a bonfire, singeing every inch of me until I'm a quivering mess.

Where the hell did that come from?

"Name's Zeb. Nice to meet you, little mouse."

Little mouse? Did he read my mind?

He doesn't release my hand, holding it far longer than a normal handshake should last. Electricity surges between us, buzzing and humming with pleasure. Raising goose bumps on my skin. Sending heat radiating up my arm where it delves deep to my core.

His gaze roams my entire body with undeniable hunger. It's a deliberate and calculated assessment, like he's drinking me in.

Devouring me.

His lips curl into a slow, dangerous smile. That smile sends shockwaves rippling through me. It might be presumptuous to be thinking this, but something tells me this is no ordinary *Hello*. The promise of dark and dangerous things—sinful things—hangs between us. I may regret giving up my single room.

I'm rooted to the spot, unable to tear my eyes away from Zeb, but then a different kind of chill runs down my spine. There it is again, movement in the corner of my eye. My skin crawls, because in my gut, I know who it is.

Scott stands at the corner by the drugstore, radiating jealousy and rage.

His gaze is like a weapon shooting through the air, aimed directly at me. For the first time in my life, I feel real fear.

Carmen's voice breaks the trance, telling me it's time to go, but I can't move. Scott's come for a fight and this is only the beginning of something far worse.

"Hey, beautiful, how about you let go of my hand so I can help the guys bring stuff in?" Zeb's words pull me out of my dream-like state, forcing me to look at him. "Is everything all right?"

"It's nothing."

"Doesn't look like nothing." The concerned expression on his face says he isn't fooled.

I run my hands up and down my arms. This time, the goose bumps aren't from the electricity pulsing between me and Zeb. It's from something else entirely.

"Where is everyone?" I look around and realize we're alone.

"They're inside." His voice is as steady as steel as he forces me to meet his gaze head-on. "You sure you're okay?"

My heart pounds away like a kettle drum and I shiver as icy tendrils slither down my spine. I try to brush off his question with a shrug, but he isn't having it. Zeb places a sturdy hand on my shoulder. He knows something's wrong. He also knows I'm too afraid to tell him.

"I'm fine."

"You don't look fine."

"Well, I am." I'm not going to debate this with a stranger. I shrug off his hand and march up the small set of stairs leading into the townhouse.

While the Guardians bring in Rosalie's meager things, I pull out my phone. To my surprise, there are no new texts from Scott. I slide down the wall and tuck my knees into my chest.

Why is this happening to me?

Because you decided to play with fire and slept with your professor.

True.

I'm my own worst enemy when it comes to men.

TWO

Zeb

What an interesting woman. The way Kaye goes from heating up to cooling off flips all the switches in my head. Talk about kicking my protective instincts into overdrive. Kaye did that in spades, and all within minutes of meeting the sultry blonde.

But how?

How did she evoke this animalistic reaction?

How did she trigger my need to ease her pain from whatever it is she fears? And what dumped ice water on that initial flash of heat between us?

No way in hell did I imagine that spark. That primal rush. That thrill of something new. Or the way it was suddenly snuffed out?

As she flees up the stairs, I can't help but watch her go.

She's an enigma. A puzzle. A beautiful woman with long, blonde hair that bounces and flows with her graceful ascent up the stairs. I could watch her all day long.

What triggered her?

Is she running from someone? Something? The way she climbs those stairs reminds me of a scared little mouse fleeing a predator.

Is it me?

No. Not me. It was something else.

Doing my best to focus on what triggered her flight, I turn to the street.

A mother pushes a stroller down the sidewalk. Her attention zeroes in on her baby. Across the street, a teen walks five dogs at once, completely oblivious to the world around him with his attention glued to his cellphone. Cars drive past intermittently; a steady stream, but not enough to choke the street. A bit of wind blows through trees planted as part of the city's attempt to turn a busy city into a park.

It doesn't work.

A man, dressed all in black, stands near the corner next to the drugstore. Our eyes lock for a moment and a flash of rage spans the gap. Before I fully process it, he turns away and flags down a passing cab. The man's gone before I blink. There are others. Small groups of people cluster together here and there, smoking cigarettes, talking quietly, but no one appears the least bit interested in this particular townhouse, except that man.

Is he the reason Kaye ran like the devil was on her heels?

There's only one way to figure this one out. The question is, will Kaye open up to a stranger? She wasn't exactly forthcoming, but I know how to warm a woman up.

After my quick search of the surrounding area reveals no threats, I head inside, taking the stairs two at a time. She left the door open, which isn't a surprise considering we're moving Rosalie in. On my way in, Hayes shoulders past me, heading to the SUV for the last of his woman's things. Rafe follows, but he stops to look at my empty hands.

"Forget something?" Rafe's lips twist in a sardonic smirk.

"Huh?"

"The car isn't going to unload itself." He grabs my arm, spins me around, and marches me out of the quaint townhouse. "I saw the way you looked at Kaye."

"I didn't look at her any which way." I brush off his comment, dismissing it with a shrug.

"Says the lion to the mouse." Rafe tosses one of Carmen's suitcases to me. "Take that, Hayes and I got the rest."

"Don't be an ass." I snag the suitcase as it flies through the air and give Rafe an unamused look.

"You may not want to chase that one, is all I'm saying." He and Hayes exchange a look, then turn their combined gazes on me filled with a heavy dose of *I-know-what-you're-thinking* and *Don't-do-it*.

"Why the fuck do you care?" I try to dismiss them.

Looks like Kaye's achieved some kind of sacred saint status with my teammates.

"Because I know your track record with women." Rafe tries to berate me, but that isn't going to fly.

"None of your fucking business who I…"

"Don't fuck with Kaye," Hayes steps in, jumping into the conversation with attitude.

"Not planning on…" Can't really finish that statement because I have every intention of pursuing that weird flash of electricity when Kaye and I touched for the first time.

"Just don't mess with her. Okay?" Rafe grabs the last bag out of the back of the SUV and gives me one of his looks. "Is it that hard to keep your junk in your jeans?"

"What the fuck is it with the two of you? Just because you're with Carmen, and you're with Rosalie, doesn't give you the right to dictate…"

"Gives us every damn right." Hayes crosses his arms over his chest, posturing like a fucking asshole. "Those women are tight. Sister-tight. You fuck with one, you fuck with them all. And if you fuck with my Rosalie, you and I are going to exchange more than words."

"The two of you are way out of line. Not to mention pussy-whipped. And it's not like I'm going to…"

"Just saying it now, so it doesn't come as a surprise later." Rafe stands shoulder to shoulder with Hayes. The two of them stare me down. "Kaye and Barbi are off limits."

"Off limits? You don't get to tell me…"

"But we just did." Hayes makes it very clear he and Rafe are united in this. "There are plenty of women jumping at the chance to ride your mythical dick. Just don't fuck with Kaye."

Interesting how he leaves Barbi out of his comment. Didn't think anyone noticed the little exchange between me and Kaye. Should've known better. Nothing gets past Rafe and Hayes. It's one of the many things that makes them good at their jobs.

Fucking cock-blockers.

"You guys are just pissed because your women didn't cave to your demands that they stay on Guardian HQ grounds. Don't take out your shit on me, and stop telling me who I can, and can't, fuck."

"And that's exactly why we're going to have a problem." Rafe pokes me in the chest, leaning into it with his pointy-assed finger pressing hard. "It's bad enough Carmen and Rosalie don't listen. Hayes and I are going to be around 24/7 until things are finished with Carmen's father. If you fuck up the vibe around here by being a dick to Kaye, that's going to make things uncomfortable both here and at work."

"Fuck you." I grip his finger and give it a good twist. "What I've done with chicks has never been an issue before, and it's never messed with the team. If something like this is going to be a problem, then we've got bigger issues than who I fuck or don't fuck, and it's not like I'm an ass when it comes to women. I'm very respectful of the women I date."

What the fuck?

The guys are lifetime-relationship-serious when it comes to Carmen and Rosalie, but where is this Nth-level protectiveness coming from when it comes to the girls' friends?

"For the record, I may date a lot of women, but I never fuck them over." Totally losing my cool that they think so poorly of me. "Everything is consensual from start to finish."

"It's the finish we're worried about." Rafe gives me a look. "The string of broken hearts you leave behind is miles long. Don't need any of that shit here."

"Maybe the two of you keep your noses out of my business?" My tone's argumentative, but only because they're right. "Not my fault your women don't listen to you. Don't take that aggravation out on me. I haven't done shit."

"Yet." Hayes mumbles under his breath.

Neither one of them is happy. They want Carmen and Rosalie to stay on Guardian HRS grounds where they can protect them from Carmen's father and any retaliation he may throw our way.

As far as Carmen's father goes, Maximus Angelo, Nicaragua's Minister of the Interior, spent barely an hour in a holding cell after our raid on his home. We rescued dozens of women who'd been kidnapped and were slated to be sold at auction. Something like that should put a person away for life. Or sentence them to a swift execution.

Evidently, if you're Nicaragua's Minister of the Interior, corruption greases the machine of a political empire that sweeps all that shit under the proverbial rug.

What a fucking shit show.

The fucker may have avoided prison, but Maximus Angelo will pay for his crimes. Guardian HRS will make that happen. Unfortunately, for right now, we're in a holding pattern while our intelligence team figures out our next move.

As for Kaye, she's in my mind as I walk back up the stairs and into the townhouse she shares with Carmen, Rosalie, and Barbi.

The moment I enter the small foyer, her choked sob pulls me to a stop. The heart-wrenching noise comes from down the hall. I take a deep breath. Hayes and Rafe's words run around in my head, but I ignore what they said. I have no intention of fucking with Kaye. I'm here as nothing more than a concerned citizen doing my best to help out a stranger in distress.

Carmen and Rosalie's rooms are upstairs. Kaye gave up her room to Rosalie and is double-bunking with Barbi for the summer. I set the bag I'm carrying at the foot of the stairs and make my way down the hall.

Sure enough, another choked sob comes from behind a half-open door.

I hate when women cry. It twists my gut and sends me into protection mode. Despite what Rafe and Hayes say, I don't break hearts. Everyone knows what they're getting when they're with me. I make it clear upfront so there isn't a problem when it's time to end things. That way, there's no confusion.

As I move closer to Kaye, the guys' words twist in my head. Shit, even I wonder what I'm doing. I'm probably the last thing Kaye needs right now.

But what if I'm exactly what she needs?

Someone to listen without judgment?

Someone to provide comfort if necessary?

Someone to lend an understanding ear that comes with no strings? Besides, showing genuine concern for another human being isn't wrong. It's the right thing to do.

When I peer through the doorway, she's curled up on the floor with her back to the wall. Knees tucked tight to her chest, she rocks slowly as a river of tears flow down her angelic face. I gently rap on the door and call out her name.

"Kaye?"

Red and puffy eyes, her nose snotty from tears, my heart skips a beat, taken aback by her stunning beauty. She also makes me wary of the undeniable pull dragging me toward her. When she doesn't answer, I move into the room.

"What do you want?" Her tone is cautious but questioning.

"Thought maybe you needed to talk. Or could use a hug?" My voice is gentle and soft. "I've been told I give great hugs." I want her to know I pose no threat, then slide down the wall to sit beside her.

"Go away." She shifts, barely, but otherwise doesn't retreat.

"After I'm all the way down here on the floor?" I keep my tone light, teasing. "Should've told me before I sat down." I nudge her gently, bumping shoulders, trying to inject a bit of humor to get her to open up. "But since I'm already here, if you need a shoulder to cry on, I happen to have one or two free."

"Don't be silly. You don't even know me."

"Don't have to know you to know something's wrong. You look like something upset you and I thought…"

"I don't like pity." She sniffs and swipes at her nose. "Especially from strangers."

"I'm not offering pity, sunshine. Just a shoulder. Or a hug. Both, if that's what you need. You look like you could use someone to talk to."

"I don't know you."

"We met outside. Or did you forget?

"Doesn't mean we're friends."

"Well, Rafe and Carmen are a thing. Hayes and Rosalie are a thing. You and Barbi are Carmen's best friends. And Rafe and Hayes are mine. Do the math. We're basically friends by association."

"What does that mean?" She swipes at her eyes.

"It's only a matter of time before we're actual friends. I say we skip ahead to the already friends part and you tell me what's got you down?"

She pauses for a moment, as if considering my words, then cocks her head. "It's Zeb, right?"

"That's my name." I thrust out my hand, offering to shake hers.

She takes a look at my hand but draws back. An odd reaction, but I don't put much into it.

"You don't like my name?" I pretend to be shocked, surprised, and a little offended.

I take my hand back like it's no big deal. My acting skills suck, so I don't really know how well I pull it off. Probably like a load of bricks, but the faintest smile curls at the corner of her rosebud lips.

"It's unusual."

"What's unusual?"

"Your name." She looks at me like I'm an idiot, but I'm keeping things light on purpose.

"It's short for Zebediah."

"A biblical name?" The way her brows scrunch is delightful.

"Cult, actually." I don't usually get to the whole child-of-a-cult thing until after sex, but here we are.

"You're in a cult?"

"My parents were."

"Your parents were in a cult?"

"Technically, my mother was in the cult. My father was the asshole who ran it."

"Wait. What?" Her hand lifts and her fingers settle lightly on my arm—like she's comforting me. "There's a story behind that."

"There is, and it's a doozy, but it's only the kind of story friends would share. Do you want to hear it?"

"Of course I do." Her eyes light with interest.

I don't blame her. It's the same reaction everyone has when I tell them about my very unusual upbringing. I leave out the darker parts. People aren't interested in the kind of shit that only brings you down. We all have secrets, and that's one I like to keep in the way-down-deep part of my past no one gets to see. Best not to dig up that crap.

"Well then, that means we're friends, and if we're friends, how about you tell me what made you run inside and hide?"

"Hide?" Her brows tug together in confusion. "I didn't hide."

"Well, one moment everything was good." Very good from my standpoint. Can't deny that spark of attraction, or the rush of heat that followed. Also can't ignore the way that blaze suddenly went out. "Then everything changed."

"How did you…" Her eyes widen. Not in alarm, but rather with a bit of awe.

"One of my strengths is reading people." I get that from my pathetic excuse of a father. Evidently, reading people is a necessary job requirement for Cult Leader. That and being a master manipulator.

"I didn't think it was that obvious." Her shoulders hunch and she curls in on herself, tugging her knees tight to her chest.

Should I tell her why? That it's only because of the power of attraction pulling us together that I notice at all? Probably too early for that.

I'll wait.

"So what's it going to be?" I nudge her with my shoulder again. This time, I prolong the duration our bodies touch, leaning in rather than bumping and pulling back.

I like the way she feels. Love the way she smells. I breathe in a deep lungful of her delicate perfume and wonder what she'll feel like wrapped around me.

"What do you mean?" she asks.

"Wondering if you need the hug, or just want to talk."

"My problems are of my own making." Her eyes squeeze shut, like she's trying to forget something.

"Doesn't mean you don't need that hug." I reach for her, wrapping my much larger hand around hers. "But I'm a great listener if a hug's too much for new friends."

"I could've used that hug a few seconds ago, but I'm good now. Thanks." She leans against me, and doesn't yank her hand out from under mine.

"I guess that means we talk it out." Only, I don't want to talk it out. Now that I'm holding her hand, that rush of sensation courses through my body, waking up things that don't need to wake up and stand at attention.

Down, boy.

Doesn't every man talk to his dick? When you're a guy like me, with a sex drive like mine, conversations such as these are a daily occurrence.

She tilts her head to look at me. Our gazes lock and snag on each other, trapped for long seconds by a flash of heat too intense to ignore.

Yeah, that spark is still there.

"I don't really want to…" She quickly cuts off her own words, but I don't need her to say it.

I'm one hundred percent positive she's talking about a man. Boyfriend, no doubt. There's no ring on her finger. No fiancé or husband to get in my way.

"Then we won't talk about him." I test the waters, waiting for a reaction.

Looking for confirmation.

She gives me exactly what I expect; a brief flash of an expression, pain she can't escape. Whatever happened is the result of someone she's involved with.

And whatever that is—it's nothing good.

Not that it's a surprise. Men have been taking advantage of women since the dawn of time. I know all too well how cruel they can be. How they can hurt and betray trust in an instant. I'm living proof of how horrible a man can be to a woman.

I give Kaye's hand a gentle squeeze and lean back against the wall.

"We'll just sit here for a bit, then. Let Rosalie and Carmen get settled."

"It's nice that you came to help."

"It's part of the job."

"Being a Guardian?"

"Well, that I suppose, but for the time being, Bravo team is on 24/7 protection detail. I'm here to do a bit of recon and get a feeling of the lay of the land." My words bring a hitch to her breath and I have to suppress a smile.

"And make new friends in the process?" She graces me with her first real smile.

Jackpot!

"We're far from being friends."

"But you just said…"

"I said you're going to be seeing a lot more of me over the next few weeks."

"Wait, what?" My comment takes her by surprise.

"Bravo team is pulling 24-hour shifts watching over you girls," I explain with a smirk.

I'm not looking for friendship. Kaye is far too intriguing for friendship, and I know better than to get myself stuck in the friend zone.

Not that I've ever been relegated to that hell.

Kaye's an intriguing mystery waiting to be unraveled, and there's nothing I love more than figuring out puzzles.

THREE

Kaye

___

"Kaye? Where are you?" Barbi's soft alto calls out from the base of the stairs.

"Shit." I wipe my hands on my jeans and rush to my feet. I've been so lost in my thoughts over Scott, and trying my best not to be a total basket case in front of Zeb, that I forgot to head upstairs and bring down the last of my things.

"Problem?" Zeb cocks his head, lips twisting in a sardonic grin.

"No problem." I try to sound nonchalant, but my words come out in a rush, and my *No problem* sounds a whole lot like I'm trying to hide something.

Which I am.

It's why I leap to my feet. No way do I want Barbi seeing me sitting shoulder to shoulder, on the floor, with Zeb. It looks too much like we're flirting.

Which I am. And maybe we are?

Not sure.

I'm totally into Zeb. Like on a cellular level of *I-want-to-crawl-inside-of-him* kind of thing. And I think he's a little into me as well. Which is why I don't want Barbi seeing us together, alone, in the bedroom.

Holding hands.

"You sure about that?" Amusement twists through Zeb's words.

He's having fun with this, and if his powers of reading people are as good as he says, he knows exactly why I shot to my feet at the sound of Barbi's voice.

Which he does. The bastard totally knows.

"I'm supposed to help Barbi finish packing my things in my room and move them down here." I rub my palms against my jeans, feeling guilty, looking guilty, just plain looking like an open book to the sexy-as-sin man lounging on the floor.

"Ah…" He slowly unfolds his powerful legs and rises to his full height. He's close. Too close. It's the kind of towering-over-me kind of close. Which makes his presence difficult to ignore. "We'd better get to it, then." His mouth curves into a half-smile while his eyes twinkle with mirth.

Yeah, he knows exactly what's going through my mind.

"Right." I take a shaky step back, needing space to catch my breath. "Um, I'll be back in a minute."

Barbi's footsteps sound in the hall.

I'm too late.

I call out to my friend.

"I'm in here." I rush over to the spare dresser we moved in last night to hold my things.

Barbi pokes her head in what's now our room. Her shoulder-length hair sways back and forth as she takes one look at Zeb then shifts her attention to me, raising a brow, before marching in.

"Thought you were gonna help with the last of your things?" She waltzes in and drops an armful of my clothes on the bed.

My clothes tumble and form a heap on top of her bed. My lacy bras, and collection of thongs, land right on the top of that pile for everyone to see. A quick glance at Zeb and heat fills my cheeks.

"What did you do, scoop my stuff out of my drawers?" I rush to the pile of clothes, pawing through them in a desperate attempt to bury my unmentionables.

"You were supposed to empty the boxes and bring the empties

up, but I got tired of waiting." Her gaze shifts between me and Zeb again.

That glint in her eye tells me she's up to no good and hints at her mischievousness. She's curious what Zeb and I were doing in here alone.

I take a deep breath and shake off my embarrassment. Keeping my voice upbeat, I pretend having a tall, dark, and gorgeous Guardian eyeing my bras and panties is an everyday occurrence.

Nothing going on here.

Except his gaze keeps shifting from the pile to what I'm wearing. And I know exactly what's going through his mind. He's debating whether I'm currently wearing a thong or lacy panties.

"It's alright." I grab one of the boxes we brought down earlier and dump those clothes on top of the pile, burying the evidence, as it were.

Zeb wanders close. His arm brushes against mine. That tingle of electricity engulfs me, making all the fine hairs on my arms stand at attention.

"Need help with that?" He rocks back on his heels and flashes a mischievous grin.

"With what?" I pretend I'm not standing in front of a pile of my half-folded clothes and try to sound nonchalant even through there's a bright-red pair of lacy panties peeking out from beneath the pile.

Just kill me now.

"Folding? Unpacking? Packing? Consider me free labor." He folds his arms across his chest, looking pleased with himself. His offer hangs in the air and no one says anything.

Barbi waits for me to react. Her attention shifts to me and she throws me a lifeline.

"Zeb, why don't you take the empty boxes to the kitchen and start breaking them down?" The twinkle in her eyes tells me my cheeks are indeed flushed and rosy red.

"I can definitely do that." Zeb grabs the empty boxes and heads for the door. Before he leaves, he pauses and twists back to look at me. "I enjoyed our talk and look forward to continuing it at a later time."

My face is on fire as I watch Zeb leave. I wait until he's gone, and out of earshot, before spinning around to smack Barbi on her arm.

"What the hell were you thinking?" I press my hands against my cheeks, mortified and a bit giddy at the same time. "Was that your idea of a joke?"

"What did he mean by *Your talk?*" Barbi props her hands on her hips and raises her eyebrows. "Were you really talking? Or was something else going on?" She ignores my question to ask hers. "Looks like something else was going on."

"It was nothing," I mumble and take a step back. I reach for one of the drawers near the bed and pull it open. "Did you really have to embarrass me like that?"

"What did I do?" She feigns innocence, but the glint in her eyes says otherwise.

It was deliberate.

"You know what you did."

"Do not."

"You dumped my stuff on the bed where he could see all my…"

"All your, what?" That impish grin of hers is back.

"You know what I mean."

"Do you mean your panties, or the thongs?" She holds up the red, silk panties in one hand and loops her finger through one of my thongs with her other hand. Holding them both up, she bats her eyes at me like an innocent.

"Both." I snatch my things out of the air, mortified Zeb could walk back in any second, and toss them in one of the empty drawers behind me.

"Hey, it's not my fault. I grabbed those first and covered them with the rest of your things so the guys didn't get an eyeful. If I'd known you were having a private tête-á-tête with your own Guardian, I wouldn't have…" A low laugh escapes her. "Why do you care? Unless…" She doesn't complete that sentence, but I know exactly what she means.

If I didn't care what Zeb thought, I wouldn't care what he saw.

"I can't look him in the eyes after that."

"Well, I'll try to be more discreet next time. For the record, I'm not the one who insists on wearing dental floss instead of panties. Don't know why you even bother with them at all."

"Oh my God, you're infuriating." Infuriating, but I love her too much to be angry with her.

"And you're funny as shit." Her expression softens. "You've got the hots for Zeb."

"I do not."

"Oh please, the scarlet in your cheeks says otherwise. That Guardian's got your panties all twisted in a knot. And you never answered my question."

"What question?"

"What were the two of you doing in here all alone? Were you talking? Or something else?"

"We weren't doing anything."

"Liar. The air crackles with the energy flowing between the two of you. I thought I had dibs on picking the first Guardian?"

"If you want him, then by all means, he's yours." I gesture down the hall, toward the kitchen where Zeb's muscular body breaks down the empty boxes for recycling. "I'm not calling dibs on anyone. Or did you forget I've sworn off men?"

"Haven't forgotten about that." Barbi moves to the side of the bed and starts folding my clothes. It's not much: jeans, shirts, shorts, tank tops, and my lingerie collection. "But you can have Zeb. Alec's got my eye. He's got this wild, animalistic thing going on." She leans in close. "I get a very sexy, fifty-shades kind of vibe from him. If you know what I mean." Her brows wriggle and it's all I can do not to roll my eyes.

"You can have Alec *and* Zeb for all I care."

"We'll see. I don't think the two of them would share a woman though." Her brows knit together as she puffs out her cheeks. "But could you imagine? Two Guardians in bed? That would be a lot to handle. You can have Zeb. I can't handle two of them."

"Don't know until you ask."

"Well, I'm not asking. And I'm certainly not poaching from you."

"From me? Did you miss the part where I said you could have Zeb?"

"Did you miss the part where I said I wasn't taking him from you?" She rolls her eyes. "Not after seeing the way the two of you look at each other." She leans back and shoves her hands into the back pockets of her jeans. "I'd kill for a man to look at me like that."

"Like what?"

"Like he wants to devour me."

"That's not—Zeb didn't…"

"Think what you will, but I saw what I saw. And don't worry. I'm not interested in Zeb. He's all yours."

"Zeb isn't interested in someone like me."

"From the way he looked at you, he's more than interested." She chuckles softly, then finishes folding a stack of jeans and places them in one of the empty drawers of the dresser. "You know, it might be a good thing."

"How's that?" I tilt my head to the side, curious.

"Well, having your own Guardian around might help with the problem of Professor Douchebag." She leans toward me, as if we're sharing a secret she doesn't want anyone else to overhear. "I doubt Scott will mess with you if you've got a Guardian by your side."

"I don't know about that, but there's something about Scott." I glance at the door and nibble my lower lip as an unsettled feeling overcomes me.

"What do you mean?" She shakes her head, confused, like she wasn't expecting the change in conversation.

"It's probably nothing, but I'm pretty sure he was watching the house from down the street."

"Watching? As in stalking?" Her eyes widen before forming a hard, angry glare. "I'm telling you the man's deranged." Her fingers clench, forming tight fists. "Hooking up with Zeb might not be such a bad idea."

"Scott's not deranged. He's just…"

"Stalking you." Barbi props her hands on her hips. "Aka—Deranged."

"I don't know about that, but it gave me the heebie-jeebies.

When I rushed inside, Zeb picked up on it and came inside to see if I was okay."

"See, already he's protecting you." She slaps me on the arm. "Way to land yourself a Guardian."

"Not mine. I'm not interested in men right now."

"You can say that all you want, but you're not being honest with yourself."

Barbi doesn't agree with me and she's not the kind of friend who tells me what I want to hear. Always a straight shooter, I've learned to respect her intuition. Doesn't mean I have to agree with it.

"I'm honest about my feelings." I can't help but argue, even when I know she's right.

"Then explain why you're pretending not to want Zeb when we both know you're totally into him."

"I'm not *'into'* him." I punctuate my comment with air quotes.

If I deny my feelings loudly enough, maybe they'll become true. Honestly, I can't think about another man when things with Scott remain unsettled.

"You've got a crush on the man." Barbi's not giving up. Not when she's got a point to prove and knows she's right.

"Do not."

She might be the Queen of Intuition, but I'm the Goddess of Stubborn. I will not give in.

"Do so, but like I said, it's not a bad thing. Zeb could be very useful to have around, and, as far as being around, have you heard we're going to be surrounded by Guardians?"

"Zeb mentioned something about 24/7 protection until this thing with Carmen's dad is finished."

"Yeah." Barbi leans against the dresser. "I can't even begin to grasp what the two of them have been through. And what happened to those other women?" Her entire body shudders as if a chill shoots down her spine. "It's horrifying."

I feel the same. Even though neither of us were directly involved, Carmen told us everything. It shook me to my core.

"Yeah, how do we handle that?"

"As far as?"

"Do we say nothing and wait for them to bring it up? Or do we just ask?" I honestly don't know how to broach such a subject. Compared to what Carmen and Rosalie endured, my life's been a cake walk.

"I say we wait for them to bring it up. If they don't, then we have a friendly sit down and ask them to share."

"Sounds like a plan."

"Now, back to Zeb." Barbi's like a dog with a bone. She's not letting this go.

FOUR

Zeb

Halfway through breaking down the empty boxes, Brady sends a group text to the team. Looks like we're needed back at HQ, which kind of sucks. I was looking forward to getting to know the beautiful blonde.

Her delicate scent remains with me: a mix of a flowers and champagne. Makes me eager to taste her pretty lips and find out if the light effervescence of champagne is really there.

Strawberries.

I bet she tastes like strawberries.

She's a vision to behold; warm, inviting eyes and long, luscious, blonde hair. Her skin glows with an ethereal luminescence and I love the confidence of her smirk.

She's got full, pouty lips; the kind that are almost too soft, like a simple puff of air is all it takes to blow a kiss. When she purses her lips, she can't help but draw attention. It's like she's begging to be kissed, but only on her terms.

The way her cheeks turn pink sets my blood on fire. I love how that rosy hue takes over her face and creeps down her neck. But I have to watch that because when my eyes travel down, they'll stop on her perfect breasts.

I get a sense Kaye wouldn't appreciate that. She's more of a *look-me-in-the-eye-not-my-breasts* kind of woman.

I can't tell if she's a natural blonde, or not. Regardless, her hair falls softly around her shoulders and cascades down to the small of her back in gentle waves. She moves like a ballerina, and her lilting laughter is carefree, like bells on a summer day. Her voice is the kind of voice that makes a man weak in the knees. I feel that pull and would eagerly go to my knees to spend another minute with her.

She's down-to-earth with those hip-hugging jeans that accentuate the flare of her hips, and it's clear her well-loved T-shirt is intimately associated with her curves. It clings to her body in a way that hints of something more beneath.

My fingers flex with the urge to cup her breasts. To see if they fit my hand the way I imagine they will.

Her blush is a thing of beauty; enough to take my breath away. The rosy hue begins in her cheeks then spreads across her face to the bridge of her nose. When my gaze follows the path of her blush, it drifts down, deepening as it travels down her neck. It grows more intense; an unstoppable wave of emotion sweeping across her collarbone and diving into the depths of her cleavage.

It's a thing of beauty, a captivating and mysterious force stirring my heart in ways I never thought possible. Something makes me want to crawl inside her head and sift through her thoughts to see if I'm the cause of her pretty blushes.

I turn to the task at hand and finish breaking down the last of Kaye's boxes. Then I head outside, missing Kaye on the way out, and meet up with the guys at the curb.

My steps slow, then drag. An invisible force pulls at me, like a line reeling me in. No need to question that. The real question is: why her? Out of the hundreds of women I've been interested in, how does she exert this pull?

I don't understand, and things I don't understand make my skin itch. If I was smart, I'd walk away and never look back.

Only, I'm not smart.

I stop outside the townhouse, feet rooted in place, and turn back, hoping for a sight of Kaye.

"You coming, Zeb?" Alec calls out, pulling me from my thoughts.

With far more effort than it should take, I force my feet to move and head to the vehicle. Keeping my voice nonchalant, I pretend as if that long stare back at the townhouse means nothing.

It should mean nothing. Kaye's just another chick. One more woman parading through my bed. Or, she soon will be. With a tightening of my jaw, I force my thoughts away from the captivating blonde and focus on the task we've been assigned.

"Any idea what's up?" I climb into the driver's seat and turn over the engine.

The black Suburban growls to life. The engine hums with power, transmitting heavy vibrations through the steering wheel to my hands.

"Brady didn't say. Just that we needed to go." Rafe snugs the seatbelt over his lap as I ease the vehicle into traffic.

"What happened to providing protection for Carmen and Rosalie?" My jaw tightens. I thought we were doing that, and it seems silly to move them in, then abandon their security detail.

"Forest is nearby. He's going to watch over them until we get back." Rafe glances in the rearview mirror, checking out the traffic around us.

"No disrespect, but he doesn't have the training we have."

"Forest should be fine, especially since he won't be alone." Rafe shifts in his seat, stretching his long legs out in front of him as much as he can within the confines of the car.

I cut him an amused sideways glare as I navigate around a pothole and merge onto the highway. "You suppose he's got another Guardian stashed somewhere?"

I joke halfheartedly because deep down I'm concerned about leaving Kaye, Barbi, Carmen, and Rosalie unprotected while we rush off on this errand with no idea what it entails or when we'll be back.

Rafe snorts out a laugh and shakes his head before checking his phone for any missed messages from Brady or Mitzy about our destination or mission parameters.

"Nah," he says after looking over the screen for a few moments before setting it aside again and returning to our conversation from before. "Looks like Forest is with Paul tonight. Sara too. I think our women are safe with them."

Paul.

An interesting man for many reasons. He's part of Forest's unique throuple; a relationship between three people with Forest at the center.

Sara is Forest's wife. Nothing out of the ordinary there, but Paul is his Dom. Which is totally weird because Forest is what I would describe as the Alpha of Alphas.

He created Guardian HRS. He's powerful, dominant, very male. White savior complex is something that fits him to a T, but he's nothing like a white savior.

The man is a survivor of some of the worst brutality I've ever seen. Which is where Paul comes in. Paul saved Forest's life.

He's the same height as Forest. Not as broad but stacked with muscle. The two of them together are a force no man in his right mind would mess with.

The girls are safe. More than safe.

Kaye is safe.

Not that I like them watching over her one bit, but I can't argue against whether Forest and Paul are capable of providing adequate protection.

They are.

End of story.

"Earth to Zeb?" Rafe pokes me in the arm.

"What?"

"You daydreaming, or what?"

"Excuse me?"

"You haven't heard a word." He looks at me like I've got a screw loose, which maybe I do.

"Sorry. What were you saying?" I have no idea what he said to me.

"A new client's coming in for the Protectors. Sam sent Chase Lawson up from HQ, but he's delayed by an accident on PCH-1.

We're to pick the client up at the airport, secure her until Chase can get to us. Or we get to him. After that, we're free to return to HQ and drop Rafe and Hayes at the townhouse." Alec sits back and adjusts the passenger side mirror to better see behind us.

"Just Rafe and Hayes?" I scrunch my nose and let the rest of that comment wither and die.

After the dressing down Rafe and Hayes gave me about Kaye, I'm not sure it's a good idea for them to know I'm in active pursuit of Kaye.

Their comments rubbed me wrong. I didn't interfere when Rafe went after Carmen, and I said nothing when it was clear Hayes and Rosalie were a thing. Why are their noses up my ass about Kaye?

She's not a client or an active case. And she's not a rescue mission. If we're going to talk boundaries, let's talk about that. Rafe and Hayes will lose that argument each and every time.

Their overprotectiveness pisses me the fuck off. I shake it off and focus on the mission. "What do we know about our target?"

"Client, not target," Rafe corrects me.

"Sorry, force of habit." Our missions generally involve taking down a target and rescuing hostages. It's in the very name of our organization. "What do we know about our *client?*"

"Sam isn't forthcoming." Rafe spits out the words with a twist in his lip. He's not happy with the lack of information.

"Why's that?" Like him, I'm curious information's being withheld from us.

The Guardian Protectors, or Protectors for short, are a new limb of our organization. The Guardians work in six man teams, highly aligned with the way we ran missions in the Navy as SEALs.

The Protectors are solo operators, providing boutique personal protection services to clients seeking something more than the average bodyguard can provide.

"Mitzy's securing boarding passes as we speak."

"We're meeting her at the gate?" It's the only reason our technical lead would purchase plane tickets.

"You're on vehicle duty," Rafe says. "Mitzy will keep up with our progress and direct you to the pickup point."

"Sounds easy enough." I've got the cushy part of this job. Not to mention, I hate airports, especially getting through security.

With that bit of information, the three of them divest themselves of their weapons. Not that it's required. Guardians, and Protectors alike, hold special assignment status with the US Marshalls. That allows us to enter places like airports and bypass security with little to no fuss.

It also raises eyebrows, incites speculation, and draws way more attention than we want. Sometimes, it's useful to flash a badge. Other times, it's better to fly under the radar.

This is more of a get-in-and-get-out-without-being-noticed kind of gig.

My part is easy. Drop my teammates off, circle around the airport until they make contact with the client, then pick everyone up at the curb.

If I'm lucky, this will take no more than an hour, or two. We only need to fill in the gap before Chase takes over Protector duties. Then it's back to the townhouse.

Back to Kaye.

And back to my growing obsession with the pretty blonde. Why, or what, is different about her? Any other woman and I wouldn't look twice, but somehow, she worked her way under my skin.

FIVE

Kaye

______

Barbi's relentless digging gets on my nerves. Not in a bad way, but in the fun, best friend kind of way.

"If you want Zeb, you can have him." I chuck one of my shirts at her face. "Now, stop teasing me."

"Well, I just need to know if we need to come up with some kind of signal?" Her eyebrows knit together, as if she's serious, but from the curve of her lips, she's totally having fun with me.

"Signal?" Curiosity replaces that niggling annoyance.

"You know—like if there's a sock on the door, it's because you and Zeb are in here doing the nasty?"

Her suggestion sends a wave of embarrassment coursing through me. My cheeks heat for what must be the twentieth time today. I hate how I wear my emotions on my sleeve.

I groan and shake my head.

"Oh my God. You're horrible. I just met the guy and you already have us in bed? We're not talking about this."

I want to ignore what she says and return to the mundane task of folding my clothes, but she's having too much fun. A surge of vulnerability rises in my chest.

"You may be done, but I'm not. I wouldn't be your friend if I didn't tell you not to let what happened with Professor Parker cloud your judgment when it comes to other men. You know you like him and don't pretend otherwise."

The hurt inflicted upon me by Scott is like an open wound. It's hard to step away from it. Hard to think about venturing into the unknown with another man.

Doesn't she know this?

Barbi goes back to making a dent in my clothes. I join her, wordlessly, losing myself to the rhythm of tidying up our room. Her words linger in my head, repeating over and over. Which makes me think about what it would be like to be with Zeb. Another flush creeps into my cheeks.

"Ladies…" Carmen's singsong voice drifts down the hall. Her light steps follow, announcing her presence. By the time she arrives, we've made a major dent in folding the pile of my clothes. Barbi and I work quickly as a team.

"How's it going?" Carmen pokes her head in our room—still weird to think of Barbi's room as mine.

"How's Rosalie?" I twist, looking over my shoulder to see Carmen better.

"She's good. Almost moved in." Carmen's smile is as warm as ever. Sometimes, it's hard to believe the trauma she's endured. She doesn't mention Rosalie has precious little to move in.

The two of them went on a major shopping excursion, buying all the things. Considering Rosalie arrived on US soil with nothing but the clothes on her back, it was a mega shopping event.

After a few days of questions and debriefings with the Guardians, Carmen and Rosalie were finally allowed to return to the townhouse, which brings us to this moment.

"And you? How are you doing?" Barbi exchanges a look with me.

We're concerned about the effect recent events have had on our friend. Carmen basically lost her home and her father in one fell swoop.

"I'm good." From the bounce in her step and the lightness of her tone, it's easy to believe what she says.

I reserve judgment. Carmen's entire world imploded and that kind of thing tends to leave extensive damage. I'm worried.

"When you say good, it feels dismissive." I plop down on the edge of the bed and give it a good pat. "Sit and tell us the truth."

"I am good." Carmen's attention shifts between me and Barbi. When Barbi crosses her arms over her chest and gives Carmen one of her looks, Carmen puffs out a breath and gives in. "I really am good."

She sits beside me and I drape an arm over her shoulder, bringing her in for a hug. "Well, if *good* means getting kidnapped and losing your best friend in the jungle…"

"The two of you are my besties too. This doesn't change anything." Carmen leans against me and Barbi joins us on the edge of the bed.

"I wasn't talking about Rosalie coming between us. That's the last thing on my mind. What I'm worried about is…"

"Your dismissive attitude." Barbi, who never beats around the bush, finishes my sentence with a sting.

"My, what?" Carmen pops to her feet and spins around to face us. "What does that mean?"

"Look, I'm thrilled Rosalie is here. I'm thrilled she's going to be living with us. But I'm concerned how you're acting like everything's normal. Like your entire life isn't in upheaval."

"Everything is normal." Carmen refuses to give ground.

"If normal is having Guardian supervision 24/7, then we need to discuss what is, and is not, normal. Don't you think you might be sweeping things under the rug? I'm worried about you." Sometimes Barbi's direct attitude is absolutely perfect and appropriate.

I applaud her for saying the things I'm thinking, but don't want to say out of consideration for Carmen's feelings.

"I'm good. Everything's good." The one quality Carmen and Barbi share is their bullheadedness. Neither one of them knows how to back down from an argument.

This usually leaves me to play peacemaker.

"Zeb mentioned Rafe and Hayes wanted you to stay on Guardian HQ grounds, but you refused." Barbi's tone stings with the weight of judgment. "I'm worried. If they're concerned, shouldn't you be too? Shouldn't we all be a little concerned?"

"Rafe and Hayes want to lock Rosalie and me up in their ivory tower." Carmen leans against Barbi's dresser. "If it were up to them, we'd never set foot beyond the perimeter fencing. I can't live like that and Rosalie needs to get used to living here before she hits campus in the fall."

Barbi and I just stare. What else can we do? We want to support Carmen—Rosalie too. "I kind of agree with Barbi. If the two of you would be safer with the Guardians, shouldn't you be there instead of here?" I hold up my hands. "I just think we need to look at things from all sides. The last thing we want is for something to happen to either one of you."

"Thank you. I appreciate that, and I know, and see, and feel, your thoughts churning." Carmen pins me down with a soft smile.

"We're just worried." I can't help but shrug.

Barbi scoots over to sit beside me. She slings her arm over my shoulder. "We support whatever you choose, but we're concerned." That's as close as Barbi will come to laying down a gauntlet.

"Look…" Carmen breathes out a soft sigh. "My father's entire operation is defunct. He's not a vindictive man."

"He's a human trafficker." Barbi scoots back on the bed and folds her legs underneath her. "Sorry, I don't mean to bash your dad, but he's a human trafficker. I kind of think that implies he's exactly the kind of man to be vindictive. Aren't you the least bit concerned about retaliation?"

"My father is the devil. He's destroyed scores of lives over countless years, all while pretending to be an agent of the people." Carmen focuses on Barbi. "I don't excuse what he did, and I hope he stands trial for his crimes, but my father has a lot on his plate right now. Lots of fires to put out. The last thing he's going to do is come after me, or come after Rosalie. My dad doesn't give a rat's ass about Rosalie. Now that Matias is dead, she's no longer worth anything to him."

"But what about you?" I can't sit there in silence. "He had plans for you."

It's not worth going into the details about the arranged marriage her father put in motion to secure his bid to take over the presidency of Nicaragua. Without his daughter greasing the political machine, his hopes have gone up in smoke.

"The Guardians think he won't bother with me." Carmen pulls at her chin. "And I agree with them. I no longer have any value when it comes to my father."

"Sheesh, I'm sorry." It's hard to internalize the horrors Carmen endured. "It's just…"

"We want to be helpful." Barbi reaches for my hand, squeezing it lightly.

"And I love that about both of you." Carmen rejoins us on the bed. She pushes us aside and squeezes in between us. Looping one arm around my shoulder, and the other around Barbi, she pulls us in for a hug. "We're going to be fine, and I can't wait for you to get to know Rosalie better. Which is why I wanted to come here in the first place." Carmen lowers her voice. "Rosalie needs normal. I thought moving in would help with that and thought maybe we could all go out tonight?"

"Out?" My brows scrunch together.

"Yeah, to the pier?" Carmen looks at me, then at Barbi. "Rosalie wants to try San Francisco's famous clam chowder."

"Sounds good." Barbi rocks back and forth in agreement.

"And…" The timbre of Carmen's voice changes; takes on a tone I know all too well. She's up to no good.

"And what?"

"Well, there's the four of us and four Guardians…"

"Oh my God!" Barbi squeals. "You're playing matchmaker?" She squirms on the bed. "Please tell me you're playing matchmaker. Alec is too hot for words, and Kaye and Zeb seem to be hitting it off."

"Really?" Carmen gives me a look. "You and Zeb?"

"Just talking. Although Barbi's already got us twisting the sheets."

"You totally want to twist those sheets with Zeb." Barbi reaches for me, tickling me in the ribs.

I squirm and leap off the bed.

"And Barbi's got the hots for Alec." Carmen isn't one to miss an opportunity. She pokes Barbi in the ribs, tickling her until Barbi squirms and giggles. They fall back in a pile, teasing, tickling, poking, and generally having fun, while I look on from a distance.

I'll miss this.

I gaze around the room, taking in the sight of my friends. Their laughter is honest and carefree. When I head to my apartment at UC Davis, these are the things I'm going to miss.

My mother used to tell me the only thing constant in this unpredictable world is that change will always be a part of it. I'll always have Barbi and Carmen in my life, but I may not always have this.

A soft knock on the door catches my attention. Rosalie stands timidly in the doorway, her eyes wide. She hangs back at the threshold, cautious and unsure. One look at her and I know she feels awkward, like an outsider. I beckon her inside to come and join us.

Barbi and Carmen are too engrossed in their tickle fight to notice Rosalie's arrival, but I go to her and fold her into a hug.

She nervously looks around the room, like she doesn't belong. Behind me, Barbi and Carmen playfully shout at each other about all the things a Guardian is good at in bed.

SIX

Kaye

———

Glancing at Barbi and Carmen, I tug on Rosalie's arm. The two of them are in rare form. Barbi says something lewd and lascivious about Rafe. Carmen screams.

Not a real scream. It's more of a *I-Can't-Believe-You-Said-That* kind of scream.

"This can go on for hours." I keep my tone light, teasing, and inclusive.

It's my goal to help make Rosalie feel welcome and a part of our zany crew. That, however, can be hard when trying to break into a friendship as thick as the one between Carmen, Barbi, and me.

Still, I'm hopeful this is the start of something new and special. I love Carmen, and Rosalie is a big piece of what makes Carmen the woman she is. There are cultural barriers between us, but I'm sure time will break all of those down.

"Has Carmen given you the full tour?"

"Two rooms upstairs. Jack-n-Jill bathroom. Living room, kitchen, and dining room down here, and of course, Barbi's room." Rosalie blinks and shakes her head. "I mean yours and Barbi's room."

I eagerly grab her arm and guide her down the hall.

"Well, let me give you the real tour. Carmen left off the best parts." I drag her into the hallway. "What happened to the Guardians?"

"They got called in. Left a few minutes ago. Hayes said Forest is going to come by to take watch."

"Ah, that explains the lack of over-protective male testosterone lingering in the air."

"They are something, aren't they?" Rosalie breathes out a sigh.

"I don't know. You spent how long with Hayes in the jungle?"

"Long enough. Although Hayes was never overprotective. I mean, he helped when I needed it, but he needed my help along the way. Honestly, we made a great team."

"Made?" I can't help but ping on her use of the past tense.

"Make." She blushes. "It's weird knowing that's all behind me. Being here?"

"Yes?"

"It's a bit of a transition."

"How so?"

"Instead of running for our lives and evading capture, we're trying to navigate the treacherous waters of who cooks dinner and whether he can open the door for me. These Guardians are strange creatures. Alpha to the core. Respectful almost to a fault. They're nothing like what I thought."

"I see that with Carmen."

"Yeah, it's hard. And I don't mean to complain, but Hayes bends over backward helping me now that we're in the States. It's almost as if he doesn't realize I can take care of myself."

"That's the Alpha-vibe taking over."

"Yeah. When we were in the rainforest, it felt like we were on the same page. Same mission. Same objective." Her sigh is wistful and full of remembrance.

"And now?"

"Now?" She flicks her eyes up and to the right before answering. "Now, he wants to buy me everything and make sure I have what I need."

"The overprotective alpha."

"Yeah." She nibbles on her lower lip. "Is it weird I don't want that?"

"Not at all, but give him a little grace for wanting to take care of you. Not every man is built that way."

"I suppose you're right."

"So, Forest? I've heard so much about him. He's supposed to be the visionary, and financial backer, behind the Guardian Hostage Rescue Specialists."

"That's what Hayes said."

"He's supposed to be some kind of savant." I'm curious about the founder of Guardian Hostage Rescue Specialists.

Carmen says he's the kind of man who makes you want to be a better version of yourself. She also says he's reached a near-godlike status among the Guardians but is also incredibly down to earth.

I don't know what that means, but I'd love to meet him one day.

Looks like I'll get that chance tonight.

Is it weird I feel a little miffed that Zeb didn't bother to say goodbye to me? I mean, there's no reason for him to tell me his plans, but I kind of feel like…

My lips twist, but before I let that thought grow legs it shouldn't, I focus instead on Rosalie.

"Let me give you the full tour. You've got the basic layout down pat, but Carmen neglected three of the best features."

"She did?"

"Yes." I take Rosalie's hand in mine and drag her down the hall to the door leading into what would normally be a garage. "City living is what it is and cars are kind of expensive to park. Since we're a trolley stop away from campus, we opted not to have a car and converted the garage into a glorified workout room."

I open the door to our workout room with a flourish and gesture for Rosalie to enter ahead of me.

"Wow. This is impressive." Her eyes light up in wonder as she explores our gym.

"Well, city living being what it is, in addition to the car thing, none of us really have the money for a gym membership." That's not true. Barbi has more money than she lets on. Carmen and I kind of go with the flow; meaning we don't ask questions. "So we created our very own gym here."

Two sides of the gym are covered in mirrors. In the middle of one wall, we inserted one of those mirror workout screens that streams on-demand workouts with the press of a button. Barbi put a treadmill in the corner, but that's the only machine in the room. There's a small set of adjustable weights and a yoga hammock I bought a year ago and absolutely love.

"This place is amazing." Rosalie bounces on the mats covering the floor, testing the cushioning.

"Yeah, you can do pretty much anything you want. With the mirror thingy, there's tons of workouts to choose from, and if you're into meditation, or just need to relax…" I pull her toward a hidden treasure the three of us found when renovating the space.

"Townhomes are pretty much a thing in the city. Most have no garages. Those that do, tend to have a single car garage. The owners before us converted the back half of what used to be an unfinished basement into a finished garage space for a second car. We didn't need that space and had more than enough room for our gym, so we converted this to a secret retreat." I press a hidden switch and a section of the back wall pops open.

"A hidden room?" Rosalie's eyes light up. "That's incredible."

"A hidden oasis." I flick on a switch and reveal our pride and joy. Salt lamps bathe the room in a golden glow. There's a mat to sit on, plush puffy cushions all around. "It's a yoga meditation room." I drag my fingers over the sound-cancelling foam on the walls. "The whole place is soundproofed. When you shut the door…" I close the door behind us so Rosalie can get the full impact of the space and stand perfectly still.

"It's quiet." Rosalie's mouth drops and she spins around.

"Isn't that cool?"

"I've never…" She places her hands over her ears, releases them, then does it all over again. "I feel like I can hear my heart beating."

"I come here to de-stress before exams or after a grueling workout when I need a bit of centering."

"It's impressive."

"Come." I lead her to the back of the space. "Time for unique feature number two."

"Lead on." Rosalie has a bounce to her step that wasn't there before.

I take that as a good sign. She's finally starting to relax. After her harrowing adventure in the jungles of Nicaragua, escaping the men Carmen's father sent after her, I can only imagine what's going through her mind.

At the back of the modified garage, there's another door. I take her to it.

"This heads outside into the back courtyard. Did Carmen give you all the codes?"

"You mean to the doors?" Rosalie's eagerness warms my heart.

"Yeah. 2-3-11. Did she tell you how we came up with that?"

"Each number is for the letter of your names. Barbi is the second letter. Carmen the third. You're number eleven."

"Yeah, and Rosalie is the…" I sing the alphabet song in my head and count my fingers. "You are number eighteen. We should change it to 2318."

"You don't have to do that." Rosalie takes a step back, revealing her nervousness and fear about breaking into our tight little group.

"This is your home now, and you're one of us." With a bit of jiggling of the lock, I open the storm door leading up into what used to be nothing but weeds. "And this is the oasis."

Once we come up the stairs, the motion-activated lights turn on and fountains bubble to life. Barbi's the one with a green thumb, but I'm the one who created the hardscape, built out the waterfalls, and dug out the meandering streams that wander through our postage-stamp sized backyard. A trellis reaches overhead, and string lights bathe the area in soft, golden light.

"Wow, this is incredible. Did you do this?"

"Over the past four years." It's my pride and joy. I consider it a bit of fancy in the middle of a city that needs something soft.

"It's stunning." Rosalie claps her hands together. "It kind of reminds me a little of this hotel Hayes and I..." Her voice trails off and her brows knit together.

When I think she's going to continue, but doesn't, I take that as a sign that memory isn't one she's ready to openly share. I move past it quickly, trying to avoid triggering anything I shouldn't.

"It's a labor of love. Barbi is the green thumb. She loves orchids and trailing vines. I'm a water lover and created all the little streams and such. I'm also kind of a dreamer. I wanted to build a little fairy garden. It's quirky, and odd, but once it gets darker, you'll see little lights twinkling in the vegetation."

"Impressive." She spins in a circle, taking it all in. "It's truly brilliant, and it hardly feels like we're in the middle of the city."

"That's why I built it. I'm a small-town girl."

"Really? Where are you from?"

"Kansas, if you can believe it. All around us for miles, when I was growing up, were cornfields and fields of snap peas. In a place like that, sometimes imagination is the only escape. I started with helping my dad with the corn mazes in the fall, then kind of branched out from there."

"Well, you've definitely got an eye for creating magic." She spins around in a circle. "I think I'll be spending a lot of time out here. You'll have to show me how to keep it all running when you leave." Rosalie stops, and I sense her unease.

"I will teach you everything you need to know. Barbi will keep the plants alive. Carmen is totally useless. If you're up to learning about how to keep water pumps pumping and the lights working, I'll happily teach you how."

"I'm sorry. I didn't mean to..." She kind of chokes up.

"Rosalie, I'm happy you're here. I'm thrilled you're going to live here with Barbi and Carmen. I don't think, or feel, for a minute that you're replacing me. Change is inevitable, and I've dreamed of being a veterinarian since I was five. Please, don't think your moving in has anything to do with me moving out." I take her hands in mine. "You and Carmen are family, and now you're our family too. We're four women who are all sisters from different mothers, learning how to make our way in life."

"Thanks. That means more to me than you know. I didn't want you to think…"

"And I don't." I pull her in for a hug. "And that's the last time we're going to think about any of that foolishness." To my delight, Rosalie lifts her arms and hugs me back. "You belong here as much as any of us, and although I'll be away it's not like I'm going that far. UC Davis is just a few hours away. When I need to escape campus, you bet I'll come right back here." I release her and take her hands in mine. "And I really can't wait to get to know you like a sister."

"I'd like that very much." Her voice is whisper soft.

I hear what she says and what she doesn't say. In my heart, I know she's going to fit in just fine.

"Barbi, they're out back." Carmen's voice pulls us out of our reverie. She calls out from the kitchen. "We've been looking for the two of you."

"Sorry, I took Rosalie on a tour through the gym, our meditation room, and I wanted to show her our little slice of heaven in the city."

"Did you hear the guys got called away?"

"I did."

"Instead of going to the pier, I thought we could order pizza and hang out on the roof? I've got wine." She holds a bottle of one of my favorite chardonnays.

"Wine sounds fine." I put my hands up to my mouth and shout. "What time is it?"

"Wine Time!" Carmen shouts back.

"What time is it?" I call out again.

"Wine Time!" Carmen sings back.

"It's one of our things." I wink at Rosalie. "Wine Time is fun time. Time to kick back and do nothing but be present in the moment and enjoy each other's company."

Elbowing Rosalie in the ribs, including her in our little ritual, I wink and grab her hand.

"And now, for the pièce de résistance…"

"What's that?" Rosalie's expression lights with excitement.

"The third stop in our magical tour." I point overhead. "To the roof!"

"To the roof!" Carmen calls out after me, then shifts her attention to Rosalie. "It's not quite the same as climbing trees in the rainforest, but you're going to love the view."

With that, the three of us head into the kitchen, where we find Barbi coming up from the gym.

"Good, you found them." She puffs at a strand of hair covering her face. "Did I hear it was Wine Time?"

"Sure did." Carmen thrusts the bottle she was holding at me, then turns to Rosalie. "You'll find wine glasses in the cabinet behind you." She opens the fridge and pulls out two more bottles of wine. "Barbi, you're on pizza duty."

"I'm on it." Barbi snaps to attention and gives a little salute. She pulls out her phone and quick dials our favorite pizza place. "Rosie, anything you won't eat?"

Something happens when Barbi shortens Rosalie's name to Rosie. I swear it's as if her entire face lights up. No, her entire body seems to glow, and for the first time, a genuine smile graces her features.

The four of us head upstairs and clamber up the fire escape that leads to the roof. Like the gym, the meditation room, and the garden, we've made changes up here as well.

Nothing fancy. Anything left to the whim of the elements needs to be able to handle what San Francisco can throw at it. We settled for plastic Adirondack chairs and matching side tables, coffee tables, and gas fed heaters for chilly San Francisco nights. But what makes the roof so much fun is the stunning view of the city when it's lit up at night.

"So, Rosie…" Barbi uncorks the first bottle of wine. She fills up Rosalie's glass, then plops down into a chair.

"Yes?" Rosalie takes a sip and her eyes close as she takes everything in. She's definitely relaxing. "Tell us all the sordid things you and Hayes did while running around in the jungle. Did you play Tarzan and Jane? Who jumped whose bones first?" Barbi's question gives Rosalie a shock. She inhales her wine and spits it out, coughing hard.

"Wine Foul!" Carmen and Barbi point at Rosalie, and we all laugh hysterically.

"Excuse me?" Poor Rosalie looks between the three of us.

"Spitting out good wine is a Wine Foul," I explain. "Which means you have to tell us nothing but the God's honest truth to our very next question."

"Wait. What?" She turns to Carmen. "Is that really a thing?"

"You're one of us now…" Barbi slings an arm around Rosalie's shoulder. "Which means, it's totally a thing. And I have questions."

"About what?" Rosalie looks unsure.

"I want to know about you and your Guardian." Barbi leans back and takes a sip of wine. "Men like that… Men stacked like that…"

With Rosalie's eyes round as saucers, we all settle back in our chairs, and wait for Barbi to ask her question.

"Yes?" Rosalie hesitates.

"Are they as good in bed as they look?"

Right as Rosalie opens her mouth to answer, the clomping of boots rings out from the fire escape below. We stop talking and look at each other.

Barbi mouths: *Did you lock the front door?* She glances at Carmen and me. I shake my head, as does Carmen. We forgot to lock the front door.

A sudden sense of dread overcomes me. Would Scott…? No, he wouldn't come in uninvited, but who else would know the code to get in?

SEVEN

Zeb

————

WE'RE FORTUNATE TRAFFIC IS LIGHT AND MAKE GOOD TIME TO THE
airport.

My phone rings and I put it on speaker.

"Yo!"

"Howzit hanging, Zeb?" Mitzy's high-pitch voice crackles through the speakers.

"A little to the left. How about you?"

"The girls are doing just fine."

"Are you going to brief us?"

"Yup. This client is high profile," Mitzy says. "There's already been one attempt on her life in WITSEC."

"Damn." Hayes gives a low whistle.

"Sounds like the Marshalls have a leak." Rafe stares out at traffic.

"Yup," Mitzy says.

"That's not good." My thumbs tap on the steering wheel.

"What's the op?" Alec glances at me and we exchange a look. "Are we taking over protection detail from the US Marshalls?"

"You got that right on the nose, and we are until they plug the leak in their organization," Mitzy says.

"We're happy to help." I merge into airport traffic. "Do we get to know anything about this client?"

"Nope." Her lips pop on the 'p.'

"Well, that's no fun." I scratch the side of my chin.

"Sorry. Compartmentalized information. Need to know only. You should be used to that."

"We're going to need to know something." Hayes shifts in his seat.

I tap out a tune on the steering wheel while keeping an eye on the flow of traffic.

"I get that." There's another pause on the other end of the phone while Mitzy confers with someone. "I'm not sending her picture. Too much of a risk."

"Then how are we gonna know which passenger she is?" Rafe presses his hand to his temple.

"Code word," Mitzy says.

"Gotcha." Rafe runs his fingers through his hair. "I take it she doesn't know we're picking her up."

"Correct. Just the code word."

No reason for Mitzy to explain the obvious. We've done this kind of thing in the past. The client's instructed she's to be met by someone, or someones, and they'll be holding up a placard with a code word on it. Very secret spy shit.

Actually, it's simple and easy. Which is what makes it perfect for secret spy shit. Not to mention, it follows along the lines of K.I.S.S: Keep It Simple Shithead. We don't need to know what she looks like because of the code word.

"Don't burden her with questions. Chase is on his way, but there's a wreck on the road that's delaying him. Once you've got her, I'll send you to Chase and him to you. You can hand her over where you meet on the road."

"How high is the risk someone will be waiting for her here?"

"High. Like I said, there's a leak in the US Marshalls. We've done our best to keep news of her movement as quiet as possible, but you know my views on that."

"Hope for the best. Plan for the worst."

"You got it." There's another long pause on the other end, then Mitzy's back. "She's not carrying any baggage. Rafe, Hayes, and Alec, you'll meet her at the gate. On the way back, take a tram to a different airline and exit at arrivals instead of departures. That way, if her flight was leaked, they'll be looking for her in the wrong place."

"Got it." I pull up to arrivals and my teammates get out. "You going to guide me in? Or am I supposed to keep circling?"

"We'll guide you in. I'm busy and signing off, but I'm turning you over to Tom." Static scratches over the line as Mitzy removes the headset she's speaking through and hands it to one of her technical team members.

"Zeb, this is Tom Slade. I'll be walking you through your next steps."

"Hello, Tom and copy that." Tom's a new voice to me.

Over time with Guardian HRS, I can identify each of the technical gang by voice alone. In person? Now, that's a different story.

Tom's got one of those serious voices. Professional to a fault, the man doesn't waste words.

"I'm circling back around. Traffic's thick."

"Copy that. I'm notifying your team to delay. Greatest threat point is exiting the building."

"Agreed."

As I wait for the cars in front of me to pull out of their parking places, and the cars behind me to find a place to stop, I slowly inch forward through the congestion of the airport, dodging cars and impatient passengers rushing here and there with arms full of luggage, not looking where they're going. It takes a little longer than I'd like for a car to pull away from the curb. I pull into the empty spot to wait.

Tom talks to both my team and myself, synchronizing our arrivals with expert precision.

It's fate that my teammates are dressed in nondescript clothing —jeans and T-shirts—which is a relief given that we have no idea who might be waiting for our new client. I don't like that they're unarmed. Other than muscle, they don't have much to offer as far as protection goes. Well, nothing except for extensive training.

"They should be here any moment." Tom alerts me that my teammates are close.

Sure enough, within seconds, a woman exits arrivals with Rafe and Hayes walking with her in protective formation. Their movements are choreographed precisely and their attention is perfectly divided.

Rafe scans left. Hayes scans right. Alec hangs in the back, scanning forward and back. If there's someone looking for our mysterious client, they don't stand a chance against three Guardians.

Meanwhile, I pay attention to the nonstop flow of traffic, looking to see if we have any interested parties on our tail. The likelihood of that is slim to none, considering nobody knows to look for us. However, there could be someone circling the airport, waiting to pounce on our mystery guest. We're paid to be paranoid for good reason.

Tom continues on the line giving instructions. Some of what he says makes me roll my eyes. When he instructs me to "Keep an eye out for anyone tailing me; they may try to blend in with the crowd and follow." It's about all I can do not to lash out and rip him a new one.

I can do this in my sleep.

Tom continues babbling away, telling me how to do my job. If I could, I'd reach through the phone and strangle him. Instead, I keep up the steady drumbeat on the steering wheel.

"If someone looks suspicious or familiar, alert me immediately." Tension vibrates in Tom's voice, indicating strain. Where does that tension come from? Is this his first op? How high profile is the client? Maybe a bit of both?

"Copy that." I keep my tone level while grinding my molars together.

The back door opens. Rafe slides in first and scoots all the way to the other side. The woman is second. Hayes is last. He slides in and closes the door. Alec wanders around the back of the vehicle, doing one last scan of the crowd around us. He opens the passenger door and gets in.

"We're good to go." Alec secures his seatbelt as I ease back into traffic.

"On our way." My comment's for Tom, who listens on the other end of our call.

"I'm sending the route." Far less strain vibrates in his voice. It's as if I hear him visibly relax. "You notice anything out of the ordinary…"

"Tom, this ain't my first fucking rodeo." Tom officially reached the end of my patience. "I know what to do. Your job is to take care of any kinks along the way. How far out are we from Chase?"

"He's past the traffic accident and making good time. I've located a place for you to make the exchange."

I turn to our guest, who's as still as a statue turned to stone. Not to mention mute. I expect some form of communication, but not one word? Makes me wonder who she is and what she's running from?

"Nice to meet you, Miss…" I wait for her to supply a name, but Miss Mystery keeps her lips closed and shrinks back in her seat. I continue on as if it's what I intended all along.

The rest of the ride is silent, other than occasional instructions over the speakerphone from our friendly tech geek, Tom. The rush of traffic outside the car window—bores me.

Is it bad I hope for something a bit more exciting? What I wouldn't give to shake off a tail? A bit of defensive driving sounds like fun, but no luck.

I transition from city streets to the freeway, and then I spot it. Someone following.

At first, I'm not sure, but after double-checking in the rearview mirror, there's a car that follows.

"Check out the tan sedan." I elbow Alec, getting his attention. "Five cars back. It's made our last four turns."

Neither Rafe, nor Hayes, react. We don't want whoever's following us to know we're onto them. Alec uses the passenger side mirror to check out the suspicious car.

"How long?" Alec asks.

"Been a few minutes." The driver stays a hundred meters or so behind us. Far enough away to be unobtrusive, but close enough to narrow the gap if need be.

"Agree. Looks suspicious." Alec agrees with my assessment, which isn't good. I'd like to think I'm being extra paranoid. "Let's shake them. Force them to reveal themselves."

"That's what I'm thinking." I wait for a gap in traffic and then suddenly veer off the freeway.

We're lucky to be at an exit with a cloverleaf. My breathing slows as a sense of profound calmness overcomes me. The beating of my heart follows, slowing down. The only part of me that tenses are my hands. They tighten their grip on the wheel as I prepare for four harsh turns taken at speed.

"Hold on." The warning isn't for my teammates but for our passenger, who has yet to utter a single word.

I approach the next exit, waiting for the last minute, then I step on the gas and yank hard on the wheel. I take the first off-ramp, pass under the freeway and take the on-ramp heading north, directly opposite the direction of our previous travel.

I don't merge back into the flow of traffic but continue to the next off-ramp. This one puts me headed due west. One more on-ramp and we're back on the freeway headed south along our previous direction of travel, but significantly back in the flow of traffic from our original position.

I keep my attention split between the road and my rearview mirror.

"Did they follow?" I lost my focus on the rearview mirror during the on-ramps and off-ramps, but Alec watched the entire time.

"Don't see them."

The driver of the tailing car either isn't very good or they're inexperienced.

"Then, they're either ahead of us, or they'll take the next exit and try to find us." I focus on the road and drive slower than the main flow of traffic. If the tail didn't exit, trying to catch us, they'll be looking for us in their rearview mirror.

My job is to make certain that doesn't happen.

When I call it in, Tom's professionalism cracks. Actually, it's his voice that cracks. Bet his ass puckers too. He's too green for this job, getting rattled like that.

"Stop jabbering." I put an end to his stream of *Holy shit's* and *Oh-my-God's*. "We lost them. If they're in front of us, that's where they'll stay. Meanwhile, might I suggest changing our current rendezvous with Chase?"

After a few miles, I take another off-ramp, looping around the city until I no longer suspect we're being followed. Only then do I relax. Not a second later, my thoughts drift back to Kaye, the pretty blonde who loves animals.

We follow the new route and eventually arrive at our destination: a small, unassuming hotel off the beaten path.

I pull around to the side entrance and park next to Chase's Jeep. He gets out as soon as he sees us and looks around before heading toward the vehicle. Rafe opens his door and gets out. Hayes and Alec follow. Miss Mystery stays inside the vehicle.

"You have her?" Chase approaches, speaking in a low voice, just loud enough for us to hear.

"We do." My reply is direct and to the point, lacking any of the many questions filling my head.

"Thanks for the assist." Chase opens the door to the backseat with no hesitation. He acknowledges our passenger, speaking quietly to her. "It's nice to meet you." He extends a hand to our charge. "Name's Chase. If you'll come with me, we can get going."

"Nice to meet you." She accepts his hand and slowly exits the vehicle.

No words for us, but she'll speak to him?

Chase takes over responsibility for our charge and escorts her into his own car before speeding away into the night. As relieved as I am that she made it safely out of danger, I can't help feeling like this was all too easy; almost too easy.

But our job is over, which means we're cut loose.

"Where to?" My fingers tap on the steering wheel. "Back to HQ? Or…" We're an hour's drive from both HQ and the city.

Alec speaks up. "I say we go back to the townhouse."

Rafe stares at me through the rearview mirror, jaw clenched, eyes fierce, but Hayes nods in agreement.

"Agree. I don't want Rosalie to spend her first night alone."

Rafe reluctantly agrees and murmurs his assent. I head back to the townhouse, knowing our camaraderie will be tested.

Kaye's piqued my interest, and there's no way I can keep my hands off the stunning blonde. I crossed that line the moment I laid eyes on her outside that townhouse.

As far as the team goes, and our loyalty to one another, only time will tell. For now, I'm content to enjoy the ride and eagerly look forward to exploring the electric chemistry simmering between me and the woman named Kaye.

EIGHT

Kaye

———

A SHOCK OF WHITE-BLOND HAIR APPEARS BELOW THE ROOFLINE. Then two pizza boxes rise up from below.

"Who the fuck ordered pineapple on their pizza?" The deep rumbling baritone sounds like boulders crashing together.

"Forest?" Carmen jumps to her feet and Rosalie follows. "What are you doing here?" Carmen reaches for the boxes of pizza, then hands them to Rosalie.

"Evidently, I'm delivering pizza." Forest Summers climbs up the fire escape, and when he rises to his full height, my mouth gapes. "Poor delivery guy kept knocking on the door, but no one was answering." Slightly out of breath, his chest rises and falls as he takes in Barbi and me.

"Uh-oh." In our excitement to bond with Rosalie, we forgot about one of us staying downstairs. We can't hear the doorbell when we're on the roof.

"You didn't order near enough." Taller than tall, broader than broad, Forest is a force of nature. That shock-white hair, however, makes him look pale. Almost sickly. He steps onto the roof and turns around to offer a hand down to someone below. "I ordered more pizza. Hope you don't mind if Sara and Paul join us."

A pretty woman with flowing brown hair steps onto the roof. She cups Forest's face and brings him down for a swoon-worthy kiss that makes my heart take off.

Talk about a hot-as-sin kiss.

But that's nothing compared to the stunning man who follows on her heels. Dark hair, lithe body, there's a sinuous grace about him, but that's not what makes my pulse race. An aura of power pulsates around him. It makes the very air seethe, and to my complete and utter shock, that dominating force has eyes for only one person.

It's not the woman. It's the man, Forest, himself.

"My name's Sara." The woman extends her hand. "Looks like y'all know Forest, and the other of our throuple is Paul."

"Throuple?" Barbi looks as confused as me.

"We're a threesome. Or rather two twosomes?" Her brow scrunches trying to explain. "Forest and I are married. Forest and Paul are…"

"Eager for your Guardians to return." Tall, dark, and handsome, Paul strides over to one of the empty chairs and lowers his towering frame into it with impressive grace. He's tall, like Forest, but lithe where Forest is massive. Nevertheless, his power is undeniable. "We're supposed to be at a club." His accusing gaze cuts to Forest.

"We're still going to the club." Voice raspy, Forest's deep voice sounds like thunder rumbling in the distance.

Desire and need thread through his voice. It's at once sexual, yet not. Almost desperate. There's no other way to describe it. But there's a frailty to him that doesn't match anything else.

"Will the two of you take a load off and chill?" Sara glances at her watch. "It's barely seven. The Forge doesn't open for another three hours."

"They'll open for me." Forest drops into a chair and glances at the wine. He turns to Paul with a questioning look. Almost as if asking for permission?

Paul gives a sharp shake of his head. A definite *no*.

I've never been more intrigued by three people in my life.

"Sorry to crash your party," Paul says, "but when Forest mentioned Bravo team was needed for a spell and this was Rosalie's first night off Guardian HQ grounds, I figured we could provide security until Bravo team is back."

"You decided all without asking me." Forest crosses his arms in a pout.

"That's right. Tonight is my night, which means you don't get a say." Paul looks around our little gathering. "Do you happen to have more wine glasses?"

"In the kitchen." I pop to my feet, completely engrossed in our new visitors. "I'll show you where they are and grab plates for the pizza. I wish we'd known you were coming. We would've ordered more pizza."

"Forest accosted the poor delivery guy. Instead of ordering the normal way, he shoved a couple of hundreds into the guy's hands with demands for more pizza."

"Now that's something I would've paid to see." I head to the fire escape with Paul in tow. Behind us, Forest and Sara continue introductions.

For a dominating force, once I get Paul alone in the kitchen, he relaxes. It's as if, without Forest, his aura shifts. I now stand beside a normal guy, digging through the cupboards for wine glasses and rifling the pantry for paper plates.

"Should I stay here and wait for the pizza, or do you girls have a way of hearing the doorbell from the roof?"

"Seeing as how we didn't the first time…" I nibble on my lower lip and can't help but laugh. "We should probably wait down here."

"I'll wait. You take these up to the roof." Paul hands me the paper plates.

"I wouldn't want you to wait down here alone."

"Don't worry about me. I'll be fine."

"But don't you want to see the sunset? The view is spectacular."

Paul's tall enough that I have to tilt my head back to look up at him.

"I do, and I would, but tonight's mine with Forest. Sara can have him for sunset."

"What's a throuple?" I shouldn't ask, but I'm curious like a cat. There's something special about the three of them, and I want to understand it.

"A throuple?" He pulls at his chin. "It's a way to say we're all in one relationship, with different relationship dynamics between us."

"I have no idea what that means."

"Well, Sara and Forest are married, and Forest and I are in a D/s relationship."

"D/s?"

"BDSM. Have you heard the term?"

"I have." I cup my cheeks and feel the heat radiating from them. "Sorry, I'm not used to such direct…"

"I tend to be quite direct."

"So you and Forest are…" Somehow, I can't make my words flow.

"In a relationship with a power dynamic as the central focus."

"And you and Sara?"

"Sara and I are still figuring that bit out. I mean there are the twins…"

"Twins?"

"Yes. We've got two amazing kids together."

"You and Sara?"

"No. Me, Forest, and Sara."

"I'm sorry; I don't mean to pry, and not that it's any of my business, but what?" I feel bad for snooping on something that has nothing to do with me, but I'm genuinely curious.

"Don't apologize for being curious. Many people don't understand our unique lifestyle. Honestly, I wouldn't recommend it. It takes a lot of communication and work. Let me see if I can explain." He pauses for a second to gather his thoughts while I wait with intense curiosity. "Forest and I are a Dom-sub pair. Are you familiar with what that means?"

"I am."

Although, from what little I know about Forest, all of three seconds on the roof and what Carmen's told me, I don't see Forest as the submissive in any relationship.

He's the founder of Guardian Hostage Rescue Specialists. His entire vision is to create a world where those who are weak are not preyed upon by those stronger than themselves. How could a man like that cede authority to another?

Paul watches me parse this in my head. He doesn't push. Doesn't force. In fact, he does nothing I'd expect from a Dom. And yes, like the rest of the world, I'm very familiar with the BDSM lifestyle thanks to the extraordinary success of Fifty Shades of Grey.

"Forest and Sara," Paul begins, "are a traditional pairing. Forest and I are the exact opposite: a male-male dyad. Sara and I are the two halves who make Forest whole. We're both exactly what he needs, yet not enough on our own to fill the void within him."

"Two halves who make him whole?" My curiosity about Forest, and his partners, Sara and Paul, delves deeper than it should. "I tried something like that."

"What?"

"A D/s relationship, but it didn't work out."

"It doesn't always." He appears sympathetic, which helps me open up to him. I have certain questions, things that have bothered me about Scott, and no one to ask. Paul may have answers.

"Is it typical for the Dom to do what he wants?"

"That depends." Paul tips his head sideways.

"Okay…" I pull at my chin, thinking I may have been too harsh cutting Scott off.

"I sense a deeper question. Please, feel free to ask. I have extensive experience in the lifestyle."

Normally, I wouldn't share any of my thoughts like this, but Paul makes me feel safe.

"It's just that I broke things off with my boyfriend."

"He was your Dom?"

"I'm not exactly sure."

"That's not something that should ever be in question."

"It was more of a gradual thing. Does that make any sense?"

"Regardless, a D/s dynamic isn't something that is a *gradual thing.* You broke things off. Why?"

"I caught him with another woman."

"In your dynamic, was that something that was allowed?"

"No." I pull back in shock. "Not at all."

"I ask because sometimes such things are a part of the exploration of power exchange. But I take it this was a violation of trust?"

"Yeah."

"And the D/s? Can you explain more of your dynamic? It may help me provide advice."

"Well, that's just the thing. I mean, I know about BDSM, thanks to Fifty Shades. Scott is definitely dominant, in bed and out. We never officially labeled it. Over time, he became more controlling, more demanding—and when I caught him, I called things off. He says I can't do that. I guess I'm wondering if I messed up. Did I misunderstand?"

"I don't like to assume, but I have this to say. First off, there should be no question whether you're in a D/s relationship. It's the responsibility of both parties to fully discuss the dynamic and consent to the exchange of power, but in particular, it's the Dom who's responsible for ensuring the details of the relationship are firmly established. Each one is exceptionally unique, so it's difficult to speak for all, but that's a minimum. It sounds to me like you were not involved in a D/s relationship. It also appears that Scott violated the trust in your relationship with him."

"He says things aren't over until he says they are, and that I'll regret leaving him."

"Definitely not a Dominant. It sounds to me like he's controlling and domineering. Those are red flags. You were right to leave him, and I wouldn't give him the time of day. You owe him nothing."

"Thanks. That's what I'm trying to do. His texts are concerning."

"How?"

"Threatening? Controlling. Sometimes, when I go out, I get a sense I'm being followed."

"You should trust your gut. You believe he's stalking you?"

"I have no proof."

"I would suggest letting the Guardians watching over this house know about the threats. They're watching for something coming from Maximus Angelo, Carmen's father, and won't know to look out for a potential stalker."

"I'm embarrassed to mention it."

"You have no reason to be embarrassed and plenty of reason to have extra eyes on it."

"Thanks. I feel a bit foolish, but this really helps. Thank you for letting me talk about it. I didn't know who to ask about the D/s stuff."

"If you have any other questions, you can ask me anytime."

"Thanks. Although, it won't be much of an issue for long."

"How's that?"

"I'll be moving in August." My tone shifts.

"You don't sound happy about that. Why are you moving?"

"I'm moving to Davis."

"Graduate school?"

"Vet school."

"Congratulations. Why aren't you happy about it?"

"I thought I was."

"I may be overstepping, and please, don't attach too much significance to what I say, but I'm a good read of other people. Can I give you a word of advice?"

"Of course."

"Do what's best for you. I've known you for just a moment, but I sense you're struggling with the move. You're not leaving anyone behind. You're leaving your friends to pursue your dream. That dream may, or may not, include them in the future. If it does, it's going to be different from what the three of you share now. Don't be afraid of change."

"Wow, that's…"

"Too much?" He arches a brow. "Too direct?"

"Yes and yes, but also no." I place my hand on his arm and feel the steel beneath his skin. The man is solid. "Your words are far more direct than I'd otherwise be comfortable with, but also incredibly timely. I've been struggling for a while, and I think I just needed someone to tell me it's going to be okay."

"Trust me." Paul places his hand over mine. "It's going to be okay. Walk your path and trust your dreams. In life, we make new friends all the time. People come and go. It's up to us to recognize the friends who anchor us and keep them around, while welcoming new people into our lives. It's the way we grow."

"That's funny." I can't help but laugh. "There's a Girl Scout song that says just that."

"I know the one."

"You do?"

"Yes, my sister Piper used to sing it nonstop." Paul clears his throat, then surprises me with a voice that can only be described as touched by God.

～

Make new friends,
But keep the old.
One is silver,
And the other, gold.
A circle's round,
It has no end.
That's how long,
I'm gonna be your friend.

～

"Wow." I take a step back, truly amazed. "How did you do that?"

"Do what?"

"Get in my head like that?"

"It's what makes me a good Dom. Barbi and Carmen form the foundation of your circle. They're your gold; the strongest bonds you'll form. When you leave, you'll make new friends.

Those will be important to you, but never as solid as your foundation."

"I feel like you're a sage. Speaking the truths of the universe."

"Don't think too highly of me. I may look like I've got it all figured out, but even I'm navigating my own minefield." His gaze flicks up, toward the roof, where Forest and Sara wait.

"Are things…"

"Forest is keeping something from us. He's trying to be strong—stoic, if you will—when he should be leaning on those closest to him. I wish I could smack some sense into him, but our dynamic follows other paths."

"You seem to be very tuned into those around you. I don't know what Forest is keeping from you and Sara, but surely you and Sara, working together, can navigate that minefield together."

"And that is perfect advice." He grips my arm and leans down to plant a kiss on my forehead. "I think we have each helped the other tonight."

Just then, the doorbell rings, breaking the odd spell hanging over us.

"That's probably the pizza guy. Why don't you head up with the glasses and plates, and I'll follow with the pizzas?"

"Sounds perfect." Paul takes the glasses and plates from me, then trots up the stairs headed to the roof.

It may be me—I've never been good at reading other people—but I sense Paul needs to rejoin his throuple.

Whatever that is.

With pizza on my mind, I head to the front door. When I pass Barbi's room—my room now—I duck inside to grab my purse and dig out a tip for the delivery person. When I make it to the front door, however, there's no sign of anyone at all.

No pizza.

No delivery guy.

No double-parked car outside.

Nothing.

I lean out, casting up and down the street, but nobody's there.

"Odd." I'm about to shut the door when I spy a small package tucked into the corner of the stoop. Not knowing if Barbie, or Carmen were expecting a delivery, I carry it inside and place it on the kitchen counter.

I turn the package over, searching for an address, but there's nothing. No identifying markings, or hints, as to who left it.

I try to shake off an uneasy feeling. This thing with Scott is making me paranoid.

NINE

Kaye

—————

Since the pizza's not here yet, I make good use of my time. I trot upstairs and duck inside my old room, Rosalie's room now. The net sum of her possessions sit on my bed. A small suitcase plus a few designer bags filled with new clothes.

There are just a few of my things left in the closet that need relocation downstairs. I fill my arms with clothes on hangers and a couple pair of shoes. On my way down, the doorbell rings.

"One second," I call out, then rush to dump my things on Barbi's bed.

This time, when I answer the door, a delivery driver waits with enough pizza to feed a small army.

"Wow. Thanks." I give him the tip, and with pizzas in hand, I climb the stairs and head to the fire escape.

"Pizza's here," I call out, needing help. Paul climbs down the fire escape and grabs the pizzas. Suddenly, the front door slams shut and I jump at the sound.

"Everything okay?" Paul looks at me eager to help.

"I think I left the front door open." Although, I'm almost positive I shut the door, but I've been wrong before. "I'll be right up. Just want to make sure it's locked."

"Sounds good, but hurry, the sun's about ready to set."

"Will do. Be up in a jiffy." I leave Paul to the pizzas and head back downstairs. Indeed, the front door is open. Which doesn't make sense. I thought I heard it slam shut.

When I look out at the street, everything appears quiet and peaceful. An old man walks his small ankle biter of a dog a block away. A group of high schoolers laughs and smokes a few houses down. Everything looks completely normal.

For some reason, however, my attention snags on a figure down the street, hanging outside the corner store. Dressed head to toe in black, he's trying not to be seen. Our gazes connect for a fraction of a second before he turns away, but in that second of contact a strange feeling overcomes me. It's that heebie-jeebies kind of feeling that screams *danger*.

Just as I'm ready to go back inside, however, a very familiar SUV pulls up at the curb. Rafe, Hayes, Alec, and Zeb all pile out of the vehicle. My heart quickens when Zeb looks at me. He runs his fingers through his hair, giving it that tousled bedhead look like he just rolled out of bed.

And now, I'm thinking about him in bed.

"Hey, sunshine." Rafe gives me a quick hug.

"I thought you were called away for a mission?"

"Was a short op," Hayes explains. Like Rafe, he pulls me in for a hug, then continues past me like he owns the place. "Where is everyone?" He pokes his head outside, asking me.

"On the roof." I take a step back, letting the large men into the townhouse. Zeb is last and when he's beside me, my heart kicks into overdrive.

"Miss me?" His left brow arches and the corner of his mouth lifts in a grin.

"Was I supposed to?" There's a little squeak in my voice.

"I missed you." His tone turns sexy and his eyes smolder with desire.

The combination of that tone of voice, those eyes, and his innate magnetism, creates a potent mix that makes my head spin.

"Everyone is on the roof. There's wine and pizza." There's

something about Zeb that makes my stomach flutter, my heart pound, and my words trip all over themselves.

"Interesting combination. What about beer?"

"None of us drink beer. Sorry."

Why do I feel bad about that?

"No problem. I'll hit the market on the corner. Care to come with me?"

Yes!

Any chance to spend more time with this amazing man and I'm on board. But that's not what I say. For some reason, I'm reluctant to show too much interest in him.

"Ummm…"

"Come on." He extends a hand. "I don't want to get lost."

"Considering the corner store is literally on the corner, I don't think you'll get lost."

"Probably, but the companionship would be nice." He definitely doesn't give in easily.

"You really want me to come?"

"One thing you'll learn about me, as we get to know each other better, is I rarely beat around the bush. I'm pretty direct."

Funny, that's pretty much what Paul said earlier. Direct. Do I like direct men? Maybe that's why I fell for Scott. He's also authoritative and direct.

"The sun's nearly ready to set. I've been told the view is spectacular on the roof." Zeb holds out a hand, waiting for me to take it. "I'd rather not miss it."

"Umm…" I drag my hands over my pants.

"Come on. I don't bite." Those eyes of his twinkle with mischief. "Unless that's what you like?"

It emboldens me to have a little fun.

"And if I do?"

"If you like that, I've got a host of other things you'll enjoy. But first, let's get beer and something for dessert."

With my heart beating like a crazy lunatic, I let Zeb take my hand. Before I know it, he lifts my hand to his mouth and presses featherlight kisses over my knuckles. An oddly intimate gesture, it somehow feels right.

I make no move to pull away and find I really enjoy his companionship as we buy beer and cookies for the group. Our little house party is definitely turning into something more, but the moment we exit the corner store, I feel it again.

That sense someone is watching me.

Zeb picks up on it immediately.

"What's wrong?"

A shiver works its way down my spine. Beside me, Zeb's relaxed posture turns tense and his entire being goes on alert. Like me, he scans the street looking for threats.

"It's nothing." I try to play it down, but the set of Zeb's shoulders and the clenching of his jaw tell me he doesn't buy my dismissive comment.

His brow furrows and his stance widens. It's a subtle change but awe inspiring. He's ready for any threat.

Instead of sinfully hot, I see a man born for combat and violence against his enemies. It's terrifying, yet oddly comforting.

"Come." He takes my hand and pulls me down the street.

The entire time, he scans for threats. Unlike me, he's focused and methodical. He takes his time to look down the street and behind parked cars. He checks for anyone hiding in doorways, but there are no threats to be found.

Once we're back inside, he shuts the front door and locks it behind him.

"What other forms of egress are there?"

"Egress?"

"Ways in and out." His gruff tone is abrasive, but the concern behind it evens out the jagged edges.

"The backdoor. Is that what you mean?"

When he takes a step toward me, my heart races with excitement.

"Show me." He crosses his arms over his chest and waits for me to respond.

I take a deep breath, then lead him down the hallway and into the kitchen at the back of the townhome. He follows right on my heels, tense and on high alert. At the back door, he checks the lock, securing it with a click. "How long has this been happening?"

"What do you mean?" I rub my hands up and down my arms, warding off a chill determined to keep me on edge.

"That's the second time something's spooked you." His dark eyes search mine. The intensity of his gaze makes me suck in a breath. It's like he can see right through me.

"Spooked me?" My voice trembles despite my effort not to break down in front of him.

He steps close. Mere inches separate us and the warmth of his body radiates all around me. He makes me feel safe, despite the weirdness going on.

"When I was here before and just now."

Instinctively, I place my hand against his chest. I love the hard planes of his muscle. Touching him seems to let me draw strength from him in ways far surpassing the physical connection between us.

"It's nothing."

"Didn't look like nothing." His expression turns pensive.

When he covers my hand with his, my heart kicks into overdrive and the fluttering in my belly returns. I take a deep breath before responding, not entirely sure how much to tell him. We've known each other for less than a day, mere hours, if not minutes. And while he appears genuinely interested in what's happening, it feels wrong to burden him with my troubles.

I hesitate, to be honest, not wanting to make Scott into some kind of villain. The man's no saint, but he's not the devil.

"Honestly, I just came off a rough relationship. Scott's not taking it well." I shrug, uncomfortable under Zeb's scrutiny.

Not to mention it feels wrong speaking to the man I'm interested in sleeping with about the man I broke up with. There's a disconnect there I haven't fully realized.

Zeb takes a step back, robbing me of the heat radiating off his large frame. He examines me with an intensity that makes my skin itch.

"What does that mean?" Low and sincere, it's almost as if he already knows, but he wants to know if I'm okay. "Not taking it well?"

I sigh and turn away from his gaze. It's too much to process. Not to mention, I don't want to see his reaction when I tell him the truth.

"He's angry at me and wants me back."

Silence stretches between us until it becomes painful. When Zeb finally speaks, it's with zero emotion. The lack of tone and inflection makes his next words terrifying.

"How angry?"

A lump forms in my throat and tears threaten to fall. A Guardian and a protector, he's wired to protect and defend. What does that mean when it comes to Scott? Am I going to make things worse involving Zeb in something I should be able to handle myself?

"Strongly worded texts." I try to play them down.

His jaw tightens as he closes the space between us, towering over me. The thing is, I am scared. Scott's escalating texts terrify me. The urge to throw myself into Zeb's arms is almost too hard to resist, but I do. I resist the urge to snuggle against him and bury into his embrace.

"Has he done anything physical?" His fierce stare never wavers from mine.

"Scott wouldn't do that." I cringe hearing the lie spill from my mouth.

"Has he ever been physical with you?"

Before I can answer his question, Zeb pulls me into a hug that feels like heaven. In Zeb's arms, no one can hurt me. They have to get through him first, and Zeb isn't going to let anyone hurt me.

"Are you asking if he's hit me?" My voice comes out barely a whisper.

"Yes." Zeb's tone is firm. His gaze intense. He wants the truth but won't force it.

"I don't think Scott would hurt a fly." I avert my gaze, unable to watch Zeb's reaction when he realizes it's a lie.

"You'd be surprised what men will do when they want

something." Zeb leans against the counter and absently picks up the small box delivered earlier.

He gives it a little shake, then his brows pull together. He brings the box close, turning it this way and that as if trying to decipher the contents. When he brings it to his nose, sniffing it, I can no longer hold back my curiosity.

"What are you doing?" Apprehension fills my voice, probably because I know who put the box on the stoop.

"Who's this for?" He continues studying the box with a critical eye.

"I don't know. It was dropped off a few minutes ago, but there's no note attached."

"Dropped off earlier? How much earlier?"

"Just before the second round of pizzas were delivered. Someone rang the doorbell. I thought it was the pizza guy, but there was just the box. No note, like I said. I was going to ask Barbi and Carmen if they were expecting something."

He studies me for a long moment, completely silent, before responding. "I have a feeling they aren't." He picks up the box again. "More likely than not, this is meant for you." His lips form a thin line and his eyes harden while he waits for what he says to sink in.

"How would you know?" I reach for the box, hands trembling.

For a split second, Zeb tightens his grip on the box. His body tenses as if getting ready for a fight, but then he hands the box to me.

"Because I know what's in the box."

"What? How?"

"You don't want to know."

"I do." I reach for the box determined to see what's inside.

For a split second, it looks like he's going to snatch the box away. When I grab a knife to cut through the packing tape, Zeb shakes his head and takes a step back. His jaw is tight and he doesn't meet my eyes.

"Remember, I warned you," he says.

Unfortunately, my curiosity is too great. The moment I slice through the tape, the foulest odor assaults my nostrils. The pungent aroma of feces is so strong it makes me take a step back in revulsion.

Zeb grimaces and pinches his nose.

"What the…" I inch forward to see what's inside. Sure enough someone packed up a pile of excrement and sent it to me. I stare wordlessly at Zeb, my mouth gaping in shock.

"Can I look at those texts?" Zeb sighs heavily and runs a hand through his hair. His expression hardens.

"Why?" My voice cracks with fear. Not to mention how surreal this feels.

"Because your ex has crossed a very important line, and I want to confirm it."

"What does that mean?" My stomach twists with dread as I dare ask a question I don't want answered.

"Not to scare you, but there's a very fine line between an angry-ex and stalker behavior." There's a calmness to Zeb's gaze. This is his way of warning me worse things might happen.

To my surprise, I hand Zeb my phone. There's a weird quivering in my gut, and a growing sense of unease. I keep silent as Zeb scans through Scott's angry texts.

I already know what he's going to say. Barbi said it this morning. Those texts are crazy; if I don't do something soon to pacify Scott, I worry he'll go from stalker to something far worse.

Zeb swipes his finger across the screen. "This guy's dangerous." Zeb gives me back my phone.

I look at an angry text from Scott, one I haven't yet seen. It says I need to get my shit together and go back to him. That I can't treat him like this. More texts follow.

"Who's dangerous?" Carmen wanders into the kitchen. "I thought the two of you got lost. We're all waiting, and it's going to be an amazing sunset. Ewww, what's that smell?"

"Scott." I haven't had much of a chance to tell Carmen about Scott. She knows he cheated on me and that I broke things off with him. She doesn't know about the texts, unless Barbi mentioned it.

"He sent her a box of shit." Zeb points to the box.

"He did what?" Carmen looks at the box and scrunches her nose. "Why would he do that?"

"Because I stopped answering his texts." I open my phone to Scott's texts and give them to her to read. "What am I supposed to do with this box?" I pick up the package, handling it with far more care than I did earlier. "I don't want to put it in the trash."

"There's a dumpster in the back of the store down the street." Zeb turns to me. "You got any pictures of this douchebag?"

"I do." I take my phone and click on one of the hundreds of photos of Scott.

Zeb peers at the photo intensely, as if memorizing Scott's face. The only emotion he shows is the storm brewing in his eyes.

"Give me the box." I scoot the box to him and he swipes it off the table with a gruff snort of disdain. "I'll be back."

Without another word, Zeb is gone.

Is it weird I miss him?

"Dang." Carmen rocks back on her heels. "That's intense."

"Yeah, Scott's gone off the rails.

"I'm not talking about Scott. I'm talking about the energy swirling between you and Zeb."

I glance at the door that Zeb just exited through and feel the sparking of electricity that seems to crackle between us fade with his departure. Although, I'm not going to admit it.

"What energy? There's no energy."

"Yeah, I said that about Rafe. Maybe it's not something you can sense when it's happening to you? Like you, I denied it at first. As for Zeb, there's definitely something. simmering between the two of you."

"How can you tell?" I feel the crackling energy, but I'm curious what Carmen sees.

She laughs.

"It's not hard. You two steal glances at each other. They linger longer than an ordinary look, and you blush when he's around. Trust me, the energy is there."

I look away, embarrassed and unsure what to say. I don't like the idea of being so obvious, but I can't deny the truth behind what Carmen says.

"I hope you're ready," she says.

"Ready for what?"

"You activated Guardian Protector mode." She jabs a finger to where the box sat moments before "And the only reason he asked to see a picture of Scott is to canvass the streets for anyone who might have seen your dipshit ex."

"I seriously doubt that's why."

"Remember that for later." Carmen's eyes twinkle with laughter.

"Later?"

"When I say I told you so."

"Good grief, Carmen, you're impossible."

"Perhaps, but why not take a chance? Would it be so bad if you bagged yourself a Guardian?" She nudges me playfully.

"Like I said, you're impossible."

"Be that as it may, we're both going to miss sunset if we don't get to the roof soon. I came down to see what was keeping you."

"The second round of pizzas kept me. I also moved the last of my things into Barbi's room."

"Awesome. Rosalie is overloaded with everything going on. If she forgets to say thank you, she's very grateful."

"She already did. And what about you? How are you feeling after everything that's happened? Overloaded? Stressed to the max?"

"Processing. Sometimes it feels like it was a dream that happened to someone else, but then Rafe will say something, or the other guys will mention the rescue. That brings it all rushing back."

"And your father?"

"He didn't stay in prison long. Not that I thought he would. Too many of the police and prison officials owe him favors."

"I'm sorry."

"It's okay. It's just a matter of time." She glances at her watch. "Speaking of time, we've got to hustle."

Carmen pulls me upstairs to watch the sun go down, but all I can think about is Zeb. What's he doing? Can he help with the whole Scott thing? Or is he only going to make things worse?

Once we're on the roof, the brisk evening air greets us. We make our way to where the gang stares out over the city skyline. A few minutes pass, then the sound of someone coming up the fire escape draws my attention.

"Did I make it?" Zeb strides over to where we stand. A smile fills his face.

Carmen nudges me in the ribs and lowers her voice to a whisper. "That energy I was talking about. It's back."

My cheeks flush, but the rapidly darkening sky hides it from everyone but Zeb. Somehow, he zones in on it. I focus on the skyline, take a sip of wine, and do everything in my power not to make eye contact with Zeb.

He steps close and the warmth radiating off him makes my knees wobble. I shift to the side, taking a small step away from him, overwhelmed and desperately trying to regain some semblance of control over myself and my emotions.

I swore off men for the time being, and I'm not ready to jump into anything new. Especially when new means a Guardian who will go above and beyond to rescue me.

Zeb closes the distance between us, brushing my arm so lightly I can barely feel it. His warmth pulses through me like an electrical charge that sparks something within me. I bite my lip and hope he doesn't notice my body's response to him standing this close.

If I let things progress, it's not a matter of whether things will get complicated. It's a matter of when, and things will get not only complicated, but dangerous as well.

TEN

Zeb

———

The package with the dog shit inside sits uneasily on my mind. Whoever this Scott dude is, he crossed a line. From ex-lover to dangerous stalker and now open threats? I don't think Kaye grasps exactly how dangerous such a man can become.

I do.

I take that seriously.

Very seriously.

I rejoin the rest of my teammates on the roof. Kaye's roommates, Barbi, Carmen, and Rosalie are there, along with Forest and his unique throuple: Paul and Sara.

It's quite an eclectic group, brought together by the founder of Guardian Hostage Rescue Specialists, Forest Summers. He's the center of the web that connects us all.

I make the rounds, greeting Forest, Paul, and Sara. I wave to Kaye's roommates who hold half-empty wine glasses and top off their wine. I hand out beer to my teammates.

This feels nice, but it's missing something.

Everyone relaxes with their drink—beer or wine, depending on preference—while looking out across the cityscape of San Francisco. The city's silhouetted against a tapestry of pink skies streaked with fire red and umber orange. With night approaching, shimmering lights appear here and there in the buildings as people flick on the lights.

A cool breeze blows in from the Bay, sweeping away the heat of the day. Overhead, there are enough clouds to make the sunset truly spectacular without blocking it completely.

Barbi lights up a gas-fed fire pit, along with several heating towers, to push back the chill of the night as it rushes in. People gather around the fire pit, laughing, joking, having fun.

Kaye hangs back from the others, standing near the edge of the roof. She stares outward, scanning the skyline, brows tugged tight as if in deep thought. The last light of the setting sun highlights her angelic features, bathing her in a golden glow.

Damn, but she takes my breath away.

Knowing I'm going to get shit from the guys, and not caring one damn bit, I cross the distance to stand by her side.

"Hey." I nudge her with my shoulder.

It's a friendly touch, an incursion into her personal space, and a test. If she pulls away, I need to reevaluate. If she leans into me, I'll continue exploring where this night might take us.

"Hey." She doesn't pull away, but neither does she lean into me. It's noncommittal which means I need to step up my game.

"Still thinking about the package Scott sent?" I normally wouldn't bring up an ex's name in conversation, but she's clearly rattled by the way things are escalating.

"I am." She turns to me, brows furrowed, lips pressed into a tight line. "Do you believe he's dangerous? Is this something I need to be worried about?"

"Not knowing much about your relationship, that's hard to say one way or the other, but those texts concern me and the box speaks for itself."

"I don't know what to do." She hugs her arms, staving off the chilly night. "Do I call him? Ignore him?"

"Calling him will only give him an opportunity to…"

"Undermine my decision to break up with him." She finishes my sentence, showing healthy insight.

I like that about a woman. Kaye's a thinker.

"That's what my head tells me. Stand strong. Be resolute. But not talking to him…" Her voice cracks. She holds up her phone and scrolls through his texts. "Not talking to him isn't making things any better. It's making things worse. I don't know what to do."

Her personal insight only serves to intrigue me further. She's a remarkable individual.

An unexpected, but welcome, warmth courses through my veins as I look upon Kaye. I can almost block out everyone else on the roof, and forget they're here.

"In cases like this, it's best not to engage." It's the best advice, but hardest to follow.

That electrical charge from before is stronger than ever. Too strong to ignore. But what do I do with it when she's clearly navigating the nasty waters of a disastrous breakup?

We stand side by side, staring out at the city lights while I ponder my next move.

She takes a sip of wine while I drink my beer. Before I overthink things too much, I reach down and take her hand in mine. She doesn't withdraw from my touch and allows me to interlace our fingers.

She looks at me with tenderness layered with a bit of fear, but doesn't pull away. Encouraged by this, I run the pad of my thumb over her knuckles and do the last thing I want to do.

I ask about Scott.

"Tell me about Scott. What happened that made him angry?"

I'm drawn to her like a magnet and can't help but reach up to lightly brush a strand of hair from her face. My thumb lingers on the softness of her cheek. It's merely a moment in time, yet feels incredibly profound. I sweep the loose strand of hair off her face, tucking the wayward lock behind her ear.

Our gazes collide and tangle together. In that moment all is quiet around us, as if time stands still. Neither of us speaks, or moves, unwilling to break the spell. But finally Kaye looks away.

She gazes out over the city, and when the moon peeks out behind the clouds, it bathes her face in ethereal glory. Silence descends between us, but rather than being awkward, it feels welcome. We're growing comfortable with each other more quickly than most would consider typical.

But eventually, Kaye breaks the silence. She takes in a deep breath and tells me about her relationship with Scott from its beginnings to its current state.

"I remember the first time I saw Scott." Her voice shakes and her body trembles. "It was the first day of class, and I sat in the front row. He was my professor and I was enraptured."

I keep my thoughts to myself, including any judgment about a professor using his power to prey upon one of his students. What a fucking douchebag.

"We started spending time together during office hours." Her voice gains in strength. "At first it was with other students, and then one day, after everyone else had gone home, it was just the two of us."

"Go on." Despite the rage building within me, I want her to continue. I value the trust she places in me far more than my anger at a professor abusing his position.

"Before I knew it, we were kissing." A dreamy look appears on her face. "He made the first move and it felt so forbidden. We broke all of the rules."

"He used his position to get into bed with you." I can't stand here and say nothing. What Scott did is wrong on so many levels.

"I see that now, but at the time, I was swept up by the moment. His authority? His power?" She nibbles on her lower lip. "It spoke to me on a level I'd never experienced before. I fell head over heels in love with him. At least, what I thought was love."

There's that rosy glow again, and my heart skips a beat because of what it says about Kaye. It tells me what she finds attractive in a man. It also reveals some important blind spots.

There's a big difference between a dominant man and a domineering asshole. I'm the first. Scott's the second. He's the kind of man I put down for a living.

As for love, it was more likely lust that drew her to him, but I keep that comment to myself.

"When did things change between the two of you?"

"Things started to change as the semester grew to a close. I asked him for a favor. Afterward, he became more possessive, telling me I owed him." Her voice is now sad, regretful, and hurt.

"How?"

"He became possessive. Controlling. He wanted me to be available to him all the time. I couldn't hang with my friends. He made me spend the weekends with him, then demanded I sleep at his place every night. I couldn't have lunch with my friends. I had to join him in his office. Do—things I wouldn't normally do. His demands felt suffocating and I felt humiliated."

She claws at her throat and falls silent for a moment before continuing with a deep breath. "I walked in on him one day when he was with another student."

"What does that mean?"

"He had this girl, Denise, bent over his desk and was fucking her from behind. When I walked out, saying we were over, it turned into a fight." Her voice drops to a whisper and she ducks her head. "He said I had no right to walk out on him. That I belonged to him. And how dare I judge him. That it was my fault he—that he..." She scrubs her cheeks and the tears that fall.

"He blamed his infidelity on you?" What a tool. Men like that don't deserve to breathe.

"He did and that turned into an even bigger fight. I walked away. Stopped responding to his texts. Then he threatened to flunk me and call Dean Alder at Davis."

"Why would he do that?" I get the flunking her from class. That's the power professors hold over their students and precisely why there are non-fraternization policies in place. But Davis?

"Early in our relationship, back when things were heating up, I asked Scott to call the Dean of the vet school at UC Davis and put in a good word for me."

"And?"

"I asked him to help with my application. I was afraid I wouldn't get in on my own. Being a vet is all I've ever wanted to be. I was desperate. And stupid." She wipes away more tears. "That favor is what Scott held over my head. He said I owed him obedience and I wasn't appreciative enough. If I really loved him, like I claimed, I wouldn't hesitate to take things to the next level." She grips her stomach, probably without realizing it, but I hear the fear in her words.

"What does that mean?"

"To become…" Her breath hitches.

"To become, what?"

"Scott likes control. He was always very strict about our roles."

"Roles?"

"Dominant male. Submissive female." Her cheeks pink with shame. "Power exchange?"

"Is that what finally broke you, or was it his infidelity?"

"Both, I suppose. I didn't mind most of what we did. I wanted to be adventurous, but what he wanted from me…"

"Yes?"

"It terrified me." Her lower lip trembles. "Honestly, Denise saved me. If I hadn't walked in on them, I'd probably still be with Scott, and I don't think he would've allowed me to go."

"It sounds like he's a very dangerous man. You did the right thing." My need to protect her is one of my core beliefs, but I need to tread carefully. I'm not into the D/s lifestyle but am familiar with it. I tend to dominate in bed, but that's where it ends. It could be a trigger for her, which means I need to proceed cautiously, if at all.

"You're an incredible woman."

"You don't have to say that. This is a mess of my making. I just have to figure a way out of it."

"From what you've shared, I have a feeling Scott would've convinced you to give up your dream to be a vet. You have a beautiful soul and it would be a crime to deny the world of your talents."

"I don't know about that." Her shyness touches me on a deeply personal level. She's not used to praise from others and doesn't know how to accept it.

"Anyone who devotes their life to animals is a saint in my book."

"I'm no saint."

"Neither am I." I debate my next move, but after she shared something so personal, I feel a need to reciprocate and level the field. "I have something I want to share with you."

"You do?"

I feel the need to switch topics, moving from something heavy to something I hope will inspire her. She needs a bit of a pick me up and to know she did the right thing in kicking Scott out of her life.

"Growing up in the commune, animals were useful only for what they provided." I gaze out toward the horizon and admire the fading glow of the sunset.

"I thought you said you were in a cult?"

"I was born into a cult and we lived as a commune."

The thought disgusts me. How someone can cede over that degree of control to another escapes me. Perhaps this is one of the reasons alternate lifestyles don't appeal to me. Too many bad memories.

"I'm sorry."

"My mother joined the cult when she was sixteen. Ran away from home. Her parents tried to rescue her, several times, but never succeeded."

"Wow."

"She became one of my father's many wives, devoted herself to serve him. Got knocked up and fell from grace."

"That sounds horrible."

"It was."

Those details are not something I'm ready to share. Not yet. If something takes off between me and Kaye, I may tell her the rest of the story. In the meantime, I tell her about the animals and why I admire her career choice as much as I do.

"You mentioned animals?"

"Yes. We all had chores. Once I was old enough, I helped take care of the animals, and like I said, they were useful only for what they gave us."

"What do you mean?"

"Milk from goats and cows. Eggs from chickens. Wool from our bedraggled flock of sheep. Pigs for the meat they provided. Cattle for leather as well as meat. We kept one bull to impregnate the dairy cows, and slaughtered all the male calves after a year."

I pause, shudders run through my body as memories of slaughter day run through my mind.

"It was brutal."

"I can only imagine. I'm an animal lover myself, but I understand the need for slaughtering animals. I'm not a vegan, or vegetarian. As long as it's humane…"

"Ours was not," I murmur softly. "I cried every year when it came time to slaughter the calves. I spent the previous year raising them in the fields, tending their injuries, making sure they were fed. I brought them in during blizzards so they wouldn't freeze."

"You took great care of them."

"I did, but one of my jobs was to slaughter them. I had to slit their throats and drain their blood as they writhed in agony."

"Oh, Zeb, that's horrible."

"They were helpless and terrified. But worse than that, they looked at me, someone they trusted, with confusion, pain, and betrayal."

"I'm so sorry." She places a hand on my arm. "I can't imagine how much that must've hurt."

A lump forms in my throat as memories of those horrific days threaten to overcome me.

"I hated it." I'm a grown man, yet recalling this brings tears stinging the corners of my eyes. "I hated their fear. I hated the way my heart broke when I was forced to end their lives."

"It wasn't your fault."

"To this day, the smell of manure and hay bring overpowering emotions front and center." My voice cracks as I recall my childhood.

On slaughter days, the coppery tang of blood brought bile rising in the back of my throat, but it was the acrid stench of fear and the pervasive smell of death that never left me, that caused the most trauma.

I shake my head slowly and sigh. "Like I said, we weren't kind to our animals. They were to be used and that was it. Compassion was seen as weakness and a sin. Which is why you inspire me."

"Me?"

She needs to know how her life impacts others.

"I can still see it." I suppress a shudder. "The sheep, their blood staining the wool. The hooks, dripping with the last drops of life from the cattle. The bleats and squeals and screams." My fists clench and I shake my head at the memory. "It's something I'll never forgive my father for making me witness, and be a part of, at such a young age."

Odd. I haven't delved down that deep dark well in ages. Why now? How did Kaye get me to reveal this much of myself? I've told no one in such gruesome detail.

Why are memories of my father surfacing now? Probably because this prick of a man, Scott—Kaye's abusive ex—reminds me of my father.

Whatever the reason, I need to pack up those memories and shove them in a deep dark hole in the farthest recesses of my mind.

"Sorry, I didn't mean to over share." My molars grind together as I try to force the memories away. "But you inspire me because you want to help animals. Not hurt them, like I did."

"Don't be sorry. Thank you for sharing that with me." She's sincere in her words and what she says resonates powerfully with me.

"If you need any help, when it comes to Scott, if things go south with him, I'm here if you need someone to talk to, or someone to beat Scott to a bloody pulp."

"Oh please…" A smile warms her face. "No beating anyone to a pulp, bloody or not, but thank you for offering. I just need to figure out how to deal with him, once and for all."

And I'll be right by your side.

At least, I'd like to think she might want me there.

Until she asks, or Scott forces my hand, I'll wait for her to come to me.

She turns to face me and a million emotions swim through her troubled gaze. It feels like ages, that we stand together, as if time no longer exists.

The wind kicks up, sending waves of chilly air across the rooftop. The sun sets in a spectacular riot of colors. Dark blues merge with fiery oranges. Those blues drift to deep purples and eventually the inky blackness of night lays claim to the world below.

The city lights up, attempting to push back the darkness, and comes alive as people continue on with their lives.

A wave of warmth spreads over me when Kaye closes the gap between us until only inches remain. I almost think she's about ready to lift on tiptoe and kiss me. There's an invisible energy pulling us together.

That energy seems to waken something deeper than mere physical attraction and lust. It's something far more ethereal…an emotional connection orchestrated by fate.

"Kaye…" My voice is barely above a whisper.

"Yes?" Her face tilts up. Those rosebud lips of hers are kissably close.

"Whatever happens with Scott—know that no matter which direction you choose, whatever decision you make—I'll be there if you need me."

The air between us crackles. My heart pounds in anticipation as we inch ever so close toward our first kiss. Our gazes lock, and like two magnets, they pull us together.

Her lips part ever so slightly as her breath hitches.

I take both her hands in mine, gently squeeze, then release them. I cup her chin, tenderly, and stroke my thumb along the curve of her jawline, enjoying the moment and soaking in every breath, every beat of my heart, and every sigh she whispers.

We remain in this suspended state for what seems forever, but is probably no more than mere moments.

Kaye breaks the trance with a sigh.

"Thank you. I appreciate it, and I can really use a friend right now."

And just like that, I get relegated to the friend zone.

What the fuck just happened?

Disappointment and shock hit me like a ton of bricks. It's a fight to keep my face impassive. I turn away, not wanting her to see the disappointment in my eyes. I allow myself one final moment before backing off completely, firmly claiming my role in the dreaded friend zone.

"Just call if you need me." I shove my hands into my pockets and walk away.

If it weren't for Douchebag Scott, I wouldn't be forced to accept friendship in place of something more.

Just friends?

Forever?

I refuse to accept it. It's not fair. Not where this night was meant to go. I want way more from Kaye, but she's not ready, too twisted by Scott's threats.

And I can't beat him to a pulp. That's not fair. It's not right. The asshole deserves a thorough ass-beating.

This sucks.

It really sucks.

I swallow my disappointment, turn away, and force myself to retreat to where the others gather around the gas fire pit. Nothing prepares me for the hollow feeling growing inside of me.

So, I grab another beer and drink myself into oblivion.

ELEVEN

Zeb

Summer speeds by as the weeks pass. I find myself frustrated both on the home front and at work.

Mitzy's technical team makes no inroads into Maximus Angelo's human trafficking operation, except to confirm the bastard's back at it. Until that's put to rest, we continue the protective detail at the townhome.

Rafe and Hayes take the brunt of the shifts providing protection for the girls. Their shifts last 48-hours each, depending on what's going on at work. That's four days out of seven when I have no legitimate reason to be around Kaye.

Brady, Booker, Alec, and I split the rest of the 24-hr shifts, which means I get to see Kaye once a week at best; sometimes far less.

It's been two weeks, and I hate it.

When not frustrated by work, I wrack my brain trying to figure out why Kaye seems so distant and remote. Something's changed in her.

After walking the perimeter, I return to the living room and fall back on the couch with frustration.

"Hey, Sexy Guardian." Barbi waves to me as I hang out in the living room. "Howzit hangin'?"

"A little to the left. How are the girls?"

"Plumped and ready for a night on the town." She stops in the hall and does a little spin in a skintight cocktail dress. "How do I look?"

"Positively sinful."

Barbi's a hot mess, but a stunning woman. She's got a great sense of humor. After hearing one of my exchanges with Mitzy, she adopted the Howzit hanging routine as her own. It's now our official greeting.

"Where's Kaye? Is she going out with you?" I hate that I have to ask. I should know, but Kaye's in her own world these days. Whenever I see her, her expression is closed and distant. I barely get a smile.

"Ah, you poor, poor man." Barbi shakes her head. "Trapped in the dreaded friend zone."

"Don't remind me." I roll my eyes in an Oscar worthy performance.

"When are you going to get off your ass and tell her how you feel?" Barbi crosses her arms over her chest and stares down her nose at me.

"You know why I haven't."

Barbi's become my confidant over the past few weeks, and a bit of a co-conspirator. Unlike Rafe and Hayes who've told me in no uncertain terms to stay away, Barbi wants me and Kaye to get together.

"Is Scott still bothering her?" It's a question I ask myself a hundred times a day.

"Why don't you ask her?" Barbi may be my confidant and co-conspirator, but she won't do my job for me.

"Because she always seems so uncomfortable when I bring it up."

"She's not seeing him. If that's what you're worried about." Barbi glides into the room and gracefully slides into the padded chair across from the couch I've appropriated as my own. "Not that you ever ask."

"Not my business to know."

"Yeah, but you want to know. As far as I'm aware, things have cooled off with him."

"Meaning?"

"Well, no more packages of dog shit for one thing." Her flippant attitude irritated me at first, but when I realized it's how she jokes around, I got over myself. Barbi's a solid friend; to me and to Kaye.

"She's rarely around." I sound like a grumpy teenager not getting his way. "How do you know she's not back with him?"

I'm in a shit mood, because I'm pining for Kaye like a lovestruck puppy dog. I'm not a damn puppy dog. I'm more of a Doberman; a fiercely protective… Why the fuck am I comparing myself to dogs?

I know why.

News flash, I'm in my longest dry spell since I was a horny teen desperate for sex of any kind.

And I'm cranky because I'm not getting any sex. Haven't since I met Kaye. Between work and guard duties at the townhouse, my social life—aka sex life—is on a definite downturn.

"Well, she hasn't mentioned it to me, and she tells me everything." Barbi yanks down the bottom of her dress. It barely covers her ass.

"There's distance growing between us." I grumble and mutter like a lovestruck fool.

"Do you think Kaye feels awkward after sharing so much?" Barbi's well aware of what Kaye shared with me that night on the roof. She makes no bones about wanting things between me and Kaye to work out.

"I don't know." I drag my hand down my face and pull at my chin. "This friend zone stuff is for the birds. I'm about ready to pull out my hair."

"Then make a point to talk to her." Barbi flicks her lashes, exacerbated by my failure to act and rolls her eyes. "Better yet, go in there and kiss her already." She makes a vague gesture with her hand. "I'm certainly not coming home tonight if things work out." She flashes a mischievous grin. "You've got the room to yourselves."

"I'm not going to go in there and molest her."

"How do you know that's not exactly what she wants? And I

didn't mean that you should molest her. I meant talk to her. Why are men such thick-headed idiots?"

"Has she specifically told you she's not seeing him?"

"No." Barbi curls her fingers and flips her hand around to admire her impeccable manicure. "Her nose is always in her books and she has zero time for me, let alone you. At night, she goes to bed early, says she's too tired to stay up. Maybe you should give her some slack?"

A studious individual, Kaye is trying to get a head start on her first semester at UC Davis's world-renowned veterinary school.

"You're right; she's probably stressed." I don't like how defensive I sound, but I'm in unknown territory.

How do I get myself out of the dreaded friend zone?

"Have you wondered whether she's waiting for you to make the first move?"

"How is asking her to watch a movie in the dark not making a move?"

"Oh my God, you're hopeless. That's exactly what a friend would do. Maybe you should stop doing that kind of shit and march in there, shove her against the wall, kiss her until her toes curl, and rip her shirt off."

"That's a bit over the top. Are we talking about me and Kaye or what you want Alec to do to you?"

She and Alec had a bit of a fling the first week we started the protective detail at the townhome. Something happened because the two of them started out strong then crashed and burned. Neither one will say what happened.

"Alec is a total tool." Barbi dismisses my comment. "I'm talking about you. Specifically about your problem."

"I'm driving myself insane. That's what I'm doing, and you know why I can't do any of that alpha-male stuff. Not after Scott…"

"Please, that douchebag is a Dom-wannabe. He's nothing more than an asshole pretending to be a man. You've got the dominant, alpha vibe down pat. Kaye obviously likes that. You just need to close the gap. Seriously, why am I even bothering?"

"She specifically told me she didn't like the way Scott treated her."

"Because he's an ass." Barbi stands and smooths out the wrinkles in her dress. "And you're an idiot. I'm telling you, get yourself back in the game. How about increasing the time you're here? One day a week is no good."

"I try to volunteer for more shifts, but Rafe and Hayes always seem to block me."

"Well, they're just being overly protective cockblockers. They know what will happen if you and Kaye spend any quality time together."

"You're right. I need more time, and I'm counting on you to give me that time."

"Me? How am I…" She stares at me, then backs away. "Oh, no way. I am not doing that."

"I haven't even asked you to do anything."

"You're going to ask me to do something with Alec so you can take his shifts."

"The two of you seemed to be having fun. He'll give me his shifts. Rafe and Hayes can't do shit about that."

"Alec and I were having fun, until we weren't. If you want Alec's shifts, talk to him. Hell, talk to Brady or Booker if you have to. Those two haven't ham-stringed you like Rafe and Hayes."

"Why don't you talk to Kaye? Do some recon for me."

"I am not playing matchmaker between you and Kaye." Barbi wanders to the hall, heading out. "She's here for two more weeks before moving to Davis. Whatever you're going to do, you better do it before she leaves. After that…" Barbi shrugs. "Don't let that door close on your ass. You're a good guy. Not my type, but definitely Kaye's. Personally, I like the idea of you hanging around, but you're not doing yourself any favors sitting on the couch, pining away, when you should be in her bed."

"I'm not pining."

"No. You're sitting on the goddamn couch while Kaye's in her room—alone."

"She's back?"

"Yeah, dude. Got back from the library about twenty minutes ago."

"Then why didn't you say something?"

"Because you're sitting on the couch like all the other nights. Moping. Go talk to her."

With that, Barbi departs. She'll be out all night. The woman is insatiable. She's just like Alec in that regard. Don't see why things didn't work out between them. They're a match made in heaven.

As for me, I'll stay up late into the night, patrolling the exterior and interior of the townhouse, while driving myself insane with the thought of getting Kaye alone and fixing this friend zone thing.

Maybe I should take Barbi's advice?

Fuck it.

I force myself to get off the couch and wander down the hall leading to Kaye and Barbi's room. At the door, I knock gently.

"Who is it?" Kaye sounds off, like she's been crying.

"Is everything okay?" I ask cautiously and slowly push open the door.

When I see her, she tenses and looks away. Shoulders hunched, she looks sad, and did she just wipe a tear from her face?

"Kaye? Are you okay?" I cautiously walk into her room.

My heart clenches and I want nothing more than to wrap her in a big hug and make her feel safe, but that's not what she needs right now.

"I'm fine." When she looks at me, her gaze is distant, her expression defeated. A heavy sigh leaves her lips and she mumbles something so softly I can't hear what she says.

"You don't look fine." My natural instinct is to comfort her, but there's an odd distance between us.

Things have definitely cooled off from that initial flash of heat when we met.

"I am." She turns away from me, giving me her back. "I'm perfectly fine." Her tone is resolute, yet broken at the same time; an empty shell of her normal vibrant self.

Discolorations around her wrists, and again at her neck, catch my eye and stop me dead in my tracks.

Something is very wrong.

"Kaye, if you need any help. Any help at all. I'm here. All you have to do is ask."

"I said I was fine. Now if you could please leave me alone? I'm tired and just want to go to bed."

My stomach clenches and it takes everything in me not to rush to her side, but Kaye's made it very clear she will handle things on her own. All I can do is wait for her to come back to me, but I know ligature marks when I see them.

And I know exactly what's got Kaye down.

"You're back with Scott." I see it in the way she moves, how distant she is, and the fear simmering beneath the surface.

"What? No!" Kaye's emphatic in her denial. "I'm not."

She turns away and takes a deep breath before facing me again. Her gaze hardens into one of determination instead of sadness.

It's weird, and very out of character, as if her emotions just flipped on their head.

"You're definitely back with him." Maybe I shouldn't press, but Scott's a dangerous man. I take a step toward Kaye.

I could end this for her. Fight her battle and free her from an abusive man. I have the skills. I know what it takes to bring down a monster, but this isn't my fight.

At least, not directly.

Ultimately, Kaye needs to battle this herself, but I can help her along the way.

"You can tell me. No judgment. I'm here. Here for anything you need. From a shoulder to cry on to a knight riding in on a white horse."

My attempt at humor opens her up by a crack. There's the faintest hint of a smile, but it's wiped clean before it can take root. Kaye's definitely hurting.

I move into the room, until I stand beside her, far closer than a friend would stand.

Fuck the friend zone. I'm in full Protector mode now.

I reach out and slowly place my hand on her shoulder. She

flinches at first, but then her body relaxes. I say nothing. Not yet. I let the silence between us speak the words I want to say.

I'm here.

I'll protect you.

You can count on me.

You can lean on me.

Through little movements, I reassure her that I'm here for her.

She lets out a long sigh, as if resigning herself to the fact I see the truth and her lie is exposed. I take that as a sign to close the distance and sit beside her on her bed.

She says nothing but leans against me. I lift my arm up and over her shoulder and pull her into a side hug. How long we sit there, I don't know, but she seems to relax.

"Kaye, I want to help you." My voice wavers with uncertainty. I desperately want to help.

No, that's not it.

I want to march out the front door guns blazing, find Asshat-Scott, string him up, and draw and quarter him for fun. But I don't do that. I'm too fearful going off on Scott will push the wrong buttons with Kaye and result in massive fallout that could ruin any chance I have at her.

"Can you…" Her voice catches, and this time she does wipe a tear from her face. "Do you think you could hold me?"

I glance down at the bruising on her wrists and the marks on her throat. Rage boils up within me, and all I see is red. All I want is to make Scott pay for destroying my Kaye.

But instead of seeking vengeance, I fold Kaye into my arms and listen to her weep. Eventually, her breathing slows and the tension in her body eases.

"Can you hold me until I fall asleep?" She sounds so broken and lost.

"Luv, I'll hold you until the end of time." I pull back the comforter and sheets and we lie down together. She tucks into me, small and vulnerable, while I curve my body around hers, protecting her while she sleeps.

Our first night in the same bed, and all I do is hold her in my arms? Not my usual, but somehow, it's imperfectly perfect.

Now, in the morning, we're going to have a talk.

There's no fucking way I'm going to sit on the couch like an idiot while Scott hurts my girl. That shit ends now.

But first, I need to know why she went back to him. What hold does he have over my Kaye?

TWELVE

Kaye

I slowly open my eyes and curl into the warmth that radiates from Zeb's body. I shift slightly and he pulls me close, holding me in a protective embrace. I remember last night and allow myself a moment to savor the feeling of being here with him.

And not with Scott.

I can't believe I'm here, in the safety of Zeb's arms.

His face is serene and peaceful as he sleeps, lips softly parted, his chest rises and falls in slow, steady breaths. I sigh with contentment, but then the events of the previous day come back to me and I cringe.

My dirty secret is out in the open, something I've tried to hide from those I care about the most.

It's time to face reality.

I gently extricate myself from Zeb's embrace and try not to wake him as I slip out of bed. I tiptoe toward the bathroom, where a warm shower awaits me.

After a few seconds to warm the water, soothing steam fills the air and engulfs me in its comforting embrace. One glance down and there's no way to deny the ligature marks around my wrists and ankles. Shame overcomes me as I stand under the water, wishing it could wash away my lies.

Lies needed to protect my roommates from Scott's madness.

My thoughts spin and twist with what happened yesterday. How I allowed Scott to do things that frightened me. How his dark eyes filled with the need to hurt me.

I wish I could make it all go away.

I wish Zeb hadn't seen the marks. My fingers press against my throat, feeling at the tender skin where Scott strangled me.

Tears fill my eyes and mingle with the water flowing over my body. I don't know what to do. I tried leaving him, but when he cornered me outside the library several weeks ago, and gave his ultimatum, there was only one choice.

A shiver creeps down my spine, making me shudder and regret the choices I made.

The hot water, however, soothes away the tension in my body; each muscle slowly relaxes as if being kneaded by skilled hands. This sense of peace won't last. I've been ordered to return to Scott later tonight, after he's done teaching for the day, where I will endure more pain.

No matter how hard I scrub, no amount of soap and water can wash away my shame. I scrub and scrub and scrub and scrub until my skin is pink and raw. As I turn off the shower, a gentle knock from the other side of the bathroom door makes me jump.

"Kaye?" It's Zeb and his mellow voice is filled with concern. "Are you okay in there?"

I take a deep breath and compose myself before answering.

"Yes." My voice sounds small, weak, and so very unsure.

I squeeze my eyes shut, as if that will make me disappear. I can't face Zeb. I can't face him because he knows. He knows where I've been and what I've done. He knows about my terrible secret.

I wish I could follow the soapy water down the drain and disappear for good.

"Are you decent?" He calls to me from the other side of the door.

Scott would never allow me the dignity of privacy. He'd barge in and take what he wanted.

"Yes." I wrap a towel around my body.

The door opens and Zeb peeks inside, concern etching his face as he takes in my dripping wet hair. While my body may be covered by the towel, my neck remains bare. My ankles and wrists too. From the widening of his eyes, and swift intake of his breath, the red marks discoloring the pale skin are visible.

I hate this. I hate having to endure the disappointment I see in his eyes.

Zeb steps into the bathroom until we're face to face. He pulls me in for a hug, holding me silently as if he can sense this is what I need right now—nothing more than to be held without judgment or expectation.

He then shifts back half a step, but keeps a hold of my hands as he looks deeply into my eyes. "This isn't okay. What he did isn't okay."

I can only nod, and stand mutely, since speaking about it would mean confessing not only what Scott did, but that I allowed it. I encouraged it.

That's something I'm not ready to admit.

Not yet.

Maybe never.

Zeb's grip on my hands tightens reassuringly, and he lets out a deep sigh.

"You don't have to go through this alone." His tone is gentle, but firm. "Do you want to contact the authorities?"

My heart stops. If I do that, I'll have to admit I let Scott do this to me. I can't.

I just can't.

Zeb should be angry that I went back to Scott. He should hate that I allowed this to happen. Instead, he asks how he can help?

I don't understand him—his motives, or what drives him—but I admit I need help.

Can I talk about what's happening without feeling ashamed or guilty?

Zeb's steady gaze gives me the courage I need to trust he won't hurt me too.

"I can't go to the cops."

"Will you tell me why not?" Zeb's compassion is what will ruin me.

He remains firm, asking for an explanation, without demanding one. His tone, the way he delivers his words, speaks volumes. He wants me to trust him, but I don't know if I can. I don't know if I've fallen too far over the cliff. There may be no way back for me.

The only thing I know is, I don't deserve Zeb's friendship. I know he wanted more.

Past tense; wanted rather than wants. How could he want me after I dismissed him? But he's here and he wants to help. My problem is I don't know how to ask for help.

What Scott does isn't okay. I don't disagree with that statement. He's sadistic and cruel, escalating day by day. He's dangerous and revels in my pain and the control he exerts when I cave into his demands. But that's the price I pay to keep my friends safe.

Zeb doesn't know what Scott said he'd do if I didn't go back to him. What he'll do if I don't let him do what he wants with me.

No one does.

"Kaye..." Zeb's voice breaks my trance. "No matter what's going on between you and Scott—what you may or may not have agreed to—it's not okay for him to do this without your consent," Zeb speaks softly. "This is against your consent, isn't it?" He pulls back, brow arched in question.

Again, without judgment.

We're both aware of how some couples enjoy consensual power exchange, bondage, discipline, and sadomasochism. He steps lightly around the issue. Again, without judgment. Without shame. But he remains firm.

He knows none of this is with my consent.

But isn't it? Isn't this the price I agreed to pay in order to appease Scott and keep him from hurting my friends?

That's not consent! My inner voice—the one that's been screaming at me for weeks—chimes in, agreeing with the assumptions Zeb makes.

He squeezes my hands, with reassurance, before continuing. "I can't help unless you let me. We can get help from the authorities. We can report this to the dean at UCSF. Or, we can take care of things off the books, but I need you to tell me what you want me to do." He leans in, placing his forehead against my own. "I need you to let me in."

My breath hitches. It's one thing to endure this abuse myself, but quite another knowing others will be made aware of it too.

"P-pl-please, don't tell the others." I don't have the courage to face my friends.

My fear is too deep, but what if Zeb can help?

I don't want to involve him in a situation of my making. I don't want to endanger him like I endangered Barbi, Carmen, and Rosalie. But I need help. He's right. Scott's taken things too far. He almost killed me.

"You can't keep this from them. They're going to find out." Zeb looks earnestly into my eyes. "And I don't know if I can step aside and do nothing. It goes against who I am at my core. I respect you, and I'll respect your decisions, but I'm struggling not to march over there and make this right."

"Please." I grip his shirt and beg. "Don't do that."

"What hold does he have over you?"

"You don't understand."

"Then help me understand."

"As long as I let him..." My throat closes up, making it impossible to speak.

"If you let him do what?"

"You know what."

"I don't like to assume, but this is where I am right now. The bruises on your wrists tell me he restrains you—or that you let him restrain you—the marks on your throat, however, tell me he does something far more dangerous. You're capable of making your own decisions, but if he's threatening you, and forcing you to do something you haven't consented to, this has to stop. If he's choking you, you're in serious danger. Life-threatening danger. I'm not going to be able to walk away from that."

"No."

"What do you mean by *No?*"

"I let him… It's my choice."

"Coercion is not a choice. It's not consent." He drags his hand down his face, pausing to collect his thoughts, then he fixes me with his piercing gaze. "I'm going to speak clearly, and I do this as someone who considers myself a dominant male. I know many couples with very healthy relationships who are in stable, consensual dynamics. Consent forms the foundation for any power exchange. Safety is paramount. It's non-negotiable. Risk is assessed and consent given free from coercion."

"You don't understand."

"Luv, I know more about what's happening than you know. Just answer one question. Will you do that for me?"

"I can't promise when I don't know if I can answer honestly."

"Fair enough, and thank you. Honesty is crucial to trust and I want you to trust me as much as I want to trust you."

I sniff and feel my heart rate dropping. With Zeb, I feel safe. I don't feel this way with Scott.

"Here's my question. Be as honest as you can. All this time, when you said you were going to the library to study, were you at the library?"

I can't look at him. I can't admit the truth.

"Okay. Let me ask a different question. Were you with him?" Zeb refuses to accept my silence.

"Yes."

"Will you answer a few more questions? You don't have to, but I really hope you do."

"I don't know if I can." I feel so incredibly defeated, but I don't want to disappoint Zeb.

"Fair enough. Did you go back because of his threats?"

"Yes." My response is barely audible. Spoken so low, I'm not sure if I said it, or thought it.

"Against you?"

"Yes." This time, my voice is firmer and a bit louder, and I really hope he stops here.

"Did he threaten anyone else?"

Damn.

I close my eyes because this is the one question I don't want to answer. It's the one that makes me sick to my stomach and makes me want to curl into a tiny ball until I disappear.

His brows tug together with thought, but the moment he figures it out his entire body completely relaxes. It's terrifying watching the change overcome him. Voice deadly calm, and absent of any emotion, his words send a chill rushing through me.

"He threatened your roommates."

"Yes." There's no way to deny it.

He already knows.

"Please, you can't tell them." My voice breaks and cracks. "Don't tell them what he's done." I wring my hands, and tuck my chin to my chest. A wave of heat and shame rushes through me.

"When?"

"The day after we met."

"How?"

"I went to the library. That wasn't a lie. He tracked my phone and met me outside." Heat rushes to my cheeks, not with shame, but with the memory of the bone-chilling fear I felt when Scott accosted me. "He grabbed my arm and shook me like a rag doll. He told me we were going to sit down and talk about what happened." My hand drifts up to my arm where he bruised me that day.

"And where did you talk? At the library?"

"He took me to his house. Ordered me down to the basement, where…" I turn my head and close my eyes as the terrifying memory rushes through me. I smell the musty dampness of the basement. I feel the terrifying chill creeping in from the cement floor. I taste bile and fear.

"What did he do?" Zeb brings me back with the calming tone of his words.

"Made me sit on the floor. He paced around me, shouting, yelling. He grew eerily calm and told me I wasn't allowed to leave.

That I would be punished for making him angry. That things would be different going forward. That I had no say in who he fucked. He—we had sex and he let me go."

"When did he start escalating?" Zeb shakes his head and folds me into his arms.

My hand lifts to explore the tenderness at my neck.

"No need to answer that." Zeb releases me and takes a step back.

There's something about the way he holds me that makes me feel safe and secure. There's a solidness about him and the feeling he's going to make things right.

Back on the rooftop, the first night we met, I imagined how things might be with Zeb. I still remember the electricity charging the air between us. That potential for more. I remember the heat of his body and the way he looked at me. The way my heart raced and the way he made my stomach flutter.

I remember the moment that was almost a kiss.

"Your immediate safety is my first concern." Something changes in Zeb. Like a switch that flips, he's in Alpha-male protector mode—a powerful force of good acting on my side.

Despite my distress, my shame, and the tears that fall, it's hard not to see him in an entirely new light.

Zeb is a powerful protector. A gallant knight in shining armor. A noble rescuer and absolutely stunning. He's my hero.

"You mentioned he threatened to pull your acceptance at UC Davis. Has he?"

My chin drops and my gaze shifts to the floor. Shame rushes through me and my entire body trembles. Scott hasn't expressly mentioned it one way or the other, but I know. I know what he craves. None of those are to watch me pursue my dreams.

"Scott wants me for himself." Tears fall from my eyes.

"Kaye, you have to let me help. This is what I do. I'll make Scott pay for everything he's done to you. I can keep you safe. I'm going to fix this."

He makes me want to believe.

"He's going to hurt my friends." My shoulders hunch as I try to disappear. I want to believe, but I'm afraid. Terribly afraid.

"He's not going to hurt anyone. Not your roommates and not you. He's finished threatening them, and he's done hurting you. This stops now. It stops today."

I roll my lower lip between my teeth and nod. I don't have the strength for words.

"There's no way I can stand by and do nothing." He takes my hands in his and a wave of warmth rushes through me. He pulls me into his embrace, and for a moment, everything feels right.

This small gesture of comfort eases the pain inside me.

When Zeb takes a step back, he's a changed man. No longer do I see him as a guy I met one night. There's a fierce protectiveness emanating from him that's unstoppable.

Zeb is a protector. A hunter of evil men. This is what he does. It's only just now starting to sink in.

"We have options." He cups my chin, gently lifting, until I meet his eyes.

When I gaze at him, his eyes are set with determination.

"Options?"

"My team's sole purpose is helping people in situations like this. Let me help you. You don't have to do this alone, and mark my word, Scott will pay."

I nod and the tightness in my chest releases. Zeb's right. I can't do this alone. There has to be a way out of this mess I created, but do I have the strength to accept the help Zeb offers? There's only one way to know. I let out a deep breath, release my fear, and search for strength.

"Okay."

"That's my girl." He leads me into my bedroom. "Get dressed. I'm going to make some calls."

After he leaves me alone, I sit on my bed in shock. It's as if a great weight lifts from my shoulders. I've never had to ask for help like this before. I almost didn't, too fearful of what my friends might think. Will they look at me with pity because I'm weak, or will they hate me for bringing trouble into their lives?

But if Zeb is willing to help, and if the Guardians have time to deal with my screwup, maybe that will make it easier to tell my roommates?

Tremendous guilt wells up within me, however.

I brought it upon myself. It's not the same as what happened with Carmen and Rosalie. They were victims. The Guardians protect them because they're trying to bring down a human trafficking ring. That operation involves scores and scores of women. Women who were kidnapped against their will.

That's not what's happening with me. This is a mess I made.

I dress slowly, still processing what happened, and dread what comes next.

Time to come clean with my roommates. Time to learn how to stand up for myself. UC Davis may be a lost dream, after Scott's done with me, but I can let that go if it means being free of him. I feel better knowing Zeb will be there for me every step of the way.

I won't be alone.

THIRTEEN

Zeb

I'VE KILLED MEN BEFORE. WHETHER IT WAS A DOUBLE-TAP WITH MY weapon, or a knife to the throat, killing is an integral part of who I was as a frogman and who I am as a Guardian.

Each man I removed from this world deserved it. Vile men. Despicable humans. Scum of the earth. I'm going to kill Professor Scott Parker. He doesn't deserve to breathe after what he did to Kaye.

Blood roars past my ears with furious rage burning through me.

Why do men feel the need to hurt those weaker than themselves? Women. Children. Innocents. It doesn't make them stronger. It makes them pathetic weaklings.

I've felt the desire to kill before, but this is different. The drive to end Scott's life is a twisted, nasty thing. Irrational and no longer human. I want him dead on a visceral level.

Kaye is a beautiful woman. Smart, funny, and full of life, I love the way her eyes sparkle like fireflies, and the way her smile spreads warmth to everyone around her.

But that is gone.

Kaye's a shell of her former self. Her smiles no longer light up the room. Those firefly sparks are gone. Sad and vacant, her eyes are hooded. A shadow of her former self, she walks around listless and lethargic. The tiniest sound makes her jump.

Whatever happened with Scott terrified her, and I know why. The fucker gets off on asphyxiation: one of the more extreme forms of BDSM edge play. People can die from the practice, which is why those involved train to be safe, sane, and consensual.

But he's not trained. It's not consensual. He tied her up, then subjected her to strangulation against her will. He took from her. He violated not only her body, but her trust. He used threats against others, and her fear, to get her to allow the unthinkable.

It's the last straw, and I can no longer stand on the sidelines. Scott is going to pay. Kaye's under my protection until he does.

The night when Kaye and I met, a spark ignited an amazing potential between us. When she later cooled off on me, I figured she was too focused on getting a leg up on her studies prior to her first semester in vet school. We all thought she spent her days at the library, getting ready.

Little did I know what was really happening. If I had, no fucking way in hell would it have gone on this long.

While Kaye gets changed, I make a few calls and test the waters of what might be possible.

"CJ, I have a problem. A Guardian problem."

"Go on." As lead of the Guardian teams, I want to loop him in first. If he bites, I'll go to Brady, then Brady and I will go to the team.

"Carmen and Rosalie's roommate, Kaye, is being intimidated, and coerced, by her former professor at UCSF. He's using emotional and physical intimidation tactics to get her to submit to edge play."

"You've got my attention." CJ's light Texas twang hardens.

"She came home yesterday with ligature marks on her ankles and wrists. Bruising around her neck."

"Could be bondage play?"

No way in hell does CJ think this is bondage play, but he's obligated to consider all angles.

"She's a husk of her normal self. Not to mention, his intimidation tactics escalated to include the other girls. He's using threats against them to get Kaye to submit. I need to get all of them to safety, then we need to deal with him."

I need to kill him.

"What are you thinking?" The drumming of CJ's fingers is unmistakable. It's what he does when thinking.

"Who's Scott?" Mitzy's suddenly on the line. Her high-pitched squeak is a jarring contrast from CJ's slow drawl.

I rattle off Scott's full name and position at UCSF. She'll look up his basic information, then do a deeper dive into his background.

"Get me up to speed." Shock number two. Sam, head of Guardian HRS, who oversees all the teams: Guardians, Techies, Medical, and the new Protector division is on the line as well. He's direct and to the point, the epitome of efficiency.

I give him the details. "I want to move the girls back onto HQ grounds."

"That's going to be tricky." A new voice comes on the line; the soft, yet powerful voice of Skye Summers, co-founder of Guardian HRS and lead of our medical team. "Carmen and Rosalie made a point of moving back to the townhome and went against our advice to stay within the safety of HQ. You're going to have difficulty convincing them to return."

"I'm hoping Kaye will convince them moving back is the safest option." I pull on my chin, a bit taken aback by who all is on this call. I only meant to talk to CJ, then go from there.

"And you think they'll agree?" CJ asks the obvious question.

"They'll do it for Kaye, if not for themselves." I continue pacing in the hall, fingers cramping from how hard I grip the phone.

"Good point," CJ says.

"I want to take a look at Kaye's injuries," Skye pipes up. "Any thoughts on whether she wants to prosecute? If so…"

"I barely got her to agree to let me help. You can ask, but she's frightened. Too scared to act openly about what he's done."

"Aren't they all?" Sam speaks and there's silence on the line. Every threat we face is real and this is exactly the kind of assignment where we do our best work.

"Ask her when you get a moment alone with her," Skye says. "If not, I'll take her aside and be as gentle as I can."

"Will do." Honestly, Doc Summers would be far better than me approaching that aspect of things. My gut twists with what Scott did to Kaye.

"Sam, what are your thoughts?" Forest Summers's deep voice rumbles through the phone.

My mouth gapes. Did CJ dial in the entire chain of command? All the way up to the founder of our organization? Forest Summers himself?

Our organization moves fast, but this is light speed.

"Zeb, have you brought this up to Bravo-One?" Sam asks.

"No, sir. I didn't want to presume we'd take this on until I discussed it with CJ."

"Well," Sam says. "You've got the green light from me. Anyone dissent?"

A chorus of *"Noes"* rings out.

"Zeb, Brady's on the line," Mitzy speaks. "Bravo-One, we've got something for the team. Zeb, you want to fill him in?"

"Absolutely." I brief Brady on what happened to Kaye and my intention to put Scott down.

"Sounds like a plan," Brady says. "But what are you going to do about Carmen and Rosalie? They threw a fit when Rafe and Hayes wanted them to stay at HQ. Now you're going to convince them to move back? Props if you make that happen. They're fiercely independent." There's a low chuckle from Brady.

"That's the goal."

Brady makes it sound like a challenge, but I've seen how the girls interact. They'll do whatever it takes to help Kaye.

As for fiercely independent, that's not a stretch. Carmen intercepted the rescue of Isabelle LaCroix by jumping on the end of a rope dangling from our helicopter. She led the charge for returning to her father's residence to rescue not only Rosalie, but scores of women who were held captive there.

During that mission, we rescued the captive women, but lost Rosalie and Hayes during exfil. The two of them escaped through the jungle, and to hear Hayes recount what happened, Rosalie basically saved herself and dragged him along for the ride.

"They'll do it for Kaye. That won't be a problem." I'm ninety percent sure it won't. If anyone can convince Carmen and Rosalie, it'll be Kaye.

Not me.

"That's all I need to know." Brady doesn't waste time with superfluous questions. "Are you at the house?"

"Yes."

"Good. You work on the women. We'll brief the team once you have the green light from them."

"I have quarters," Mitzy says. "We have four empty TLQs in the dorm. Sending the requisition in now. As for Professor Douchebag, this isn't the first time he's done something. There are complaints filed against him."

"He has other complaints? How is he still on the faculty?" My words come out an animalistic growl. I'm beyond pissed. Way beyond.

Murderous comes to mind.

"Tenured, for one, and for the other?" I can practically see Mitzy shrug. "All the complaints were dismissed. Sounds fishy to me. I'm going to sign off this call and do some digging. I'll have something to report back by tonight."

"Anything else we need?" Sam gives everyone a chance to speak before ending the call.

As soon as I'm off with all the bigwigs, Brady calls me on a separate line.

"How bad is it?" he asks.

"Asphyxiation play. Tied her down. Could've killed her. He sent that box with the dog shit in it the day Rosalie and Carmen moved back in. The next day, he cornered her at the library. This has been going on for weeks. Now, he's openly threatened all of them if Kaye doesn't submit."

My guts twist and churn thinking about how long this has been going on. Kaye's red-rimmed, unblinking stare, completely vacant of emotion, tells me how much damage she's sustained.

When I held her, she looked miserable with the abrasions and bruising, but it was the way she curled against me that broke my heart.

I should've known. I should've been out there protecting her. Instead, I've been moping around the townhouse during my weekly watch because I thought I'd been relegated to the friend zone.

News Flash.

We're done with that.

"Fucking-A." Brady curses on the other end of the phone. "I have a bad feeling about this."

"So do I."

"Your thoughts on the previous complaints?"

"All dismissed? And there's more than one?"

"Yes."

"Looks like a pattern."

"I'll reserve judgment until Mitzy gets us intel," Brady says. "In the meantime, we're in full lockdown. No one in or out, except for the team. I texted Rafe and Hayes. They're on their way and pissed. Had to talk them down. Booker is with me at The Facility; we're training the rescues from the raid on Carmen's father's place. Alec's on liberty for the weekend. We'll meet up when you get to HQ."

"Copy that." I don't like that Brady triggered on the same thing I did. We end our call. My molars grind together and my muscles tense.

I brace for what's coming.

Unfortunately, I've been at this game far too long. I won't be the least bit surprised if Mitzy comes up empty in her search for whoever submitted formal complaints on our professor. Something tells me Scott is far too practiced at manipulation, torture, and potentially murder.

My molars grind as I think how close Kaye may have come to never coming home again, and I curse myself for not recognizing what was going on sooner. With my call complete, I return to Kaye.

I knock and wait for her to answer.

"Yes?"

"It's me. May I come in?"

"Of course."

I enter her room with newfound purpose. She looks at me with wide eyes filled with fear, but also a sense of hope. She looks miserable and pathetic.

Lost.

Somehow, she already knows I bring good news. I love her faith in me and aim to live up to every bit of it.

"What are we going to do?" She gives a slow blink and swallows thickly.

I like this—taking action—far better than watching the light go out in her eyes from a distance.

I approach her bed, where she sits. She looks up at me with puffy eyes rimmed in red. Her cheeks glisten from new tears.

I kneel on the floor to make myself less threatening and on the same level as her. My hands grip either side of the bedframe as I take a moment to compose what I want to say.

"I called Guardian HQ and spoke with the team. We think it would be best if you and the others come down to Guardian HQ until we can figure out how to put a stop to Scott and his threats."

"What does that mean? Put a stop?"

"Neutralize the threat."

"You're not going to…" Her voice drops to a whisper, and she leans in. "Kill him?"

"No." I take her hands in mine. "No one is killing anybody." I'm totally going to watch Scott take his last breath. "Are you aware there have been complaints regarding misconduct filed on him before?"

"No." She shakes her head.

"More than one, and each one was summarily dismissed. It may be nothing, but it's concerning. The tech team is looking into it." I speak in an increasingly urgent tone and can't help but reveal how much concern there is for them all.

"I didn't know." She tucks her chin.

"I need your help." I brush the back of my thumb against her outer thigh. It's a test of how much physical contact she'll allow after the trauma she endured. She doesn't pull away.

"Me?" She tilts her head, confused.

"It's too risky for the four of you to stay here. With Scott's threats, you need to convince Carmen and Rosalie to come back and stay at HQ. As I understand things, they were quite vocal about not staying there."

"I can do that." She nods and curls in her lower lip. Her voice sounds less timid. More sure about herself. This is what I hoped for. Kaye needs to restore control over her life and what's happening around her.

"Good. Talk to them. We need all of you to get your things together. I don't know how long this will take; a week or two for sure. Rafe and Hayes have been alerted, and you know what's going through their minds."

"Oh, I can imagine. I hear the *I told you sos* already." The tiniest curve of her lip shows the hint of a smile.

"Exactly."

"And this has nothing to do with Carmen's father or our ongoing mission surrounding that. This is about…"

"Me." She cuts me off. "It's my fault."

I give her hand a squeeze. She needs to hear the truth and internalize it rather than blame herself for what's going on. Scott's the one who carries the blame.

"You did nothing wrong. Do you know where the others might be?"

It doesn't escape my notice that Barbi didn't spend the night here last night, and no one is moving around upstairs. Kaye glances at her watch.

"Carmen and Rosalie are probably out for lunch. As far as Barbi? She didn't come home last night, so I have to call her."

"Good. We'll need to get everyone here. You get them to agree, then we move everyone out. We need to act fast, before Scott gets wind of anything unusual happening. Is he expecting you any particular time?"

"He's at the Decomp farm."

"The, what?"

"It's part of his research on human and animal decomposition?" She looks at me like I should know.

"On, what?"

"Scott and his friend, the dean of the vet school, have a research grant to study decomposition of humans and animals. They spend the first Saturday of every month at the farm. That's why he sent me home."

"That's seriously gross."

"True, but important. Especially in the field of Criminal Science."

"If you say so."

"Anyway, he sent me home, but I'm supposed to be back no later than five tonight. Moving Rosie and Carmen out shouldn't raise too much concern."

"How's that?" I disagree on principle, but I'm interested in her thoughts.

"He knows about Carmen's dad and how she and Rosalie are in danger. It won't be weird for them to move back for protection. We can probably extend that to Barbi as well."

"And you."

"If I'm not back by five, he'll come looking for me."

"Can't you tell him you're busy? We can say Carmen and Rosalie are leaving and you want to spend the evening with them."

"He'll know something's up. He always does."

"Then we don't give him that chance."

I love seeing her engage. Her voice is stronger than it was moments before. She sits straighter, no longer curling in on herself, and she no longer wrings her hands, twisting her fingers.

The tears stop. She's still overwhelmed but nods as I go over the plan.

FOURTEEN

Kaye

I call my friends and tell them it's urgent. Unfortunately, Carmen and Rosalie went to Napa for brunch. It's four in the afternoon before they come home. We all gather in the living room. They sit on the sofa while I pace. Zeb leans against the wall.

I have yet to get a hold of Barbi. Almost five, I'm getting more and more worried. If we're not out of here soon, Scott will come looking for me.

"What's up?" Carmen picks at lint on the arm of the sofa, while Rosalie keeps looking between me and Zeb. She knows something's up, but waits for me to explain.

"Have any of you heard from Barbi?" I look to my friends.

It's not unusual for Barbi to be out all night. She's a party girl and enjoys single life. This wouldn't be the first time she stayed out all night, but she's usually back by now.

"I'll text her." Carmen pulls out her phone and taps on the screen. "Meanwhile, what's up?"

I rub my palms on my jeans, trying to find the courage to speak.

"You've got this." Zeb flexes his biceps and that poor shirt strains over the muscles of his chest. There's a potency about him. An air of strength and power restrained only by his will.

It's different with Scott. He doesn't carry himself with the same confidence that oozes from Zeb.

With Zeb, I know he'll look after my well-being above his own. With Scott? It's exactly the opposite.

I can't describe it any other way.

"Well, one of you needs to start speaking." Carmen glances at her phone, frowns when there's no text from Barbi, then looks to me. "What's up, Kaye? Spit it out."

"It's Scott." I know what needs to be said, but I don't know how to begin.

"What happened?" Carmen leans forward.

Rosalie tenses but doesn't speak. She's still figuring out her place with us.

"Show them." Zeb gestures with a flick of his chin. His eyes zero in on my wrists.

I stare at the bruises and cuts, sick to my stomach that I allowed it to happen.

"Show us, what?" Carmen scoots to the edge of the couch. "What's he talking about?"

I glance down at the long-sleeved shirt I wear. When Zeb told me to dress, I moved like a robot, methodical and half-aware of what I was doing. Evidently, some part of my brain knew enough to toss on something that covers the bruising.

Slowly, I roll back my sleeves. First on the left. Then on the right. Words fail me as I extend my arms and reveal the ligature marks on my wrists.

Carmen gasps and hops off the couch. Rosalie looks from me to Zeb, then to Carmen and finally back to me.

"Scott did this to you?" Rosalie slowly rises off the couch and comes for a closer look.

"What did he do?" Carmen grips my hands and flips my wrists back and forth.

"He used Zip Ties." Rosalie's voice is flat, with zero emotion. "That's how the women your..." Her voice catches, but she clears her throat. "That is what the wrists of the women your father imprisoned looked like after a night of…" Her voice trails off as if she can't continue, but Rosalie doesn't need words. She takes one look at my neck, then pulls back the collar to expose my skin. "He strangled you. For pleasure?"

A wave of intense shame overcomes me. My entire body trembles with the sensation. My face heats with shame. I don't know if I can do this.

"He did, what?" Carmen raises her voice, alarmed. "When did this happen?"

Rosalie doesn't appear surprised. She turns to Carmen and takes her hand. Then reaches out to hold mine.

"Scott is a bad man. Dangerous." She looks to Zeb. "Kaye needs protection."

"That's what we want to talk about." Zeb kicks off from the wall and comes to stand beside me. "I've talked this through with the team and Guardian HRS leadership. We need time to investigate Scott, and…"

Rosalie bows her head, then she fixes her gaze on Zeb.

"We're here because Scott is a threat to us." She glances at Carmen. "They want us to go back."

"Back?" Carmen's half a step behind Rosalie.

"Back to HQ." Rosalie tugs at the collar of my shirt looking at the extent of the marks.

"Us?" Carmen glances at Rosalie. "Why us?"

I take in a deep breath, not ready to admit everything to my friends, but knowing it's necessary.

"This was not done willingly." Rosalie steps in with profound understanding. "I've seen other women do things such as this to protect the younger girls."

"What are you talking about?" Confusion pulls at Carmen's face.

"Tell her." Rosalie turns to me, giving me the chance to explain.

Carmen looks to me, not understanding. I swallow my pride and explain.

"Scott ran into me a few weeks ago. It was the day after you moved back and Rosie moved in. He told me what would happen if I didn't talk with him. I thought nothing of it, figured we'd talk and that would be the end of it."

"But it wasn't the end," Rosalie speaks without judgment. Her affect is strangely flat.

"No. It wasn't. He told me if I didn't stay with him, I would regret it. At first, I thought it was just a threat against me, but then he threatened you."

Rosalie covers her mouth with her hands.

"Yes." I nod. "He told me what would happen if I didn't. Every day I told you I was studying at the library, I was in his office. Then he would take me home. Things got weird. The sex…" My voice breaks, and I have to clear my throat.

It feels wrong to talk about having sex with Scott in front of Zeb, but things can't get any worse than they already are.

"He became more violent. More controlling. He already was controlling, but things changed. The sex got rougher. He punished me for random things."

"Punished?" Carmen's eyes grow as big as saucers.

Do I tell them he beats me with his belt? Punches me in the stomach? Grabs me by the throat and shoves me against the wall? Do I tell them about the rest?

I can't. I just can't.

"Kaye, why didn't you tell us? We could've done something to help." Carmen takes both my hands and squeezes tight.

"He said if I mentioned it to anyone, he would make one of you suffer. I couldn't do that." Especially now that I know what it means to Scott to make someone suffer.

"You were protecting us." Rosalie puts her arm around Carmen's shoulders, hugging her. "Just like the women did for the younger girls—when they could."

"How did we not know?" Carmen's eyes shimmer with tears. "Kaye, I'm so sorry. I should've known."

"How could you?"

"I've been so focused on my father and what he's been doing

that it never occurred to me something like that could happen here. Let alone to you." She looks to Zeb. "So what now?"

"Guardian HRS wants the four of you to return to HQ. We'll keep you on HQ grounds until we can investigate and neutralize the threat from Scott. We've classified him as extremely dangerous, and we can't provide the level of protection you need here. I know you and Rosalie didn't want to stay at HQ, but…"

"Of course, we'll go." Carmen doesn't hesitate. "There's no question about it. When?"

"As soon as possible. Tonight." Zeb's tone is firm. Serious. But he doesn't alarm Carmen and Rosalie. "You need to pack your bags. We're leaving as soon as Hayes and Rafe get here. They'll take you and Rosalie back to HQ."

"I bet they're pleased." Carmen rolls her eyes. "They've been waiting to say I told you so."

"Rafe and Hayes know this has nothing to do with your father or your decision to leave HQ. This is because Scott is a threat to the four of you." Zeb looks between us. "Has Barbi responded to any of you?"

Carmen looks at her phone, as do I, but there's no response from Barbi.

Which is odd. A small tendril of fear uncoils in my gut. Has Scott…? But no, he would have no reason to act against Barbi. She was probably up all night and is sleeping it off in some one-night-stand's bed.

"No." I glance at my phone, as if she answered us in the last second.

"Okay, that's not an issue. Mitzy will be able to locate her." Zeb wraps his arm around my shoulder. He pulls me in and kisses the top of my head.

I don't know why, but that tiny bit of tenderness makes me believe everything will be all right.

"How?" Carmen asks the question I want to know.

"As long as her phone is on, and charged, Mitzy will work her Mitzy Magic and find her. We'll send Alec out to fetch her. In the meantime, the three of you have bags to pack."

The moment Zeb gives us something to do, Carmen and Rosalie spring into action and head upstairs. I stay with Zeb in the living room. His arm is still wrapped around my shoulder and I don't want to move.

I lean against him, turning in slightly, loving his rich, warm scent. Zeb completes my turn, guiding me in, until we're face to face. He places his hands on my waist and tugs me tight against his body.

"Don't worry about Barbi. We've got the best people on the planet looking for her, and she's probably right where you think she is."

"And where is that?"

"In bed with whomever she met last night." He cups my chin and tilts my head back until I'm looking up at him. "Don't worry about Barbi. We'll pack your things and hers. Then we'll head down the coast to Guardian HQ."

"Okay." I smile, feeling tremendous relief flowing through me. "I don't know what to say."

"You don't have to say a thing. There's no way I'm going to let anyone threaten you, or those you care about."

"Thank you."

"You don't have to thank me."

"Yes. I do. You've been—just wonderful." My lips tremble, as emotion overwhelms me. "Incredibly wonderful."

I lift on my tiptoes, thinking to place a chaste peck on his cheek, but some strange force brings our lips together. At first, our lips barely touch, but then a surge of passion takes me by surprise. A million volts of electricity surges between us, sparking and igniting a firestorm.

Sparks fly.

The air heats.

I pull away in shock. As if I don't want the explosion of sensation to continue. The truth is, I never want this feeling to end, but a silent warning bell rings in my ear.

"I'm sorry." I spring out of his arms and place my fingers over my lips as if I can capture the moment and hold it forever. Already, I miss the taste of him. "I didn't mean to kiss you. It was an accident."

I inhale, filling my lungs with the scent of him, wanting more, but I back away as if what I did was terribly wrong.

A low chuckle makes his shoulders shake. He takes a step closer and I find myself rooted in place until he closes the distance. He towers over me and his lips curve into a small smile, the kind that holds secrets.

He gazes at me with such intensity, my heart kicks into overdrive. "If that was an accident, it was the best accident I've experienced in a very long time." His voice rasps from the effort it takes to control it. "Maybe next time it'll be intentional, and we can finally explore what might happen if we don't stop." He takes my hands in his and stares at me with smoldering heat simmering in his eyes. "You should pack."

"Aren't you going to help me?"

"I'd love to follow you to your bedroom, but if I do, you won't be packing a suitcase. I'm going to stay here and cool off from that amazing, and beautiful, accident."

I swallow thickly, realizing I want exactly that, but he's already made up his mind to stay here while I walk down the hall.

That kiss lingers on my lips, and something indescribable takes root in my heart. I pack my bags, and Barbi's too. That kiss is still with me, unforgettable and burned into my memory. It will stay there until I can find the courage to do it again, and I promise myself next time won't be an accident.

I've wanted to kiss him from the moment we met, and it's ten times, a thousand times, better than I thought it could be. My heart pounds as I place the packed bags in the hall and hurry back to the living room. Zeb is there, lounging on the couch. He looks up when I enter and a satisfied smile fills his face.

"You're packed?"

"I think so."

"Good. Rafe and Hayes are thirty minutes out. We'll wait for them to get here before loading your bags. Any word from Barbi?"

"Not yet."

We speak as if nothing happened. As if that kiss didn't fundamentally shift things between us.

But it did. It absolutely did.

FIFTEEN

Zeb

———

A low chuckle rumbles in my chest. Definitely didn't see that kiss coming. Now that I've had a taste of her, and feel the energy surging between us, any doubt about the attraction lingering between us is gone.

Typically, I wouldn't back off. I would've followed Kaye into her room, stripped her down, and spent the next few hours drowning her in pleasure.

But I can't do that.

Not after what Scott did. Kaye needs time to process and heal. Which means, I spend thirty very uncomfortable minutes waiting for her and the others to finish packing.

Kaye takes a seat on the other end of the couch, maintaining distance between us. Noise from the stairs has me popping to my feet.

"I'm going to help them with their bags." I want to stay with Kaye. I want to scoot over and sit next to her on the couch. I want to hold her hand in mine and lean in for a kiss that is no accident.

But I can't do any of that. Not yet.

What I can do is get everything ready for when Hayes and Rafe arrive. Once they're here, we'll do a bit of recon on the street, then move out.

At the top of the landing, Rosalie struggles with a large suitcase. When she arrived several weeks ago, she had far fewer possessions.

"Here, let me help." I grab the suitcase and carry it downstairs. Then I head back up to help Carmen with her things. By the time I'm back downstairs, the front door is open and a heated conversation fills the air.

Rafe and Hayes confront Carmen and Rosalie. The exchange between Rafe and Carmen escalates.

"This is why I wanted you to stay. You don't listen." The anger radiating from Rafe clashes with the fierce stare Carmen shoots back.

Rafe worries about her father retaliating, kidnapping her, or worse. Carmen downplays that risk, and they can't find common ground.

They fire off angry words back and forth in rapid succession, like a battle being waged. It's too fast to follow.

Rosalie stands off to the side, wringing her hands. Every now and then, she glances over to where Hayes stands in the entryway. The muscles of his jaw clench, but he's wise enough to stay silent.

Although, with Rafe and Carmen's argument escalating, there's no room for him to interject, or say anything to Rosalie.

I take a step forward, ready to break up the argument, but before I can say anything, Kaye steps in.

"Rafe… please." Her soft voice cuts through the anger and confusion. "This is my fault. It has nothing to do with Carmen's father."

Rafe's mouth gapes as he bites back whatever it is he wants to say. He takes a deep breath, still frowning, but no longer shouts at Carmen.

Carmen does the same, except she keeps her glare focused on Rafe. There's more to the argument between the two of them than what we see on the surface.

I stand silently beside Kaye, supporting her with my presence.

"If we can all just quiet down and let me explain." Kaye tells

Rafe and Hayes what happened and how I recommended the girls move to Guardian HQ until things are settled with Scott. "So you can see, this move is because of me. There's no new threat from Carmen's father."

"The fact he still breathes is threat enough." Rafe bites out the words, unwilling to let the argument fade. "At least you were able to talk some sense into her." His angry glare nearly sets off another argument, but Kaye smooths things over without raising her voice.

"That may be." Kaye sighs, her eyes fill with concern, but fatigue mutes her voice. "But we need to agree we're going to disagree about that. I feel awful for putting Carmen and Rosalie in danger because of the choices I made. If you could try to step back from your thoughts about her father, and whatever threat he may or may not pose, and focus on helping me, I would really appreciate it."

"You're right." Rafe heaves a heavy sigh. "I'll sidebar it for now." The look he exchanges with Carmen says only that their argument will continue when they're alone.

"Thanks. I really appreciate it." Kaye smiles gratefully. Her gentle yet firm authority still amazes me. All she wants is for her friends to be safe.

For the time being, the argument is put aside. Rafe and Hayes help me load the luggage while the women pack last-minute things. There's still no word from Barbi, which worries me, but Kaye and her friends don't seem too concerned.

Once outside, I speak freely with Rafe and Hayes. "Keep a look out for Scott. If he's here, I want to know about it."

"You really think he's slinking around watching the house?" Hayes scans the road and nearby buildings.

"His escalation concerns me. Honestly, I'm surprised he allowed Kaye to come home in the first place."

"Well, I'm going to feel better having Rosalie back at HQ." Hayes shares a glance with Rafe. "Carmen refuses to believe her father is still a threat. Rosalie feels he's no threat either, because Matias is dead. Neither of them understands their value. This is a blessing in disguise."

"What he's trying to say…" Rafe pops the back of the vehicle. "Is this whole situation sucks, and I wouldn't wish it on my enemy, but we're thankful for it as well."

"That she's got a stalker and potentially murderous monster out to kill her?"

"Not that. Dude, that is not what I meant. I only mean to say, this keeps all of them safe."

"I know what you meant. That was sarcasm." I load the suitcases I carry into the back of the car.

"We're here for you and will do whatever it takes to protect Kaye. She's one of us now." Hayes grabs me by the shoulder.

"Thanks. I appreciate it. Anyone know where Alec might be?" I rub my hands on my pants and scan the street.

"Not sure." Rafe shrugs and looks to Hayes. "Do you know?"

"Nah, but I heard him talking about heading to Napa for the weekend."

"Alone, or…?" I let my voice trail off.

"With him?" Hayes laughs. "You know it's a chick. And if he didn't tell us, that means he doesn't want us to know."

Something shifts in the air.

"I feel eyes on us." It's unlikely Scott would be here. He thinks Kaye is defeated enough to do whatever he says, but I glance at my watch. "Shit."

"What's wrong?"

"We're losing the day. Kaye's supposed to be back in less than thirty minutes."

"Surely a few minutes…" Hayes says.

"Are a few minutes too many. How are we going to get them out of the house without him knowing where they go?"

"You think he's here?" Rafe takes a look down the street, scanning.

"It's probably nothing." I rub at my neck. "I'm just anxious to get them to HQ." Something across the street catches my eye; something that shouldn't be there. Turning my back, I keep my voice low. "Second tree on the left. Black box tied to the trunk above the third set of branches. Is that a camera?"

Rafe and Hayes know better than to look at the same time. They wander around the car, kicking tires, opening up the doors, as if pretending we're getting ready for a trip.

"Definitely a camera," Hayes speaks first. "Direct line of sight on the front door."

"Shit. That's what I thought."

"If that is him, and you bring Kaye out the front door…" Rafe says what we're all thinking.

"Yeah, I'm with you." I rub at the back of my neck. "He shouldn't care about the four of you taking off. It looks like you're headed on a weekend retreat."

"How do you want to play this?" Rafe pulls up his phone and pretends to take a selfie of the three of us, but the camera shoots outward. He'll send the photo to Mitzy and her team to see what they make of it.

Less than a minute later, all three of us receive a text with the make, model, and capabilities of the surveillance camera installed, along with the most likely direction of the lens. No surprise, it's the front door of the girls' townhouse.

"Fuck." I close the back and gesture to the guys. "Back inside and let's figure this out." They seem to understand the urgency in my voice, and follow me in.

Inside, I explain the situation to the women. "It looks like Scott has eyes on the house. We can't walk out the front door without him knowing about it."

"I can." Kaye's face is pale with worry over her friends' safety. "It's what I normally do when I leave to go to him."

"No way am I putting you on the street at this hour."

"Why not?"

"There's no way to know if he's not waiting to grab you. Too risky."

"Carmen and Rosalie can walk out with Rafe and Hayes," she says. "It'll look like the four of them are going on a long trip."

"True. It's you that will raise an alarm. The last thing I want is to tip Scott off before we have a plan of action."

"What about the back yard?" Kaye offers a suggestion.

"I thought of that, but if he has the front under surveillance, he probably has the back as well."

"What do we do?" Kaye asks.

"What about the roof?" Rosalie pipes up.

"The roof?" I press my fingers against my temple, staving off the beginnings of a headache. Why can't things be easy? There's always a wrinkle. What I wouldn't give for one easy day.

"Yes." Rosalie sounds like she knows what she's talking about. "There's that oak growing between the buildings. You can use it to get to the roof next door. I haven't looked closely, but it should be sturdy enough."

"Rosalie and her trees." Hayes laughs. "If I've learned anything, it's to trust my woman. We should check it out."

I glance at Hayes, who gives a noncommittal shrug, then back to Kaye to see what she thinks. Not as sure about it as Rosalie; she's scared enough to try almost anything.

That worries me. The pressure she's under could lead to her taking risks where she shouldn't.

"Let's take a look before making a decision." I gesture up the stairs.

Rosalie moves first. She takes Kaye's hand in hers. "It looks scary, but it's easy enough. Just don't look down."

We ascend the stairs as a group and clamber up the fire escape to the rooftop terrace. Keeping Kaye out of sight, Hayes and I go with Rosalie to look at the tree.

Last time I was up here, I don't remember seeing the large oak, but it had been dark and I was more interested in checking out Kaye.

The oak grows between this building and the neighbor's. Its branches reach high. There's a narrow gap between the roof's edge and a branch about as thick as my arm.

"See." Rosalie points at the branches. "You can cross directly over to the other roof."

"Looks good." I'm not against this plan, but then Hayes taps me on the shoulder.

"It's in the camera's line of sight." Hayes gestures toward the street. "This won't work."

"Shit." I drag my hand down my face. "Alternatives?"

We rejoin the others, who lounge on the patio furniture, trying to make it look like the six of us came up here to enjoy the afternoon.

"The tree is a no-go." I hate giving bad news, but we'll find another way.

"So that's not an option?" Kaye's face pales when I give her the news.

"It's too risky if Scott is watching." I scan the street and rooftops, searching for some other way out. "Any other ideas?"

Then Hayes claps his hands. "I got it. We rig a rope here and connect it to that building." He points directly behind the townhouse. With the hill sloping downward at an insane angle found only in San Francisco, the roofline is below this one. "We swing her across. If there's another camera out back, it won't be pointed up, but at the courtyard below."

"What?" Kaye's face is a mixture of fear and more fear. Her face pales and her eyes widen. "You want me to do what?"

"A zip line from here to the other house?" I cross my arms and think it through.

The best option would be for Carmen and Rosalie to leave with the guys. Kaye could then walk down the street, just as she would when going to meet Scott. Only, I refuse to leave her alone, and no way in hell am I walking with her. I don't want to give Scott any reason to punish Kaye; in the unlikely event he gets his hands on her.

Which means, we need a plan B.

"I'm game if you are," Hayes offers encouragement. "We just need someone to set the anchor on the other roof."

"That should be Zeb." Rafe points at me.

"I was going to stay and talk her through it." I don't like separating like this.

Rafe raises his hand. "Which I would normally agree with, but our pattern over these past weeks is for only one of us to stand guard. Since Hayes and I just arrived, you're relieved of your shift. Go out the front door, saunter down the street, make it look like you're done for the day. Hayes and I will get her set up and talk her through it. Once the two of you are back together, we'll pick you up. Then the four of us will leave on our presumed trip. It'll look like Kaye's still here."

"No need. My motorcycle is parked down the street." I drove it over last night, never realizing we'd find ourselves in this situation. "Which works. I drive off. The five of you hang on the roof. We set the anchors, send Kaye to me, and we'll ride back to HQ. Scott will have no reason to think Kaye isn't still inside."

I don't like leaving Kaye behind, but this makes better sense than climbing the tree.

"And, since Hayes and I were working the rock wall at HQ when Brady called…" Rafe rubs his hands together in anticipation. "We happen to have the rope and the harness she needs. This is totally doable."

"Harness?" Kaye takes a deep breath and exhales slowly. "I don't know about this."

"Do you trust us?" Hayes offers his most comforting smile.

"Yes," she answers without hesitation.

"Then you know we won't let anything happen to you." Rafe looks pleased with himself.

I nod in agreement as I step forward and put a hand on her shoulder. "If you're ready, let's do this."

"Is there any other way?"

"We've done this a thousand times with people in far worse shape than you, and we haven't lost one yet. Besides, you're in the best hands, and it's perfectly safe. I trust these guys with my life, and they'll make sure you're safer than safe."

"I guess." She looks up at me with a flash of fear in her eyes.

"I'll be with you every step of the way. Okay?"

"Okay." She nods and squares her shoulders. "Let's do this before I lose my nerve."

Rafe, Hayes, and I quickly get to work rigging the zip line. It takes creativity to get the anchor rope set on the other roof, but we figure it out after a few false starts.

Once the anchor on the roof is set, I leave like we discussed and hop on my bike. I park it outside the building we picked for the other end of the zip line. I make my way to the rooftop of the designated building with a smile for an elderly woman who lives there and a story about inspecting the roof.

Once on the roof, I signal to the guys.

We run the rope, make sure it's secured, and draw out the slack.

I wish I was with Kaye, talking her through things, but watch from a distance as Rafe sets her up and steadies her for the ride.

He fits her with the harness and shows her how to use it. In no time, we're ready to go.

"Is she ready?" I talk to Hayes through my phone.

"As ready as she can be," he says.

From across the distance, Kaye turns to me and gives me two thumbs up.

SIXTEEN

Kaye
____

RAFE AND HAYES CHECK THE ROPE. IT'S ANCHORED TO THE ROOF through a series of knots I don't understand. Rafe looks at me, his eyes warm and friendly

Reassuring.

Understanding.

"Are you ready, Kaye?"

I take a deep breath before responding.

"Yes."

But the real answer is: *No way in hell am I ready.* I'm not like Carmen or Rosalie. They're brave and fearless.

Carmen jumped on the end of a rope dangling from a helicopter, literally hanging onto Rafe for dear life as they flew over the rainforests of Nicaragua.

Fear didn't stop her.

Rosalie, grew up in those same rainforests and she escaped through them by using the trees as her highway. She not only climbed through the trees, but swam down rapids and climbed down a waterfall.

They face their fears.

Me?

I run.

And there are two things I fear the most: heights and dangling from a rope as I glide from one roof to another.

I give a reassuring smile and thumbs up. Inside, I'm nauseous and sick to my stomach. There's no way I can do this.

Rafe checks the tension in the line one more time while Hayes adjusts the harness they wrapped around me. Rafe comes over and double-checks Hayes's work, then they both look to me.

"Remember," Hayes says, "you don't do anything. You can hold the rope that goes from your harness to the line, but don't grab the line itself. You'll injure yourself."

"And if I flip upside down?" This is what I fear the most. What if I fall out of the harness while I'm a gazillion feet in the air?

"You're not going to flip." Rafe pats me on the back. "It's like every other zip line. All you do is slide down and go for a ride."

"I've never been on a zip line before." I swallow the lump of fear congealing in the back of my throat. "Just tell me I'm going to be fine."

"You're going to be fine." Hayes grabs the end of the short piece of rope that connects my harness to the line stretching between our roof and that of the building down the hill.

"Remember—" Rafe goes over things one more time. "Do not grab the rope overhead. You can hold this one here." He places my hands where they will be about chest high once I'm on the line. "Close your eyes if that helps. Zeb will catch you on the other side." He gives me a quick demo one more time on how to sit in the harness correctly.

And he's right. All I have to do is sit.

"Okay." My hands tremble and fear grabs hold of my heart. I can't help but feel like I'm hurtling to my death.

"Are you ready?" Hayes cocks his head. "We're going to help you to the edge of the roof."

"No, but yes. Better now than never." I force a smile; certain I look like a fool.

"Come on." Rafe laughs. Not at me, but with me. "Take my hand. You've got this."

I don't believe him, but I place my hand in his. It's nice. Warm. But feels nothing like when Zeb holds my hand.

Zeb's hand fits. Rafe's doesn't.

They walk me to the edge of the roof. Rafe helps me to sit down on the edge. One peek over the side and it feels like the world spins beneath my feet.

Note to self: *Do not look down!*

I give myself a little pep talk. Like: *You've got this,* and *It'll be over before you know it,* and *Zeb wouldn't have you do this if he didn't think it was safe.*

Of course, he and his teammates climb rock walls for fun. I don't do that and am happy as a clam when my feet are on the ground right where they belong. None of this dangling-in-the-air stuff.

While Rafe holds me, Hayes clips the other end of the line to the rope stretching between the buildings.

I gulp and try to swallow that knot of fear lodged firmly in my throat.

"Now, just hold onto the rope with both hands." Hayes shows me exactly where to put my hands and demonstrates how to keep a firm grip. "When you're ready, scoot off the edge. Gravity will do the rest."

"You realize you're asking me to literally jump off a building."

"Yeah," Hayes grins, "but in a really cool way. Remember, people do this for fun."

"And they're all crazy."

Rosalie and Carmen walk up behind me. They squat and give me a hug.

"You've got this," Carmen says.

"Don't look down and keep your eyes on Zeb," Rosalie gives me one final pep talk. "Your Guardian is down there, waiting to catch you. Failing that, close your eyes, but whatever you do, don't scream."

"Why?"

"No one needs to look up and see you flying through the air." She's right, of course.

I take another deep breath before nodding. I turn toward Hayes for one last look of reassurance before leaning back.

"We'll count from three to one." Rafe places one hand on my hip, the other under my arm. Hayes kneels down on my other side and does the same.

"Now three, two…" I wait for one, but Rafe and Hayes lift me up and toss me into the air.

I bite back a scream, knowing I'm going to die, but then a sharp jerk stops my fall.

I'm moving.

Wind whistles through my hair, blowing it back, and swallows the tiny shriek I make.

I open my eyes, then promptly close them tight. I don't want to remember any of this. The carabiner hisses as it slides down the rope. I glide through the air, toward Zeb, who waits for me on the other side, ready to catch me.

It feels like forever but is less than a few breaths when strong arms wrap around me and I come to a sudden stop with bone-jarring force. As soon as both of my feet are firmly planted on the roof, I open my eyes.

Zeb works to unclip me from the line. I step free, and he releases the anchor. The line slips over the roof, falling to the ground, where Rafe and Hayes gather it in.

I breathe a sigh of relief as my entire body shakes. When Zeb wraps his arms around me, his skin is warm. His muscles tense. The strength of his body makes me feel sheltered and safe.

"I never want to do that again." I look up at him, trying to make light of that terrifying ride, and find his dark eyes glittering with admiration.

"It takes a brave person to do what you just did. Never doubt yourself."

He releases me but holds my gaze for a moment longer. His smile turns into something else—something warm and tender that burns all the way through to my soul.

I'll never forget this.

For the first time, I feel truly alive.

The cool evening air brushes against my skin as I stand on my toes and loop my arms around Zeb's neck. His dark eyes twinkle and a small smile tugs at the corners of his lips.

"Admit it," he says, "you secretly enjoyed that."

"Never."

He breathes out and the heat of his breath tickles my skin while sending shivers down my spine. He dips his head until our lips crash together, soft at first, but the kiss transforms from heated passion to a beautiful harmony where we're perfectly in step.

As if we've done this a thousand times before.

He cups the back of my neck, controlling my head, and uses his hand on the small of my back to obliterate any space between us. Deepening our kiss, each flick of his tongue sends sparks of pleasure coursing through my body, and a delicious trickle of heat builds in my core.

I cling to him, as tight as I can, never wanting this feeling to end.

And while it feels as if time stands still, as we lose ourselves to the kiss, we finally break apart to catch our breath.

"Now that was definitely worth the wait." His dark eyes smolder with desire. His gaze lingers on mine before he takes a step back and releases me. "As much as I want more of that, we should probably get off this roof."

We share one last lingering gaze before he reaches for my hand.

With night falling, the lights of the city make the sky glow, twinkling like a million tiny stars. It's not much different from the night we met. All around me, life goes on as if I didn't experience the most intense few minutes of my life.

I wish I could stay right here, right now, with the whole world on pause.

But time rushes on. Zeb escorts me off the roof. We head down three flights of steep stairs. He makes me pause at the door.

"Stay here. Let me check the street."

"You don't think he's here?" My stomach clenches with fear.

"I don't, but I'm still going to check. If I wave, it's clear to come out. If I head back, that means it's not safe." He lifts my chin with his finger and places a tender kiss on my lips. "Yeah, way better than an *accidental* kiss."

With that, he heads outside where he parked his motorcycle. He glances up and down the street, taking his time, then pulls two helmets out of pannier bags draped on either side of the back wheel. He waves and I exit the building.

Without wasting time, he dons his helmet, then helps me with mine. Swinging a leg over the bike, he gestures for me to get on the back.

This is another first for me.

"It's about a two-hour ride to HQ from here. If you get too cold, let me know and we'll stop and get you something warm to wear."

Why would I need a jacket when I plan on leaning against him the entire time?

All around us, the constant hum of traffic flows by. Sirens wail in the distance and the roar of the freeways, with their never-ending stream of vehicles, makes the night come alive.

The deep, growl of the Harley fills the night. Zeb reaches back, grabs my hand, and places it around his waist.

"Hold on, luv. I hope you love a ride on a Harley better than a ride on a zip line."

"I'm definitely looking forward to this."

I wrap my arms around his waist and lean against his back. Without any shame, I take in a big breath, inhaling his uniquely warm scent as I close my eyes. He engages the clutch and we merge into traffic.

SEVENTEEN

Kaye

THE WIND RUSHES PAST MY EARS AS ZEB'S HARLEY ROARS DOWN THE street. The Harley is an adrenaline-fueled, gas-fed, living, breathing thing, coming to life beneath me. It rumbles through the city streets, holding back its power until it can unleash itself on the open road.

I cling to Zeb from behind, feeling his strong back through the thin fabric of his cotton T-shirt. I peek over his shoulder, letting the wind whip my hair. The smell of oil and exhaust, rather than noxious, somehow enhances the ride.

Night has truly fallen. Stars shine brightly, peeking out from beneath ribbons of clouds streaking across the sky.

We exit the city, then find our way onto PCH-1. Two hours of driving along the coast lie ahead of me. To my surprise, the air is warmer than I would've thought, and some heat rises from the motor beneath me to beat away the chill.

The engine hums between my legs, singing a lullaby. The first hour is exhilarating. The only sound is that of the engine, the wind whipping through the air, and the occasional car ahead of us.

After the horror of yesterday with Scott, I feel free. At one point, I let go of Zeb's waist and lean back in my seat. I stretch my arms out wide, letting the wind whistle between my fingers. It feels like I'm flying, free from the constraints of my life.

Free from Scott's abuse.

Free to do as I please.

I soar down the road, leaning into the curves, then I wrap my hands around Zeb's waist and place my cheek against his shoulder. Eyes closed, it feels like I'm in a dream.

It's as if the Harley can carry me to new adventures and places where I truly am free.

The front headlight illuminates the dark highway, but that only makes the experience more invigorating. To my right, steep cliffs drop down to the ocean below. Every now and again, the pounding surf penetrates the low rumble of the Harley and reaches my ears.

I've never felt more alive.

Euphoric.

About an hour into our ride, Zeb stops at one of those scenic lookouts. When I climb off the bike, the soreness in the muscles of my legs comes as a surprise. The wind swirls around us, chilling me, but I barely feel it.

Overhead, a full moon shines down on the ocean. Dark and mysterious, the black waters surge below us, crashing against the rocky coastline booming like thunder. White froth dances on the tips of the waves, glowing in the moonlight, and every now and then, a bird dives down to plunge into the water, seeking its evening meal.

"It's beautiful, isn't it?" Zeb comes up behind me. He wraps his arms around me and stares out into the ocean. The heat of his body warms me and my senses grow hyper-alert. I inhale his rich scent, a mixture of leather, gasoline, and something uniquely Zeb.

"Absolutely stunning." I lay the back of my head against his chest and grip his arms as they wrap around me.

"I love coming to places like this, especially at night," he says.

"You do?" I twist my neck to look into his eyes, mesmerized by him.

"Fewer people. I can sit alone with my thoughts. The smell of the ocean, the salt and brine, and the constant movement of the water soothes me."

His words resonate with me. Something about the ocean just centers me.

"It's amazing." My voice comes out soft and almost a whisper.

"You're cold." He shifts behind me, releases his grip around my waist, and runs his hands up and down my arms in an attempt to warm me.

"I don't feel cold." I feel absolutely perfect. As for cold, a chill ripples down my spine, but it's not from the chilly air. It's from the heat of his hands running over my skin.

I turn to face him and see the silvery reflection of the moon in his eyes, making them mysterious and captivating.

"Here. I've got a jacket in the saddle bag." He leaves me to grab the jacket. He shakes it out and holds it up for me. "Put this on."

I spin around and love the weight and feel of his jacket on my body. He takes my hand in his and leads me near the edge of the cliff. We stand behind the guardrail and stare out at the ocean as a companionable silence envelops us. The rhythmic lull of the waves creates an almost hypnotic state.

"It's beautiful, isn't it?" Zeb's deep voice sends a shiver of anticipation rushing along my skin.

"Gorgeous." I turn my face to the night sky, basking in the glow of the full moon high overhead, loving the way the wind whips through my hair.

With my eyes closed, Zeb surprises me with a gentle kiss to my forehead. My eyes open and I can't help but smile. He pulls me close, arms wrapped tight around me, as we listen to the waves.

I don't know how long we stand there, taking in nature's beauty, but eventually, Zeb clears his throat.

"We should get going, or they're going to wonder what happened to us."

"Reality calls." I breathe out a sigh. "Can't we stay just a little longer?"

"Come on. There's plenty more of this at The Facility."

I've heard about The Facility from Carmen. It's some kind of halfway house/recovery facility for those Guardian HRS rescues. It sits along PCH-1, oceanside, and is supposed to be an amazing place to recover and rebuild.

He tugs gently at my hand and leads me back to the Harley. We mount up and continue our journey with the Harley growling like a beast as it chews through the curving road. Eventually, we come across a small diner perched over the rocky cliffs. The sign over it says, "Bill's Burgers - Best on the Coast."

An inviting little hole in the wall, my stomach rumbles with the promise of a great greasy burger.

"Are you hungry?" Zeb pulls to a stop in the small parking lot.

"Famished."

We step off the Harley and head inside, holding hands. The moment we open the door, mouthwatering aromas attack our noses.

"Oh my, I think I've died and gone to heaven." I place my hand over my belly, hoping my stomach will behave until we can order food.

Bill's Burgers is a small burger joint with a linoleum floor, stressed wood tables, and hard plastic chairs, but the floor sparkles and the tables are clean.

"Have a seat anywhere you like." A woman with curly hair drawn up in elegant disarray on top of her head looks like she just stepped out of the fifties. "I'll be with you in a moment."

Zeb guides me over to a booth at a window. When I try to slide in, he places his hand out to stop me.

"I sit there." His voice snaps and I jump.

"Why?" A little taken aback by the brusqueness of his tone, I flinch involuntarily.

"Sorry." He pulls me in for a hug. "Didn't mean to startle you. I sit here because I can see the exits. I like to keep my back to the wall and my eyes where I can see who's coming and going."

"It's okay. I was just startled."

"Startled or stress response?"

"What does that mean?"

"Like a trigger. I don't know how Scott treated you and I don't want to do something that triggers you."

"Oh, I get it. Um, maybe a little?"

"If I ever do something that makes you jump, or flinch, or react in a negative way, just tell me. If you can't tell me, just tap my arm three times. I'll know I pushed a trigger and can fix it in the moment."

"I'm sorry. I'm still a bit keyed up."

"I mean this in the best way possible, but you have no reason to apologize for your feelings, or your reactions to the stimuli around you. Especially, when I'm the stimuli. I can sometimes snap orders without realizing I'm doing it. I don't want you to ever feel uncomfortable with me."

"I'll try." He remains standing while I slide into the booth. Once I'm seated, he slides in opposite me. We exchange shy smiles, lost for words, for the moment, until the waitress appears with a pad of paper tucked into her apron. She yanks it out, clicks a pen, then licks the ballpoint end.

"What can I get you?" She scratches on the pad, leaving me wondering what she would write when we haven't said anything. I open my mouth to answer, but Zeb cuts me off.

"How good are Bill's burgers?"

"Why, they're the best on the coast." Nearly twice his age, the waitress flirts with Zeb. She props a hand on her hip and cocks out a leg. "Is that what you want? One of Bill's famous burgers?"

"We'll take two. If they're the best, we can't miss out."

"Darling, you are going to love them. Cheese? Bacon? Want to make yours a double?" Her ballpoint scratches over the pad.

"How do you recommend them?"

"Cheese. Double for you. Bacon. Of course." She's spectacular at the double eye roll. "I usually skip the lettuce, but the tomatoes are a given. Bill only uses the best beefsteak tomatoes."

"Then that is exactly what I want." He turns to me. "What about you, luv?"

"Single for me. Love beefsteak tomatoes. No bacon."

"You sure about that?" She nibbles the end of the pen. "Everybody loves bacon."

"Okay, bacon it is. How can I not?"

"Exactly, dear." The pen scratches against the paper. "Fries or tots? Our fries come well done. None of that floppy half-done mess. We fry them twice, so they're extra crispy, but I prefer the tots."

"What's it going to be, luv?" He reaches across the table and interlaces his hand with mine. Staring deep into my eyes, my stomach does a little flip.

"I love tots."

"Tots it is for the lady. How about you?" She turns to Zeb.

"I'll do the crispy fries."

"Drinks? We've got water, soda, and coffee if you're looking to be up late at night. We don't do that decaf stuff here."

"Water's good for me." Zeb distracts me, rubbing tiny circles over the back of my hand with his thumb. Such a tiny thing, it sends tingling sensations racing along my nerves.

"Miss?"

I give a start and shake my head to clear my thoughts. My eyes pinch, trying to remember what the question was.

"She'll have water too." His deep rumbly laughter brings a smile to my face and heat to my cheeks.

"Coming right up." She leaves us and I lean back in the booth.

"That's not fair." I cross my hands over my chest and try to give him my fiercest stare.

"What?"

"You were distracting me."

"All I was doing was holding your hand." Zeb leans across the table and extricates one of my hands from where I hold it tight to my chest.

Our hands are still clasped together when the waitress comes back with two glasses of cold water. She takes a look at us holding hands and smiles. When she leaves us again, I take a deep breath and try to clear my head. It's been an eventful day.

"Penny for your thoughts?" Zeb caresses the back of my hand with his thumb again.

"I was just thinking about how much we've done today. It feels like a dream."

"You've conquered quite a few things."

"I don't know about that."

"Well, our improvised zip line is definitely a new thing."

"And not something I want to repeat."

"Never say never."

"Why's that?"

"Because I think you secretly enjoyed the thrill of it. Now, if you really want a thrill, I can take you skydiving?"

"Never." My voice squeaks and Zeb laughs.

"Never say never." He winks and a smile turns his rugged face into something stunningly handsome.

"Well, I've had enough excitement with the zip line. Thank you very much. There's no way I'm ever jumping out of a plane." I nibble at my lower lip and my free hand rises to my throat. Zeb follows the path of my hand and his eyes harden. I try and shift the focus of our conversation off what Scott did to me. "Now as for fun, today is the first time I've ridden on a bike and it's amazing."

"Harley virgin?" He leans back.

"Yes."

"I'm thrilled I was your first."

The sound of burgers sizzling on the grill and pops from the fry grease fills the burger joint with tantalizing aromas. My mouth waters in anticipation. I can almost taste how amazing the burgers will be.

"First time on a Harley and first time on a bike."

"What did you think about it?"

"I've always been afraid of bikes. Felt like an unnecessary risk, but after feeling the engine roar and the wind whip across my skin. I definitely see why people like them."

"Maybe I can teach you how to drive someday."

"No need."

"Not your cup of tea?"

"No. It's just, why would I want to ride my own bike when I can sit behind you? Tell me you didn't enjoy the way my arms wrapped around you."

"Luv, it's not your arms that revved my engine."

"It's not?"

"No." He stares at me with heat simmering in his gaze. "It's the way your legs wrapped around me that I couldn't get out of my mind."

There's too much to unpack with that comment, but his interest is clear. As are the tiny jolts of electricity shooting up my arm as he traces those light circles over my knuckles. I'm completely mesmerized when moments later, the waitress returns with two plates piled high with a juicy burger, tots for me, crispy fries for Zeb.

All conversation about my legs wrapping around his body goes to the wayside as we dig into our sizzling burgers stuffed with cheese and bacon. A generous portion of golden fries fills his plate while savory bite-sized tater tots fill mine.

The burgers are greasy, but that's what makes them great. People don't stop at places like this if they're worried about clogging their arteries. Sometimes, the food is worth the risk.

"Well?" Our waitress is back after giving us a few moments to dig in.

"Best burger ever, here or otherwise." Zeb gives a thumbs up and takes another bite.

EIGHTEEN

Zeb

———

WE MAKE IT TO GUARDIAN HQ LATER THAN I THOUGHT, BUT THEN Kaye and I stopped to eat. When we roll in, Carmen and Rosalie are already moved into their dorms. Barbi is still MIA.

"Well, you made it." I hold the door for Kaye, ushering her into her temporary quarters. "The dorms at HQ are meant to house employees, either as they onboard to the organization, or if they're temporary hires working on any one of the hundreds of projects Guardian HRS has ongoing. Your quarters are functional, but plain, one-bedroom apartments."

"I'm too thankful to be picky. This is wonderful." Her soft voice stirs dark cravings.

"While you're here, you'll have access to all of our facilities. The gym is top-notch. There's an amazing cafeteria, and while it sounds like something you'd get from a school lunch, our chefs are five-star."

"Impressive." Kaye smiles softly, but there's strain in her expression; a weariness and heaviness that stoops her shoulders.

"Most people commute from home, off base, but we have some who are here temporarily for one reason or another. Feel free to wander around. I'll be here as I can, barring other duties. The only restriction you have is, please, don't leave Guardian HQ grounds."

"What if I need something?" The hitch in her voice gives me pause. Guardian HQ is a phenomenal facility, but she's not exactly here by choice.

"Let me know and I'll get it for you, or we'll have it delivered."

"Thank you, and that drive was amazing." Her eyes sparkle and some of that weight on her shoulders lifts.

I hope she's not just saying the ride was fun to make me feel good.

Kaye closes the distance and lifts on tiptoe to plant a delicately light kiss on my lips. "Do you want to come in?" Mischief flashes in her eyes.

Her lips curl into a playful smirk and curiosity dances across her face. She gives me a very thorough once over, taking her time to check me out from the tip of my toes to the top of my head. Her gaze lingers below my waist and then again at my chest.

I don't mind. I like that she's comfortable checking me out.

"I'm afraid of what might happen if I do." I take three steps back and hold my hands up.

"What if that's what I want to happen?" Her hands stay by her side, fingers twitching. "Don't you want to stay?" Her uncertainty makes me realize how my comment may be taken the wrong way.

"Without a doubt." I correct that error immediately.

"Then stay." She gestures for me to enter.

"You're a temptress, but we're not staying."

"We're not?" Her brows furrow as she stares at me. "You mean, you're not staying." Her eyes search mine and her lips part slightly, waiting for me to answer, or kiss her.

I'd rather kiss her, but there are things to do. Needless to say, the air around us thickens with anticipation. There's no denying the attraction surging between us.

"Actually, both of us." A hint of frustration highlights my words.

"Why?" Her brow lifts with a question.

"Doc Summers wants to examine you, and before you say no,

she's an exceptional physician. You can trust her to be thorough and discrete, but afterwards Skye, Mitzy, Sam, and CJ want a SITREP." I'm resigned to an evening of briefings rather than cuddling with Kaye. I'd love to spend the night in her quarters, but it's better to wait.

"A what?" Her brows pinch in confusion.

"Situational report. It's basically a report on the situation."

"What about sleep?"

"It's barely nine. What time do you normally go to bed?"

"Lately, it's been early. Scott gets up at four in the morning to work out. Sorry," she replies with sadness and dips her head in shame. "I didn't mean to…"

"It's okay." I place my finger under her chin and reassure her about my feelings. "Stop apologizing for what happened, but I will say one thing."

"What's that?" Hesitation fills her voice.

"For now, it may be in our best interests not to have any more sleepovers like last night."

"It's not like we did anything." Her soft whisper sends desire coursing through my veins. She's a delicious torture I endured last night, but I don't plan on suffering through that again.

"The next time you're in my arms, we won't be kissing."

"We won't?"

"Well, we will, but there'll be a whole lot more going on. If that's what you want." I'm not reading her wrong. I know where things are headed.

Self-control may be a strong suit for some, but my control slips around Kaye. I kiss her again. And once more for good measure. It's the perfect reminder of why I can't spend the night.

Her face turns the prettiest shade of pink which makes me grin, but her smile falters.

"Sorry. Couldn't resist."

"Well, you know one thing about me for certain."

"What's that?"

"I blush." She shrugs, but a wicked smile dances across her face. "Which isn't fair. I can't control it."

"Which is why I love it, but don't worry. I won't use it against you."

"So, you won't be staying with me tonight? What if I have nightmares? What if I can't sleep?"

"Now you're pushing it." Thoughts of spending the night with her make my cock jump. Reason number one why I need to get her out of here and down to medical ASAP. If I stand here any longer, we won't be leaving her room for a week.

"Well, I have orders and those say to bring you to medical for a meeting with Doc Summers, and then to the Tech building to discuss next steps."

"What a bummer. Think about the fun we could have."

"Tell me about it." I make no effort to hide my arousal. I want her to know I find her attractive. I also want her to know I can control myself. With a grimace, these next few days are going to be challenging.

After a short walk, Kaye and I arrive at Medical, where Guardian HRS personnel receive all medical care. There's no one at the front desk at this hour, but I know exactly where to go. I take Kaye down a sterile hallway until we reach Doc Summers's office.

"We're here." I glance at Kaye, only now noticing how terrified she is. Her eyes are wide and unsure. Her hands shake, although she tries to hide it from me. "Hey, you've got this. It's just an exam."

"I know." She wraps her arms around herself and stares at the polished floor.

When I knock on the door, we're welcomed by a friendly voice.

"Come in," Doc Summers calls out, her voice light and cheery. When we step inside her office, Doc Summers wears a white lab coat with her name embroidered on it. She smiles warmly at us both. "Kaye, it is very nice to meet you." She turns to me and I already know what she's going to say. "If you don't mind waiting in the hall?"

"No problem, Doc." I turn to Kaye. "I'll be right outside. You're in good hands."

"Thanks, Zeb." Kaye looks a little more relaxed. That's Doc

Summers's doing. The woman has the best bedside manner, always putting her patients at ease.

With that, I excuse myself while Doc Summers takes Kaye through a range of medical tests checking for any physical trauma that could have resulted from Scott's abuse.

It's my hope she'll check Kaye's mental state as well, offering advice and tips on how to cope with her situation, plus keeping herself safe in the future.

Finally, the door to Doc Summers's office opens.

"We're all done here." She escorts Kaye out into the hall. "No major injuries. Just the few contusions. I mentioned taking self-defense classes while she's here. It's a great way to work through some of the trauma." She glances at Kaye. "And I told her you would be able to teach her."

"Oh, definitely." My voice rises with excitement. "I mean, if that's what you want?" I look to Kaye.

Why didn't I think of that sooner?

Carmen and Rosalie should get the same self-defense training as our rescues at The Facility. It would certainly help to pass the time. Barbi too.

I think that's why Carmen and Rosalie decided to leave HQ. In many ways, we basically locked them up in what's essentially a minimum-security prison without much to do. No wonder Rosalie and Carmen wanted to get out.

"Great." Doc Summers claps her hands together, signaling an end to the visit. "The others are waiting in Mitzy's office. Kaye, do you mind if I talk to Zeb alone for a minute?"

"Um…" Kaye looks between the two of us. Hesitant at first, but then nods.

"Thanks, it won't take but a second." Doc Summers gestures to me to join her in her office. The moment the door closes, I jump in.

"She's going to be okay?"

"Yes, like I said, only contusions from the ligatures. You already know this, but I don't like to assume. She's emotionally scarred by Scott's behavior, leaving her at high risk for PTSD. Precautions are necessary. Be on the watch for symptoms and let me know if anything concerns you. Physically, she's fine. The self-defense will help as well."

"It's a great idea. I'm annoyed it didn't occur to me sooner."

"Don't beat yourself up about that. I understand what happened is new?"

"Yes."

"Well, then how would you have known?"

We head to the Tech building next, where I introduce Kaye to Mitzy, CJ, and Sam.

"Welcome to Guardian HRS." Mitzy pulls Kaye in for a hug, even though it's the first time they've met. "I'll give you a brief overview of what we can do for your unique situation. CJ will explain how the Guardians fit in. Bottom line, we'll not only protect you from Scott, but by the time you leave, he will never threaten you again."

"Um, it's nice to meet all of you." Kaye glances around those assembled, her voice meek and unsure.

"Ah, don't let the testosterone affect you," Mitzy says. "They're all over-protective to a fault, but good, down deep where it matters. Did you check into your lodging?"

"Yes. Rafe and Hayes put her things in her room." I answer for Kaye, taking some of the burden off of her, considering she's the center of attention, something Kaye doesn't like.

"Good." Mitzy runs her fingers through her psychedelic hair. "I promise we'll get you back before midnight. We're just starting to build out a package…"

"A what?" Kaye turns to me.

"It's all the important tidbits." Mitzy flaps her hand. "That's my job. I lead the tech crew. We do intel and recon. This is CJ."

"Good evening. It's nice to meet you." He extends a hand which Kaye takes.

"CJ leads the muscle. That's Zeb and the others. We have four Guardian teams; Alpha, Bravo, Charlie, and Delta. Zeb and the others are Bravo team. This lug in the corner is Sam. He's kind of like the CEO of Guardian HRS, meaning we all report to him. You came from Medical, so you met Skye, and you met Forest some time ago."

"I did. He was intimidating." Kaye clasps her hands in front of her.

"Intimidating, yes." Mitzy shakes her head. "But stubborn as a mule. He and Skye created Guardian HRS."

"Yes. Carmen and Rosalie told me. It's beyond amazing, and I can't thank you enough for helping me. Compared to human trafficking, I'm small potatoes."

"No life is small potatoes." The deep rumbling voice of Forest Summers sounds from the hall. Our illustrious leader pokes his head through the doorway. "Nice to see you again, Kaye."

"Likewise," she says.

"Hey, I can't stay. Got things to do, but don't think you're not worth our help. You're one of us now, and we take care of our own." With that, Forest leaves us.

"Well, there you go." Mitzy wrangles our attention back to the front of the room. "So, here's what you can expect. My team is going to build out a package around Scott. While we're doing that, Zeb and the rest of Bravo are going to work with you and your roomies on basic self-defense. We'll provide basic personal safety tips every woman should know. Our job is to leverage what we discover regarding Scott to neutralize the threat he poses. Once that's done, you and your besties will be cut loose. Any questions?" Like always, Mitzy speaks a mile a minute. It's a wonder Kaye keeps up at all, but she nods with understanding.

"Well, I really appreciate it, and I'm kind of excited to poke around HQ."

"Girl, there are so many cool places to poke around here. You come find me tomorrow and I'll give you the backstage exclusive, one-of-a-kind tour." Mitzy glances at me and winks. "We're going to have a ton of fun."

After introductions are done, we're excused. I'm a bit confused, to be honest. I thought there would be a lot more about Scott discussed, but it seems as if Mitzy's not ready, which is odd. Mitzy's always got something to say. Maybe they found something they didn't want Kaye to know?

I walk Kaye back to her lodging, holding her hand the entire way. We stop outside the building. If I go inside, I won't have enough restraint to leave.

"I really appreciate everything you're doing for me." Kaye spins around to face me. She takes my hands in hers and gives a little squeeze.

"You're worth it."

"I'm incredibly lucky to have you."

I offer her a small smile. "Well, I hope you sleep easy tonight. You're safe. He can't hurt you."

"Thanks. That means the world to me."

Scott's been a problem for too long. I'm happy I have the resources to help her. Not many women have that.

"We'll figure this out together. You don't have to suffer alone anymore."

She smiles back at me, then glances at the building. "Will you walk me to my door?"

"I thought I'd stop here."

"Why?"

"Because, if I go inside, I may not have the strength to leave."

"If I promise to keep my hands to myself, do you think you could stay a bit longer? I-I'm not ready to be alone, especially in a place I don't know."

"You're not the one I'm worried about."

"I'm sure you can keep your hands to yourself." She gives a timid smile. "Let me put it like this, so we get it out in the open."

"Sure?" I'm not really certain what she wants to say, but I'll play along.

"You make me feel things I've never felt before."

"Things?"

"I feel like I've known you my entire life. There's chemistry between us. I never knew what that meant until I met you."

"I feel it too." I rock back on my heels and shove my hands deep into my pockets.

"It's not a stretch to say things will progress."

"Progress?"

"Don't make me say it."

"Why not? I love watching you blush."

"You're horrible. I'm trying to have a moment here."

"Okay. Sorry." I wipe the grin from my face and give her my full attention. "You were saying things will progress?"

"Yes."

"To sex?" I can't *not* go there.

"Yes." Her eyes flare with annoyance, but it's not real. Her smile tells me she's having fun with me. "Are you saying you don't want to spend the night with me because you don't want…"

"Want, what?"

"To go there."

"Go where?"

"Oh, you're impossible." She stamps her foot and flicks those long lashes of hers in irritation.

"I'm just trying to clarify. And who's to say I'm the one who's going to have problems keeping my hands to myself? I saw the way you were checking me out earlier. My eyes…" I point to my eyes with a dramatic flourish. "They are up here. Not here." I point to my chest. "Or here." I gesture below my belt. How do I know you won't try to ravish me?"

"Ravish?"

"That's what I said." A grin fills my face.

"You would love it if I ravished you." She shakes her head and laughs.

"True."

"Okay, at some point, we're going to have sex."

"Hot damn. Best words ever."

"But not tonight." Her smile slips into a laugh.

"Buzz kill."

"Stop it." She can't stop smiling.

"You're the one talking about sex."

"No, I'm talking about *not* having sex."

"Potatoes, tomatoes."

"Have nothing to do with it. Will you be serious for a minute?"

"I don't think I can." I scrub my face and plaster on a flat, expressionless mask. It lasts all of five seconds before her laughter fills the air.

"You're hopeless." She holds up her hands. "Will you…"

"Yes?"

"I haven't asked the question yet."

"Okay." I put on my serious face and rock back on my heels. Her lips twitch into another smile.

"Will you please come inside and stay the night? Not for sex." She holds up her pointer finger. "Not for sex, but for comfort, so I don't have to sleep in an unfamiliar bed, in an unfamiliar building, in an unfamiliar place?"

"Yes, luv."

"You will?"

"How can I say no? I would love to sleep in your bed, but don't get handsy with me."

"For the love of…"

"Hey, that's my condition." I hold up my hands in front of me.

"Fine. I won't get *handsy*, but seriously, I really could use…"

"No need to explain. I'm just having fun." I gesture toward the door. "Do you want to check in with Carmen or Rosalie?"

"I'm sure they're busy."

"Well, we could be busy too, but the *no handsy* rule is in effect."

"You're a total goofball."

"I try." I'm really trying whatever I can to help Kaye relax. It's been a trying day on more than one level, and now that she's here, Scott is on the hunt—out there looking for her. I'm sure that's on her mind.

We head to her room and enjoy relative silence as she unpacks her things. After she changes into very unflattering PJs, I strip to my boxers, keep my shirt on, and we crawl into bed together. Me with a major boner and her with flannel PJs that cover up all the good bits.

I curl my body around hers and drape an arm over her hip. I avoid her erogenous zones because my restraint is only so strong, and wait for her to relax. After she settles down, I close my eyes and breathe in her light floral scent. It's going to be one hell of a long night.

"Thank you," she says softly.

"For what?"

"For being here. For helping."

I find myself unable to find any words that suffice as an answer. Instead, I squeeze Kaye's hip in reassurance. "How about we get some sleep?"

"And for staying. So I don't have to sleep alone."

"Whatever you need, luv, I'm here, and I'll do whatever it takes."

"I don't deserve you."

"Nonsense." I give her a gentle kiss on her temple. With my arms wrapped protectively around her, I wait for her to drift off to sleep, before closing my eyes and allowing sleep to claim me. This feels good. It feels right.

NINETEEN

Kaye

───────

MORNING SUNLIGHT FILTERS THROUGH THE SHEER CURTAINS, casting a warm, yellow glow over the room. The soft light highlights the contours of Zeb's face leaving me with butterflies fluttering in my stomach. I take a moment to gaze at him and try to keep those butterflies in check.

If I'm not careful that fluttering will grow into something bigger, something far more complicated and impossible to control.

Here I am, waking up in his arms, like this is my new normal, when nothing about my life right now is normal. I should be filled with apprehension, anxiety, and dread. Instead, I feel comforted, safe, and incredibly relaxed.

Not wanting to wake him, I extricate myself from his embrace and slip out of bed as carefully as I can manage. Tiptoeing softly to the bathroom, I open the door quietly, and close it behind me, hoping the click of the latch doesn't wake him.

When I catch my reflection in the mirror, I give myself a little pep talk.

You can do this.

The words come, but I don't feel them. I've never felt this out of control in my life.

Determined not to let my emotions get the better of me, I close my eyes and focus on my breathing. In for a count of *one-two-three-four.* Hold for seven. Push out my breath for a count of eight.

When I open my eyes, I feel better. Calmer. Ready to face the day. Or at least try.

I can do this. I've got this.

Most of all, I'm going to attempt the impossible.

It's not healthy to jump from one man to another, but I'm going to try. Despite how fast I've fallen for Zeb, I resolve to take things slow and enjoy getting to know him. It's too easy to jump into bed, and rush physical intimacy, without laying down a proper foundation.

I reach for my phone, then remember it's in Mitzy's possession. A wave of anxiety washes over me. Normally, I check my phone a half dozen times or more before my feet hit the floor. It's become an automatic habit to check texts, email, social media, and more, before getting out of bed. Without my phone to distract me, and jumpstart my morning with a dopamine surge, I'm alone with my worry.

Take another breath.

Focus on the present.

It's strange being without my phone; something essential is missing, but it's necessary. Mitzy's going to use it to deal with Scott.

Honestly, it's best I don't have the phone. I can only imagine the string of nasty texts from Scott, threats against me, threats against my friends. Just thinking about it gives me that queasy, shaky feeling.

Did Barbi ever respond to our texts?

I make a mental note to ask Carmen and Rosalie when I see them. Putting my anxiety aside for a moment, I take advantage of Zeb sleeping to use the bathroom. Unlike the rest of my temporary quarters, which is functional to a fault, whoever designed the bathroom knows exactly how to pamper its guests.

The separate shower and tub are a nice addition. I'm not one to soak in a tub, but I love a roomy shower. There's something about letting the steam build and how it wraps around me in a comforting fog of warmth. I'm also that chick who sits down in a shower to enjoy the steam. I won't sit in a bath, but I'll sit in the shower until the water runs cold.

It's a quirk, don't judge.

I do that now, and while I sit there, I let the anxiety building within me swirl down the drain. From now, until things are over with Scott, I'm not going to think about him, his threats, or any of the nastiness surrounding him.

And that lasts all of ten seconds.

UC Davis is a wash. There's a lesson there.

I cheated the system and used Scott to secure my place. Now, I pay the price with it being ripped away.

Which leaves me where?

My entire life, I've wanted to be a veterinarian. Generally considered more competitive than medical school, I have the grades, recommendations, and scores to be a competitive applicant. But I lack the confidence to believe in myself. Meaning, I jumped at an opportunity, exploited what Scott could do for me, and never looked back. There is no backup plan because I didn't apply anywhere else. I didn't need to when my spot was secure.

But that doesn't mean I won't get into another program. Like I said, I'm a competitive applicant. I can apply again. I'll have to get another faculty recommendation to replace Scott's, and I may not get into the school of my choice. I'll have to wait a year to apply, but I can accept that as my punishment for working around the system.

If I thought Davis was far from my friends, the other options are even farther away. I might wind up in Idaho, or Arkansas, or somewhere on the east coast.

I think back to the words of encouragement Paul gave me what seems like forever ago. He made some great points.

If I want this, I have to put fear aside and go for it. Carmen, Barbi, and now Rosie are my anchor. That sounds like they'll pull me under. I need a better analogy.

They're my beacon. The light guiding me home.

Yeah, I like that analogy much better.

I'll make new friends, other lights in the darkness, but keep the old. My friends will always guide me home.

I can't help it, but that silly Girl Scout song plays through my head. Turns out, it's not so silly after all, and holds some sage advice.

Finally, it's time to get on with my day. I dry off and wrap myself in the fluffy white robe provided for guests and pad back out to the main room.

"Good morning, sunshine. I thought I lost you to the luxuries of the bath." Zeb sits in bed with two pillows propped behind him.

He turns off his phone and sets it to the side. The entirety of his attention turns on me and those butterflies react with a tumultuous surge of frenetic energy.

"Shower." I tug at the belt keeping the robe closed and try not to let my mouth gape.

Zeb climbs out of bed and yanks off his T-shirt, revealing rippling muscles across broad shoulders and rock-hard washboard abs. My heart gives a little flutter of appreciation with how gorgeous he looks with his hair still tousled from sleep and that heart-stopping smile of his.

He stirs all kinds of cravings within me, more intense than before, probably because we're alone.

"Are you hungry?" He's definitely a morning person with that cheery disposition.

I need a little more time to wake up. Mornings are my grumpy times. At least until I can fuel the tank with caffeine.

"Famished." I place a hand over my belly and pray my stomach doesn't growl and embarrass me.

"If you're done in there…" He points toward the bathroom. "I'll get ready, then I'll take you to breakfast."

"That would be amazing." I step to the side and bite my lower lip as he saunters past me.

But Zeb surprises me, grabbing me and pulling me in for a kiss on the cheek.

The cheek?

Talk about disappointing.

"I—uh," There's that smirk of his. "I need to release some tension. I may be awhile." He says it teasingly, then winks before his gaze slants down to the growing bulge behind his briefs.

He disappears inside the bathroom with a chuckle while my face heats with embarrassment. Then he turns that molten gaze on me, letting it roam all over my body while the unmistakable outline of his arousal continues to grow.

A delightful heat rises inside of me.

Did he…?

Is he…?

I can't believe he said what he said.

Suggested what he suggested.

But he did. He absolutely did.

He leaves my head spinning and my body aching for his touch.

No way did he imply he was going to… But didn't he? That sly, suggestive smile spoke volumes.

What else can it mean?

His audacity sends a thrill shooting through me.

The moment the door closes, and I'm alone, I can't help but imagine what's happening in the bathroom. I slump against the wall and desperately fan myself while trying to think of something to distract me from what he's doing in there.

Why is that so damn sexy?

And talk about unfair?

He leaves me hot and bothered while he's in there—*releasing the tension.*

The anticipation is too much. I can't resist.

Do I?

Dare I?

You only live once.

I place my hand on the doorknob, bite my lower lip, and twist it open. The door creaks, ever so softly, announcing my presence.

And there he is facing away from me, briefs pushed down to mid-thigh. Powerful shoulders top his broad back. All that muscle angles down to a swimmer's waist. My eyes rove over his body as he stands before me. The taut curves of his backside clench. His briefs ride low, shoved down in the front, while his arm moves rhythmically out and back, stroking himself.

Zeb pauses and turns toward me, revealing the long, engorged length of his cock. He says nothing, simply stares into my eyes with an intensity that sends shivers of delicious heat shooting through me.

Strain pulls at the muscles of his neck as his hand slowly glides from root to tip, twisting as it glides up the turgid shaft. His thumb rubs over the tip of his glans as a low moan vibrates in the back of his throat.

He finally breaks eye contact and his hand speeds up, stroking his cock.

Twisting.

Tugging.

Faster and faster.

I stand motionless for a few moments until I remember to breathe. I take a few deep breaths and steady myself before stepping backward, wordlessly, with wide-eyed awe.

"Come here." Husky and aroused, his command stops me in my tracks.

My heart bangs away in my chest as I close the distance between us, marveling at how beautiful his body is, how strong and perfect and virile.

His breath tickles my neck as I step close. He wraps one arm around me, pulling me tight while the other keeps moving over his shaft with stiff, sure strokes punctuated by soft grunts of pleasure.

The sensation of his arousal pressed against me makes me burn and ache in the most delicious way possible.

"Do you want to touch?" His words come in short bursts as his arousal grows. His breaths quicken, telling me he's close. "Or do you want to watch?"

I find myself transfixed by him pleasuring himself. It feels deliciously naughty to watch. Not something I've ever done before.

His hips jerk as he thrusts into his hand. A deep groan builds in the back of his throat.

"Feel me." He takes my hand and places it so that I cup his balls. His hand twists as he pumps up and down. That groan deepens and grows.

Suddenly, his entire body tenses then releases as a shuddering wave travels through him. He presses his forehead against my shoulder as the aftershocks of his release pulse through him and his body shakes with the force of his orgasm.

Eventually, he grows still, except for his heavy breathing. He makes eye contact while my heart beats wildly, erratically, after the most intense sexual experience of my life.

That says something, considering he didn't touch me.

His gaze moves over the features of my face. He pulls me close as we both catch our breaths.

"Thank you." He presses a chaste kiss on my lips, then whispers, "For sharing this moment with me."

I can only nod wordlessly in response. Before I know it, the spell breaks and reality crashes around us.

I pull back, unable to speak, feeling suddenly shy, and unsure.

"Don't." He grabs my arm, holding me.

"Don't, what?"

"Don't turn away, not after that." He ducks down until we're eye to eye. "I'm not ashamed to pleasure myself while you watch."

"It's just…" How to find the words? "I've never…"

"Never, what?" He encourages me to express myself.

"Just not like that. So open." I look around and gesture toward the lights. "It's always been under the sheets and in the dark."

"Luv, when you and I are together, there's no way we're hiding anything from each other. I want you to know how you make me feel, how my body reacts when you're around. This is our time, something intimate and powerful. Something, we only share with each other."

I nod, realizing the truth of his words. I've never had a lover pleasure himself in front of me like that before. It was an experience unlike any other.

I'm still reeling that he's here at all, with me, and that he wants me. Even if this is only temporary, this is a moment that will shape my life forever.

No matter what happens down the road—whether I get into vet school here, or move far away—I'll always have this incredible moment.

With him.

I peek up at him and twist my fingers in my robe as nervous anxiety threatens to overwhelm me. "I don't know what I'm supposed to do now."

Zeb's lusty laughter breaks the spell. "Get dressed while I clean up. We've got a full day ahead of us." He spins me around and gently escorts me out of the bathroom. "I'll be out in a second. We'll get breakfast, then I'll take you on a tour of the grounds."

"Don't you need new clothes?"

"I've got a change of clothes in the bullpen. We'll stop there along the way."

My skin heats at the sight of him bare before me. The man is unashamed, but for good reason. His body is the embodiment of male perfection.

He's a warrior. A Guardian. He's a hero to so many. And the man is hot as sin.

"You should probably go." He grins and turns on the shower.

"Why?"

"Because I'm not doing round two alone." He raises an eyebrow. "And the longer you look at me like you want to eat me up, the more likely it is there will be a round two."

No need to say more. With a squeak, I spin around, heart beating wildly, while his lusty laughter chases me into the other room.

He leaves the door to the bathroom open, which means after I get dressed, I've got the best view on the planet as he lathers up and rinses off.

The electrical chemistry between us surges with power and anticipation. Our connection has grown even stronger over the past twenty-four hours; our lives colliding in the most beautiful way possible.

What started as a simple friendship is gradually building into something much deeper, something special—something more than I ever dreamed possible.

Or dared to hope for.

TWENTY

Zeb

____

I can't help but smile as Kaye runs from the bathroom. That was totally not what I intended—having her watch me fuck my hand—but it was so fucking hot.

I came hard. Harder than I ever do with the five-finger hustle.

I can't wait to turn the tables on her and torture her with my fingers, my tongue, and my cock. But for now, it's time to put sex on the back burner. We'll get there when we get there.

I step out of the shower and grab a towel from the rack, wrapping it around my waist. Kaye waits for me on the small sofa, peeking up from beneath her long lashes.

She's embarrassed, but excited by what she saw.

I grin and take my time to stroll across the room, not bothering to hide anything from her gaze. She got an eyeful in the bathroom. No point in pretending fake modesty now.

I pull on my jeans and sniff my shirt from last night. It smells like a mix of sweat, oil, and fumes from the bike; definitely not something I want to wear again. Fortunately, my gear locker in the bullpen has several days' worth of clothing in my Go Bag to choose from.

"I say we grab breakfast, then I'll give you the full tour. I have a briefing at noon. I'll bring you back here so you can change before sparring practice." I keep my voice soft, trying to ease some of the sexual tension swirling in the air. Not an easy task.

"Excuse me? Sparring, what?"

"Time to learn how to defend yourself, luv." I place my finger under her chin and tilt her head back so that I can press my lips against hers. Her sweet scent brings a groan to the back of my throat and my cock stirs, wanting more.

Down, boy!

"Your afternoons will be filled with classes on self-rescue and defense. Your mornings are free to do as you please, but first… How about food?"

"I'm famished." The corners of her mouth twitch, lifting into the prettiest smile I've ever seen.

"Good, because if we don't leave in the next thirty seconds, I don't think we'll be leaving for a week. Don't think I'm going to be satisfied with you just watching." My eyes crinkle with my smile.

"Umm…" Kaye blushes and nods in agreement. "I agree."

"To which one? Breakfast or…"

"Both."

I pull her into my arms and lightly kiss her forehead. I don't dare do more than that.

"Then, if you're hungry, I suggest we leave."

"Yes." She doesn't meet my eyes, looking instead toward my crotch.

A grin fills my face and I can't help but push her buttons. "I meant for food…" Stepping forward, I place the tip of my finger under her chin. "My eyes are up here, luv. You're going to have to wait to get a taste of that."

Just as I expect, her blush turns her face scarlet red.

Damn, I love that color.

She ducks out from under my touch before I can do anything more than smile at her reaction.

I can't help but laugh when her embarrassment deepens.

"I hate that I blush so easily." She shakes her shoulders and looks everywhere but at me.

"It's one of the things I love the most about you," I speak softly, hoping she hears what's important.

There's nothing more sexy than seeing her innocent side peek out every now and then.

And nothing hotter than the way she looks at me.

"It's embarrassing." She takes a deep breath and seems to have difficulty composing herself.

I pause and take in her beauty. The desire to possess her is too strong to resist, but I need to wait for the right moment.

I'll be patient if it kills me, or makes my balls turn blue.

"It's beautiful." I let out a breath of admiration. She's going to be mine—is mine already—but it will be a while before I can truly claim her.

But that's okay. She's worth the wait.

"Don't do that." Her lashes flutter as she looks away.

"Do, what?"

"Look at me like that."

"How am I looking at you?" I study her face and my gaze lingers over her delicate features.

"Like you want to devour me." Her cheeks redden and she looks away.

"That's exactly what I want." A mischievous grin spreads across my face. There's no hiding my desire. I reach out and slowly take her hand in mine. Drawing a heart on the palm of her hand, I reassure her with a single look. "But I'm in no rush. We're not doing anything until you're ready."

When her gaze shifts to the bathroom, a rush of heat burns through me. We're so close to giving in and taking things further, but that will only complicate matters.

I take a deep breath, count to five, and calm myself before speaking.

"We should probably go." Throaty and hoarse, I clear my throat and start making my way to the door. If we stay much longer, neither one of us will be leaving for the rest of the day.

She follows me out of her temporary quarters, then loops her arm through mine as we greet another one of California's spectacular days. I guide her to one of the cafeterias on HQ grounds as a comfortable silence settles between us. We're each lost to our own thoughts until Kaye speaks up softly.

"Where are we going?"

"The Mess Hall. You said you were hungry. I thought that meant food, but we can go back."

"You said you were in no rush." She shoves me playfully.

"I lied." My wink turns her cheeks pink. Damn, but I love that. "But I'm content to wait, until you're ready."

We meander through the grounds and I point out various buildings along the way, showing her the medical facilities we visited last night as well as Mitzy's fiefdom where the techies rule.

"And this is the cafeteria. Or Mess Hall. People use the two interchangeably."

"Looks busy."

"It is, and it's bigger than it seems. Plenty of food and plenty of tables. Come on."

We push through the cafeteria doors and are immediately greeted by the savory scents of breakfast sizzling away and the low background noise of people talking while sharing a meal.

"Oh my, this place smells amazing." Kaye's eyes brighten and she places her hand over her stomach. "What do they have?"

"Anything you can think of."

"Waffles?"

"Yes."

"With butter?"

"Yeah, I think we have butter."

"And whipped cream?"

"Someone loves their waffles." I love learning these little things about her along the way. It's like stealing peeks into her innermost thoughts.

"I haven't had waffles in forever. Too much mess to clean up at home, but if they have it, and I don't have to do the dishes…" Her eyes light with excitement.

"Not only do we have waffles, there's an entire station dedicated to them. Pancakes too; plain, blueberry, chocolate chips…"

My mouth waters thinking about chocolate chip pancakes. Those are my absolute favorite. Not something we ever had in the commune. We weren't allowed frivolous things. I learned about chocolate chip pancakes only after joining the Navy.

"You're kidding?"

"Nope." I pull her over to the waffle station, where I leave her to make her selections. After she's set, I get in the main line, grab a plate, and pile it high with eggs, bacon, and biscuits with gravy.

She loves waffles. I love biscuits with gravy.

I rejoin her just as her waffles finish and guide her to a private table, where we take our seats and enjoy our meal alone.

"So, how do we pay for this?" She twists in her seat, checking out the dining area. "I don't see any registers."

"We don't."

"What?"

"It's part of our salary. Food, medical, and the gym are all employee perks. We're responsible for bussing our dishes and wiping down the table, but that's it."

"You're kidding?"

"Nope, and I can't wait to show you around the rest of the place."

"But I'm a guest, not an employee."

"We'll just leave it as it's included with your stay, don't worry about it." I can see the wheels turning in her head, but see the moment she relents and decides to change the subject.

"Since this is my home for the time being, I definitely appreciate the tour. Not to be a buzzkill, but any idea what happens next?" A cloud falls over her, darkening her expression and dimming the light in her eyes.

"You mean the tour? I thought I'd show you Bravo's bullpen." Only after the words leave my mouth do I realize that's not what she's talking about. It took a beat too long to figure out.

"I meant Scott," she says. "Like, what are the next steps?"

"That lies with Mitzy and her team and my noon meeting. Once they build out a package, Bravo team will plan tactics and execute."

"What about me?"

"You get to enjoy waffles." I don't mean to be dismissive, but it's the truth.

"I mean the briefing. Earlier you said you were going to take me back to my quarters because you had a briefing. If it's about Scott, shouldn't I be there?"

"Not at the initial meetings. We have certain ways we build out a package for an operation. At this point, speed and efficiency are our allies. I know you want to be involved, and no one means to keep you in the dark. That's not it at all, but we work best in the rhythm and tempo we train with."

"You're saying I'd be a distraction."

"I'm trying to say that without sounding like a jerk, but that's basically it."

"I don't like it."

"I knew you wouldn't, but it's not something I can change."

"I don't mind if you have a certain way of doing things, but please don't keep me in the dark. I'm scared and my entire life's been turned upside down."

"I know, and I'll do my best to include you as we're able. In the meantime, there are some things we can teach you that are great life skills."

"You mentioned sparring."

"Every afternoon." I glance at her plate. "Your waffles are drowning in whipped cream. Best to eat them before they dissolve."

Her role in what comes next will be exceedingly small. Fortunately, she laughs at my waffle joke, and I breathe out a sigh of relief. I got her smiling and she's not pushing as hard as I thought she would about Scott.

I take the win.

To use Kaye's words, talk about Professor Scott Parker is a total buzzkill. Although, I'm eager to see what Mitzy and her team have discovered.

After we finish breakfast, I take Kaye to the Guardian building and point out the different teams' quarters. We stop at Bravo team's bullpen and I gesture for her to enter the private space where only members of our team are allowed.

"Are you sure I should be in here?" She looks around in awe.

"Can't exactly leave you outside, and my change of clothes is in here."

I open the lock to my gear locker, which holds all of my personal gear. Inside is a Go Bag with several days' worth of spare clothing.

"Now, no funny business while I change." I tease her lightly. "I'll be in enough trouble if we're caught by one of my teammates as it is. Add in hot and heavy sex, and we'll never live it down."

Her eyes round with that comment. Not that I would ever be so crass to risk exposing her like that, but her reactions are too much fun not to tease her about it.

"And each team has a bullpen?" She wanders around the room, running her fingers over the fencing surrounding each of our personal gear lockers.

"Four teams. Four bullpens. And we each have our own gear locker, but we call them cages."

"I can definitely see why." She peers through the fencing. "There's a lot of stuff in there."

"Anything that's tailored specifically to each of us is kept in our personal lockers."

"Like, what?"

"Favorite weapon, body armor, boots, rucks, our helmets with night vision goggles. Stuff like that. Go Bag." I point to my bag.

"It's impressive. I'm finding it difficult to imagine the scope of an operation like this."

"We're funded by billionaires. You met Forest and Skye, plus there are many other sources of grants and private funding."

I grab a clean pair of jeans and shirt and quickly change clothes. As I do, I can't help but laugh under my breath. If Brady, or any of the others walk in and see Kaye in here, and me in my skivvies, I'll never hear the end of it.

"We really should leave before we get caught. I'm not kidding about the amount of flack they'll give me if they know I brought a woman into our sacred spot."

We hustle out of Bravo's bullpen and I show her the central briefing room in the center of the building. Chances are, she'll be here again for updates on whatever progress we make with Scott. Kaye listens with rapt attention, her eyes wide as she takes it all in.

We once again step outside, and the bright California sun beats down on us as we tour the different facilities. I explain some of the things Bravo team does here. How we train and test out new weapons, tactics, and the tech Mitzy's gang thinks up.

We stroll along one of the many paths scattered throughout The Facility until we arrive at Mitzy's fiefdom, the tech facility.

A metal door stands closed against a white wall and a posted sign reads Omega Tech Testing Facility.

"Omega?" Her eyes sparkle and she can't help but peer inside.

"Mitzy says her team is the tail that wags the dog, and since that's the end—Omega."

"Funny, but who's the dog?"

"The Guardians." I roll my eyes, but it's for show.

"A bit of rivalry?"

"You'd think, but not really. We prefer being called the pointy tip of the spear, but Mitzy's trying to get everyone to switch to calling us the dogs."

"That sounds horrible."

"You'd think, but it's because of the Rufi."

"Rufi?"

"Yes, those are her Robotic Ultra Functional Utility Specialists, or R.U.F.U.S. It's the name of a dog in some kid's book. Her pack of Rufuses was too hard to say, so we call them Rufi. She hates it and retaliated with Omega."

"That's kind of funny."

"Maybe, but it's not catching on. Mitzy's trying, though. She renamed the Tech building to be the Omega Tech Testing Facility to try and push the change." I press on the access panel and the outer metal door opens with a hiss.

We step into the cool, air-conditioned interior, where I give Kaye the nickel tour, letting her peek in on all the cool projects Mitzy's team is currently working on.

After spending a little over an hour with the Techies, I take her to the gym facilities. Her eyes widen as we enter the main area, which is larger than a stadium.

"This is where you'll meet me after lunch for our first sparring lesson."

I give her a moment to take it all in. Our gymnasium is larger than a football stadium with a retractable roof far overhead. Inside, the space is partitioned into scores of training spaces for different things.

"This is insane." She grabs at my arm and tries to look at everything all at once.

We pass the massive rock wall, where we train for missions. It spans the length of the football field and soars nearly all the way to the roof overhead.

"How tall is that?" She cranes her neck, taking it all in.

I pull at my chin. "I honestly don't remember."

"And it runs the entire length of a football field."

"It does."

"Why?"

"For various training activities. We have something running almost all the time."

"This place is… Wow. Just wow." She releases my arm and spins in a slow circle. "When Rafe and Hayes said they came from the climbing wall, this is not what I pictured."

I guide her into the center of the field, where dozens of sparring mats spread out in a grid over the ground.

"We'll train over here."

There are enough sparring stations for all four teams of Guardians to split into pairs and face off against each other, plus many more for ongoing skills maintenance of non-Guardians.

"Train? What do you mean?"

"Self-defense. Remember what Doc Summers said?"

"I don't remember much of last night. I was overwhelmed."

"Well, she thinks, and I agree, that you and your roomies should take advantage of our self-defense training while you're here. We start this afternoon."

"Oh, that makes sense, and you're going to train me?"

"It involves a lot of close, physical combat, lots of holds and grabs. There's absolutely no way I'm letting the guys get that close to you."

"You're funny."

"It's the truth."

"Possessive?"

"Yes, but not in a bad way. To be honest, our best trainers are Jinx and Lily."

"Who's that?"

"They're former DEA agents. Lily was a field agent. Jinx was in crypto, but she's got this badass Brazilian fighting style that we're all trying to learn. I've yet to beat her."

"I find that hard to believe."

"You'll understand when you meet her."

Silence drops between us as Kaye tries to absorb everything around us.

"Come on. I think you'll like this next bit."

"What's that?"

"Look overhead."

She cranes her neck but doesn't make out the wires running overhead.

"What am I trying to see?"

"Zip lines." I grin and point to the lines. It takes a moment before she makes out the thin lines against the dome overhead.

"And why would you think I'd like that?"

"Because you're a zip line queen." I try to make light of how we got her out of the house yesterday.

It takes a minute, but she eventually smiles.

"I'm good with my feet on the ground, thank you very much. Why do you have zip lines? Seems odd."

"We use them for urban training scenarios, doing exactly the kind of thing you did. We also train for midair operations."

"Midair? You're kidding me?"

"No."

"You willingly go on a zip line from one aircraft to the next? I thought that only happened in action movies. You know, when everything is bigger than big? Badder than bad? And physics doesn't matter."

"Where do you think those directors thought that shit up?"

"Wow, I guess you really do learn something new every day. I thought it was fiction."

"We do a lot of things that are very cutting edge. I'm constantly surprised by some of the tech Mitzy's team comes up with. In your downtime, ask her to show you the VR suite. Now *that* is fucking cool."

I bypass the diving facilities where we train for water ops and take her to the weapons arsenal, eager to show her everything all at once.

Exhausted by my extensive tour, just before noon, we find a quiet spot in the middle of the Quad and rest under a tree. The shade relieves the heat of the day as we sit side-by-side.

"Thanks for showing me everything." Kaye reaches for my hand. "I've had the best time."

"We only hit the highlights." I turn her hand over and interlock our fingers.

"I'm beyond impressed." She tips her head back and sighs with contentment.

"Guardian HRS is an amazing organization. I'm happy to be one small part of the work they're doing in the world."

"You must have saved so many lives. That's an incredible legacy to leave behind."

"Well, I'm not ready to leave it behind just yet, but yeah, the life of a hero…" I lean back and lock my fingers behind my head. "I love laying on the grass and staring through the branches of a good tree."

"It's a great day for it." She settles down beside me.

"Unfortunately, our little jaunt is coming to an end."

"It is?"

"Yeah, I have to meet with the team."

"About Scott." Her lips twist, and I think she's going to ask to join us, but to my surprise, Kaye's silent on the matter.

"I'll walk you back to your quarters. We'll meet after lunch and we've got something special cooked up for dinner."

"Are we going to the cafeteria? Do they make waffles at dinner or is it a breakfast-only event?"

"I honestly don't know, but we're going someplace far better than that."

"I don't know if anything is better than those waffles."

"Well, you've never had one of Rafe's homecooked meals."

"I didn't know he cooked."

"I'm surprised Carmen didn't mention it. His parents are world-renowned chefs and taught him everything they know. He kept it secret from all of us. It's a mistake he pays for now."

"How?"

"We make him cook dinner at *Insanity* on the first Saturday of every month. It's become an unofficial Guardian event. That's tonight."

"What's insane about that?"

"*Insanity* is a place."

"A place called *Insanity*?"

"Yup."

"And where is this place?"

"Now that is a surprise you're going to love."

"How mysterious." She rubs her hands together, having fun. "I can't wait."

And I can't wait to see her reaction to *Insanity* and the guys who call it their home.

TWENTY-ONE

Zeb

WHEN I ARRIVE AT THE CONFERENCE ROOM, IT'S ALIVE AND BUZZING with activity. Mitzy's there with four of her team, gathered around the conference table, talking amongst themselves. She's at the head of the table, not leading any conversation but arguing over which of the dozens of screens she wants information displayed on.

A familiar energy fills the room: anticipation melding with apprehension. It's always like this when we launch a new operation. This first session is about building out a basic profile and looking for anything concerning that might point to difficulties down the road.

Mitzy notices my entrance and smiles. Her psychedelic pixie hair sparkles under the bright halogen bulbs that light the room. The aroma of ozone from multiple computers, as their servers chew through data at an incredible speed, laces the air. Mixed in with that are the various smells of cheap cologne and breath mints from Mitzy's team.

Bravo team avoids artificial scents. It's one of any number of things with the potential to alert the enemy to our presence. As for Bravo team we're all here, minus one. Brady, Booker, Rafe, Hayes, and I sit around the table. Alec's on leave, doing whatever it is he does for fun.

"You're the last one here." Mitzy points to one of the chairs. "Take a seat."

"Where's CJ? Sam?" I look at Brady, concerned they're not here, but then maybe Kaye's crazy stalker-ex isn't important to the top brass?

"Working another issue." Brady rubs the back of his neck.

"Are we waiting for them?" I glance around the room, listening to the half-dozen side conversations going on between Mitzy and her team.

"No." Brady leans back and shifts in his seat. "They said to get started."

I slide into a chair and make myself comfortable.

Mitzy opens up several screens that line the walls, pulling up demographic data and pertinent information about Professor Scott Parker. The data scrolls in a near-endless stream, too fast for me to pick up on any particular details.

"Got anything good?" I expect little from this first meeting. It's focused on establishing a baseline more than anything else.

"Nothing good," Mitzy mutters, fiddling with her display, pulling up multiple files. "A forest of red flags."

I love the way her fingers fly over the keys. It's nearly hypnotic and too fast to follow.

Booker shakes his head as he reviews Parker's social media accounts. "This guy is a total tool. No shortage of ego." He taps his tablet, sharing the screen with Rafe. "Thinks a lot of himself."

"What do you see?" Sitting opposite them, I can't see what they're looking at.

Booker flips the tablet around and I jerk back in alarm. "What the fuck is that?"

Desiccated human remains fill the screen. Parker stands proudly next to a pit dug into the ground and several buckets holding the remnants of mummified bodies. Human bones fill the pit and appear to be in various stages of decomposition.

A huge smile fills Parker's face and the caption reads, *Funded for another three years. Thank you, NIH.*

Standing next to him is a man I've never seen before. He holds a bucket filled with human skulls, tilting the bucket outward so the camera can take the picture. Inside, dried and mummified, human heads stack up like cantaloupes. They're a morbid, and graphic, representation of what they once were. Skulls covered in brittle, leathery skin with wisps of hair falling into empty eye sockets.

"That," Mitzy says, "is Professor Scott Parker celebrating the renewal of his NIH funding."

"And who is the other guy?"

"I'll give you two guesses." Brady pulls at his chin, eyeing me.

"Two guesses? How the fuck would I know…" Then it hits. The pit in the bottom of my stomach opens up as dread slithers down my spine. "That wouldn't be the dean of UC Davis's vet school?"

"Dean Robert Jones Alder. Nice work." Booker curls his fingers and checks out his nails. He flicks a ragtag button toward Brady, who catches it midair. "Took me three guesses, and you got it in one."

"Kaye mentioned Scott was friends with the dean. I didn't realize they were research buddies. What the hell are they doing grinning like lunatics, holding human remains, and posting the whole gruesome thing on social media? And isn't he a veterinarian? What's he doing with human remains?"

"That is something we're trying to piece together." Mitzy takes a seat at the head of the table. "You know, one day—just one day…" She lifts her pointer finger for emphasis. "One day, I'd love to come to work, and have myself proven wrong."

"What do you mean?" I drum my fingers on the table, not liking the direction the conversation heads.

"Professor Scott Parker is creepy. He's a small, creepy man, taking advantage of his students, and playing with human remains," she says.

My gut raises all kinds of red flags on its own. No need for Mitzy to raise any for me.

"Instead of killers, human traffickers, and thieves, I'd love to come across some boring average Joe who wouldn't hurt a fly." Mitzy leans back with a sigh. "Just another day in the office, and it sucks. I'm telling Forest I need a raise."

"Are you saying Professor Parker isn't an everyday Joe?"

"I'm saying he's a creepy ass and a bastard." She gestures behind her. "Suspicion, conjecture, and a healthy dose of realism has me heading down dark paths. Every time, I think I'm going to prove myself wrong—that there are still good people in the world—I reconfirm this is a shitty place to raise my kids." Her voice trails off, and she holds up a hand, palm facing out. "I digress, and I'm getting ahead of myself."

"Meaning?" I look to Brady.

"Meaning, we've got our work cut out for us on this one." Brady shifts in his seat. "Not a good day in the office today, boys."

"What are you not saying?" I don't like the tone in his voice. It's feels like I got here too late and am half a step behind. I missed out on the important bits.

"Maybe we could take a few steps back?" I look around the conference table, looking for clues in the expressions of those gathered. "I need a recap."

"Conjecture only at this point, based on patterns of behavior." Mitzy closes her eyes and pauses before continuing. "Nothing solid. Definitely no proof. But it's sketch, and you know how I feel when things don't add up."

"You dig until you get to the bottom of it." We all know she's the best of the best, a tenacious opponent. For the hundredth time, I'm glad I'm on her side.

Mitzy runs our technical team, but there's far more than that involved. She oversees an intelligence team rivaling what the CIA or FBI have combined. Then there's her team of eclectic technical geniuses. Recruited from across the country, they lead the forefront of up-and-coming technologies. From her VR suite, to her drones— her dragon Smaug to her tiny dragonflies—to enhanced optics, robotics, and invisibility shields, her operation is impressive.

"His posts on social media show soft signs of paranoia, anxiety, and God complex." Mitzy takes a breath. "The man isn't lacking when it comes to thinking he's better than the rest of us." Mitzy rolls her eyes with that comment. "But he's sloppy as shit. It's only a matter of time before he makes a mistake." She pushes back from her chair and claps her hands. "Anyway, let's do this the right way and start from the beginning."

"Are we doing this without Alec?" It feels wrong to build out a mission without him.

"Don't worry about Alec. I called him back." Brady leans back and folds his arms over his chest. A huge grin fills his face. "He's supposed to be in Tahoe off-roading. Should be here later tonight."

I do a double-take. "What do you mean by *supposed to be*?"

Mitzy snorts, then covers her face. "Sorry."

"What's so funny?" I look between her and Brady, confused.

"We're going to have fun tonight." Booker turns off his tablet.

"Why?" I glance around the table. Once again, I'm missing a key piece of information. Then it hits me. "Because he isn't in Tahoe?"

"Exactly." Mitzy presses her fingertip to the tip of her nose, telling me I got that on the nose.

"So he's not where he said he would be. Who cares? If he's off-duty, he's off-duty. He's a grown man, and how would you know…" I cock my head and give Mitzy the eye. "Unless…" My voice is full of accusation and outrage. "I thought you didn't track us like that?"

One requirement of being a Guardian is allowing Guardian HRS to implant two tracking devices in our bodies; one to find and one to hide. It's an issue of safety, in case we're ever captured or killed. No matter where we are on the globe, Mitzy's team can find us, or our body.

"Cool it," Brady speaks up. "I asked her to locate him."

"Why?"

"Because he wasn't answering my calls." Brady gives me a look, calling me out for calling Mitzy out. "I needed to track him down, and good thing I did."

"Why?"

"Because we were wasting resources trying to locate the fourth roommate." Mitzy taps on the keyboard. Those lightning fast fingers draw my eye while her words sink in.

"Barbi?" I rub my nose as it all falls into place.

"Turns out, Barbi's with him in Vegas. Not Tahoe," Mitzy

interjects. "We've been trying to track her down, wasting time—and you know how I feel about that." She props her hand on her hip and shakes her head.

"Looks like the two of them have been sneaking around. Not wanting us to know they've been hooking up." Rafe glares at me. "Like you've been doing with Kaye."

"I know nothing about any of that." I hold my hands up in defense. "And I haven't touched Kaye. I'm keeping things professional."

"Seriously?" Hayes shakes his head. "You're such a terrible liar. The two of you are totally hooking up. It's not like we didn't see you leaving her room this morning." The muscles of Rafe's jaw clench.

"Are you stalking her? Me? Isn't that what brought us here? Stalker behavior?"

"Not stalking, but it was kind of hard to miss." Rafe's eyes narrow down into two slivers. He's fucking pissed. "Getting caught up with a woman in the middle of an operation puts your head in the wrong damn place."

"Says the pot to the kettle." I slam my hand on the conference table and stand, raising my voice. "You of all people…" I stop and point to Hayes as well. "The two of you have shit to say to me about that, and for your information, Kaye asked me to *hold* her while she slept, emphasis on *sleep*. There was no fucking going on. She's scared. Terrified over what Scott might do to her friends. Not knowing where Barbi is only makes things worse. She asked me to hold her, and that's exactly what I did."

"Zeb…" Brady raises his voice, not to shout, but to end the back and forth. Basically, grab our attention and tell us to shut the fuck up. "Sit down. No one is accusing anyone of anything. Or judging one another." He points to Rafe and Hayes. "It's none of your business what Zeb does, or doesn't do, and if Kaye asked him to hold her while she slept, then leave it be. It's not like either of you haven't done the same. Alec is on his way, or will be once he reads his texts. Barbi is with him. We can stop looking for her because we know she's with him. As for making Alec pay, we'll have fun with him tonight. Right now, let's get down to business and stop wasting time."

"Now that we're done with the macho, testosterone bullshit…" Mitzy presses a tiny remote. The images of six college-aged women pop up on the screen at the far end of the room.

"Who are they?" Rafe, Hayes, and I aren't finished with this conversation, but we put it aside for now.

"They are the women who filed complaints against Professor Parker," Mitzy says. "He's one of those assholes who finds himself in a position of power over young, impressionable college coeds. He uses that power to prey on his victims and feed his depraved fantasies."

"Kaye was terrified when I saw the ligature marks on her wrists and the bruising around her neck. The look on her face…" I drag my hand down my face, remembering that moment. Bile rises in the back of my throat, feeling her fear, her desperation, and the betrayal that went against everything she knew about Scott. "He's into dominating women and forcing them into dangerous situations." I'm going to teach this asshole a lesson when I see him.

"That's how predators work," Mitzy says. "They lull their prey into feeling safe, then pounce when least expected."

And that was Kaye.

Prey.

"So what do we do with the women?"

"I want to question them. Find out *why* they dropped their complaints and see if I can dig up any dirt on Professor Parker."

"Bastard had Kaye tied to a chair, while he strangled her." Saliva floods my mouth and bile rises in the back of my throat. "Seems like that could shut someone up."

"Exactly why I want to talk to them." Mitzy props her chin in her hand and stares at the pictures of the women."

Kaye has no idea how close she came to never coming home again.

TWENTY-TWO

Kaye

After Zeb drops me off, I want to check in on my friends. I knock on Carmen's door, my knuckles rapping against the wood.

"Who is it?" Carmen's crystal clear voice calls out.

"It's Kaye."

"Oh, come in."

Carmen and Rosalie lounge on the couch, reading books. They pause to look up at me, their faces warm and welcoming

"What's up?" Carmen asks.

"I just wanted to check on you guys," I reply. "And see how you were doing."

"Oh, we're alright," Rosalie interjects, her voice light and melodic. "Just reading and passing the time. What about you?"

I do a slow spin, checking out Carmen's quarters. "Looks like they didn't get fancy on the decor. It's a mirror image of mine and just as plain." I glance at the furnishings and grin. The furniture's functional, but utilitarian and in the same uninspired beige palate.

"I guess they spent all their money on all the high tech stuff and don't have any left for interior decorating." Carmen pats the cushion next to her. "Come, have a seat and tell us what you've been up to all day with Zeb."

"It wasn't all day." I sit beside Carmen, feeling a little embarrassed. "He gave me a tour."

Carmen and Rosalie exchange glances before Carmen speaks. "That's it? No romantic strolls? Stolen kisses?"

I shake my head and laugh. "No, nothing like that, but we had fun talking and getting to know each other better."

Rosalie grins knowingly and nudges me with her elbow. "So, what did you two talk about? Anything juicy?"

I glance away, suddenly very interested in the pattern of the carpet beneath my feet. "Oh you know—stuff. Nothing special really. Just normal conversation." I shrug nonchalantly, trying to play it off as no big deal when really my heart is pounding out of my chest at the thought of telling them more details of our conversations.

"Well whatever it was," Carmen says, "it must have been interesting from that blush on your face. Don't worry though, we won't pry too much." She winks as she leans back against the couch cushions and picks up her book again.

Rosalie follows suit and a wave of relief washes over me. Or at least it does until Carmen shuts her book and tosses a pillow at me.

"Come on, you have to spill. Tell us about the night you spent with him."

Rosalie puts down her book and gives me a most innocent look. Her eyes glint with mischief and she shares a knowing look with Carmen.

"Nothing happened." I roll my eyes and sit next to Carmen, trying to play it cool.

"Nothing?" Rosalie's eyes widen. She leans in, her voice an excited whisper. "Really? Not even a little bit of something?"

I shake my head and feel the heat of embarrassment rise to my cheeks. I was hoping she didn't notice.

"If nothing happened, then why was Rafe ready to kill Zeb when he saw him leaving your room this morning?" Rosalie's innocent look turns into a smirk as she raises her eyebrows expectantly.

My stomach drops at her words and I resist the urge to bury my head in my hands.

"I asked him to spend the night with me." I shrug and cozy up on the couch, trying to play it off as no big deal, but my heart races with embarrassment.

"Finally." Rosalie claps her hands and laughs delightedly. "We've been betting on how long that would take."

"So what happened? Did you two share a passionate night of romance, or what?" Carmen tosses her book aside and grins mischievously at me.

I groan and bury my face in a pillow before answering them truthfully. "No, nothing like that." I can't meet their eyes. "We just talked until we fell asleep."

The two girls exchange a look before bursting out laughing and reaching for their books again.

"It's ok," Carmen says between giggles, placing a reassuring hand on my shoulder. "You don't have to rush into anything unless you're sure about it."

"We're going to have to reset the bet again." Rosalie nods in agreement before adding teasingly, "But if it does get serious—we want all the juicy details!"

Her words finally make it through my dense head.

"You've been betting?" I look at each of them in turn, my eyes widening in shock. "On whether he and I hook up?"

Rosalie nods, her eyes bright as she grins.

Carmen clears her throat before answering. "We placed a bet the first night the two of you met." Her smile falters when she sees the look on my face. "Oh, it was just in fun."

"I know." They mean no harm. It's just an innocent bet.

Carmen and Rosalie exchange a guilty glance before Carmen extends an olive branch. "Do you want to talk about it?"

"No, but I appreciate it." I turn to Carmen. "How worried should I be about Rafe's reaction?"

"He'll get over it." Carmen gives a dismissive wave. "As for our bet, we've had to reset, and reset, and reset the bet again and again. I will say, the two of you have been quite restrained this past month.

I gave it a day. Rosalie said a week. It's been agony watching the two of you dance around each other, but I'm glad you finally gave in."

"We haven't…" No need to finish that sentence. We haven't had sex, but I watched him stroke himself and watched him come. Whether that counts as sex lies somewhere in the gray zone.

"But you're interested, right?" Carmen looks hopeful, and I can see why. She and Rosalie are head over heels in love with their Guardians. They just want me to feel the same. "The two of you would make a great couple."

"I was preoccupied with…" Scott. No need to say his name. They know.

The mood shifts and my friends exchange a worried look as they take in my silence.

"Well, we were wondering why you didn't jump Zeb's bones." Carmen's gaze dips to my wrists where the ligature marks are still horrifyingly present. "I wish you'd told us about Scott." Her tone shifts, no longer teasing, she's concerned and worried.

I take a deep breath and wipe away the tears that form in my eyes. "I was too ashamed. Then when he…" I can't bring myself to finish the sentence, but my friends know what I mean. "I couldn't let him hurt you."

Rosalie shifts on the couch, moving to give me a hug. "I don't know how I feel about that, to be honest. On the one hand, I want to hug you. On the other, I want to shake some sense into you. You should have trusted us enough to talk about it. Instead, you let him hurt you."

Carmen nods in agreement and glances at Rosalie before continuing. "We understand why you kept it from us, but it doesn't make it right for you to suffer alone like that. Don't ever feel like you can't confide in us."

"I was scared."

"All the more reason to tell us. We aren't here to judge you. I love you. I love you like I love Rosalie, and Barbi too. We're a family, the four of us."

The two of them offer me comfort with their words and I try to hold back fresh tears as they embrace me in a joint hug. I'm lucky to have such amazing friends who are always there for me no matter what.

"Thank you," I whisper before pulling away, wiping away any remaining tears on my face with the back of my hand. "I'm sorry for keeping it from you."

Carmen smiles at me while Rosalie nods. They both stand up from the couch, giving me space to process all of this information.

"You don't need to apologize," Carmen says firmly before looking pointedly at me again. "But if Zeb ever does something to hurt you, promise you'll tell us immediately so we can help."

"I promise." I cross my heart, making it official. "And now we're all safe, although my actions brought you back to Guardian jail."

"Yeah, Rafe and Hayes are thrilled about that." Rosalie shakes her head. "Couldn't wait to say *I told you so*, even if this has nothing to do with Carmen's father."

I take in a deep breath and blow it out as slow as I can. "Honestly, I can't believe I let Scott manipulate me like that. After all the time I've put into being a strong and independent woman, I cave to a bully of a man."

My friends exchange a knowing look before Rosalie speaks up. "Sometimes it doesn't matter how strong we are, some situations just have us feeling helpless. We've all been there."

Carmen takes my hand in hers and squeezes it reassuringly. "We've all been in relationships that weren't good. Don't beat yourself up about it. It's not healthy. You need to focus on the future instead of dwelling on the past."

I nod slowly as her words sink in, feeling better knowing they understand what happened and that they don't judge me for it. That's one of the best things about having such amazing friends; they always have my back no matter what I've done.

Rosalie furrows her eyebrows and slowly shakes her head, her gaze turning away from Carmen and toward me. The memories of her own abuse parades across her face as she relives some of the darkest moments of her life. Her fingers clench into fists.

In that moment, Carmen communicates an entire story with a

flash of her eyes. Rosalie was a victim of abuse. And Carmen is silently expressing her unwavering support for her friend.

I know what it's like to feel alone in the darkness, but thankfully, Carmen and Rosalie remind me I am not alone. That no matter what pain I've been through, or will go through, they will always be here to pick me up when I need it most.

Rosalie was never in a relationship with her abuser, Matias. He collected her when she was ten, to be Carmen's maid, raped Rosalie that night, then spent the next decade terrorizing her as she was forced to endure his presence day in and day out.

He never touched her again, but only because Carmen convinced her father to grant Rosalie a protected status as Carmen's playmate. In the end, Rosalie killed Matias in self-defense, after he captured her with the intent of doing vile things. We sit in silence for a moment, each lost in our own thoughts. Finally, I speak.

"When it comes to men, we've all had it rough, but I picked the man harassing me. I chose Scott. Which means I'm responsible for everything that's happened since." As I speak, my voice fills with guilt and self-loathing, and my body slumps as if the weight of my words is too much to bear.

Carmen and Rosalie both look at me with compassion and understanding.

Carmen speaks softly, "Stop."

"But…"

"No. Stop beating yourself up about it." She gives me a look, telling me she's not going to let me blame myself. "It's not healthy."

Her words are a reminder that I'm not alone, and that I have their support and understanding. I take a deep breath and a sense of calm washes over me.

I have the strength to move forward.

"Well, I'm sorry the two of you are back here."

"You mean back in Guardian jail?" Carmen arches a brow and a smile tries to work its way free.

"I don't know why you think this place is bad. Zeb gave me the tour this morning. That's where we were. He took me to breakfast, then we visited Bravo's bullpen; I got to play with some cool tech gadgets at Mitzy's Omega Facility, then we went to the gym and I've never seen anything like it."

Carmen's eyes round in shock. She and Rosalie exchange glances and cover their mouths.

"What's wrong? What did I say?" I'm truly confused.

"Never say that out loud again." Carmen places her hand on my shoulder.

"Say, what?"

"That Zeb took you to Bravo's bullpen." Rosalie takes a deep breath before answering me.

"Why not?" My eyes widen in surprise.

"It's this unwritten rule the teams have. No women in the bullpens. Well, except for Delta. They have women on their team. But no outsiders are allowed. You can get Zeb in big trouble with his teammates if they find out."

"I didn't realize." I cover my mouth. "Shoot, he did mention…" I look at the two of them. "You're not going to tell Rafe and Hayes are you?"

"Never." Carmen places her hand over her heart. "Your secret's safe with us."

"I feel bad." It didn't take me but a second to betray Zeb's trust. "I'm horrible at this. I'm not used to keeping secrets."

"Don't worry. We're not going to tell." Carmen turns on the couch, pulling her legs up in a crisscross. "But I think we need to have a conversation about Zeb."

"Why?"

"It's a warning." Rosalie's voice hushes.

"About Zeb?"

"Well, he is a Guardian," Carmen says. "If he's like all the others, he's going to be possessive and Alpha to the core. Not in the creepy Scott kind of way, but in the loving and supportive kind of way." She holds up her hand. "I mean, he totally has our stamp of approval, but I just want you to know what you're getting yourself into." She scoots closer and lowers her voice to a whisper. "Now, back to the bullpen. Tell us everything you saw."

"Not much to tell, to be honest. For the life of me, I can't figure out why it's *restricted*." I use finger quotes to emphasize my point. Briefly, I give them the rundown of what I saw.

We laugh about the absurdity of the restriction and make a few plans of our own. Then I ask the one question I'm most worried about.

"Have you heard from Barbi? Mitzy took my phone to monitor this thing with Scott, but I'm really worried."

"Barbi's fine." Carmen gives a dismissive wave of her hand. "Evidently, we were taking bets on the wrong couple." She and Rosalie exchange another glance.

"What does that mean?" I look between them, getting a headache with all the twisting back and forth.

"Only that Barbi and Alec—evidently—have been hooking up since that first night."

"They what?" I give a little shriek. "I don't believe you."

"Believe." Rosalie brings her knees to her chest and props her chin on her kneecaps. "And you should've seen Rafe and Hayes when they found out."

"Why?"

"Let's just say they're acting like overprotective older brothers, and seem to think, since they're with us, that they have a say about who you and Barbi date. If Alec and Zeb aren't good enough, there's not a man on earth who'll pass whatever rigorous standards they have." Rosalie shakes her head. "Men. Am I right? Can't live with them. Can't live without them. And you surely can't understand them."

"Yeah, I don't know where they got the idea they could dictate who you see, or don't see. Sleep, or don't sleep with." Carmen giggles. "They put the two of you on the *Do-not-fuck* list."

"Oh lord." My cheeks heat remembering the whole bathroom and shower thing this morning with Zeb. "Well, I'll have to absolve them of that notion." I shake my head. "And I can't wait to watch Barbi go off on them when she finds out they told Alec not to touch her, and knowing Barbi, you know she was probably the one who touched first."

Barbi is notorious for living fast and living loose. I still remember when she proclaimed it wasn't fair for men to sleep around and be called studs, when she was called a slut, or whore, for having a healthy appetite for sex.

It's hard not to agree with her when she puts it that way.

"So…" Carmen sidles up to me, "are you going to tell us why Zeb was seen coming out of your room if the two of you aren't hooking up?" Carmen blinks innocently at me.

"I asked him to."

"That's it?" Carmen doesn't look convinced.

"That's it." I completely lie to my friends.

"I don't believe you." Carmen shoves me on the shoulder. "What else happened?"

"Nothing."

"Nothing, my ass." She looks at Rosalie. "She's lying."

"Am not." I shift, feeling a bit uncomfortable with the lie. Although, technically, it's more of a half-truth. I'm going to stick with that. "I was scared, feeling vulnerable. This whole thing with Scott is insane. I needed a hug, and asked him if he wouldn't hold me until I fell asleep."

"And that turned into him sleeping over?" Rosalie exchanges another look with Carmen, then they both break out in laughter. "Now, that's one way to get a man in bed."

"It wasn't like that." I playfully punch Rosalie in the arm. "We were fully clothed, if that matters."

"So nothing happened?" Carmen doesn't look like she believes me.

"Nothing happened." I defend myself, although I don't know why.

It's probably because a lot did happen. We definitely crossed a threshold this morning. I look to each of them again, and remind myself why I'm here.

Carmen raises an eyebrow and Rosalie cocks her head to the side, but neither call me out on my fibbing. Instead, they exchange a knowing look that tells me they know better than to press the issue right now. Despite their curiosity, and our friendship, they can tell when I don't want to talk about something and, for once, give me a pass. We switch back to safer topics, like what we should do for lunch.

"Zeb dropped me off for a meeting. They're talking strategy about what to do about Scott. I was wondering if you wanted to grab a bite to eat and what you're doing this afternoon. Zeb says he's going to teach me self-defense."

"Ah, the dreaded self-defense class." Rosalie rocks back and groans. "They are relentless."

"It sounds like a good idea. Don't you want to know how to defend yourself?"

"I do, it's just sparring practice with a Guardian is intense. Hayes wants me to be an expert, and I'm just not." Rosalie vents a frustrated sigh. "It's not in my wheelhouse."

"Oh, come on." Carmen gets up from the couch. "Kaye's right. It's a good idea."

"Hey, Zeb mentioned going out later tonight." I sense the stress in Rosalie and figure a change of topic is a good idea. "Said Rafe is some secret chef and is cooking at insanity. What does that mean?"

"Oh, that's right. I don't think I mentioned it, but Rafe's a master chef and *Insanity* is probably the coolest place on earth."

"What is it?" I look at Carmen, confused.

"It's Angel Fire's home," Carmen says.

"The rock stars?" I've heard of Angel Fire. Everyone with a pulse has heard about Angel Fire. They're a worldwide sensation, and I'm definitely a fan. I'm way more than a fan. I'm secretly obsessed.

"You do know that Skye and Forest live there, right? She's married to their lead singer? And Mitzy's married to Noodles? The keyboardist?" She looks at me like I'm an idiot.

"I had no idea."

"Well, Rafe and I went there when I was preparing for how to return to my father after my whole jump on the rope thing. He wound up cooking lunch and they loved it so much, he now cooks for them once a month. He asked if Bravo team could join and they said yes. Then Alpha team wanted to get in on the action. It's now an unofficially official Guardian get-together. Super cool and tons of fun."

Carmen takes my hand and squeezes it gently as if to reassure me that everything's going to be all right. "Final words, because we should probably get lunch before sparring practice, but we're all here for each other. What's the saying? All for one and one for all? We're the Four Musketeers." She releases my hand and stands. "Now, let's get out of here before Rafe and Hayes come back with reinforcements." We all laugh at this, but soon enough, the laughter fades away as we make our way outside.

Guardian HQ is an amazing place, but for us, it's Guardian Jail. Realizing once more just how fragile our lives are and how quickly things can change in an instant, I'm grateful to be here. I'm grateful I have this as an option.

If not for Carmen and Rosalie, what would I have done?

As we step out into the fresh air, I take a deep breath. This is a second chance for me, and I'm determined to do better this time around. I'm going to make better decisions. No more shortcuts.

It's not worth the risk.

TWENTY-THREE

Kaye

———

Sparring with Zeb can only be described as intense. If intense means tons of hands-on, physical contact. I try to keep from drooling as he explains the basics of what I need to know about self-defense.

"Krav Maga is all about instinctive movements, aggressive counterattacks, and an anything-goes attitude." Zeb weaves his hands through the air.

I stand on the balls of my feet, ready for anything, but not really sure what that might be. "I've never been in a fight before."

"That's okay. We're starting with the basics. Form a fist." He forms a fist, locking his pointer and middle finger down with his thumb. "A straight punch is the core building block of any effective striking system. We're going to work on this the most. Really ingrain it into your head so you don't have to think about it."

"Makes sense." I look at my hands with doubt. They're teeny-tiny compared to the massive battering rams Zeb holds up for demonstration.

He looks at me, staring dubiously at my fists, and his voice softens. He smiles reassuringly and approaches. "Like this." He wraps his hand around mine, moving the position of my thumb and refolding my fingers.

I swallow with the contact. The warmth of his hand moves through my palm and into my wrist. Tiny electrical sparks of energy make my nerves tingle. The latent sexual chemistry between us builds without relief.

"Keep your fingers curled and your thumb over the top of your fist. Come at me." He signals for me to attack. I don't know what I'm doing. All I can think of is to raise my fists in what I hope is a defensive position.

I punch out, but he sidesteps me as if I move in slow motion. He puts a hand on my hip.

"Keep your feet together, just like this." He shows me what he means and I follow his movements as he rocks me back and forth on the balls of my feet. "Now throw a punch."

He flicks his eyes up to mine, waiting for my attack, then explains further when I arch a brow.

"Like this." He moves to stand beside me. "Step into your punch and make sure your hips align with the movement."

I throw another half-hearted jab, feeling all kinds of self-conscious, certain my movements are far too jerky and awkward.

"I'm hopeless." I drop my arms and shake out my hands.

"We all start somewhere. I prefer this, actually."

"What does that mean?"

"You don't have any bad habits we need to break. You'll learn proper form from the beginning. Just don't give up on me, okay?" He stoops down until our eyes are at the same level. "They did not build Rome in a day."

"Fine. I'll try."

"Trying is lying." The corner of his mouth twitches up in a smirk.

"Isn't that Yoda's line?"

"No. He said, *Do or do not. There is no try.*"

"Then I will *do* my best." I swallow, my voice small and uncertain. "How do I do that?"

Zeb meets my gaze squarely. He lowers his right hand and

curls his fingers into a tight fist. "We'll start with the fist." He points to his hand. "Keep your fingers curled, and lock your pointer and middle finger down with your thumb." He waits for me to do what he says, then continues. "What you don't want to do is put your thumb inside your fist, and don't let it hang over the top."

I do what he says and he rewards me with a smile.

"That's the first step. Congratulations, you successfully made a fist."

"*Yeehaw.*" My voice lacks enthusiasm. We've been at it for ten minutes and all I've successively done is form a fist. Haven't hit anything. Haven't been hit. Haven't ducked, dodged, or kicked.

"What did I say about Rome?" He lifts my chin with his thumb.

"I know." I take in a deep breath. "What's next?"

Zeb looks at me. "When you throw a straight punch—you can use either your forward or rear hand…"

"I thought I only had a left and right. Which one's which?"

"From your stance. If your front leg leads, that's your forward hand."

"Okay."

"You're going to use your legs for leverage. Drive off the ground and rotate your hip and shoulder forward." He demonstrates what he means, holding his fists up and ready. "Try it."

"Like this?"

He repositions my feet, widening my stance.

"Now, this is important and the most common mistake I see beginners make. Your arm alone won't generate enough power. It's all about using the momentum of your body: shoulder, trunk, hips, legs, and feet. To direct your punch, turn your shoulder toward your chin and cheek.

He moves into position, demonstrating what he means. "See how far forward my left shoulder is turned?"

"Yes." I mimic his position. "This feels weird. My shoulder's basically touching my chin. Is this right"

"Yes. It's the rotation of your body that throws the punch and generates power."

"Okay." We try that out a few times. I punch. Zeb corrects. I punch again. Slowly, it begins to feel more natural.

"Let's work on your fist."

"Am I not doing it right?" I show him my fist. My thumb is where he said to put it.

"Yes. What I want you to focus on is striking with the top two knuckles." He points at his first two knuckles, then taps mine.

I stab at the air, pretending I know what I'm doing.

"We call this the striking surface. It's a direct extension of your hand, through your wrist, to your arm, and to your shoulder."

"When do I actually get to punch something?"

"We're getting there. Form over function. We work the basics. Now, as far as what to hit, your target areas are eyebrows and below."

"Why?"

"The skull is thick and can take a hard hit."

"Gotcha."

"As you punch, move slowly and deliberately. Remember your legs drive off the ground, your hips rotate your shoulder forward. That momentum is what throws the punch and generates the power. Your arm is weak when used alone. You have to engage your entire body."

"Never knew there was this much behind a punch." I try it out a few times, feeling more comfortable and almost like I know what I'm doing.

"We talked about eyebrows down and you asked why. Not only is the skull thick, but eyebrows down is what we consider the soft areas of the face. Effective punches there will affect vision and breathing. More importantly, you'll create a pain response in your opponent. Which means, these are the areas you're going to want to protect on yourself."

"Oh lord. I've barely figured out how to punch and now I have to defend?" I shake my head. "How do you make it look so easy?"

"Because I have hours, weeks, months, and years of practice."

"I don't have that."

"All we're trying to do is get you to minimal proficiency. Your entire goal isn't to engage in a fist fight, but to learn how to escape an attack. Failing that, how to fight for your life."

"How about a break?" I nibble my lower lip, but I know what he's going to say.

"You get one break every half-hour. We've been at this less than twenty minutes. Come on, you've got this."

"And how long did you say we were going to train?"

"Three hours a day sparring and another hour on basic physical conditioning."

I blow out a puff of air. "When you said relocate to HQ, I didn't think I'd be doing hard time."

"Hardly." He shakes his head and laughs. "What else are you going to do to pass the time?"

"I don't know? Sit on the couch and eat bonbons? You could spend that time ravaging me."

His gaze heats with that comment, just like I hoped. Anything to get his mind off training and to something far more exciting.

"We've got all day…" I gesture around the gym, which is relatively empty this time of day. "Who's going to know if we slip off and…"

"I'll know, and there's no way I'm going to be the reason you're unprepared for a fight."

"But for how long? How long are you going to insist we hang out at Guardian HQ? The summer is passing us by and I don't understand what's taking so long. Can't Bravo team head over to Scott's place and intimidate the hell out of him?"

"That doesn't work with people like him. He'll back down, then attack when we least expect it."

"But Rosie got her acceptance at UCSF. What's she going to do when the fall semester starts? She can't do it from here? Same for Carmen and her graduate studies. Barbi too. She can't miss out on her first day at Law school."

"We're working it."

"I know you're working it, but you've basically cut me out of the whole thing. I have no idea what's happening, and while I won't be starting this fall, I'm going to have to do something this coming year until I can apply to other programs."

"Take your frustrations out on me. Come on." He pivots sharply and heads to a gear locker.

I follow along, jogging to keep up with his long stride. He stops at the gear locker and pulls out two padded helmets. He puts one on and adjusts it, while tossing the other one at me. I falter when I realize what he means.

"You mean, like literally take my frustrations out on you?"

"Exactly."

"I'd rather you just filled me in, rather than keep me in the dark."

"I'll make you a promise."

"Okay?"

"Give me your absolute best for the next two hours. Do that, and I'll take you to our next briefing."

"Serious?"

"Fair warning, you may not like what you hear, or where the investigation is taking us."

"What the hell does that mean?"

"Two hours." He shifts to the nearest mat. "No questions for the next two hours, unless directly applicable to our lesson."

"Fine, but for the record, I should be involved. I'm the one at risk."

"Which is exactly why you're not involved and precisely why you'll be on this mat three hours a day, with me, or with the others for physical conditioning. You'll also attend our new employee education."

"But I'm not an employee."

"It's the education on how to endure torture and how to escape. Basically, Guardian HRS's equivalent to SERE training."

"I know what that is." And I gulp. Should I be nervous Zeb wants me to know how to survive, evade, rescue, and escape? What the hell is going on?

Zeb cracks his knuckles, steps back, and calls out to me. "We start with technical drills, focusing on form and technique.

I assume the fighting stance Zeb taught me and we begin with basic drills on punches to the eyes and chin. As we work through the strikes, Zeb continues to instruct, correcting problems with my form and layering on new skills as I develop basic proficiency in the ones we work on.

My progress is slow, and I slog through the next hour. What did Zeb call it? Minimally proficient.

We take a break at the top of the hour and all I can manage is to lie flat on the mat, staring at the retracted dome far overhead.

"Are you ready to start incorporating some footwork?" He sits beside me and leans back.

"No." I shade my eyes with my arm, but peek up at him.

"Come on. Break's over." He extends his hand, which I take, and pulls me nearly off my feet. Without any preamble, he gets right down to business.

We're training again.

"Remember, the goal is to dodge any incoming strikes, but you must be ready to counterattack."

"Right. The don't get hit part."

"Exactly." He huffs a laugh. "I showed you a few blocks, and we're going to work on those, but the real skill is to avoid them completely. That starts with your feet."

The next hour is a slog. I consider myself an active individual. I'm not an athlete, or a runner, but I can endure a somewhat vigorous hike. I'm not a total couch potato, but by the time we wrap up the afternoon, Zeb's put me through the proverbial wringer.

My arms are useless noodles. I'm a ball of sweat. My heart begs for relief and my lungs wave the white flag in surrender. When I stand, I sway on my feet and blink away the salty sweat pouring into my eyes.

We finish with different defensive tactics that take into account different scenarios, then finally, blissfully, Zeb calls an end to our very first training session.

"Come on." Once again, he extends his hand.

I've spent more time flat on my back this last hour than I have on my feet. There's definitely a lot more to learn.

"How did I do?" I sway while the ground spins beneath my feet and hold onto Zeb for support.

"Exceptionally well. You get a gold star."

"I deserve a stiff drink." My gaze cuts to his shorts and I think back on this morning. "Or something else that's stiff?"

I can't help but insert innuendo. All morning, during breakfast, the tour of The Facility, and our afternoon sparing, images of Zeb stroking his cock have flooded my mind.

"Something else?" His lusty laughter makes me ache in the worst possible way. "We decided we were going to take things slow in that department."

"I don't think we were in our right mind when that decision was made. I've had all day to think about it."

"You have?"

"I have, and if I'm going to get a gold star, I know exactly what kind of reward I want."

"As much as I'd love to spoil you, we barely have time to get you back to shower and change before heading out to *Insanity*."

"We could kill two birds with one stone?"

"What do you mean?"

"Shower sex? Slippery and wet?"

"Damn, when you put it like that. I want to say a very definite yes."

"But?" There's too much hesitation in his voice.

"We're already going to be late as it is."

"Late? For what?" There's literally no place I need to be. "We've got all night."

"We're supposed to be at *Insanity*. Or did you forget your evening with rock stars?"

"Holy shit! I thought that was a joke. Are we really going to their home?"

"Yes. It's not a joke. And, it's a beautiful night, which means we'll have a bonfire down on the beach, but if you don't want to hang with Angel Fire…"

"I *want* to do both, but there's no way I'm missing out on spending a night with rock legends."

"That's what I thought. Go on up. Get showered and dressed. It's casual; jeans and a T-shirt are fine."

"And where are you going?"

"Not up to your room." His husky laughter curls my toes. "I'm headed to the bullpen to shower and change. I'll meet you back here in thirty minutes. Is that enough time?"

"Plenty."

With the briefest of the briefest kisses in the world, Zeb jogs off in the direction of the Guardian building, while I head upstairs to shower by myself and think about how amazing it's going to be when Zeb and I finally have sex.

TWENTY-FOUR

Kaye

Less than an hour later, Zeb and I are on our way to Insanity with Brady and Booker. Carmen and Rosalie, with Rafe and Hayes, travel in a separate car.

My stomach flutters with a mix of excitement and nerves.

"I can't believe we're actually invited to have dinner here." I place my hand against the window and press my nose against the glass.

My eyes widen in amazement as the gates to *Insanity* swing open. Our car meanders up a long, tree-lined driveway. Although I can't quite imagine what such a prestigious estate might look like, nothing could have prepared me for the sheer size and opulence of the sprawling grounds.

Immaculately kept, with perfectly tended gardens that stretch on for acres and flowing water features that sprawl across the grounds, there's a definite Zen vibe to the grounds, making me wonder who designed them.

As we make our way up to the front entrance, my heart races with excitement. Not only do I get to visit *Insanity*, but I get to meet the rock legends of Angel Fire.

This is definitely going to be an experience I'll never forget.

"I'm excited to meet Angie and Izzy." Trying to make conversation and ease my nerves, I catch Brady's eye through the rearview mirror. "Although it feels like I already know a little about them through Carmen."

Angie and Izzy will meet up with us at *Insanity*. Everyone from Bravo team will be here tonight, with the exception of two missing people: Barbi and Alec.

So far, there's no word on them.

"Excited?" Zeb grabs my hand and raises it to his mouth for a featherlight kiss.

"Yes."

But more so to meet the rest of the Bravo team family. I already feel connected to Angie and Izzy, even if I've yet to meet them in person. We make a very unusual, yet spectacular, family founded by circumstance and choice.

Angie and Izzy were taken hostage by the *Coralos* cartel in Nicaragua while working with Doctors Without Borders. They were unknowing pawns, carrying millions of diamonds hidden in rabbit's feet. In addition, those rabbit's feet held the accounting of hundreds of women trafficked by Maximus Angelo, Carmen's father.

Carmen had been working for nearly a decade to take down her father's network. When Matias kidnapped Izzy, to get the diamonds back, Guardian HRS launched a mission to rescue her. That's the mission Carmen hijacked. She ultimately helped Guardian HRS crack the encoded list of names. That information launched a new mission; the one that brought Rosalie and Hayes together, eventually leading to Rosalie living with us.

Which makes me pause. I was supposed to start at UC Davis this fall. Which is why I gave up my room to Rosalie. I wasn't supposed to need it anymore. But now, all that's up in the air.

My assumption is my spot at Davis is gone; ripped out from underneath my feet by Scott and his rage. I'm going to need a job; something to pay the rent while I reapply to vet school.

"Hey…" Zeb gives my leg a little shake. "What're you thinking about? Looks like you've got the weight of the world on your shoulders." His brow furrows with concern.

"Oh, sorry." I let out a weary sigh. "I was trying to figure out what I should do with my life."

"Life?"

"Yeah, like what I'm going to do for the next year."

"What happened to UC Davis?"

"I fully expect to receive a letter rescinding the offer. I guess I'm trying to figure out what to do next year while I reapply, but I don't want to think about it tonight. Besides, we're here to have a good time. I'm excited to see *Insanity*, meet the band; maybe I can get them all to sign my boob."

Zeb chokes at that comment. "No fucking way any man is signing any part of your body without going through me."

Brady chuckles from the front seat. Booker nearly spits out his drink. I exchange a look with Brady through the rearview mirror and can't help but grin. It was the perfect set up and Zeb fell for it.

"Calm down. I'm not going to do it, but I'm interested in the rock star life. And this group home thing is interesting as well."

"They're a tight group that's for sure." Booker glances out the window, staring off toward the horizon.

We pull up outside the front entrance. Ahead of us, Rosalie, Carmen, Rafe, and Hayes spill out of their car. The four of us join them on the steps.

"Why are the walls so tall?" Rosalie spins around, looking at the tall walls between the estate and the highway. "I assume it's to keep the paparazzi out?"

"Forest says they're always trying to snap pictures," Brady says. "Tried to use drones, but Mitzy let loose a swarm of hers and that stopped."

"Drone wars." Rosalie giggles. "I can totally see Mitzy going postal on the poor drones sent over those walls to spy."

"I can't wait to see the beach." I loop my arm around Zeb's bicep and lean into him, loving the way he feels: solid, strong, and perfect.

Rafe and Hayes give us the eye, not happy about Zeb ignoring their ultimatum to keep his distance from me.

Sorry, guys, you don't get to decide who I date.

I'm a bit miffed they feel they get a say in who I date, or don't date.

"Beach? I want to see inside." Rosalie's eyes are about ready to bug out of her head.

I get the excitement. I'm interested too.

"Is it true the entire band lives here?" I tap Carmen on the shoulder. She's been here before.

"Each couple has their own living suite, like personal apartments, but there are common living areas." Carmen acts as our unofficial tour guide.

"That's kind of cool." Rosalie lets out a low whistle. "As for this place… Wow."

A deep inhale brings the subtle scent of the ocean and fragrant flowers flooding my senses.

Zeb rocks back on his heels. "Told you it was impressive."

"It's totally insane." I understand why this place is called *Insanity*.

Carmen, Rosalie, and I exchange excited glances. We extricate ourselves from the men and walk together arm in arm up to the front door.

The distant booming of the surf echoes off the rocky cliffs surrounding Angel Fire's massive estate, and the sun hovers the width of my hand above the horizon, not quite ready to give up the day.

"It's going to be an amazing sunset." Zeb comes up to stand behind me. He props his chin on the top of my head.

"Do we knock—or?" Rosalie looks unsure.

"Go ahead and go inside. They're expecting us." Rafe gestures for all of us to enter.

"How long have you been doing this?" I turn to Rafe, intrigued by all the new things I've learned about him.

"As far as cooking?" he asks.

"Yeah."

"It wasn't long after Carmen hitched her ride on me, to be honest." He pulls Carmen to his side and kisses her cheek. "It was lunchtime and for some reason, all anybody wanted was PB&J sandwiches."

"I love PB&J." I rub my belly. "But how did that impress them?"

"What Rafe's not telling you…" Carmen lifts on her toes to kiss Rafe's cheek, "is that he took over their kitchen and whipped up this amazing meal. It was mouthwatering and ten thousand times better than any PB&J. Didn't Ash try to hire you on the spot?"

"Yeah." Rafe rubs the back of his neck. "We settled on the first Saturday of the month and invited all the Guardians." Rafe holds the door while we all hold back our gasps as we enter the grand estate.

"Kitchen is this way." Carmen grabs Rosalie and me by the hand and yanks us down the long hall until we enter the largest living room I've ever seen.

A glass wall soars far overhead to a peaked roof. The view looks out at the wide expanse of the Pacific Ocean. From the top of the hundred-foot cliffs, we can't see the waves crashing against the shore, but the ocean clearly extends off in the distance where it finally meets the sky on the faraway horizon.

"This view is stunning." I can't keep the grin from my face. "The sunsets must be phenomenal."

Too focused on the view, we completely miss the interior. I take a second to rectify that and turn around. The living room is a massive space. It holds several separate groupings of sofas and coffee tables. Each one could be its own living room. Together, they kind of flow into one another.

I like it. Seeing as how there are five band members, their wives, and an assortment of children, the arrangement of separate spaces makes perfect sense.

"The nights are just as stunning, especially when the full moon floats over a black sea." I've never heard a melodious voice like that, and spin around in shock.

TWENTY-FIVE

Kaye

I DON'T WANT TO ADMIT TO ANYONE I'M AN ANGEL FIRE SUPERFAN, but I am. The man belonging to that voice is none other than Blaze, lead singer of Angel Fire, although he's been transitioning to his real name, Ash, lately. My belly does a little fluttery thing. Which makes it impossible to play it cool.

"Welcome to *Insanity*. My name's Ash."

Mouth open, jaw agape, I'm beyond a little star struck, and can't help but stare at the iconic tattoo decorating his neck—a black spiderweb dripping in blood. A dragon perches in the very center of the web, holding a raven in one of its claws.

"Um, thanks for opening your home to us." Somehow, I manage to stammer out something that doesn't sound like I'm hopeless. "This place is…"

"Insane?" He rubs the back of his neck. "We get that a lot. *Insanity* is Forest's brainchild. We let him run with his crazy ideas and this one just worked. Between you and me, we believe he wanted all of us living in one spot so he could have us all to himself." Ash's hypnotic green eyes hold me enthralled and render me speechless.

I can't believe I'm standing in front of a rock legend, in his home, and get to spend the entire night here.

"It's definitely impressive." Rosalie sticks out her hand. "I'm Rosalie and this place is crazy, insane, and absolutely stunning. This one…" She nudges me in the ribs, "with her mouth hanging open, is Kaye."

"This is surreal." I gather enough nerve to shake hands with Ash, while Zeb, Rafe, and Hayes chuckle at my expense.

"Let me give you the nickel tour." Ash gestures for us to follow, then pauses and looks at Rafe. "The kitchen is yours. Forest bought everything on your list. It should be all there."

"How many do we have tonight?" Rafe asks.

"Forest said Charlie and Delta are out on missions, so that only leaves Bravo and Alpha. Our menagerie is all here. They're down on the beach with the kids checking out the tide pools. Forest and his throuple will be here as well."

"Cool." Rafe looks to Zeb and Hayes. "Congratulations. You've just been drafted to help with dinner."

"I'll be back to help after I show the girls around." The smile on Ash's face is enough to make any girl swoon.

I don't know how Skye doesn't live with constant jealousy considering the charisma rolling off Ash. The man's got one of those magnetic personalities. "Ladies, we begin the tour with the garage."

Ash begins with a garage that's nothing like any garage I've ever seen.

"This is Forest's pride and joy." He pats the sleek hood of one vehicle. "He's a collector of every supercar built."

"I hate to ask, and don't mean to be rude, but what does something like that run?" I remind myself to not gape.

"Millions."

"For the collection? Wow." There's simply too much to look at, and I'm not about to open my mouth and reveal how little I know about cars. They've got pretty colors. That's as far as I get.

"Oh, no. Millions for each car. They range in price from a few hundred thousand to several million." Ash gestures to a few of the more expensive cars.

Dozens of cars easily fill what must be the entire basement of the main building. I try to count, but lose my way several times when I get to double digits and keep going. There may not be a hundred cars in Forest's collection, but it's close.

And it's totally insane.

We move to the recording studios, plural.

"This is where all the magic happens," Ash explains.

"I got to use that one…" Carmen points to one of the smaller recording booths. "When I called my father, before the raid that…" Her attention cuts to Rosalie and there's no reason to finish what she was going to say.

We make our way to the kitchen, where Rafe's busy whipping up a gourmet meal.

"Someday, I'm going to walk in here and say 'This is my chef—the best in the world.' For now, though, I can only claim him one night a month." Ash winks at us, sharing the inside joke.

"Hah," Rafe snorts. "You're going to have to pry me away from the Guardians and I don't think you can afford me."

"I'm sure we could come up with something reasonable." Ash sounds hopeful, but Rafe shakes his head.

"You could tempt me with a shitload of cash, but…" His eyes shift to Carmen where they soften with love, affection, and an unbreakable bond. "I don't do it for the money."

"Aww…" Rosalie and I flank Carmen, and we both hip-check her as we pitch our voices high, using a singsong voice. *"That's so sweet. He loves you."*

"Stop it." Carmen playfully slaps at us, which only encourages us to sing it over and over again. For once, I'm not the one with red cheeks.

We settle down and hang out in the kitchen for a bit. We watch Rafe cook, offering unhelpful advice, but then Ash asks us to join him outside.

"I want you to see this before the sun sets. The view is lost once it's dark." He shows us the patio—although I'm not sure something that size can be called a patio—with its breathtaking view of the ocean and its massive infinity pool.

"Holy wow." Rosalie steps right to the edge, where two rows of safety glass have been installed. She props her arms on the metal railing and stares down the sheer cliff face. Knowing Rosalie, she'll want to try climbing it.

Not me. I'm not a fan of heights. Which brings back memories of that terrifying zip line and Scott. I can't help but wonder what he's doing now.

Did he give up on me and move on? I hope so. Actually, I don't hope so. Moving on means he's got someone new to terrorize.

"And down there," Ash points to the beach far below, "is where we have our bonfires." Several people gather around what looks to be a pile of dead wood stacked up in a fire ring. He heads toward a gondola propped on the edge of the cliff. "This is your ride down to the beach."

"Wow, a gondola." Rosalie gives a happy screech. "It's safe, right?" She peers down the steep incline, looking concerned.

"Built by Forest, so you know it's over-designed and can withstand a hurricane. Not that we have those here."

"This is phenomenal." I step inside the gondola and stare out the glass walls. "Not recommended for anyone afraid of heights." Glass covers every surface except the floor. "The view is spellbinding."

If there's something solid beneath my feet, heights don't bother me. It's only when I'm dangling in midair that I have a problem.

"Here, let me show you how it works," Ash explains the controls.

"You're not coming with us?" Carmen's eyes grow very round.

"Don't worry. It's literally the push of a button, and I'm going to go back and help Rafe with dinner. If he won't come cook for us, I need to learn everything I can from him. Can you tell Skye that everyone's here? She's already down there. Tell her to go ahead and light the bonfire. We'll be down shortly."

"Absolutely." I look to Carmen and Rosalie, waiting for them to climb on board with me. "Come on. Don't be scared."

I laugh, because the one thing Rosalie is not afraid of are

heights. Carmen too. But for some reason this gondola gives them pause.

They finally join me and I press the button that says Down. Ash isn't lying about how simple it is to operate. There are only two buttons that control this thing. One says Down and the other says Up.

Pretty simple and breathtaking.

"Come." I wave for them to join me at the front of the gondola. As it begins to slowly traverse down the cliff face, we stare out over the expanse of the ocean.

The gondola rattles against the rails as it descends. An exhilarating, but slow, ride, my heart pounds the entire way. The sun hangs a handbreadth over the horizon and begins its nightly display turning the sky into a fiery halo and tinting the clouds with streaks of red. Beams of sunlight pierce the clouds to shine down on the water below, forming an ethereal cathedral in the sky framed in golden-orange.

With our noisy descent, seagulls cry out from their nesting spots along the cliff's face. We spot a few of their nests on tiny ledges as we pass. They flap their wings to scare us away, which works as the gondola takes us down the cliff. With irritated squawks they balance on the jagged cliff face and settle down to tend their nests.

Color spreads across the sky, shades of light pink and sunflower yellow. Waves crash against massive rocks below us, booming with power, and the salty breeze carries hints of charred wood from previous bonfires to our noses.

Before we know it, we come to a gentle stop. The door to the gondola opens and we step out onto the rocky beach. We head toward a massive stack of wood where the others are gathered.

Overhead, the clouds deepen their colors with plumes of vibrant orange and deep ochre red. Soft yellows and pinks still frame the backdrop, but will give way to dark blue and eventually black as night grabs hold of the sky.

For now, however, the sun is just beginning to set. Laughter and music fills the air as we approach the firepit and those gathered around it.

"I can't believe we're going to meet the rest of the band." I grip Rosalie's hand and give a squeeze, far more nervous and starstruck than I'd like to admit.

"Hey, you made it." Skye jumps up from her seat on a large log of driftwood. I remember her from my first night at Guardian HQ and the awkward conversation we had regarding what Scott did to me.

I cringe a little, unsure of how to mix that professional interaction with this much more casual setting. However, there's no reason to be worried, because Skye says nothing that relates back to that conversation.

"I wouldn't miss this for the world." I rub my hands on my jeans, far more nervous that I want to admit.

"Well, let me introduce you to everyone. We'll start with the band." Skye gestures toward Bash, Spike, Bent, and Noodles. "You already met Ash upstairs. This is Bash, our drummer."

Bash comes over to meet us.

"Bash, this is Kaye and her roommates Carmen and Rosalie. Barbi should be joining us later." Skye mentions our missing roommate, but continues on without missing a beat.

"Hey there." Bash greets me with a warm smile. When I stretch out a hand to shake, he grins and pulls me into a hug. "Sorry, but you're one of ours now." He does the same with Rosalie, leaving us both speechless. Carmen gets a hug too, but she's already met the band.

"This is Spike, our lead guitarist." Skye continues the introductions.

"Nice to meet you." Spike also hugs each of us in turn. Up close, his multiple facial piercings are wicked and insanely attractive.

"This is Bent, our bassist." Skye gestures toward a bear of a man with a mop of curls on his head.

"Welcome." Bent wraps us up in a massive bear hug, making us laugh.

"And this is Noodles, keyboardist, Zen guru, surfer, and friend to Old Joe who has yet to take a bite out of him." From the grin on Skye's face, she references an inside joke.

I have no idea who Old Joe might be.

"Ignore her. Nice to meet you." Noodles makes the rounds with the hugs.

"You already know Mitzy." Skye points to Noodles. "If you can believe it, our hyperactive pixie and Mr. Zen are married. Piper…" Skye scratches her head. "Not sure if you've met her, but she's our lead physical therapist. Phenomenal woman. Bent claims her. She's with Holly and Angel, and will be back once the sun sets. They're on gremlin watch, which means they've got kid duty and are out terrorizing the denizens of our tide pools. Holly's with Bash and Angel's with Spike."

Skye props her hands on her hips and glances at a second group of people, the members of Alpha team; none of whom I've met.

One of them stands and approaches. "Nice to meet the new ladies of Bravo team. Name's Max and I'm very pleased to meet you. Let me introduce you to Alpha team."

Over the next few minutes, Carmen, Rosalie, and I meet Max, Knox, Axel, Griff, Liam, and Wolfe. Like the men of Bravo team, they're tall and solid, packed with muscle. Drool-worthy and heroes, they're kind and gentle to us, but I can only imagine how ferocious and terrifying they would be on the battlefield.

When Rosalie, Carmen, and I don't move, Max heads to several coolers. "Ladies, you might as well get comfortable and take a load off. We've got beer, wine, water, juice—pretty much whatever you want. Hard liquor too. What can I get you?"

We give our drink orders—all wine—and take our place around the firepit. Max hands out plastic wine glasses, then pours our wine.

"Thanks." Carmen takes a sip, then her eyes widen. "This is really good."

"Nothing but the best." Max fills up my glass. "Now, where's Bravo team? They're slacking, leaving their women alone."

"Lay off the girls." Skye shakes her head and laughs. "Rafe's got Bravo team helping in the kitchen, and don't go stirring up trouble." She looks over her shoulder and points to the gondola. "I bet they're coming down now. Which means, food will be here soon. Bash, you want to round up the gremlins?"

"On it." Bash jumps to his feet. Bent joins him, and together they wander toward the water and the rocky outcroppings where several children squat around the tidepools with a few adults.

The gondola picks up its passengers and makes its way back to the beach. Max, along with the rest of Alpha team greet Zeb, Rafe, and Hayes with friendly smiles and fresh cold beers. The men carry food to several spots around the fire, chatting and laughing with each other like family.

"Hanging in there?" Zeb comes to check on me.

"Yeah." I scoot over, making room for him to sit beside me.

"Still nervous?" He glances at the crowd gathered around the bonfire.

"Not like I thought I would be. You work with some really amazing people.

As the sun dips closer to the horizon, Skye lights the bonfire. It casts a warm, comforting glow over the group, and wards off the chill blowing in off the ocean.

Is it weird that I feel an incredible sense of belonging as I sit down with these strangers, listening to their music, and watching the flames dance as the wood crackles and pops?

As the sun sets, Angie and Izzy come down the gondola with Forest, Sara, and Paul. Forest looks paler than I remember and his smile looks forced, not as warm as I would expect, but it's heartfelt.

He takes his time, gazing at friend and family alike, with nothing but joy filling his face. Paul sits to his left, Sara on his right. He leans on Paul, or maybe Paul holds him up, while he and Sara interlock fingers. She lifts Forest's hand to her mouth, kisses his knuckles, then exchanges a look of concern with Paul. Across the way, I catch a frown on Skye's face as she stares at the three of them just like me.

I nudge Zeb and whisper in his ear, "What's up with Forest? He looks…"

"I know." Zeb slings an arm around my shoulder. "But we don't ask."

"Why not?"

"Forest is a strong man. A proud man. He's endured more pain than anyone should in ten lifetimes. We don't bring up anything that says otherwise."

"But if something's wrong…"

"Leave it to Paul and Sara, Skye too. They can handle him."

"This is really nice." I lean into him, curling into his warmth. I don't agree with what he says about Forest, but I'm an outsider. "You have an amazing group of friends. Feels like one huge family where everyone likes everyone, and it's not just for show."

"We have our spats." He points the tip of his beer bottle toward Rafe and Hayes. "We had a conversation after you left."

"About us?"

"About them butting in where they're not welcome and staying out of what we're trying to make happen."

"And what *are* we trying to make happen?" I press the palm of my hand against the hard planes of his chest. "Why are you getting involved with a woman who has notoriously bad taste in men?"

"Because, you deserve to know how a real man treats a woman. Not to mention, you make me ache in the best possible way. Remember this morning?" He fists his fingers in my hair. "Or should I remind you how hard I came?"

In the ruddy glow of the firelight, it's fifty-fifty if he can see my blush, but Zeb laughs and reveals the truth.

"Luv, I can feel the heat radiating off those cheeks. How about we skip this party and let me put a smile on your face for real?"

My heart races as Zeb's words wash over me. I can't believe he's talking to me like this, but I can't deny the way my body responds to his touch. I nod, unable to form words, and follow him as he leads me away from the fire and toward the ocean.

As we walk, Zeb keeps a firm grip on my hand, pulling me closer to him. The warmth of his body staves off the chilly wind and I can't help but imagine what it would be like to be wrapped in his arms.

As we leave behind the bonfire, and those gathered around it, we reach the edge of the beach. Rocky outcroppings extend out into the water forming myriads of tidepools. It must be low tide. I imagine these rocks get covered when the tide comes in.

Zeb turns to me and cups my face in his hands, looking into my eyes. "I've wanted to do this since the moment I laid eyes on you."

"Kiss me?"

"Yes," he murmurs, leaning in for a kiss.

"You've already kissed me, silly."

"Shush." He wraps his hands in the long lengths of my hair, grabbing a fistful and giving the slightest tug.

He bends down and the light of the fire catches the arresting features of his face. Every nerve in my body wakes up, thrumming with anticipation as he lowers his mouth and captures mine.

I part my lips, inviting him in, as I burn for him, wanting more. My fingers claw at the fabric of his shirt, as his powerful arms wrap around me.

The world spins and my heart races. Equally tender and demanding, Zeb's lips move over mine, then travel along the sweep of my jaw with tiny nips and flicks of his tongue. Each tiny jab elicits a riot of sensation as my body heats and my blood boils.

The heat of his mouth and the relentless flicks of his tongue make me moan as the relentlessness of his attack turns me into a quivering mess of want and need.

It's not enough. I need more. My arms loop around his neck, and I lift on tiptoe and pull him down to meet my passion.

When did my body start trembling?

"You taste like heaven." Voice hoarse, breath tugging deep, his desire builds, rising to meet mine.

I could kiss him forever, but Zeb pulls away. He towers over me, looking down with eyes blown black by lust. He brushes a strand of hair from my face and smiles.

"Come, let's find a darker, quieter spot where I can ravish you."

"But what about..." My words trail off as I glance toward the bonfire.

"I could care less about them, or what they think." He grabs my hand and presses it against the length of his erection. "I want to make you mine. Say yes." His plea is one I can't refuse, because I feel the same dizzying need.

"Yes." My answer comes out a breathy moan, one of dozens

that spill from my lips, and I bet there will be scores more before this night is through.

Off in the distance, near the horizon, flashes of lightning hint at a storm brewing over the ocean. Overhead, the clouds thicken, blotting out the stars one by one. Zeb takes my hand and leads me away from the party.

TWENTY-SIX

Zeb

———

I LEAD KAYE AWAY FROM THE OTHERS AND EXCITEMENT BUILDS within me. Before this night is done, she'll be mine.

I've wanted her from the first moment I laid eyes on her outside her townhome. Undeniable chemistry electrifies the air and tingles when we touch.

Now that she's here, with me, I can't help but feel like I'm on top of the world.

And she said '*Yes.*'

The heat of her hand warms my palm. Already, a torrent of heat surges through my veins, coiling at the base of my spine, and stiffening my cock. It's an all-consuming sensation, rocking me to my core.

Most of all, I can't wait to feel the heat of her body wrapping around me, clenching tight as I plunge deep and seat myself fully within her, but there's no rush.

Not when it's inevitable.

As we reach an outcropping of rock, large enough to hide us from the others, I pull her around the edge, where we disappear from view.

It's just me and her now. I turn to her and cup her face in my hands. "Tell me you want this." Low and throaty, my voice is raw, barely restrained, and eager to begin.

Desire swirls in her eyes. She wants this as much as I do, but I need her to say it. I need to hear the words and know this is what she wants.

I'm cautious and mindful of what she's been through.

I want there to be no confusion in her mind, nothing linking what we do with what that bastard did to her. It's enough to make me pause where I would normally forge ahead.

If Kaye calls an end to this, I'll take it in stride, and take things as slow as she needs, but my dick has plans.

It has needs.

It wants Kaye with a desperate hunger.

It weeps for her and I don't think the fucker is going to like standing down.

I lean in to kiss Kaye and she melts into me, her lips parting under mine.

"I've never had sex on the beach." Low and sultry, her voice is like crack to my dick. It jerks in response as blood races to engorge it. "I've heard sand is not our friend."

"Then we're in luck. *This* beach has very little sand." And there's no way in hell I'm lying her down on the rocks. I may like things harder than most, but vigorous does not mean dangerous.

Like what Scott attempted. A feral growl rumbles in the back of my throat. It's primal and raw, intent on tearing Scott apart.

"Kiss me." She tugs me down to kiss her, and I eagerly oblige.

Electric, full of passion and fire, her lips burn and stoke my desire. I wrap my arms around her, pulling her closer as I deepen the kiss.

As I take control.

She gasps as I move my hand between us and slip my fingers under the fabric of her shirt.

Her tiny whimpers drive me forward as I push aside the fabric of her bra and finally get to feel the weight of her breast in my palm. Using my thumb and forefinger, I gently roll her nipple, stimulating it until it's peaked and tight. Her delicious moans encourage me as I continue my exploration.

A sigh overcomes me as my patience falters. But Kaye surprises me by reaching down and grabbing the hem of her shirt. Eyes locked to mine, she pulls the shirt over her head. Her head disappears and her long hair spills around the fabric as she struggles to remove it—and fails. Poor thing is caught up in the twisting fabric.

"You're killing me, little mouse." I free her head, her hair, and extricate her arms from the sleeves. Bunching up her shirt, I carefully place it on the rock beside us, trying to keep the fabric as clean as possible.

Her chest heaves and her breasts rise and fall in a hypnotic rhythm. I could watch her tits all day. Biting her lower lip, she reaches behind her and unhooks her bra. Holding the cups against her breasts, the shoulder straps slip off her shoulders and hang on her arms.

"Give it to me." Hand out, my command isn't one she can refuse.

To my delight, she bends to my will, peeking through long lashes framing her eyes. Ever so slowly, she hands me her bra. A shy thing, she trades her hands for the bra.

Covering her flesh.

Like I did with the shirt, I place the bra where it will stay dry and mostly sand free. Then I take a step back and slowly shake my head.

"Arms down. Tits out. I want to drink you in. Don't hide from me."

In the darkness, it's hard to tell, but I'm certain her cheeks turn beet red.

I love that.

Absolutely love her responsiveness.

Feeling my way through this, I navigate treacherous waters, finding out not only what she does and does not like, but what turns her on and turns her off, as well. She likes dominance. Absolutely loved when I took charge. She yields beautifully.

Is this why she allowed Asshat-Scott to get away with murder? My anger rises with the near-literal implication of that thought. The fucker could've killed her. He didn't, but I give no grace for that. The fucker needs to go down.

With a breath in, I focus on the beautiful woman in front of me, instead of a man I want to rip limb from limb.

I reach out and wrap my fingers around her delicate wrists. Applying enough pressure to make a statement—a show of dominance and test of my theory—I pull her hands away from her breasts and place them at her side.

I graze my knuckles over the creamy expanse of her curves, loving the way her breath hitches when I stroke her nipple and give the tiniest flick of sensation.

"Keep your hands down and don't move."

She jumps when I cup her breast.

Leaning down, I cover her nipple with my mouth and drive her crazy with tiny flicks of my tongue. She rises on tiptoe, and despite my command, both hands lift and dig into my hair, curling and tugging as her little whimpers turn into deep, throaty moans.

I don't correct her for moving her hands, because I love the way her fingers twist and pull my hair.

Alternating the heat of my mouth with the cool night air, she responds beautifully when I place my hands at the waistband of her jeans.

"Last chance. We stop now, or we finish this. Which will it be?"

I hold my breath, waiting for her answer, fearful she'll say no, but certain her answer will be a definite yes.

"Please—don't stop." Her plea is almost desperate, more desperate than I hoped.

"Tell me you want this." Sharp and commanding, I eagerly await her answer.

"I want this…" Her words end on a breathy sigh. "Please…"

I won't stop, but there are some logistical issues we need to navigate.

With a flick of my finger, the button of her jeans releases. The rasp of her zipper sounds loud in my ears but is nothing compared to the pounding of the surf behind us.

I can't wait to sink inside her wet heat, but for right now, something tells me she needs to take the edge off.

I'm more than happy to oblige.

I take my time slipping my hand down the front of her pants. My fingers explore the cotton of her panties as I move down the outside of the material and glide over her heated core.

"You're wet for me." A thrill of excitement zings down my spine.

Kaye's strung out, squirming and panting as I trace the outlines of her pussy with the tips of my fingers.

"Please." The heat of her breath feathers against my shoulder.

"Please, what?"

"Please…" Hesitant at first, her words bring a grin to my face. "I need…" Her voice is nothing but a whimper.

"You need, what?" I lift my finger from her clit, where I've been pressing tiny pulses. It's enough for her to feel my touch, but not enough to do anything more than frustrate her.

"Show me what it means to be yours." She presses her forehead against my shoulder, ceding control.

Fuck, her words send a blast of heat shooting through me. I almost come in my jeans like a one-pump-chump.

"With pleasure." I walk my fingers back up to the edge of her panties.

Slipping first one finger, and then the rest, my fingers glide under her panties and feel the heat of her skin.

When I reach her folds, I hold back a groan and bite my lower lip. Cupping her gently, my cock jerks, growing longer and thicker.

Readying itself—for her.

Kaye stands as still as she can, but considering the way her entire body trembles, she's going to need support. I wrap my free hand around her waist, preparing to hold her when her legs give way.

I take my time tapping her outer folds, stimulating her, while enjoying how wet she is for me.

Her tiny whimpers drive me wild, and I finally sink a single digit inside her pussy. She cries out and lifts onto her toes. Her hips sway as she rubs against me.

"Stand still, or this ends." I pause, loving the feeling of her wrapped around my finger, and wait for her body to still. "Good girl."

The moment she obeys, I pump my finger in and out as her panting intensifies. Adding a second finger, I search for that tiny spot of roughness that will make her fly.

She cries out the moment my finger strokes over her G-spot, then pants and mewls with joy and pleasure. I thrust harder, heating her up. I probe deeper, until she trembles and her legs shake.

Raw sexual energy courses between us, moving from me to her and intensifying. I thrust harder with my fingers and continually stimulate her G-spot, until her entire body tenses, and tenses, and tenses.

With a final flick of my fingers, I send her flying over the edge. Her fingers dig into my muscles as her body shakes and her orgasm rolls through her, moving outward in expanding waves of pleasure.

My fingers continue to move, caressing her through her orgasm, until she's a moaning puddle of pleasure in my arms. Then I increase the tempo. Doing it all over again.

My thumb lashes savagely against her clit as my fingers delve deeper; pumping and stoking her desire as I seek the limits of her body's arousal. I build her release as she clings to me, driving her higher and harder until I carry her up and over through a second orgasm chasing the heels of the first.

"Oh—my…" Kaye's body shakes and her legs finally give way. But my woman doesn't fall.

I hold her securely in my arms as her eyes close and her mouth opens. Hauling her close, I claim her lips as I'll claim her body.

Her breath stutters in and out. It hitches with the waves of pleasure coursing through her body. Slowly, she returns to her senses and her lids flutter open. The prettiest smile curves her lips. Kaye looks at me with an expression that nearly knocks me off my feet.

I meet her gaze, staring down at her with insatiable hunger

churning within me. Not to mention my driving need to conquer, claim, and command. Which means, I'm going to fuck any memory of Scott out of her brain.

She swallows thickly as she looks up at me. Her hands lift to rest on my biceps.

I push a wayward strand of hair off her face and can't help the crassness of the words falling from my lips. "Fuck, but you're magnificent."

Her eyes shimmer and appear to glow now that the full moon's out.

"I've—never…" Out of breath, she struggles. "That—was…"

I take her wrist and slowly lower her hand to my groin. My eyes never once disengage from hers. "Feel me, little mouse." I press her palm against my raging erection, hating the denim separating us. "Do you feel how much I want you?"

"Yes." Her eyes widen as her fingers explore the full extent of my arousal.

"Are you ready to feel me inside of you?"

"Yes." Her fingers squeeze, eliciting a slow moan from my mouth.

"Free me." Raw and throaty, my command hangs in the air between us.

She blinks once, slow and still incredibly aroused, then she unbuttons my jeans.

The rasp of the zipper makes me jump.

"Pull my cock out."

When she slides her delicate fingers under my briefs and touches my skin, I grab her by the hair and lay savage claim to her mouth.

She strokes my shaft, fully engorged, with desperate, but sure, strokes. At the tip, she runs her fingers over the head of my dick, then her grip slides back down the shaft in a firm spiral hold that rocks me to the core.

"Condom." I can barely speak. "Back left. Now."

She reaches around me, locates the condom wrapper in my back pocket, and sheathes me while I shove my jeans over my ass and halfway down my thighs.

I can't wait to impale her on my cock. While my mind works out how to divest her of her jeans, Kaye surprises me when the heat of her mouth wraps around my dick.

I stagger back half a step in surprise, but Kaye doesn't release me. She lowers herself to her knees and places her hands on my thighs. She takes me in, all the way to the root, while my toes curl and my balls draw up.

There, she pauses, and does the one thing that turns me into an animal. Kaye looks up at me, her mouth filled with my dick. Her eyes soft and submissive.

"Fuck." I reach down and grip her hair, taking control. "I won't go slow." I make a final ask for this evening.

She answers with a nod. Her eyes disengage and her head shifts to better take me in. Using my grip on her hair, I rock forward, seating myself fully inside the wet heat of her mouth. Then I slowly pull out to just the tip.

I wrap one hand around the base of my dick, to protect her from me going too deep. The fingers of my other hand twist in her hair.

Leaning my head back, I groan as I rock forward and force her to take me as deeply as she can. Toes curling, I rock back, then plunge forward. Time stands still as pleasure races through my body, building in intensity, until my entire being catches fire in an explosive release. I shake from head to toe, and have to brace myself against the nearby rocks to avoid collapsing entirely.

I wanted to turn her into a quivering puddle of need, but she's the one who brings me to my knees.

My kneecaps protest the hard rocks as I fall. Kaye wraps her arms around me, and I do the same for her. I don't know how long we kneel on the rocks; it's at once an eternity and the blink of an eye.

Finally, I lean back and cup her face.

"Now *that* was worth the wait."

Kaye giggles, and just like that, everything shifts between us. No longer is there uncertainty about whether I'm in the friend zone, or acting the part of a protective bodyguard.

Kaye is finally mine.

And I'm hers.

"So what do you say? Hang out here and make them wonder what's keeping us? Or do we stay here for round two?"

Kaye bites her lower lip and smiles. "I think they already know."

"Hmm, then we have something of a problem to overcome."

"What's that?"

"Your pants need to come off, because there's no way I'm fucking you on these rocks." I shift from my knees to sit on my ass. "And those rocks…" My gaze shifts to the jagged rocks that hide us from the others. They're rough and jagged, not smoothed down by the waves. "Those rocks will slice your skin if I hold you against them."

"Then I suppose you'll have to wait until you take me home?" Her impish grin returns.

"The fuck with that." I leap to my feet and yank up my pants. Reaching down, I haul Kaye to her feet and point to her pants. "Zip up. We're leaving."

"What about the bonfire? And Rafe's dinner?"

"Fuck food. The only thing I want to eat is you."

Once we're both decent, I grab Kaye's wrist and drag her back around the rocks. Instead of returning to the bonfire, where we'll catch flack, I march us straight to the gondola, which takes far too long to climb up the hill.

I practically drag Kaye through *Insanity* to the vehicle.

"Get in."

"But what about Brady and Booker?"

"They can find their own damn ride."

The wind kicks up as we climb into the car. That storm is closer now, building strength as it nears land.

The tires skid as I speed down the long drive. Fortunately, *Insanity* isn't very far from Guardian HQ.

TWENTY-SEVEN

Kaye

WITH MY HEART BURSTING WITH EXCITEMENT, AND A WARM FLUTTERY
feeling from the two best orgasms I've ever experienced, I can't
believe what just happened.

Or what's soon to happen.

I finally get to have sex with Zeb.

We race to the car, and Zeb speeds away from *Insanity* in a rush
to make it back to Guardian HQ. We merge into traffic on PHC-1
and wind our way along the dark highway.

But not all is quiet on the drive home.

"What's wrong?" The muscles of my jaw tighten as Zeb's entire
body goes on high alert.

"Someone's following us." Zeb drives with focus and intensity.
His jaw sets and his hands tighten on the wheel.

I fight rising panic as my heart hammers away inside my chest.
That fluttery sensation from two powerful orgasms is replaced by
fear punching at my gut.

"Who do you think it is?"

"No idea, but the fucker put on the high beams." Zeb's eyes
narrow against the blinding glare coming through the rearview
mirror. "Let's see how interested he is in following us."

I tense as Zeb floors the accelerator. We take off with a roar from the engine, leaving the mystery car in our dust.

Zeb expertly maneuvers around sharp turns while I frantically smash down on a brake pedal that doesn't exist. My stomach twists with dread as fear crawls into my throat, lodging firmly in place.

The thought of accidentally going over the edge of the road does not sit well with me, especially since there's nothing but rocks and the deadly surge of the ocean down below.

I twist in the passenger seat to look out the rear window. In what seems like slow motion, the mystery car accelerates, careening toward us on a collision course.

"Zeb!" A scream escapes me an instant before the car slams into us, sending us off the road. Our rear bumper crumples under the force of impact, groaning from strain.

The car swerves wildly, but Zeb regains control moments before we crash into a guardrail. Fortunately, the guardrails keeps us from launching into the air.

Zeb yanks us back onto the road. He increases our speed beyond what's safe. There's no escape from whatever lunatic drives the other car.

A quick glance shows the driver busted out one of his headlights, but otherwise, the grill of his vehicle appears undamaged.

My heart aches from the frenetic drumming against my ribcage and the coppery tang of blood fills my mouth from where I bit into my lower lip when we hit the guardrail.

Eyes focused on the road ahead, Zeb navigates the turns with expert precision.

The tires screech against the pavement as we take one turn after another. Panic takes hold of me as the lunatic driver follows closely behind, his remaining headlight blazes through the darkness.

Zeb's grip on the steering wheel tightens, and he exchanges a glance with me. A silent understanding passes between us.

"Eyes forward," Zeb calls out. "Brace!"

The car once again slams into us. This time, our rear window shatters from the impact. Sparks fly between the two cars as we drift into a turn on two wheels.

I'm thrown against the door, but Zeb manages to right our vehicle before we launch over the edge and into oblivion.

His impressive reflexes are the only thing keeping us alive. He doesn't let up on the accelerator, desperately trying to outrun our pursuer.

"Fuck." Zeb miraculously keeps us on the road. Behind us, sparks fly as the twisted metal of our crumpled bumper grinds against the road surface.

I take another look at our pursuer.

"Zeb…" Terror twists at my stomach.

"I see him." Terse and brusque, Zeb doesn't waste words. "Don't worry."

Don't worry? How does he expect me not to worry when we race toward an inevitable crash at alarming speed?

My heart accelerates with each turn of the wheel. My hands tremble as I take in our pursuer. My anger ignites as I look into Scott's eyes and find murderous rage twisting his face.

"What do we do?" I wipe the sweat from my palms on my jeans in an effort to stop the trembling in my fingers. It does no good. Instead, I hold my breath and prepare for whatever happens next.

The car slams into us again and again. Each time, Zeb struggles to regain control. But then, the worst thing happens. The next time Scott hits us, the mangled mess of our bumper and the grill of Scott's car become entangled and entrapped.

Our car jumps forward as a scream erupts from my throat.

"Hang on!" Zeb battles for control as our car slams against the guardrail. More sparks fly, illuminating the dark sky as our cars grind together. Zeb smashes the brakes, desperate to keep us from breaking through the protective barrier, but Scott guns his engine.

I brace for the worst as our car breaches the safety of the guardrail.

We're thrown forward suddenly as our vehicle comes to a jarring halt. My body slams against the seatbelt as the nose of the car tips forward.

The only sound is the hiss of steam rising from the engine, punctuated by the occasional groan of metal from the guardrail.

"Kaye, are you okay?" Zeb checks with me, his calming voice pulls me out of my fear-induced stupor.

"Y-yes." I barely process his question and manage a quick assessment for injuries and find nothing life threatening.

"We've got to get out of here."

The car tilts precariously over the edge of the cliff, threatening to plunge us into oblivion at any moment. I make the mistake of looking down and see nothing but waves crashing against the rocks far below us. It's a deadly surge we will not survive.

My heart races as the car rocks back. I want to move, but my body refuses to budge.

Zeb reaches for the clasp of my seatbelt, but I shake my head too terrified to speak. "Kaye, we need to move our weight back." He glances out the shattered back window with a grimace. "We're running out of time."

With that, he unlatches my seatbelt as the car tips forward. Gravity takes hold of me and I fall forward, but Zeb sticks out his arm, pushing me back into my seat.

"Pull the lever to push the seat back. I need you to crawl over your seat and out the back window."

My body's frozen in place.

With me not responding, Zeb leans over me and pulls on the adjustment for the seat back.

When the back of my seat falls back, Zeb practically lifts me up and out of my seat, moving me back.

"Move!" He barks the command and my body reacts on its own.

Before I know it, I scramble into the back seat and crawl out the back window. The car rocks back. Zeb's right on my heels, pushing me up and through the rear window.

Adrenaline shoots through my veins imbuing me with superhuman strength. I slide out of the back window, onto the hood of Scott's vehicle.

Spiderweb cracks in the front windshield radiate outward from where he hit his head. Blood drips down the front of his face. While I stare at him, he opens his eyes and glares at me.

Behind me, Zeb has more difficulty climbing out of the back window. Our car tilts toward the abyss. Without thinking, I spin around and grip the opening of the window, placing all my weight on the back of our window until Zeb works his way free.

Twisted metal groans and shifts. Zeb grabs me by the waist and vaults off our car as it tilts forward and slides a foot over the edge.

Scott's eyes widen as the guardrail finally gives way. The SUV falls forward, dragging Scott's vehicle with it. It slips closer and closer to the edge and the deadly drop.

Scott's face contorts with fear. He moves fast, unbuckling his seatbelt and barely manages to get out of his car before both vehicles tip over the cliff's edge.

Gravity wins this fight as the three of us look on in horror. Both cars plummet over the side, disappearing into the darkness below. They crash against the rocks, making the ground shake, squeals of twisting metal bring my shoulders to my ears, then there's a loud splash as they hit the water below and disappear beneath the raging surf.

If we'd been in that car, no one would ever know where to look for us.

I clutch at Zeb's hand as we turn to face Scott.

"What the hell do you think you were doing?" Zeb rages at Scott. "You could've killed her."

"She doesn't deserve to live." Scott stalks toward us, hatred burning in his eyes. "Not after you left me."

The tension between us is so thick, I can barely breathe and it's as if time slows down. I cling protectively to Zeb.

"I don't belong to you. What do you think you're doing? Just let me go." I try to reason with Scott, but Zeb pushes me protectively behind him, shielding me with his body.

The air around us crackles as Scott takes a step closer. Rage burns in his eyes along with madness.

Zeb faces off against Scott, ready for battle. The men remind me of two wild animals facing off. Neither will back down or run away, not when I'm the prize.

Scott blinks first and launches at Zeb, fists clenched in seething fury. His breathing is uneven and wild as Zeb steps protectively between Scott and me.

He's a wall of steel—a force no man can break.

I've never seen Zeb this way before—powerful, deadly, and unyielding. It's both awe-inspiring and disturbingly frightening all at once.

Despite the danger posed by Scott's madness, Zeb makes me feel safe beside him; knowing I can depend on him to protect me even if it puts himself in jeopardy.

Scott stops short when he sees the deadly intensity radiating off Zeb.

"She's mine." Spittle flies from Scott's mouth. He launches forward, head down, charging like a bull intent on knocking Zeb off his feet.

But Zeb is ready for that. His muscles twitch, and he waits until Scott's close enough. He throws a vicious right uppercut that meets Scott's jaw.

It's enough to lift Scott off his feet and dump him down on his ass in a tangle of limbs, but Scott doesn't stay there. Up and back on his feet, Scott blinks twice, staggers until he regains his balance, then he stands straight, shaking it off.

"This fight is over." Zeb's tone is at once a threat and a promise.

Scott stands still, tall and proud, enraged and filled with jealousy. His nose bleeds; hard to say if it's broken. Then he takes a step toward me.

"She's mine. She belongs to me." Scott shifts his attention to me; a deadly glare.

"Sorry, but she's made it abundantly clear she doesn't want you." Zeb matches Scott's step.

It's like watching a train wreck and already knowing the outcome. Zeb's a trained killer and takes down men ten times worse than Scott.

But Scott can't see that. He feints left and throws a snap right, aimed low to hit Zeb in the solar plexus.

But Zeb sees it coming a mile away. He twists at the waist, taking the hit and absorbs the momentum. His body rotates, coiling like a spring, winding tight until releasing energy in an explosive burst of violence and speed.

Unlike Scott, Zeb's attack is precisely timed and controlled. It starts with his returning elbow, moving in an arc of destruction. The backward rotation of his center of mass feeds it, adding extra velocity and force until he chops down sharply against the side of Scott's neck.

The hit drops Scott to his knees.

This time, it takes Scott longer to get up. His legs wobble when he straightens, and his hands go out wide, as if seeking extra balance.

Zeb doesn't wait.

He steps in and hits Scott again, same arm, same ferocious force, but coming from the opposite direction. Instead of his elbow, Zeb backhands Scott below the left eye, knuckles to bone. Scott staggers back, but recovers. He blinks and swings, aiming at Zeb's face, but fails to touch Zeb who sidesteps the sloppy hit.

Zeb grabs Scott by the shoulders, squares off against him, then jabs his knee up and into Scott's midsection again and again.

Scott goes down and this time, he doesn't move. That doesn't stop Zeb.

"Help me get his shoes off."

"Why?"

Zeb rips off Scott's sneakers and tosses them at me. "I need the shoelaces."

Rolling Scott face first into the dirt, he grabs Scott's arms and secures his wrists at the small of his back.

"Hand me the laces." He holds out his hand and I give him one set of the laces.

One of Scott's eyes opens. His voice slurs and I can only make out every other word. "You'll-regret… Find—her."

"Hand me the other one." Zeb gives a little flick of his fingers as I hand him the second shoelace.

Satisfied with his work of hog-tying Scott's hands and feet together, Zeb steps back and pats down his shirt. He looks at me and cocks his head.

"Lost my phone." He jerks his thumb over his shoulder toward the cliff and the mangled mess of what remains of the guardrail. "Please tell me you have yours?"

I bite my lower lip and shake my head. The wind whips at my hair and a flash of lightning illuminates the ground where Scott lies in the dirt.

"Well shit." Zeb scratches his head and blows out a breath. "We can stay here, or walk. Guardian HQ is still a few miles from here." He glances down at Scott and nudges him with the toe of his boot. When Scott doesn't move, Zeb turns his attention to me. "He's not going anywhere. We can walk to HQ, or wait for someone to stop and call the cops?"

TWENTY-EIGHT

Zeb

I stare in awe as the night sky morphs into an ominous canvass of thick, billowing clouds. Flashes of lightning illuminate the sky, followed by the rumblings of distant thunder.

Roaring waves precede the fury of the storm, crashing against the jagged cliffs, making the ground shake and the air boom with each powerful strike. The power of the waves grows with every passing second; the tiniest reflection of what that storm will bring. I take a deep breath, feeling my chest tighten, and turn away from the horizon.

"I don't like being exposed like this. We need to find somewhere safe to ride out the storm. Hope you don't mind getting drenched." My gaze casts up and down the deserted highway, then I take another look at the sky, trying to gauge the speed of the incoming storm.

My stomach twists with unease as I debate the merits of staying here, with Scott, or leaving him and hoofing it down PCH-1.

Guardian HQ isn't that far by car, but on foot, it's still a hike. And there's no shelter between here and there. No homes perched on the cliffs. No businesses clinging to the edge. Nothing to protect us from the elements.

"We can't just leave him." Kaye glances at Scott with a worried frown.

She wraps her arms around herself and shivers with the blustering wind. Strands of hair blow wildly around her face, making her grab her hair and gather it in a fist. She glances at Scott with a worried frown, her gaze lingering on him as he lies face down on the dirt, right where I left him.

With the way I hog-tied his hands and feet, he can't flip to his back. Fucker gets to eat dirt and I don't feel bad about that.

He deserves a bullet to the brain for endangering Kaye's life like that. If I'm lucky, a stray bolt of lightning will land on the fucker's ass and fry him to charred bits from the inside out.

It would solve a lot of problems.

With that thought in my head, another bolt of lightning ignites the sky. Closer than the previous strikes, the thunder shakes the ground.

Damn, the storm's moving faster than I thought. The first fat drops of rain fall on my face and I wish Kaye and I hadn't left *Insanity*. If we hadn't, we'd be with everyone else, abandoning the beach and bonfire, and retreating to the safety of the massive estate.

Instead, we're out here, lucky to be alive, after asshole Scott tried to kill us.

No phone.

No car.

And, evidently, we're the only people on the road. What happened to the traffic?

"Whether we stay or go, we're going to get wet. Be prepared," I warn Kaye, not that there's a need. She stares at the sky, concerned, but not frightened.

Honestly, stay or go, both options are shit.

"I'm not worried about a little rain." Kaye shivers as the temperature drops. That storm is determined to slam into us.

"Me either, but I'm not keen on being out here with lightning striking all around us."

"Even more reason we can't leave him." Kaye tugs at her hair, wringing her ponytail in distress.

I can.

I have absolutely no heartache leaving Scott to his fate, but if I leave his sorry ass hog-tied on the side of the road, there will be tons of red tape to be sorted out. He could charge me with assault. Which will immediately be thrown out after the whole running us off the road thing comes out.

I glance at the road, disturbed by the lack of traffic.

"Wish I had my phone." I pat the rear pockets of my pants for what must be the tenth time, as if doing so will make my phone magically appear. It wasn't there the last nine times. Don't know why I think it'll be there now.

"There." Kaye points down the winding coastline and the deserted highway. "Lights. I'm sure if we flag them down, they'll stop."

She has far more confidence in the goodwill of the common man than me. No one in their right mind would stop for me. I'm a big man, tall and packed with muscle. That makes me a threat, but Kaye on the other hand…

"You should flag them down." I grab her hand and tug her toward the edge of the road where the car will see us.

"Me?" She points to her chest. "Shouldn't it be you?"

"If you saw me on a dark, deserted highway, would you stop? There's no way to know who might be in that car. If female, she'd be stupid to stop. Men are fifty-fifty, depending if they're more beta than alpha."

"Good point." Kaye hurries to the edge of the road while I check in on Scott.

She stands to the side, waving her arms wildly at the approaching car. I have little faith it'll stop, but to my surprise, it does. The car slows and pulls off the road, coming to a complete stop. The driver steps out.

"Do you need help?" The man looks harmless enough, but I move to stand protectively beside Kaye.

"Dean Alder, it's so good to see you." Kaye answers before I can reply and relief floods her voice. "We had an accident."

"Is everyone all right?" He sweeps the area with a penetrating stare. "How can I help?" His left brow lifts as he takes in Scott and the gaping hole in the guardrail where our car went off the road.

"Can we use your phone?" This is the Dean who did a favor for Scott, getting Kaye into his veterinarian school. The fine hairs at the back of my neck lift. I feel naked without a gun.

"Absolutely." The man's attention lingers on Kaye a bit longer than necessary, making me bristle. So far, he doesn't seem to care about Scott.

Talk about red flags.

His brows bunch together and he nods. "Just let me get it." He turns back to his car and leans in.

Something sinister swirls in his gaze. A chill runs through me when I realize what's happening, and my feet move of their own accord.

The unmistakable slide on a handgun being racked makes my heart stop. My gaze snaps to the dean, eyes narrow as time slows to a crawl.

"Get down!" I shout at Kaye, lunging to protect her as a deafening gunshot pierces the air. My body shields Kaye, taking the bullet instead of Kaye. Searing pain slams into me, knocking the wind from my lungs. It forces me back and my knees buckle. I fall to the ground in a sea of agony, my breath coming in shallow gasps.

Kaye's scream echoes around me as I clutch my chest, pain radiating through every inch of my body.

Through my haze of pain, the man grabs Kaye.

"It wasn't supposed to be like this." His hard gaze cuts to Scott with accusation. "I knew you'd fuck it up."

"What are you doing?" Kaye struggles in his grip, then pleads with him. "You don't have to do this."

Dean Alder slaps handcuffs on Kaye, and manhandles her into the back seat of the car while she desperately fights for her life.

My vision tunnels and I struggle to remain conscious. My mind scrambles to make sense of what's happening, but I'm losing the fight to remain conscious.

Kaye needs me, but I can't think. I can't get my legs to cooperate. I try to crawl, but my body resists. My head swims through a thick fog and my limbs grow heavier with each labored breath. Every movement is a battle against the searing pain that radiates through me.

Dean Alder straightens, his gaze turning to Scott with a hint of something smug in his expression. Scott looks away as the dean strides confidently toward him. He pulls out a pocketknife from his belt loop. With lightning speed, he slices through the shoelaces restraining Scott and steps back.

"Get up." The command comes naturally to the man, as if he and Scott have had some version of this same conversation many times in the past.

Scott rubs at his wrists where the shoelaces bit into his skin before standing on shaky legs. His gaze darts around nervously, but then lands on Kaye trapped in the back seat and his eyes light up in victory.

Kaye struggles in the backseat, eyes wide and frightened.

The stranger says nothing, but he watches Scott like a hawk. There's no doubt in my mind the man is a predator, and this isn't the first time such a scene has gone down between the two men.

My heart races as Dean Alder moves toward me. A sickening sense of dread washes over me. I've never felt this helpless and realize what he has planned for me.

He crouches beside me, a cruel smirk playing on his lips, but to my surprise, instead of killing me, he carefully tucks his gun into his waistband. Then he takes a step back with a satisfied smirk.

"You have to stay here for now." As he turns away, he mutters something about needing bodies for leverage later on down the road, sending chills up my spine. The fucker strolls back to the car like he's got all the time in the world. He slides into the driver's seat as Scott approaches me.

He stares down at me with murder in his eyes and a sneer contorts his face. "Kaye belongs to me, and you're never getting her back." With that, he kicks me in the gut.

Scott goes to the car, and when he opens the passenger door, Kaye's screams fill my ears, but they're silenced the moment Scott shuts the door, trapping her inside with the two of them.

The engine roars to life and they peel away in a flurry of gravel spitting in my face. I sink back to the ground, losing track of time, going in and out of consciousness as fat drops of rain splatter on my face.

My mind races with a million thoughts as I lay there, drenched in my own blood. What the hell just happened?

In the distance, the car with Kaye inside it, disappears into the night. I grit my teeth and struggle to stand but collapse as pain slams into me.

It's a struggle to breathe, becoming more difficult with each attempt. Thankfully, a surge of adrenaline floods my system, pumping through my veins. I force myself to stand, laboriously pushing myself to my feet, determined not to give up until I find Kaye. It's a hike to Guardian HQ, but I'm determined to make it.

Intense pain consumes me, but I stagger and limp down the road with nothing but murder on my mind.

Blood streams down my arm. All I can hope is someone stops, but who will stop for a man like me, bleeding out from a bullet to the chest? With each passing second, my chances of survival decrease.

I don't know how long I stumble along the side of the road. In a fog of pain, I barely register the loud squeal of tires behind me. I look around, surprised to find myself staggering in the middle of the damn road. All around me, the fury of the storm rages.

A car screeches to a stop. The doors open. Four people jump out. They race toward me.

"Zeb? What the hell happened?" Brady catches me as I fall.

TWENTY-NINE

Kaye

My heart races as I watch the road pass by, not knowing what lies ahead. All I can think about is the way Scott stared when Dean Alder grabbed me and pushed me into the car.

It was the rage of intense jealousy, with the promise of retribution layered on top. Dean Alder, on the other hand, preens with victory, as if claiming me is some great prize.

With each passing mile, anxiety builds inside of me. I want to scream. I want to cry. I want to launch myself out of this car.

I did at first, scream and cry, but both men ignored me. With my hands behind my back, and the way I'm strapped in, the whole launching out of the car thing isn't a possibility. Not that I would at sixty miles an hour. That would invite certain death.

But what do I do?

I can't find the courage to scream anymore. All I can do is sit in the backseat silently, with my hands cuffed behind my back, and try to calm myself down. I need to be clear-headed to fight my way out of this.

We drive for what feels like hours. The entire time, my captors don't exchange a single word. The tension is stifling.

We head north, but I have no idea where they're taking me or what they will do with me once we get there.

Scratch that. I know exactly what Scott wants. As for Dean Alder? That's another question entirely, and I don't want the answer.

Alder looks back at me occasionally. Each time, a smug expression fills his face. His beady, black eyes simmer with malevolence and something darker. Something I don't want to acknowledge.

The man's a killer, and he greedily laps up my fear. My heart races as I take in the sickly-sweet smell of his cologne. My stomach churns, and I fight the urge to retch. He smells of death, and a shiver slithers down my spine each time he looks at me. It's as if he savors the moment, cataloging it, and filing it away for later.

Scott is a sadist. He gets off on inflicting pain. Dean Alder is something far worse. He thrives on creating fear.

The longer I'm in the car, the more certain I am that Scott and the dean plan to kill me. Maybe that's why they don't speak to each other? Maybe Scott isn't done with me and doesn't agree with killing me?

Is that something I can use against them?

The thing is, I've watched enough television, and read enough books, to paint a vivid picture of what comes next. Knowing their depravities—or at least Scott's, I'm extrapolating to Dean Alder— it's not a stretch to connect the dots.

While the dean greedily laps up my fear, savoring every bit of it, Scott glares at me from the passenger seat with a face set in stone.

At the mercy of two psychopaths, my mind turns to escape. It's the only thing keeping me from dropping into the pit of despair.

But what do I have that can help me?

With my wrists shackled at my back, even if I had a key or a hairclip, I couldn't use it.

I come up empty and more scared than before.

After what seems like an eternity, the silent ride finally comes to a stop. My heart pounds in my chest as I look out the window.

There's nothing but trees and darkness. We're in the middle of nowhere, far away from civilization.

Dean Alder turns to me with a leer and speaks to me like I'm barely human. "This is where we're keeping you until I figure out what to do with you. Don't try to escape. I'll find you, and you'll wish you were dead." With that, he gets out of the car. Scott follows. The car doors open and close, leaving me inside.

Alone.

A wave of terror washes through me and a chill penetrates deep into my bones.

The two of them step some distance away. Their aggressive gestures, and the harshness of their yelling, tells me everything I need to know. They're fighting over me.

It's also clear who's in charge.

It's not Scott. He's not the one in control here—it's Dean Alder; a far more menacing man than Scott could ever be. I turn away from the window, unable to watch anything else. My heart beats faster as I wait, powerless to change my fate, trembling from fear that clots the very air, it's so intense.

That fear intensifies, becoming a heavy weight pressing down on me. I've never felt this powerless. I've never felt this scared. I want to scream, but I can't bring myself to do that and waste my breath. I'm completely at the mercy of my kidnappers, ensnared in a living nightmare of my own making.

And Zeb?

Tears sting my eyes as I wonder about Zeb. He's alone and wounded, left to die on the side of the road. Visions of his body and far too much blood, flash through my mind like the lightning of that storm. I want to howl with grief and rage with fury.

There was so much blood.

Is he alive?

Something inside of me snaps. My sanity unravels knowing he might be dead because of me. My choices led us here. I'll never forgive myself for destroying the man I'm falling in love with.

My hands are like ice, so numb I can barely feel my fingers. My wrists ache from the metallic bite of the cuffs. My back is a twisted pile of knots. My mind races with all kinds of possibilities, but I can't seem to make any sense of anything.

What is Scott going to do to me?

Why does he defer to the dean like he does?

Is there some reason he's so loyal to Dean Alder?

What does the dean want with me?

Every cell in my body screams that he definitely wants something from me, yet I can't fathom what that might be.

I try to keep calm, but it's getting harder and harder. I'm consumed by fear; all I can do is pray Zeb survives, and that somehow I'll escape this too.

Without warning, the back door opens. Scott grabs me violently, yanking me from the vehicle. His grip is like an iron vice: cold and unforgiving. He drags me through the woods, never once saying a word. The trees overhead tower over me like eerie specters who stand witness to what very well may be my last moments on earth.

I scream, desperate to save myself. He rewards me with a punch to the gut that leaves me gasping for breath. Then he hauls me, stumbling and in pain, to a small clearing where a decrepit cabin snuggles beside a burbling brook.

A chill runs down my spine as the dean opens the door. "Welcome home, my pet."

I try to take a deep breath, but my lungs don't cooperate. It's as if fear paralyzes me, leaving me mute and unable to move.

Dean Alder steps aside and motions for me to enter the cabin, as if I'm an honored guest instead of a prisoner. The musty air inside the cabin is thick with death. The floorboards creak beneath my feet as I shuffle inside. Scott follows on my heels, closing the door behind us with a thud as he slides a locking bolt closed. Meanwhile, the dean flicks a switch.

A sickly light flickers, then flares to life, but it fails to push back the sinister shadows shifting and dancing in the corners of the room. My stomach churns as I look around. I want to run, but I can't. I want to scream, but I don't.

I want to disappear, but I'm truly here.

I feel like a mouse in a trap, waiting for the inevitable.

Dean Alder turns to me and smiles, his eyes gleaming with a sick kind of delight. "You're not going anywhere. Not until I get what I want from you." He leans in close, his breath hot on my neck. "I can't wait for our games to begin."

The threat hangs in the air, heavy and menacing. When a shudder runs through my body, he smiles. It's the most terrifying sight I've ever seen.

My throat tightens until I can barely breathe. Trapped like a mouse in a maze, my heart pounds with the realization there's little chance I'm getting out of this alive.

THIRTY

Zeb

Pain blinds me. My vision swims in and out of focus. Brady shouts my name.

He shakes me.

Slaps me.

I can't focus on anything beyond the infinite agony pounding inside my chest. Well, that and breathing. Each breath is harder than the last.

I fade and slip away.

"You're going to be okay." Strain fills Brady's voice.

Booker appears at my side and barks orders at the others. He rips open my shirt and quickly assesses my injury.

I gasp in agony as he presses his fingers to the bullet wound in my chest.

"His chest is filling up with blood. He needs a chest tube STAT." Booker is calm, but his voice is determined. "Grab my bag in the back of the car."

I can barely see through the pain fogging my head. Then something cold and sharp presses against my skin. I flinch as Booker inserts something between my ribs.

Fucking agony.

My lungs burn and I struggle for every shallow breath.

But—the pain ebbs as the tube relieves pressure in my chest. Air moves in and out of my lungs, easier than before.

"Where to?" Brady asks.

"We need to get him to a hospital." Booker leans over me, his intense gaze never leaving my face as he works. "I've got you, brother. How are you feeling?"

"Like—shit." Each breath robs me of strength, but it's definitely getting easier to breathe.

"I'm on the phone with Skye." The soft voice of Izzy sounds incredibly far away. "She says take him back to *Insanity*."

"He needs a hospital." Booker argues with Izzy.

"Skye says she's closer and she's prepping."

The men help me to my feet and I lean heavily against Brady, who supports me as we make our way to the car. My toes drag against the blacktop.

"Kaye…" I gasp, trying to keep my eyes open.

Brady stares at me, concern filling his eyes.

"Trouble," I croak, my voice barely a whisper. "Scott—and…" My vision blacks out and I slump into Brady's arms.

Brady's grip tightens, and he helps me into the car. Booker climbs into the driver's seat, and the rest pile in.

The engine roars to life and we race down the road. My vision comes and goes as I fade in and out of consciousness. Booker takes corners at high speed as the SUV careens around each bend. Brady remains quiet, his eyes constantly checking in on me. Izzy is on the phone with Skye, giving updates on my condition.

"Thready and fast." Angie cradles my head in her lap and checks my pulse. "He lost a lot of blood."

Angie's a doc like Doc Summers, but she's an eye doc, not a trauma doc. Right now, I need Doc Summers.

Whatever Booker put in my chest tugs with the weirdest sensation. It doesn't belong there. I try to take it out, but Izzy bats my hand away.

I drift in and out of consciousness, but we finally come to a stop outside *Insanity*.

I'm dimly aware of a flurry of activity around me.

Doc Summers is there, waiting. She oversees Brady and Booker as they carry me inside.

"Put him here." She's got one of those soft voices, but when she's in doctor mode, it carries absolute authority.

Brady and Booker lay me out on a table.

Doc Summers examines me and mutters something about infection, before quickly setting about cleaning and dressing my wound as best she can with limited supplies.

"It was either that or he'd be dead." Booker defends his actions, making me wonder what he shoved inside my chest.

"It'll do for now." She moves quickly, taking out whatever Booker put in me, then inserts something that feels like a goddamn garden hose. I practically levitate off the table, it hurts so damn much.

The pain is unbearable, but I'm so far gone, I can only watch as my life slips away. People shout all around me. Then there's a beep, and another beep. Sounds like a heart rate monitor, but I'm too far gone to make sense of it.

The room spins as I continue to drift in and out of consciousness. Every now and then, snippets of conversation reach my ears, but it feels like it's coming from a thousand miles away.

Brady tells Booker he did a great job.

Doc Summers mutters about infection.

Booker defends his decision.

Others are there, but their voices are too indistinct to make out.

I have to tell them about Kaye, about the danger she's in, but each time I try to speak, they tell me to be quiet and save my strength.

A strange calm comes over me. My vision fades as I slip into a deep sleep.

I'M DIMLY AWARE OF A BRIGHT LIGHT AND THE SOUND OF MACHINES beeping away. My eyes flutter open, and I find myself in a bright white room, lying in a hospital bed. I blink a few times and take in my surroundings.

"Zeb, you're awake." Doc Summers stands over me, taking notes on her tablet as she inspects my chest tube.

"Welcome back to the land of the living." Her soft eyes are gentle and kind. "You had us all worried." She pats me lightly on the hand before continuing with her examination.

I try to speak, but my throat is too dry, so I nod in acknowledgment.

"Your vitals are better." She steps closer and checks the monitors. "Stable."

My vision clears, but my memories remain fuzzy, like fog on a windowpane. All I know is Kaye is in danger somewhere out there. I try to speak, but all that comes out is a dry croak. I try to get out of bed, my only thought that I need to rescue Kaye.

"Easy, there." Doc Summers places a hand on my shoulder.

"I need…" My mouth's too dry and my tongue's thick and twisted; noncompliant when it comes to forming words.

"What you need is a few days of rest. Do you remember what happened?"

"Scott—shot." The words don't come.

"It's okay. Let me fill you in. Brady and Booker found you wandering in the middle of the road with a bullet wound to your chest. You were delirious from losing too much blood."

"I…" My hands explore something protruding between my ribs.

"Don't touch that. You yank out my handiwork and we will have words." Doc Summers gently takes my hand and moves it away from the chest tube.

"Kaye…" I try to wet my mouth, get rid of the cobwebs, but I only succeed in making things worse.

"Here. Have a sip." Doc Summers notices my discomfort and offers me some water from the cup beside my bed. "You were pretty out of it. Booker had to improvise. Used a straw, if you can believe it, as a modified chest tube. That man is definitely resourceful. Saved your life."

I don't doubt that.

"Whoever shot you, nicked one of the blood vessels in your chest. Your chest cavity filled with blood and collapsed the lung on that side."

I nod, if only to keep her talking. I'm not a fan of these holes in my memory. She holds the cup of water as I suck in the liquid.

"They brought you to *Insanity*, where I performed minor field surgery to stabilize you, then we moved you here, back to HQ. We gave you blood and antibiotics for infection, then took you to surgery to remove the bullet and fix the damage. You've been out of surgery for a day."

"A day." I bolt upright, ready to get out of bed, desperate to get to Kaye.

"Hold on." Once again she presses me back into bed. It's a testament to how weak I am that she can move me at all.

"They took Kaye."

"They?" A high-pitched voice calls out from the hall.

My vision's blurry, but not too blurry that I miss the riot of colors on top of the woman's head.

"What's Mitzy doing here?" I manage a few words, then suck on the straw again, needing to hydrate and get rid of the cotton in my mouth.

"Well, hello to you, sunshine." She flits inside my hospital room like she owns it. "What do you mean by they?"

"Scott…" I take in a breath, surprised at how winded I am. "Ran us off the road." I pause and suck wind. It feels like I'm in the middle of a sprint trying to hold a conversation.

"Save your breath." Mitzy's tone sounds sarcastic, but that's just how she speaks. "We followed the blood back to where he ran you off the road. The guardrail's busted and there are two cars in the water. So we already figured that bit out. Highway patrol isn't happy you fled the scene, but we're handling them. I take it both you and Kaye survived?"

I nod, but anger builds in my veins, spiking my heart rate and raising my blood pressure, if the angry beeping from the monitor is any indication.

"I take it she's with him?"

"Yes." The word comes out more of a growl than anything else. I choke up, but get out a few words between sobs, "Scott and the other man took her."

"Other?" Doc Summers looks at Mitzy.

"We assumed there was another car." Mitzy taps her chin, thinking hard. "Unfortunately, there aren't any cameras near there. I wasn't able to track anything, but if you can give me details, I can try to work a bit of magic."

A grin tips the corner of my mouth up. The Guardians call it Mitzy Magic, because none of us understand how Mitzy accomplishes what she does. The woman is a whiz when it comes to anything tech related, but computer systems is where she truly shines.

"I don't know—seemed familiar…" I close my eyes and drift.

"Make and model of the car would help. A license plate would be best. If you remember." Mitzy's voice pulls me back.

I grimace, because that was the last thing I was thinking about when that fucker pulled up pretending to want to help us.

"Not us." My teeth grind together as fury burns through me.

"Excuse me?"

"He came to help Scott." I grip the scratchy hospital sheets and swear bloody murder to Scott and the man who helped him. "It was the dean who came to help Scott. Like they were a team, stalking Kaye, waiting for the right moment." I turn my attention to Doc Summers and tug on the tube shoved between my ribs. "You gotta let me out of here."

"You need time to heal." Her expression says what I want isn't up for discussion.

"No."

"You need two weeks, but I know a Guardian's mind when his woman's in danger. I'll let you up in a few days. No sooner."

"But…"

"It's non-negotiable. You'll more likely kill yourself trying to help Kaye if you go now. Then who is she going to kiss when we rescue her?"

"Where's my team?"

"They…" Mitzy pushes my legs to the side and sits on the foot of my bed. "Are in the waiting room. Give me an hour, and we'll make this Guardian central. We'll find your girl. Now…" Mitzy leans close. "Make and model?"

"Black Audi."

"Any detail on the plates?"

"None."

"California plate? Or another state?"

"California."

"It's a start." Mitzy looks to Skye. "It's going to get packed in here. Anyway we can move him to a larger room?"

Doc Summers nods. "We'll find a larger room."

"Great." Mitzy claps her hands. With a smile, she points to the IV. "I'll take care of everything. We'll find your girl but listen to Skye. You're no use to Kaye if you're dead. Stay in bed like a good little Guardian. Rest and heal."

She's right. I'm no use to Kaye like this.

"Two days."

"I said a few." She gives me a look that says *non-negotiable*.

I glare at Doc Summers and show her I mean business in the only way I can. I sip from the cup and finish my water. Those antibiotics had better do their thing.

As for healing?

The moment Doc Summers gives me the go ahead, I'll be up and out of this bed.

Nothing will keep me from finding Kaye.

THIRTY-ONE

Zeb

I should rest and follow doctor's orders, but it's impossible when all I can think about is rescuing Kaye.

"If you stopped helping me, this would go a whole lot faster." Doc Summers chastises me when I get in her way again, but she comes through like a champ.

With the tube in my chest, a long tube snakes back to the wall, where it attaches to a suction canister. That suction drains the blood from my chest and allows my lung to heal.

What that means is, I'm tied to the wall by that tubing, like a leash keeping me in place. Doc Summers disconnects me from the wall and, with the help of her medics, wheels me and my hospital bed into a larger room. It's not a patient room. It's more of a general procedure area.

"You know," Doc Summers says, "we could've just had you join virtually."

She's right about that. We could do this virtually—patch me into the meeting held in the Guardian building—but Doc Summers gets me. She gets what it means to be a Guardian.

"It's not the same." I'm in a grumpy mood, tired of others telling me what I can, and can't, do.

"I know, and that's why I don't mind making this work." She backs my bed up against the wall, then bends down to disconnect my chest tube from portable suction and connects it back to the suction coming from the wall. "Besides, it gives Mitzy a chance to mobilize her team and test their mobile setup."

"I thought she kind of jumped on the chance too easily." Talking makes me cough, and coughing hurts like a motherfucker when you've got a piece of plastic shoved between your ribs.

But pain is good.

Pain is life.

Pain reminds you that you're still alive and have something to live for.

Still weak post-op, coughing leaves me breathless. I'm getting stronger, however. Some of my exhaustion fades. Most likely, because they pumped me full of blood after what I poured all over the highway.

"You okay?" Doc Summers pauses and gives me a once-over. Before I can complain, she sticks her stethoscope in her ears and places the cold metal of the diaphragm on my chest.

"Take a breath."

"Doc, do we need to do this now?" People are looking at me and I hate feeling helpless.

"Deep breaths." She doesn't put up with my shit and waits with infinite patience for me to comply.

I take in a shallow breath but wind up coughing instead. Splinting against the pain, I squeeze my eyes shut and tell myself, *It's just a flesh wound.* Somehow, that seems to help.

A little.

"Here." She shoves an inspirometer into my hand. "Keep up with your exercises."

Technically called an incentive spirometer, the device measures the volume of the air inhaled during a breath. It has three plastic balls in three successive chambers. The harder and deeper I breathe, the more balls pop to the top of the chamber. I'm supposed to do that and keep them there as I strengthen my breath.

So far, I can lift only two balls, but I can't keep them up there.

Doc Summers knows this, and it's a not-so-gentle reminder of how severe the bullet to my chest was.

"Use it. If you don't, there's no way I'm letting you out of this bed for a week." Her tone tells me this is where she draws a line in the sand.

"Come on, Doc…" I try to complain, but when Doc Summers is in doctor mode, she's a ballbuster and takes none of our flack. "I'll do it later."

"Then I'll let you out of bed—later." She gives me one of her looks and I roll my eyes. There's no arguing with her.

My gaze shifts to the room and those who fill it. Using the damn inspirometer makes me feel like an invalid, and I don't like that one bit.

"Do it." She props her hands on her hip, and although a diminutive woman, manages to stare me down until I place my lips on the device and inhale in a breath like a dutiful patient.

"How're you holding up?" Booker saunters in with Brady. He pulls a stool beside my bed and takes a load off.

I keep breathing in, barely keeping two of the three balls in the air, and feel like an idiot. Out of breath, I lay the damn thing in my lap.

"Alive, thanks to you."

"No problem, man." Booker waves his hand like what he did was nothing.

"Did you really shove a straw between my ribs?"

Most of that night is filled with moth-eaten holes. Big gaps in my memory, which bothers me way more than taking a bullet in the chest.

"Yeah." Yet again, Booker dismisses what he did.

"Like one of those wrapped in paper? Or a used one from an exercise bottle?"

"Yup."

"Which one?"

"Paper straw."

"Kind of an odd thing to have laying around."

"Bring that up with Isabelle. I'm always on her about leaving stuff like that in the car, but thanks to her…" He shrugs and doesn't bother to complete the sentence.

"At least it wasn't full of your spit." I look to Booker, realizing only after the words leave my mouth, that may not be a question I want answered, but I can't help myself. "Please tell me it wasn't used."

"Dude, I wouldn't put a used straw in your chest." Booker shakes his head and swivels in the stool.

The thing is, he totally would. If it meant the difference between saving his teammate or watching me die in front of him. He'd lick the damn straw clean, then do what had to be done.

This isn't the first time Booker's saved my life.

Or the lives of the rest of our team.

If not for him, Brady would be dead, burned to a crisp in that explosion that nearly took all of Bravo out of action over a year ago in Cancun. Rafe wouldn't be with us either. He lost a leg in that explosion, and only because of Booker's quick actions managed to *only* lose a leg instead of his life.

Hayes and Alec each lost some fingers. I'm lucky to still be walking with the amount of shrapnel that peppered my body. Booker's the only one who made it out of that shit show without injury.

"The tech team moves fast." Booker changes the subject and jerks his chin in the direction of the nonstop stream of people moving equipment into the room.

"I'd move fast if Mitzy was on my ass." I try to laugh but end up in a coughing fit instead.

Booker glances out the door where Mitzy's high-pitched voice can be heard pushing her team to move faster.

"She's like a pint-sized drill sergeant." There's an honest-to-goodness smile on Booker's face.

"Never seen a drill sergeant with rainbow hair, but she does get them to double-time it."

Booker snorts and shakes his head. "Ain't that the truth."

As Mitzy promised, the room fills with her tech team and all their gear. The rest of Bravo team and Doc Summers hold up the walls, trying to stay out of the way.

"What did she say?" Booker points to Doc Summers.

"Says two weeks at least, but if I'm a good patient, she'll let me out in a few days."

"Damn. That's rough." His face twists with emotion. Concern paints his face and the corners of his mouth pull down. "You know we'll get her back." Booker looks away, his face a stone mask.

"I know."

But I want to be the one to save her.

Not enough to delay a rescue mission, but I have plans for Scott. Fucker's going to eat lead.

Another twenty minutes pass before Mitzy and her team are set. Like Doc Summers mentioned, in addition to finding Kaye, Mitzy's testing the operational readiness of her team.

Not unlike the Guardians, they're required to be ready to move on a moment's notice. Nearly all of our missions require tech support on the fly.

Already, her technicians scour CCTV footage along PCH-1.

"You ready?" Mitzy strolls over to where I'm tied to the wall.

"As I'll ever be. I can't thank you enough." I gesture at the room and the array of technology before me.

"Listen up, everyone." Mitzy claps her hands and the room falls silent. "CJ and Sam are working another issue. I'll fill them in when we have something actionable. Our mission is to find Kaye and build out a package to bring her home." Mitzy turns to me. "Zeb's going to tell us what happened, then we're going to work our magic." She gives a nod, telling me to go ahead.

The room falls silent except for the humming of the computers and the whirring of the fans cooling the massive computing power gathered in this room.

I take in a breath and begin.

"We left *Insanity*…" I leave off why we left and a sharp pain stabs at my heart. If I had more restraint and hadn't been so eager to get Kaye in bed, she would still be safe. "Drove a mile or so when I picked up on a car following us. It was Scott and he ran us off the road. He attacked me, but I trussed him up like the pig he is. Our cell phones went over the cliff with the cars; we were lucky to make it out the rear window, wasn't thinking of phones. I wanted to walk to HQ, but Kaye saw a car approaching. We waved it down, not realizing who it was. Alder got out of his car, seemed like he was going to help, then pulled a gun and shot me. Next, he's dragging Kaye into the car, then cutting Scott loose. Don't remember much after that. I passed out. Got to my feet. Next I knew, Brady and Booker were there."

"The only thing we have to work on is the car is a black Audi with California plates." Mitzy shakes her head. "Locate all potential areas where CCTV might have footage along PCH-1. He and Scott have to have some kind of relationship that goes beyond casual friends or a professional relationship. The question is, what ties them together? You mentioned Scott deferred to Dean Alder?"

"Like a beta to an alpha. It was weird." While my memories of that night remain fuzzy, some things are crystal clear. The first is the fear rimming Kaye's eyes as the dean dragged her into the car. The second was the sickening way Scott deferred to Dean Alder.

"I'd say." Mitzy shakes her head.

"They thought this through." I tip my head back against the mattress. "Scott knew exactly where we would be. I don't know if he intended on driving us off the road, but it's clear he was there to get Kaye. Dean Alder had to be nearby to provide an assist. It's the only thing that makes sense, but what do we do now?"

Mitzy and I exchange looks for a long moment before she speaks again. "I want everything on both Scott Parker and Dean Alder, from the moment they took their first breaths to what happened two nights ago. Find a connection. Find that car. We need to know where they would take Kaye. Where would they feel safe..." She taps her chin as her team gets to work.

Something from the last time we met to discuss Scott makes my blood run cold.

"Mitzy, the women who filed the complaints against Scott. They disappeared. Are there any who filed complaints against Alder?"

"Good question. Let's see if anyone from the vet school

submitted any complaints against the dean. Anything suspicious, we track it down."

I nod, feeling a renewed sense of purpose as we work on a plan of action.

Mitzy and her tech team get to work. Some of them focus on CCTV footage. Others hack into student records at UC Davis. My teammates close in around me, lending silent support.

Until her team finds something, we have little to do. Can't build out an operational plan when we don't have anything to go on.

With every passing minute, my anxiety grows. We're losing precious time. Time I'm not sure Kaye has left before Scott decides she's a liability.

Or worse.

All of a sudden, there's commotion as one of Mitzy's tech guys shouts that he found something on the CCTV footage. All eyes turn to him as he puts the footage on every screen in the room.

"Fucking-A." Brady whistles in awe. "We got him."

"Not yet." Mitzy rushes to her technician's workstation. "Follow that car as far as you can. Trace the plates. I need anything you can get. Track it down to the sixth degree." She spins around and looks at me in victory.

The atmosphere in the room shifts from anxiousness to determination as her team works their magic.

"Won't be long now." Brady stands on the opposite side of my bed from where Booker twists on the stool. "We'll kit up with full tactical gear. All the bells and whistles. As soon as we have a location, we roll."

I bite my tongue as my teammates acknowledge what Brady says.

"Boys…" Mitzy joins us with a grin on her face. "We've got him. They're headed to Deadwood; an abandoned town three hours away from here."

With renewed strength, I sit up in bed. "You bring her back to me. As for Scott, I want him alive."

"We've got your back." Brady squeezes my shoulder. "Bravo, to the bullpen. Gear up and wheels-up in sixty. We're bringing Zeb's woman home."

I clear my throat and the room falls silent. "Thanks." It's all I can manage, too choked up with emotion, and too short of breath to say anything else.

Except, I wish I wasn't tethered to a damn wall.

THIRTY-TWO

Zeb

Hours later, I sit in my hospital bed, growing more and more anxious by the second, waiting for my teammates to report in.

They arrive in Deadwood, an abandoned mining town in the high desert of California near Redstone Valley. It's a desolate and eerie place, heavy with dust and sand. Light on people. I imagine I'm with my teammates, where the only sound is the faint whispering of wind against the rocky cliffs.

"Bravo in position." Brady's voice sounds loud and clear. Not a hint of static. The display from his headset is likewise clear. Shades of green fill the monitor as his night vision goggles scan the small ghost town.

"Copy that." Mitzy peers at the screen closest to me. Then she turns to me. "What do you think?"

"Check for thermal signatures." I wait while Brady and the others adjust their HUDs to incorporate thermal imaging into the feed they send to us.

"We're splitting up." Brady keeps us informed.

My teammates split up to search for Kaye in the various buildings that make up the abandoned mining camp. There's only the four of them. I'm stuck in a hospital bed and Alec's yet to report in from his leave.

The main structure is a large, two-story building, made from crumbling brick and mortar.

"Signs of recent activity." Booker's voice comes through. "Footprints, cigarette butts, and discarded beer cans." He shows us signs of life, but the building remains frustratingly empty.

With the thermal imaging imposed over the infrared, we see the green bones of the main building but not the reddish glow of people inside.

"They must be holding her elsewhere." I scratch my head and rub my eyes. Fatigue pulls at me. It's my body demanding rest, but I won't sleep until Kaye's safe.

In addition to four screens streaming live footage from my teammates' HUDs, a swarm of Mitzy's tiny dragonfly drones infiltrate the space. They slip through cracks and explore beyond what Bravo can see with their augmented vision.

All the windows of the main building are covered with plywood. Seems a strange thing to do, but I suppose it keeps the sand and grit out of the interior. There's little rain in Redwood valley.

"I'm getting nothing," Brady reports in.

"Same here." Rafe updates Brady on what he and Hayes find. They search several outer buildings that are in the process of being reclaimed by nature.

"Same for the dragonflies." Mitzy pulls at her chin. "I have no heat signatures. And no sign of the Audi."

My chest tightens and my gut sinks.

"Orders?" Brady asks.

"Return to base." She turns to me. "Sorry, Zeb, but she's not there."

"Then where the fuck did they take her?"

"I don't know, but we'll find her."

Brady and the others leave behind the empty shell of what used to be a bustling mining camp. There may be signs of life, but no sign of the one person's life that means the most to me.

"What now?" I twist on the bed, needing to do something—

anything—to find Kaye. "We've wasted an entire day." It's been three since she was taken.

"I'll find her." Mitzy blows out a puff of air.

"And you need to rest." Doc Summers enters the room. She watched everything from the doorway, but when we came up empty-handed, she moved purposely into the room.

Toward me.

Her patient.

"Sorry, Zeb, but have faith. Guardians never fail, and right now, that means I need to take care of my patient and get you back to fighting strength." Doc Summers turns her attention to Mitzy. "I need you to either clear the room, or I need to move him out."

"I'm staying." No fucking way is she pulling me from the action. If I can't be with my team, I want to be right beside Mitzy.

"You need rest if you're going to rejoin your team when they go out again."

"Excuse me?" I do a double take, wondering if I heard her correctly.

"You're healing faster than I thought." She sets to work, checking my vitals, and changing the bandages on my chest.

"What are you saying?"

"I'm saying, do as your doctor says. Get some rest and there's a small chance you can go out with your team next time instead of watching from the sidelines."

"But I thought you said weeks?"

"I said you should recover for two weeks, but if you did what I said—to the letter—I might let you out in a few days. Do you want to save your girl?"

"Hell yes." There's no hesitation in my voice.

"Well, then you're lucky I'm the one who stitched you back together. That bullet didn't do as much damage as it could have done. It nicked a blood vessel, which bled into your chest and caused your lung to collapse. We stitched up the blood vessel, drained the blood, and your lung's reinflated. Your breath sounds are clear and equal. There's no sign of fresh bleeding, which means the operation is a success. You'll get winded easier than you might otherwise, but there's no reason I can't let you back out into the field." She pauses, then adds. "It's a good thing Guardians heal fast."

"We'll leave our gear here and continue back at HQ. That way he can get some rest." Mitzy turns to me and lifts a finger. "I'm not giving up. We will find her." With that, she claps her hands and gets the attention of her team.

In less than a minute, they clear the room, leaving me alone with Doc Summers.

"Here, this will help you sleep." Doc Summers injects me with a painkiller and an antibacterial agent that will help speed up the healing process. Then she hands me the inspirometer. "Do the work. Rest. Work on your lung. I'll check in on you through the night."

Under her intense scrutiny, I dutifully lift the device to my mouth and inhale. For the first time, all three balls lift within their tubes and hang there for a few seconds before I can no longer hold them in place.

"Nice improvement." She places an empty urinal beside the bed. As I'm tied to the wall by the tubing snaking from my chest, I'm effectively a prisoner and bed bound. "Now, get some sleep. I'll see you in the morning."

"Yes, Doc." I dutifully breathe in and lift the blue balls like a good little patient.

Skye rolls her eyes, then leaves me alone, flicking off the switch on her way out. That's another thing I can't reach with the way I'm tethered to the wall.

And to my chagrin, with the darkness and whatever she put in my IV, I go out like a light.

Throughout the night, my dreams fill with everything Kaye— her smiling face and gentle laughter fill my dreams. When morning comes, I feel ten times better. Nowhere near normal, but getting there.

As if waiting for me to wake, a soft rap on the door pulls my attention from the inspirometer to the door. Not only do I get all three balls to rise to the top, but my breath's strong enough to keep them there for thirty seconds.

Definitely a win.

When I look up, CJ saunters into the room. Sam follows on his heels. I'm about to greet them with a grin and show off the amazing progress my body made healing overnight, but the expressions on their faces are grim.

Afraid for the worst, I can't help the next words out of my mouth.

"What's wrong?"

Sam pulls a stool over to the side of my bed and takes a seat.

"What?" I struggle to keep my voice from shaking.

CJ and Sam look at each other, then turn back to me. CJ takes a deep breath before he speaks.

"We found something," he says. "It's not good."

My stomach knots in fear as I wait for him to continue. My heart gallops like a racehorse, faster than ever before, because if it's bad news about Kaye, I don't want to hear it. I force myself to take a few calming breaths before CJ starts speaking again.

"When your team came up empty-handed at Deadwood, I asked Mitzy to locate the other students who lodged complaints against Scott."

"And?"

"They were all reported missing after they graduated from UCSF. Within days of going home."

"I thought we checked that?"

"No. That's the thing." Sam rubs the back of his neck. "We asked Mitzy if any other complaints were filed. She found them. Each girl stayed in his class, passed with flying colors, then graduated. We stopped there because it appeared there was no retaliation against any of the women. Each complaint was rescinded a week before finals, and as I said, all the girls passed his class. We didn't take it further."

"Until last night." CJ paces up and down the length of the room.

"What happened last night?"

"When Deadwood didn't pan out, Mitzy tried contacting the women to see if Scott might have taken them someplace other than

Deadwood." CJ stops at the foot of my bed. His knuckles turn white as he grips the hard plastic of the footboard.

"When she couldn't get a hold of *any* of them, she went digging." Sam grabs the metal rim of the stool and rocks forward. "Like I said, they were all reported missing less than a week after graduation." He leans back with a stony expression.

"How are we just discovering this now?" It's a major fail for Mitzy and her team, if true. "Wouldn't there be a report filed? How was this missed by the authorities?"

"None of the women are locals." The muscles of Sam's jaw bunch. "Their disappearances were reported, but only to local officials. None of the girls lived near each other. Three were out of state. One was from Crescent City, near the Oregon border. Another from San Diego. The last from Needles near the Arizona border. That's six disappearances. All reported. None linked together…" Sam pauses and looks toward me.

"Until now." I don't need him to finish his sentence. I do it for him.

"Mitzy's piecing together what she can from their disappearances, but this looks exactly how it sounds." Sam's lips twist.

"I don't believe in coincidences. We have every reason to believe these men are responsible for the disappearances. We've contacted the FBI to assist."

"I take it that means the BAU is involved?" It's the obvious next step.

The Behavioral Analysis Unit is a division within the FBI focused on serial murders, sexual assaults, kidnappings, and other criminal acts targeting adult victims.

"Correct." Sam nods.

"Where does this leave us?" I don't like the direction this is taking one bit.

"As of an hour ago, a joint task force was formed. Guardian HRS will be acting in an ancillary role, serving as deputy US Marshalls on the task force."

I feel a bit relieved with this news. Although, it solves nothing.

Kaye's still out there. This won't be the first time the Guardians assisted the FBI, and our collaborations are always top-notch. Delta team works with the FBI almost exclusively, taking on missions the FBI can't take on directly, or simply assisting where our unique skillsets come in handy.

"So where does this leave us?" I sit up in bed, needing to move. To do something, and suddenly realize the tether attaching me to the wall is gone.

The chest tube is still stuck in me, but it's attached to a Heimlich valve: a portable device used for transport.

"There's something else." Sam exchanges a look with CJ; it's one of those looks you never want your bosses to share.

"What?"

"Alec's missing." CJ pauses to let that sink in.

"What do you mean—missing?"

Missing is impossible, unless you're like Hayes, who lost both of the embedded trackers every Guardian is implanted with before being allowed to operate.

"He's not the only one." Sam swivels on the stool, expression grim, gaze cast down at the floor.

It's as if he doesn't want to look me in the eye. Which means whatever it is, isn't good. But what could that be…

"Holy fuck." My eyes widen in shock. "Please tell me it's not Barbi."

"Told you he'd figure it out." CJ holds up a hand.

Before I know it, Sam flicks a raggedy button toward CJ, who catches it in the air. CJ pockets the button while rage builds within me.

"How certain are we about that?"

"Considering the threat Scott made on Kaye's roommates, we're treating it as real." Sam's mouth twists. He's not happy.

"Alec would've told me if he was with Barbi." I don't believe them. "He's not the kind of man to keep something like that secret. It could be true, but unrelated?" I say the words, knowing they're wrong. "How certain are we?"

"Both he and Barbi have charges on their credit cards in Vegas.

Same day. Same place. Within minutes of each other. Then nothing. It's too coincidental not to be true."

"But his trackers?"

"His trackers blipped out." CJ pulls at his chin.

"Blipped out?"

"Stopped responding." Sam rubs his temples.

"So, it's not just Kaye they've taken?"

"Afraid not." Sam tugs at his ear.

"Fuck." I lean back in the bed, frustrated and agitated by how helpless I feel. "What now?"

"We find what links the two men together. Use that to find where they take their victims."

"Okay." I take a breath. "Any chance I'm getting out of this place? I want to help. I need to help."

"Actually…" Doc Summers raps on the door and enters with a smile on her face. "I'm going to pull the chest tube, then you're free to go."

"You're kidding?" I don't believe her.

"Would I ever kid a Guardian?" She folds her arms across her chest and shakes her head. "I've learned to be brutally honest. That way, when I say you have to stay, you know I mean it. And when I say you're free to go, you'll pay attention to my discharge orders so that you're not right back in one of my hospital beds." She looks at CJ and Sam. "Gentlemen, if you don't mind?"

"Not at all." Sam pushes the stool back and stands. He moves out of Doc Summers's way and stands against the wall with CJ while Doc Summers lifts my hospital gown and removes the bandages over the chest tube. "Now, I want you to take in a deep breath and hold it."

"Why?"

Doc Summers just gives me a look but doesn't explain herself further. I dutifully suck in a breath and hold it. While I do, she yanks the chest tube out from between my ribs.

"The stitches come out in five days. He can operate, but…" She huffs a soft laugh and puts away her suture kit. "Who am I kidding.

Just try to take things easy. I know you won't, but maybe try not to lead the charge? Let your Bravo buddies support you."

"Hell, I'll do whatever you tell me to do as long as I can get out of this bed and get to work."

"You're free." She places a new bandage over my side.

"Thanks, Doc." I turn to Sam and CJ. "Am I really free to operate?"

"Only because she says." CJ folds his arms over his chest. "If it were up to me, I'd give it two weeks, but we've got work to do. We'll take you to the war room."

No doubt, Mitzy and her team are deep at work figuring out what connection ties Scott and the dean together.

THIRTY-THREE

Kaye

I LAY ON THE COLD, HARD FLOOR IN THE CORNER OF THE ROOM, trying to ignore the chill that seeps into my bones. I've lost track of how long I've been here. All I know is that it's been far too long.

Day and night have no meaning anymore. Time passes in a never-ending cycle of boredom, restless sleep, and sprinkles of intense fear whenever Scott or Dean Alder come into the room to check on me.

If I go by the number of times I've been fed, I'm on day three. Maybe four?

And I'm completely, and utterly, alone with my thoughts.

The only sound is my breathing and the occasional drip of water from somewhere in the concrete walls. Then there's the creak of a floorboard on the other side of the door which precedes a visit from either Scott or the dean.

Like Pavlov's dogs, I'm conditioned to that sound. It sends tendrils of fear clawing their way deep into my heart, where they twist and writhe until I can't breathe. My mind races with questions. Where am I? What do they want with me? Why haven't they raped me? Killed me? How can I get out of here?

Will I die alone?

After everything they've done, there really are only two options.

They either kill me or I escape.

There's no way they'll ever let me go. They can't afford what I'll say to the authorities.

Death or escape.

Those are my options.

They come every few hours to either bring food and water, or take me to the small bathroom to relieve myself. I hate that the most because they stand in the hall, forcing me to keep the door open while I pee. It's degrading and dehumanizing.

But today, something feels off. It's in the air. In the way this house creaks. It's in the weight of my fear as I listen to other sounds. Scott and Dean are anxious about something, arguing about what to do with two hostages held captive somewhere else.

When Scott brings a cup of water, he looks at me with regret, almost as if he's sorry.

"Please, you don't have to do this."

He's done vile things to me, but he may be the only one to save me from Dean Alder.

"Please, I'll do whatever you want. I was wrong to leave you. Wrong to question you. I'll stay. I'll behave. I'll do whatever you say, but please… Please, don't let him hurt me."

Dean Alder wants me.

It's the one constant that gives me hope I may actually survive, but the look on his face hardens as my hope shines. It's as if he can read my mind and knows that I lie.

"Don't." Scott shoves the water toward me. "It's too late for that."

Is it my imagination, or is there the faintest regret in his words?

I feel more helpless than ever before.

My thoughts turn to escape, but my rational mind shoots those thoughts down. There's no way out of here without help. I need Scott to see me as someone he still cares about; if that was ever the case in the first place. Or pray Zeb finds me before it's too late—

before Scott and Dean Alder make good on whatever they've been arguing about.

When I do sleep, Zeb is in my dreams, calling out words of comfort and strength. Those words become a mantra.

Don't give up. You will survive. You'll make it out of here alive.

"Thank you." I take the water from Scott with shaky hands, gulping it down because I have no way to know when I might get more.

Suddenly, the air shifts. We're no longer alone. The dean stands in the doorway, armed with a gun pointed directly at me.

"Time to go. You're coming with us."

"Coming? Where?" I turn to Scott, pleading for my life.

But he grits his teeth and squeezes his eyes shut. "I thought we were moving her in the morning?" His voice grinds the words, spitting them out with barely restrained fury.

"Change of plans." Alder waves the gun. "Get her ready to move." Eyes narrowing, the man is evil incarnate. When he smiles, it's not comforting.

It's terrifying.

Scott makes me afraid, but Dean Alder shows me true evil exists in this world. My world has become a very strange place when I look to Scott to protect me from the dean.

Scott releases me from the chains that bind me. They fitted me with a wide belt and collar. A strap connects them together, and two locks secure them. One at the back of my neck. The other in the small of my back. Which makes it impossible to free myself, even if I knew the combinations.

When I'm in the room, chains secure me to bolts on the floor. Thick leather cuffs circle my wrists and they lock those too.

Scott helps me out of the room, barely touching my arm. He stands outside the bathroom, door open, as I relieve myself, then guides me down the stairs and to the back door. Before we exit, he secures my hands behind my back.

We move swiftly through a dark path in the woods, ultimately emerging at a small field where a Cessna waits in the darkness. We board the Cessna and Dean Alder orders Scott to sit with me in the back seat.

Before I know it, we're taking off into the night.

If I knew fear before, it's nothing compared to what I feel now. Not only is there no escape from this living hell, there's no way Zeb, or his Guardian brothers, can find me now.

We fly for what seems like hours before landing in pitch blackness at a small airfield. There, we refuel, then we're back in the air again.

More time passes. The droning of the plane's engine vibrates my teeth and there's nothing to see outside the windows. No lights. No cities. Just blackness. Then we descend again.

This airport is smaller than the last. I don't know how the dean knows where to land. Everything is black on black.

But we do land. We land with a bump, then a jarring ride over uneven ground as we brake and come to a stop.

"The truck's out there," Dean Alder says. "I have to stow the plane. Pick me up at the hangar."

Without acknowledging what the dean says, Scott opens the door and hauls me out of the plane like a piece of baggage.

"Where are you taking me?" I stumble out of the plane and turn to Scott, desperation in my voice.

But he remains silent.

Dean Alder stays with the plane, driving it toward something that looks more like an oversized shed than a hangar.

Scott takes my arm and leads me toward a waiting truck. "Everything will be okay."

It's the first time he's spoken to me with kindness.

I cling to those words, hoping desperately that he's right, but in my heart, I know it's a lie.

He makes me climb inside the truck where I sit in the middle of the bench seat. Then Scott drives toward a hangar where the dean waits to be picked up after stowing the small Cessna inside.

He climbs into the passenger seat, sandwiching me between himself and Scott.

The truck rumbles along a dirt road, the darkness deepening around us. Stars twinkle above, more than I've ever seen in my life, which is bad.

Very bad.

We're nowhere near civilization. Nowhere near city lights that make the sky glow and hide the stars. The moon is only a sliver in the sky, making the darkness the deepest black.

After a few more hours, we come to a stop at yet another small cabin tucked away in the woods.

Dean Alder steps out of the truck and heads inside without a word. Scott helps me out of the truck and then follows after the dean. My body quivers with fear as I look around. While I can't see much in the darkness, it feels even more remote than the previous cabin.

I take a deep breath and look around for anything that might give me some kind of clue as to my location, but there's nothing.

I step inside this new cabin with trepidation, my heart racing as I take in my surroundings. It's dark and musty. Dean Alder turns on a light, revealing a small living space with two bedrooms, a kitchen, and a large, stone fireplace at one end of the room. Next to that fireplace is a large, steel crate for a dog.

"Put her in." Dean Alder gestures to the crate and I balk. When Scott doesn't immediately force me into the dog crate, the dean's eyes narrow. "Do we have a problem?" He taps his gun against his leg as he speaks, emphasizing his point.

I swallow hard as I try to process what's happening. Fear engulfs me like never before.

Scott steps forward and speaks up. "I'm not putting her in a cage."

"Why not? It's secure."

"I'll chain her to my bed." His voice is softer than before. More timid, but he doesn't back down. "She's not going anywhere."

"You take risks you shouldn't." Dean Alder points to my feet. "You want her chained to your bed instead of the crate? Then give me her shoes and strip her down." He turns his hawkish gaze on me. "If she tries to escape, she'll die out there; either from exposure, wolves, or bears."

"She won't run." Scott looks directly into my eyes with an intensity that takes my breath away. His gaze is both comforting and threatening all at once; it's like he's saying *trust me*.

But do I dare?

THIRTY-FOUR

Zeb

___

The walk to the Omega Facility, leaves me out of breath. Doc Summers may have released me from the hospital, but it's clear I'm not at the top of my game. When we walk into the conference room, it's a buzz of activity, with the FBI and Mitzy's team working side by side.

Monitors cover every wall, displaying photographs of each girl. They look so young and vibrant, filled with promise and hope for a bright future; all of which is gone. It's heartbreaking and infuriating all at once.

"We need to find what connects these girls." Mitzy stands at the front of the room, directing the combined efforts of Guardian HRS and the FBI. "Anything other than they were students in Scott's class and lodged complaints against him. Anything can point us in the right direction, so keep an open mind."

The general noise level in the room picks up as everyone gets back to work. Monitors cover every wall. Six in a row display pictures of the missing girls.

When Mitzy notices me, she gives a jerk of her chin, then waves for me to join her at the front of the room. Sam and CJ follow as we wade through the press of people.

"Nice to see you out of bed." Mitzy flashes a pretty smile.

"Good to be on my feet. Heard the FBI was called in."

"We stumbled upon something Scott and Alder have tried hard to hide." Her lips purse, but she says nothing else.

"I need more than that."

"Working theory is serial kidnappers or serial killers. Either way, it doesn't look good. And now that Alec and Barbi are missing…" She doesn't complete her thought, leaving me reeling.

"What can I do?" I feel helpless standing around doing nothing.

"For now, I'd say head to your bullpen. Get your gear ready."

"Where's my team?"

"Bravo's back," CJ answers instead of Mitzy. "They're on mandatory downtime until we spin you guys up again. I agree with Mitzy. Pack your gear and you might as well rest while you can."

In his own way, CJ lets me know he noticed how out of breath I got during the short walk over.

"Copy that." I turn to leave, but my feet don't move right away. There's too much going on in this room for me to walk away without processing it somehow.

"Okay, we've combed through every detail of these women's lives," Mitzy mutters to anyone listening. "Student records, social media, web searches, you name it. But we haven't been able to find any direct links between the missing girls."

"Professor Parker and Dean Alder didn't just wake up one day and decide they were going to work together. How are they connected?" I scratch at the bandage over my side, then stop, not wanting to irritate the wound.

"We're looking into that." One of the FBI agents leans in close.

"What about that grant they share?"

"Which one is that?" The FBI profiler looks at me.

"They share a research grant to study the decomposition of humans and animals. I don't know how something like that works, but it seems like a good place to dump a body." Sometimes, I hate this job. Didn't take but a second to make that leap. There's simply too much evil in this world.

"I had the same thought," Mitzy jumps in. "But that decomp

farm is highly regulated. It would be like shitting where you live. I already ruled it out."

"Maybe we need to take another look." The profiler pulls up information on the decomp farm as we watch.

"You start messing with their research and it's basically sending up a red flag. The last thing we want is for them to know we're onto them."

"I think they're aware we're onto them." I brush my fingers over the bandage on my side. "They didn't bother to ensure I was dead, and they're smart enough to know what we do. We are the Hostage Rescue Specialists, and right now, they have three of our team: Kaye, Barbi, and Alec. Which means…" I massage my neck. My entire body's a mess of sore muscles.

"Which means, what?" Mitzy props her hands on her hips.

"I don't know. That's your job to figure out, but they've been at this a while."

"What tells you that?" Mitzy cocks her left hip forward. She hates being challenged.

"You didn't see the way they interacted." I roll my head to the side and attack a knot of muscle. "It was weird. Dean is the alpha. Scott the beta. Men like that don't just fall into that kind of dynamic. Something triggers it. You've just got to find it."

"Zeb, I love you like a brother," Mitzy says, "and I'm telling you, we're doing everything we can. We will find them, but you look like shit. Pack your gear, then get some shuteye. If we find something, I'll…"

"When you find something," I correct her.

"*When* we find something," she says, "Bravo and Charlie teams will go."

"Charlie?" I look to CJ and Sam.

"The moment Alec went missing, we escalated. This is a two-team mission now." Sam's gruff voice breaks through the quiet. "I disagree about the decomp farm."

"Why?" Mitzy cocks her head to the side.

"Zeb's right. They have every reason to think we're onto them. I say give them a show." Sam turns to the FBI lead agent.

"What do you say? Do you have a team that can work that angle?"

"Absolutely. It'll take a day, but I can have my people on it at first light."

First light? If Guardian HRS was in charge, we'd have people there within an hour. But I know when to keep my thoughts to myself. We're not in competition with the FBI, and turning this into a pissing contest helps no one.

"Zeb…" Sam clamps a hand on my shoulder. "I want you on this mission. Prep your gear and get some rest." He doesn't mention he'll yank me at the first sign I'm not physically up to it.

"Copy that." I take in a deep breath, look around the room once more, and remind myself these are the best geeks on the planet. If anyone's going to find Kaye—Barbi and Alec too—it'll be someone in this room.

As I take it all in, CJ steps up beside me and speaks quietly so only I can hear him.

"Seriously. Get that rest. Skye was generous letting you out of the hospital. We don't know how long things are going to be like this, but take advantage while you can."

"Heard. Loud and clear."

He's right, of course. If Mitzy's team figures out where these girls were taken there might be a chance we save not only Kaye and Barbi, but maybe one or more of the others might still be alive when we get there.

"I'll be in the bullpen." With that, I execute a sharp about-face and leave Mitzy and her team to their task.

It takes ten minutes to pack my shit, which leaves me spinning my wheels in Bravo's bullpen. I take advantage of my time, hit the showers, then dress out in my black tactical fatigues. Tired and strung out, I sling my hammock in my personal gear locker, and immediately fall asleep as the grim realization sets in.

Scott and Alder have been murdering young women for years and no one noticed because they picked their victims well: women who lived far from campus, and none near any of the others.

It's brilliant, in a macabre kind of way.

But what links the men together?

When I wake, I'm calmer and more determined than ever to find Kaye and put an end to this nightmare.

I'm so lost in my thoughts, I don't notice when the bullpen lights flick on and off. The silence is broken by a quiet tap on the locker door.

"Who's there?" Instantly alert, I'm on my feet in less than a second.

"It's Mitzy. Permission for a female to invade the oh-so private bastion of male testosterone?"

"Give it a rest. We know you come in here all the time when we're not here."

The unwritten rule about no women in the bullpen isn't one that's followed very well. At least Mitzy has a reason to tinker with our stuff. She's always testing out some new prototype or another.

"So, that's a yes?"

"Yes, Mitzy."

When Mitzy strolls in, her eyes glow in victory. "We found something." She hands me her tablet. "We're not sure where it'll take us, but it's a start."

"What am I looking at?" The screen's filled with a bunch of little kids. "An old school photo?"

"Second grade, to be exact. The two boys on the far left are none other than Scott Parker and Robert Jones Alder. You were right. They've known each other their entire lives. Swipe left."

I find myself staring at older kids, mostly boys, in military uniforms.

The cadets are in their mid-teens, most with pimples and wispy peach fuzz on their chins. They wear green flight suits with yellow trim and mirrored sunglasses. There's a small prop-driven plane in the background.

"What organization is this?"

"At first, I thought it was Civil Air Patrol, but it's not. That is a private aviation club. That's Dean Alder, and that's Professor Parker." She points to two of the boys.

"How does this help?"

"Because the dean happens to own a plane, and I have the tail number."

"And…?" I feel it in my gut, that adrenaline surge right before everything comes together.

"Guess who failed to file a flight plan?"

"You're kidding."

It never ceases to amaze me how the tiniest thing can crack a case wide open.

"Guess he hasn't kept up with technology." Mitzy rocks back with a smug look on her face. "He landed at a small airfield in Oregon. Don't know where he started from. I assume, and you know how I feel about that, but I assume it was a farmer's field and not an airstrip, but he landed at a small, rural airport and took off after refueling. I tracked him from there."

"I'm going to kiss you if the next words out of your mouth are you know where they landed."

"You said it. Not me." She covers her mouth, but her eyes twinkle.

"Don't give a damn." I pull her hand from her mouth, cup her cheeks, and lay one on her. It's fat, messy, and sloppy as shit.

And I don't give a flying fuck she's married to a rock star.

With her smile growing even wider, she makes a show of wiping her mouth, but it's all in fun.

"Wheels-up in thirty. Charlie and the rest of Bravo are already locked and loaded, we're just waiting on you."

"Why didn't you tell me sooner?" I grab my things and rush out of my gear locker.

"Because they're still fueling the bird, and I wanted to tell you myself. We've got them, Zeb. We found your girl." She gestures to the door. "And I've got a car waiting to take you to your team."

"Fuck yeah."

She steps back as I race out the door.

I'm coming, Kaye. I'm coming for you.

THIRTY-FIVE

Zeb

Bravo team moves like death toward the small mountain cabin; our steps cautious and measured. Charlie team fans out behind us. With them, plus five of the Rufi, Mitzy's robotic dogs, we set up a perimeter defense no man can pass.

I admit I wasn't a fan of the Rufi when they were first introduced, but I'm definitely a convert now. It relieves some of the stress knowing the robots monitor any escape Scott and Alder might attempt.

My breaths come easily, slow and steady. I may not be up at fighting strength, but I'm not a complete liability. We did make concessions. I wanted to be first man through the door, but I'll hang back. Hayes will be first, followed by me.

"Bravo in position," Brady reports our progress to Command. Not that Command doesn't know our precise location and isn't following our every step through our HUDs.

The wind disturbs the needles of towering pines and the branches sway far above us. Overhead, the sun claims dominion in a cloudless, blue sky. It's absolutely beautiful; in stark contrast to the decrepit cabin sitting in the middle of the field. Nothing moves in the woods, except for the occasional crack of a branch or the rustling of leaves as squirrels scamper through the underbrush.

"Hold, Bravo. Dragonflies deploying," CJ orders us to a halt as Charlie team deploys a fleet of the tiny drones.

"Holding." Brady responds for the team.

Bravo team surveys the expansive clearing around the cabin from the tree line. That's going to make it difficult, if not impossible, to approach during the daylight without being seen.

It's a toss-up between rushing in now, announcing our presence, or waiting it out until we can approach at night and keep the element of surprise.

My gut wants to charge in. The thought of Kaye enduring another minute with those monsters brings bile rising to the back of my throat, but waiting gives us the greatest chance of a successful rescue.

A small dirt road runs up to the cabin, and a truck parks out front, obscuring our view of the front door. The tracks are fresh, less than a day old. Someone's here, but we won't move until we know exactly how many people are inside and where they're located. That's up to Mitzy and her drones.

"Three adults inside." Mitzy sends us the infrared feed from one of the drones. "Two in the front room. A third in the back bedroom on the left. Smaller, presumably female."

My heart races. She's alive. Kaye's alive. But where are Alec and Barbi?

"Bravo…" From the tone of CJ's voice, I know I won't like what comes next. "No go for approach. I repeat. No go for approach."

Son of a bitch.

I curse under my breath, but it's a good call. It's the right call.

"Copy that," Brady answers for our team.

Tex, leader of Charlie team, replies in the affirmative as well. "Good copy."

"Sorry," CJ says, "but it's too risky to approach in the daylight. We wait for night."

So fucking close.

But I'm a trained operative, and the call is sound.

"Orders?" Brady checks for commands.

"The Rufi are on patrol. The dragonflies will alert if they exit the house. Set up sniper positions and wait for the call."

"Understood." Brady waves to us and we fade back from the edge of the clearing, becoming one with the forest.

Using hand signals, he directs us to spread out and position ourselves in an arc around the front of the cabin.

Charlie team will watch the rear, and the Rufi will do what they do best.

I snuggle into a depression in the ground and sight my weapon on the front door. With the shutters drawn, we're blind to the movements of Scott and Alder, but only in the visual spectrum.

Mitzy feeds us everything the dragonflies see and maps out the interior of the cabin.

Meanwhile, we wait.

For hours.

But eventually, the sun sets and darkness falls.

We continue to wait, however, until we're in the thick of night. I blink against fatigue, but there's enough adrenaline flowing through my veins to push back my exhaustion.

The smaller figure in the back room, Kaye, hasn't moved all day. Scott and Alder, on the other hand, pace the length of the cabin. The IR feed isn't as discrete as our night vision goggles, but it's clear the men alternate between arguing and sitting still.

"Bravo One—report." CJ's voice snaps me to immediate alertness.

"Ready to roll."

"Mission's a go. Repeat. Mission's a go." CJ shouts through the comms and I snap to full alert.

Time for Bravo team to do what we do best.

Brady gives the signal and we cross the open space of the meadow, blending in with the shadows. We move as a unit, a single organism with our weapons raised and ready to fire.

Brady leads the way, followed by the rest of our team. Brady and Booker creep up the steps of the front porch, careful not to make a sound. Rafe follows with a ram.

I move into position with an enhanced night vision scope mounted to my rifle. I train my weapon on the door.

Rafe holds the ram against the wood door, and nods to Brady, signaling he's ready.

Brady holds three fingers in the air.

The countdown starts.

Three-Two-One.

Rafe takes a deep breath and slams the ram against the door. It splinters under the power of the ram, instantly snapping open with a loud crack that echoes through the night.

The first few seconds of an assault are critical. We have to get inside before Scott and the dean can react.

Hayes is first man in. He crosses the threshold and takes up position against the wall, aiming his weapon at the man on the right, who happens to be Dean Alder.

I'm right on his heels, but instead of moving into the main room, I shift left.

It puts me closest to the hall leading toward the room where Kaye's being held. We take care of hostiles first, but I'm not wasting a second more when it comes to Kaye. I train my weapon on Scott, and slow my breathing, ready to take the shot.

Brady and Booker fold in behind me while Rafe guards our backs.

We catch Scott and the dean by surprise, and by surprise I mean Scott's no beta to Dean Alder's alpha. He's an omega, and we catch him performing fellatio on the dean.

The men cry out in surprise. Dean Alder springs back, tucking his dick into his pants as Scott reaches for a weapon.

"Don't do it." I give him a chance—a choice really—we need one of them alive.

But only one.

There's no sign of Alec or Barbi, which is something no one voices out loud. Not that we need to.

We'll sort that out later.

"On the ground." Brady barks orders at the men. "Hands behind your head."

Scott barely moves, but it's enough. His fingers twitch moments before he makes a fatal mistake. The man lunges for his gun. I shoot first and my bullet hits him in the center of his chest.

Scott's eyes widen in surprise, but then he's dead before he drops.

Dean Alder makes the same mistake. Rafe shoots him in the shoulder; a nonlethal shot. With Scott dead, we need the dean alive.

The dean screams as the gunshot echoes through the room. With Scott eliminated and the dean contained, I move deeper into the building, weapon raised and ready to fire if I have to.

But there's only one person left.

Hayes follows on my heels.

Behind us, Brady orders Dean Alder face down on the ground. I don't envy him the pain he's about to endure once Brady and Booker truss him up and neutralize any threat he poses.

I move quickly toward the bedroom where Kaye's being held, taking point, weapon raised and ready. My heart races as I approach the door, but I keep my breathing level and narrow my focus to the job at hand.

Hayes and I exchange a look, communicating our intent without the need for words. I jiggle the doorknob, but it's locked. I take a step back while Hayes moves into position.

I give him three fingers and count down silently. Hayes kicks down the door.

The room is dark, but Kaye's there, lying on the bed, huddled against the bedframe, eyes wide with fear, but very much alive. When she sees me, her fear fades and overwhelming relief follows.

"Kaye." I rush to her side.

She reaches for me and her eyes fill with tears. Disgusting leather wraps around her throat, her waist, and nasty D-rings anchor the chains that bind her.

"It's okay. You're safe." I pull her into my arms while Hayes works to free her from the chains.

Once she's loose, I scoop her into my arms and carry her out of the room.

"It's over, luv." The moment she's in my arms, she trembles and cries uncontrollably. Her entire body shakes.

There's nothing to do about the mess in the living room. Moving as fast as I can, I try to spare her the trauma from having to see Scott's body. Fortunately, she clings to me so tight, tucking her head against my chest, that I make it outside before she can see the mess I made of Scott's chest.

"Any sign of Alec? Barbi?" CJ's tone is gruff, irritated.

He already knows the answer to that. But I get it. We're missing a man and another woman's still at risk. This shit show is far from over. For Kaye, however, the entire nightmare is over.

"We're looking now." Booker marches a wounded Dean Alder outside while Brady, Rafe, and Hayes search for any sign of our missing Bravo team member and Kaye's best friend.

The *thwomp, thwomp, thwomp* of a helicopter's rotors cut through the air. I cradle Kaye close to my chest as I carry her out to the helicopter.

I keep murmuring *I've got you. I've got you,* but the rotor blades drown out my voice. I help Kaye into the helicopter, then hop in beside her. After securing her belt, I strap myself in for the ride back to our staging area. Hayes and Rafe join me, while Brady and Booker stay behind to wait for the FBI task force and turn over custody of the dean to their team.

As the helicopter lifts off, I steal one last glance at the cabin. We still have to find Alec and Barbi, but at least Kaye's out of there.

Lights in the distance wind down the dirt road leading to the cabin. It's the FBI task force coming to search the area for evidence and take over from here.

I'd like to say I can only imagine the horrors she's lived through, but the truth is I've seen far too many victims in my line of work.

She'll need to work through what happened, and navigate the treacherous waters of recovery until she finds a new kind of normal. Until then, phantoms of this trauma will linger. Left alone for a moment, we find ourselves in a bubble of relative quiet.

"I knew you'd find me." She places her palm against my chest.

"I never gave up hope." She curls against me and her breathing slows.

Finally, Kaye closes her eyes. I whisper a prayer of thanks, grateful we got to her in time.

Thankful, we got her out alive.

THIRTY-SIX

Kaye

After my rescue, Zeb takes me to a small church where the Guardians set up Command and Control.

"They're going to ask you a ton of questions." Zeb guides me inside, palm lightly pressed against the small of my back. All the pews inside the church are shoved to the center, separating the worship hall into two distinct spaces.

On the left, Mitzy and her technical team work around monitors. On the other side, men and women, wearing dark suits, look a little lost.

The moment I enter, there's a pause in conversation as everyone looks up from what they're doing. It makes me want to shrink in on myself. I don't enjoy being the center of attention, especially with this many people I don't know.

"Are you doing okay?" Zeb rubs his hand against the small of my back, providing what reassurance he can.

If he only knew how much it means to me that he's by my side at all. I don't think he understands how deep my feelings for him run.

"I'm okay. Why is everyone looking at me?"

"You represent the success of the mission, but there's something you need to know." The tone of his voice sends a lick of fear down my spine.

"What?" I rub my arms, feeling suddenly chilled.

"There's a room where you'll be debriefed. I'll tell you there."

There? Whatever it is, he doesn't want to tell me in front of all of these people. I both love and hate that consideration, because now, all I want is to know what he needs to tell me.

Zeb steers me through the crowd, keeping people away. Mitzy looks up and moves with us toward the front of the worship hall. We head down a narrow hallway until Zeb stops in front of a nondescript door. He opens the door and ushers me into a small room with clean, white walls, bare except for a cross hung prominently on the wall. Inside, Sam and CJ stand once they see it's me.

"How are you doing?" CJ approaches and takes my hands in his. He gives a light squeeze, a polite substitute for a hug. Sam follows suit.

"We're glad you're back with us." Sam gestures to a chair. "If it's okay, we have a few questions."

"Sure?" I take a seat and place my hands on my knees, nervous beneath the scrutiny of the leaders of Guardian HRS.

Sam looks at Zeb. "Have you told her?"

"I didn't want to in front of the others." Zeb gives a sharp shake of his head.

"Tell me, what?" A swarm of butterflies takes flight in my stomach, making me feel anxious and nauseous at the same time.

Zeb sits next to me. He takes my hand. His gaze drops to the floor as he tugs in a deep breath. Then he lifts his gaze to meet mine. His jaw bunches, but he doesn't make me wait for long.

"It's about Barbi." Flat, with no emotion, those three words take the bottom out of my world.

"What about Barbi?" My heart sinks like a stone while the room spins around me.

Zeb takes in a deep breath, then speaks slowly, carefully, picking his words with great care. "She's missing."

"Missing?"

"She and Alec went to Vegas." Zeb keeps his voice level, with no emotion. "Then they disappeared."

"But that can't be." My entire body shakes with fine tremors.

"We don't know where they are, or what they're up against," Sam speaks, his tone grave, and far more serious than I like. "We're doing everything we can to find her. Our concern is Scott took her in retaliation."

Zeb wraps his arm around me, pulling me close. His warmth and comfort provide a small bit of relief from the news about Barbi. I can't believe she's missing.

"What did Scott say?" I lay my head against Zeb's shoulder as tears fall from my eyes.

"He didn't make it." Zeb's tone remains flat.

"Didn't make it?" I know what Zeb means, but it's too much to process.

"We're questioning Alder, but he's not talking." Sam's grim tone speaks to far more than the dean not talking.

"I don't understand." But I know all too well what they're trying to tell me.

"We're working the problem," Sam provides reassurance. "Doing everything we can. We will find your friend. The FBI's involved." Sam looks on with a grim expression of sympathy etched on his face before saying anything else.

"The FBI? How does that help?" I look between Sam and CJ, not understanding, but Sam explains.

"More resources. Agents trained in behavioral analysis," Sam answers.

"Kaye, we have every reason to believe you're not Scott and Dean Alder's first victim."

"First?" I clutch my belly and try to process what they're telling me.

"We believe they've been working together for years," Sam says. "And we identified several potential victims."

"Several?" The hits keep coming. "But you're going to find Barbi?" I look to Zeb, begging. "Right?"

"We won't stop until we find her." Zeb wraps his arms around me, providing the strength I need. "But if you could answer a few questions, it would really help."

The others in the room fall silent for a moment, but then the questions begin.

I spend hours answering their questions until they've wrung everything out of me. Finally, I'm released and head home with Zeb, Brady, and Booker.

More time passes on the flight back to Guardian HQ. Hours where I snuggle against Zeb.

By the time we reach Guardian HQ, I'm beyond exhausted. My body aches from my time held captive by Scott and Dean Alder, but physical exhaustion is nothing compared to the psychological trauma I endured.

I'm completely unprepared for the wave of emotions that wash over me as we drive through the gates of Guardian HQ. It's a sense of profound relief.

Zeb seems to understand. He comforts me as I hyperventilate and come apart in his arms.

Thoughts of Scott and Dean Alder fill my mind. Their cruelty and the way they treated me like I was an animal.

I don't understand why they took me when neither one of them touched me while I was their prisoner. I suppose I should be grateful for that. I also don't understand why they argued all the time.

Was it about Barbi? Me?

Did I hear anything that might be helpful?

That answer is a sad *No*.

"Almost there." Zeb squeezes me as we pull up outside the temporary quarters Guardian HRS loaned me.

To my surprise, Carmen and Rosalie wait outside.

"Did you text them?" I look up at Zeb with fatigue and a smile.

"Thought you could use your friends."

"Do they know about Barbi?"

"They do."

Brady pulls to a stop and Zeb and I climb out. He hangs back with Brady, pretending they have something to say.

I know the truth.

He's giving me space to reunite with my friends.

"Oh my God." Carmen wraps me in a full body hug. "We've been so worried."

"Are you okay? Do you need to see Skye?" Rosalie hugs me too. "Are you hurt? Injured?"

I don't know what I say. It's a mumbled mess of tears and joy.

"Did they tell you about Barbi?" I pull back and wipe my tears.

"She's tough and if Alec's with her, she's going to be all right." Carmen glances at Zeb. "I'd say it was a PJ and sofa night, but I have a feeling a certain Guardian wants to spend some time alone with you."

I steal a glance at Zeb and catch him staring at me.

Using both hands to wipe my face free of tears, I look at my friend. "You don't mind if I…"

"Girl, he's exactly what you need right now." Rosalie grabs my hands and smiles. "And he's coming this way." She squeezes my hands and bounces a little on her feet. Sharing an excited look with Carmen, they squeal with excitement then take several steps back.

"You look like you need to sleep." Zeb takes my hand in his. "Come, let's get you in bed."

Somehow, I have a feeling me, bed, and Zeb have very little to do with sleep.

He guides me inside the building and I pause on the threshold. After what happened, I'm grateful to be back within the safety of Guardian HQ, but mostly, I feel as if I've come home.

When we reach my quarters, Zeb closes the door behind us. "How about a warm shower? Then bed?"

"We? Or me?" I twist my fingers, incredibly nervous.

"What do you want?"

"I don't want to spend the night alone, but I don't know if I'm ready for anything more than that."

Zeb leans against the wall. "I'd love to stay and hold you through the night."

"And that's it?"

"Not for a lack of interest on my part, but how about we start with that shower? I'll be right out here if you need me." He pats the bed.

"You won't leave, will you?"

"After everything I went through to get you back?" He arches a brow. "Never."

"Isn't that what you do? Rescue people? Eventually you have to leave them behind."

He kicks off from the wall and prowls toward me. "That may be, but I've never done this to one of my rescues."

The temperature in the room rises sharply as Zeb cups my cheek. I lean into his touch, loving the tenderness of his fingers on my skin. What I'm not prepared for is the way his lips crash over mine. Or the way he plunders my mouth with primal power, claiming me as his own as he takes what he wants.

He makes all the bad thoughts in my head disappear.

My entire body ignites with sensation, and all of that sensation courses through me, until it becomes an inescapable ache between my legs.

No one has ever kissed me with such passion, such ferocity, and such overwhelming desire. But as soon as the kiss begins, Zeb takes a step back, chest heaving, pupils blown black by lust. He stares at me, letting the moment stretch, then jerks his head toward the bathroom.

"Go, before I take this too far. Don't make me break a promise before it's even said." His arm sweeps to the side, the message clear.

I hear what Zeb doesn't say. My kidnapping is too recent. My trauma yet to be faced. We need a moment to cool off before finishing what we started on that beach during what feels like another lifetime ago.

I lift my hand to place it against his chest, but draw back at the heat radiating from his body.

"What if this is what I want?"

"You've been through a lot, I don't think…"

"That's the thing. I don't want to think." Without a word, I take his hand, pulse pounding with anticipation. "I just want to feel."

And pretend nothing happened.

If only for a moment.

"Kaye…" His voice turns hoarse as his desire builds. "Are you sure this is what you want? There's no rush. We have our entire lives to…"

"This is not just what I want. It's what I need. Right here. Right now." I lead him into the bathroom and turn on the shower. As the water heats, steam fills the room. His gaze never leaves mine as I reach for the bottom of my shirt and slowly pull it over my head.

His hands grab my hips as he pulls me against him, pressing his hard body against mine.

"You're sure?" He waits for a response, but I can hardly breathe.

I reach out and touch his chest, letting my fingers explore every defined ridge and each sculpted muscle of his chest and abs.

"More than anything in the world."

His lips find mine again, this time gentle and loving. He cups my face, then lets his fingers explore every contour of my face as if burning this moment into his mind.

His fingertips make my skin tingle, but when his lips trail down to my neck, my entire body comes alive.

Zeb slips my bra straps off my shoulders, then unlatches the clasp in back. My bra flutters to the ground between us as first his fingers travel down my body, only to be followed by the heat of his mouth and the roughness of his tongue. He uses his tongue to trace circles around my nipples, making me moan softly and tilt my head back as a surge of pleasure builds within me.

Zeb grabs my butt and yanks me against his body, grinding his hips against mine.

This time, my gasp is filled with delight and anticipation.

His kisses become more feverish as his hands wander freely over my body, exploring every curve as he teases my nipples with flicks of his tongue and nibbles at my neck as moans of pleasure wash through me.

His hands move lower. With his help, I lose my jeans. He slips a hand under the fabric of my panties to gently tease my clit. With each press of his finger, my excitement builds.

Suddenly, he takes a step back. Kicking off his shoes, he removes his shirt and the rest of his clothes. With a grin, he pulls a foil pouch out of the back pocket of his jeans.

My eyes widen at the size of his cock, then he suddenly lifts me into the air and carries me into the shower.

The water is hot on my skin, but his fingertips are hotter as he explores every inch of my body. He bends to kiss my neck, and I melt into the exquisite sensation.

Desire flows through me. My legs tremble. My heart pounds. My breaths surge in and out.

Needing to touch him, I trace my fingers down his back, then sweep around to his chest. Moving down, past an eight-pack of washboard abs, I find what I'm looking for and wrap my fingers around his cock.

His hands tighten around my waist before he shoves me against the wall. A thrill runs through me with the sensation of his hard body pressed against mine.

He kisses me hungrily, the intensity of his desire too much to bear. I arch against him, needing more friction as our bodies slide against each other in perfect harmony.

Zeb opens the foil pack and quickly sheathes himself. Then he grabs one of my legs and wraps it around his hip. The head of his cock presses against my opening.

He pauses and dips his head. "Last chance to back out."

"Never." I loop my arms around his neck and lift off my toes as he wraps my other leg around his hip. With my back pressed against the tile wall, Zeb makes my breath catch as he slides inside of me. Inch by inch, my insides tighten until he's seated fully inside of me.

"You're so damn hot. So fucking tight." He tilts his head back and bites his lower lip as we stay like that for a few moments, but then Zeb rocks forward, going deeper, before pulling out and slamming forward, thrusting deeper and faster as my body responds.

Waves of pleasure crash over me. My body tightens around him as he fills me completely and drowns me in pleasure. I surrender to the sensation and cry out in ecstasy as pleasure takes me to a different realm entirely.

Zeb's not too far behind me. The pace of his thrusts intensify as his climax builds until suddenly, his pleasure peaks, taking him over the edge.

He holds me there, breathing heavily, as the steam from the shower builds all around us. Finally, Zeb sets me back on my feet. He turns off the shower and hands me a towel. After we dry off, he carries me out of the shower and lays me down in bed.

I shiver with the loss of his body's warmth, but he climbs in on the other side of the bed and drags me to him until he can wrap his body around me.

"That was…"

"Yes?"

"Amazing," I whisper softly.

"Most definitely." He holds me close and kisses the tip of my shoulder.

While I've been through a lot over the past few days, I'm determined to put it all behind me. What happened will always be a part of me, but I vow to become a stronger person as a result.

And there's no doubt in my mind I will, just as there's no doubt in my mind the gorgeous man beside me is as deeply in love with me as I am with him.

I take in a deep breath and let it out as the full impact of what happened crashes over me.

Not only did I survive, but I found new friends.

A new home.

I have a chance to start over.

Not many people are that lucky.

With a smile on my face, I close my eyes and dream about a new, brighter life. With our bodies a tangle of limbs, I drift off to sleep in complete bliss.

THIRTY-SEVEN

Kaye

A few days later, I bask in another glorious morning of the best sex of my life that makes my body ache in the best possible way. It's a wonder I'm not walking bowlegged with how much sex we've been having.

As for the sex?

No one has ever fucked me so fiercely. Every kiss, caress, and thrust expertly applied, until I feel Zeb's presence inside every cell of my body. The exquisite warmth of his breaths feed a stream of heat and desire that lick along my skin and ignite a blaze that will never be extinguished.

"You like that?" Zeb looks down at me as he rocks in and out.

"Yes." My fingers dig into his biceps as pleasure spikes within me.

The pressure in my belly grows as he slides in and out, intensifying my pleasure, while delaying his.

It's always like this. He's everywhere, in my body, around my body, above me, below me. Sharing breath as we come together, literally and figuratively.

My insides burn and tighten. Nerve endings sizzle, and it's as if my very soul shakes with the pleasure sparking in my veins.

Our gasps mingle together, twining until they're one and the same. A moan escapes me as my insides tighten and burn.

Zeb falters above me.

"Please don't stop." I wrap my legs around his hips, loving the way he rocks reverently in and out.

It's our second time making love this morning. Unlike the fury and passion of our first coupling, his cadence is slow and unhurried, as if he wants this moment to last.

I agree with that sentiment. I never want to forget how I feel when he's fucking me, or when his lips press against mine.

His breath hitches as he hits a telltale rhythm.

"Do you feel me?" Low and husky, his voice sends licks of flames shooting down my spine.

His invasion within me swells as his cock seems to grow impossibly thicker.

"I feel you." I grip his arms as he holds himself off my chest, loving the slow drag of his cock in and out. I tilt my pelvis, needing to feel him deeper than ever before.

My legs tremble and my breath hitches as he sends me up and over the edge. My orgasm crashes all around me as the pace of his thrusts increase. Zeb chases his release, fucking harder, faster, desperate to join me in pleasure. His body tenses then jerks, as he comes deep inside of me, then he collapses over me, breaths tugging, chest heaving.

"That was…" My entire body feels strung out, tingling everywhere at once. My pussy throbs, part pleasure, part soreness, from the vigor of Zeb's efforts.

"Incredible." Zeb brushes the hair from my forehead and leans down for a kiss.

I don't know how long we stay in bed, but I close my eyes for a moment, then find myself waking up hours later, alone in bed.

Lying on my back, I stare at the ceiling, feeling incredibly and wonderfully alive. When I move my hand to Zeb's side of the bed, the sheets are cold, but his unique scent remains. I roll over and grab his pillow, bringing it close to my chest. Even though he's not here, his presence lingers.

Memories of our passionate morning bring a smile to my face. The way we made love with such intensity, losing ourselves in the other? It was like the rest of the world didn't exist.

We're connected now. On a level I've never experienced with another man.

Lazily, I climb out of bed and stretch, then head to the bathroom to take a long shower.

After getting dressed, I meander into the living room where my sight snags on a letter Zeb left. Curious, I pick it up and start reading:

> My dearest love,
> You are more beautiful than words can say. This morning was amazing. You're amazing. Unfortunately, work calls me away.

My heart swells with Zeb's words and tears of happiness prick at my eyes. The love letter continues with Zeb telling me how much he loves me and how happy he is. How he loves sharing these intimate moments and how he never wants them to end.

> Don't forget sparring practice this afternoon, and don't eat a big lunch. Remember our bet.
> Love
> Zeb

Ah, my cheeks flush. Yes, I remember the bet.

By the time I finish reading his letter, happy tears stream down my face.

Using an app on my phone, I arrange for Guardian's internal transport system to pick me up and take me to The Facility, where I'll meet with therapists and begin the work managing my trauma.

For the most part, life is slowly getting back to normal. To fill my time while Zeb's away, I volunteer at the local animal shelter, and

I'm looking into working at a veterinarian's office, doing whatever they need me to do.

I've got a few months before applications for next year go out, and I need to secure new recommendations. I'm not giving up on my dream.

Someday, I'll be a vet, but until then, I'm enjoying life.

But there's tension in the air.

I continue to stay in the quarters given to me at HQ, which makes it easy to attend my therapy appointments at the Facility. Our townhouse feels different with Barbi missing. I don't like spending time there when she's not there. Zeb says the Guardians are hard at work, and I feel it. There's tension and energy swirling in the air as everyone works desperately to find Alec and Barbi.

I feel it too, and better understand the worry Carmen and Rosalie felt when I went missing. I understand what Zeb felt when Dean Alder shoved me into the car and left him for dead, but I have faith in the Guardians. They'll find Barbi. Alec too.

Until then, I do the work to manage my trauma, and secretly plan how to beat Zeb at his own game.

He doesn't know it, but there's no way I'm losing our bet. With a smile on my face, I get to work, and when I come home, I know there will be a Guardian in my bed who loves me more than life itself.

And I love him just as much.

We've been through hell, but I look to the future with renewed hope, excited for whatever comes next. With Zeb by my side, whatever that will be is going to be wonderful.

~

Dear Reader,

I hoped you enjoyed reading about Zeb and Kaye.

Are you interested in the woman the men of Bravo team picked up at the airport?

Cara's Protector is another nonstop romantic adventure

and is best read before *Rescuing Barbi*, the final book in the Bravo Team series.

Now is the best time to grab both books and finish out the Bravo Team series.

Grab your copy of *Cara's Protector* and *Rescuing Barbi* today.

Ellie

~

HAVE YOU MET THE MEN OF ALPHA TEAM? THEIR SERIES IS complete and full of all the sexy, swoon-worthy, action and romance, with all the gritty suspense you love.

If you haven't check them out: Guardian HRS Alpha Team series.

Turn the page for a sneak peek of *Cara's Protector*.

Cara's Protector

SNEAK PEEK

For the second time in my life, I walk away from everything I know and venture into the unknown.

After a harrowing escape, and enduring several agonizing hours wedged into a cramped middle seat in the back of economy, I find myself in another unfamiliar place, with no name, and utterly clueless about what comes next.

The moment I disembark the plane, the pandemonium of San Francisco's bustling airport amplifies my already frazzled nerves.

I close my eyes, regulate my breath, and steel myself to face what comes next.

I'm here.

I'm alive.

That's all that matters.

It's time to start life number three—maybe this time, I really will disappear from those who want me dead. I scan the crowd, looking for my newest protector.

The airport teems with the hustle and bustle of hundreds of lives, if not thousands. People dart around me in all directions. Public announcements blare over the public address system, people shout, kids wail, tired parents attempt to navigate the chaos without losing a bag, a child, or a spouse. Occasionally, a runner sprints by frantic to make their flight. Harried gate agents strive to keep the crowd in check while placating disgruntled passengers with unwavering smiles.

The sheer energy of the place is overwhelming. My constant companion, anxiety, spikes my heart rate, tightens my chest, and turns my palms into a sweaty mess.

After the Witness Protection Program failed to safeguard my new identity, another organization took over my protection. Although I'm not sure what to think about the Guardian Hostage Rescue Specialists, they're the ones who stepped up to protect me. It's a daunting name, but I'm neither a hostage, nor do I need rescuing. What I require is protection from men who want me dead.

One man in particular: Artemus Gonzales, a wealthy Nicaraguan businessman involved in human trafficking.

I'd ask if these people are qualified, but my last handler gave me specific instructions in case things went south. With his dying breath, he gave me a number and instructed me to call Guardian HRS .

Which I did.

Chase.

I look for a man holding a sign at the gate with the name Chase written on it. Not at baggage claim. The voice on the end of the line was clear about that. My personal protection specialist will meet me at my gate and take it from there. I scan the crowd, seeking the stranger whose sole job is to keep me alive until I testify.

What happens after that?

Does the FBI's protection of its witnesses end after they put away the bad guys? Do I get to return to my old life? Do I continue in limbo with a fake name and fake life?

A multitude of people throng the gate area, preparing to board the next flight. I think that's going to be a problem until I glimpse an opening in the crowd. Not quite open, but filled by two formidable, intimidating men. Their military bearing is unmistakable and people unconsciously create an empty zone around the men.

To my surprise, one of them holds up a placard with CHASE scribbled over it.

I approach cautiously. No one should know that name except for the man sent to protect me. There aren't supposed to be two men.

What do I do?

I take a deep breath and moved forward, attempting to project as much confidence as possible, even though my heart pounds and my palms slick with sweat. The men sense my unease, telling me I'm horrible at feigning confidence when I'm anxious. One of them steps forward with a reassuring smile on his face.

"Name's Rafe. This is Hayes." The man has a gruff but friendly voice. "We have a third, Alec, scouting the crowd."

"Um, where's Chase?" This isn't what was supposed to happen, but I'm stuck now.

"Do you have a laptop? Cellphone? Any electronics in that bag?" The man does not answer me. Instead, he points to my purse.

I nod.

"If you could hand them to Hayes, please?" The command in his voice compels me to surrender my belongings without questioning why.

"An accident delayed your Protector. Guardian HRS asked us to provide security and take you to your Protector."

I exhale a sigh, relieved that I'm in the right place, even through I'm not with the right men. "How do I know you're—"

"Who we say we are?" Rafe cocks an eyebrow.

"Yes."

"You shouldn't." He reaches into his pants pocket and pulls out a phone. "Do you remember the hotline number you called?"

"I do." I'll never forget it.

"Call it now. Confirm they cleared Bravo team to escort you to Chase." He hands me his phone while the man beside him—Hayes, I think—holds my purse and scans the crowd.

Quickly, I dial the number. A woman picks up on the other end.

"Hello, this is..."

"I'll stop you there. No names, please. From the phone you're using, I assume you're with Rafe."

"Um..."

"Your Protector is stuck behind a wreck. Bravo was sent to fill the gap and take you to him. There should be two other men there; Hayes and Alec. A fourth is the driver and will pick you up at the curb. His name is Zeb."

Stunned by how smooth the person on the other line is, I stare at the phone, then glance up at Rafe. Everything he said matches up, but I need more reassurance. There's one name Rafe didn't mention.

"What's the name of your driver?" I grip the phone and hold my breath.

"She's a smart one." Hayes grins and holds my purse in front of his chest.

"Agreed." Rafe turns toward me. "Zeb is the fourth in our party. Smart checking that out." He extends his hand, requesting his phone back.

"Now what?"

"Do you have luggage to claim?" Hayes asks.

"Hank said no luggage. Nothing they could track."

"Excellent. And your electronics are in your purse?" Hayes continues to interrogate me.

"Yes."

"That's a beautiful watch. May I see it, please?"

An odd request. I surrender my watch and furrow my brow as Hayes takes a closer look. "It was my grandmother's. It's nothing special and barely keeps time. It has to be manually wound every day."

"No electronics." He hands it to Rafe, who completes a similar inspection before handing me back the watch. "Completely analogue."

"If you'll follow me." Rafe signals for me to accompany him and I step in beside him. Hayes stands a little behind us, still holding my purse.

When we arrive at an intersection of terminals, Rafe halts in front of one of those exorbitant boutique shops that charge an arm and a leg, as well as your firstborn for their wares. The clothing is aesthetically pleasing, but not my style.

"This looks good." Rafe glances at me. "Forgive me for asking, but what size do you wear?"

"Excuse me?"

"What size?" He gestures to the store.

"Um, I don't think we have time to shop, and I certainly can't afford that."

"We have the time. Chase is still stuck. Furthermore, this is on Guardian HRS's tab." Rafe crosses his arms over his muscular chest and stares me down.

"What Rafe's means to say, and is totally blowing," Hayes interjects, "is everything you're wearing needs to go."

"Go?"

"Correct."

"Why?"

"Because we don't know how your identity was compromised. Everything you brought with you stays here."

"What do you mean by stays here?"

"Did I stutter?" Hayes gives me a stern look, and takes a step back when I reach for my bag.

"I'm not leaving my things here."

"This is nonnegotiable." Rafe jumps in, trying to soothe me. "It's for your protection."

"Everything?" I glance at my grandmother's watch. It's the only thing I have left of my real life.

"The watch can stay. We're worried about trackers and bugs. We don't have time for an exhaustive search of your things. Anything you need will be provided and anything identifying the woman who walked off that plane will be destroyed. Your new life started the moment we met. Now, we have time to buy a change of clothes, but we don't have time to argue about it."

"Fine, but not here." I scan the row of shops. "Over there. That store."

One of those general all-purpose stores, it sells everything from newspapers, to bottled water, to San Francisco themed apparel.

"That one? Are you sure?" Rafe looks at me like I've gone crazy.

"Positive." I take back a tiny modicum of control and march toward the store. Rafe and Hayes trail behind me.

I continue to scan the crowd, but so far, I haven't made out the third man.

It takes all of three minutes to find a matching hoodie, tee-shirt, and leggings. I glance at my Coach purse I adore and how Hayes clutches it possessively. I hastily grab a cheap purse, lip balm, and other necessities. I walk out with a traveller's dream kit of comfy clothes, travelling essentials, two books, a neck pillow, new purse, and snacks for the road. Rafe covers the expenses, and together with Hayes, they escort me to a public restroom.

"Not that it needs saying, but put everything you're wearing back in the bag after you change. We'll take care of it from there."

I eye my Coach bag with longing, but I've been through too much to resist their efforts to protect me. I could object, but that's not my nature. Instead, I head into the women's bathroom, switch outfits, check my appearance in the mirror, and brace myself for whatever comes next.

Upon exiting the restroom, Hayes no longer holds my belongings.

"Where's my..." I don't complete my sentence, since they were clear about not leaving the airport with anything I had on, or carried into it.

My anxiety intensifies, and I've never felt more lost and adrift.

As we thread our way through the throngs of people, Rafe and Hayes shield me from the crowd, but that uneasy, panicky sensation grows.

I loathe crowds. Crowds hide threats. Anything can happen inside a crowd.

My breaths turn progressively shorter and shallower as we board a packed tram. I must appear confused because Rafe leans in and whispers into my ear.

"We're shifting to another terminal and meeting our driver at arrivals, in case your flight was tracked."

I nod shakily and clutch the metal pole in front of me as the tram follows its endless loop of the busy airport. We disembark three stops later and head toward the exit. It's peak travel time, and I don't know whether it's fear, apprehension, or both, but there are more people, more noise, and just more of everything.

Rafe moves at a steady clip and it's a struggle to keep up with him. With each step, the crowd seems to push back harder than before. Fear takes over, and panic rises within me.

"Take deep breaths." Hayes grasps my elbow and pulls me close. "We're almost there."

But I can't take deep breaths. It's as if my body has forgotten how to breathe.

"What's wrong?" Rafe looks at me.

"Panic attack." Hayes tugs me to his side, doing what he can to shield me from the throngs of people all around us.

"Miss, we're almost there." Rafe steps closer, forming an impenetrable wall around me as the faces in the crowd blur into a mass of hostile eyes and cruel intentions. The air crackles with tension and a desperate urge to run fills me with dread.

About to break free of my guardians, Hayes' grip on my arm tightens. "Almost there." He tries to inject confidence into his tone, but all I hear is a droning hum. "Step up the pace."

Rafe's pace quickens, and I scurry to keep up. They keep me close as we exit the airport, where there's a vehicle waiting for us at the curb. On high alert, they scan the area as I slide into the middle of the back seat. That's when I finally see the third man. I think Rafe said his name was Alec.

The men climb in and the driver, Zeb, eases us into the flow of airport traffic.

"En route." Zeb's comment isn't for me, or the others, but to someone on the phone.

"You notice anything out of the ordinary..." The voice on the other end sounds strained.

"Tom, this ain't my first fucking rodeo." Zeb's irritation shows in his abrupt response. "I know what to do. Your job is to take care of any kinks along the way. How far out are we from Chase?"

"He's past the traffic accident and making good time. I've

located a place for you to make the exchange." Tom replies, rebuffed by Zeb, who looks at me through the rearview mirror.

"Nice to meet you, Miss…" He waits for me to supply a name, but I don't know what new name I'll take. Safe in the car, the weight of my circumstances settles on my shoulders. This is not how my life was supposed to go.

It may be rude, but I'm tired and my nerves are fried from the events which led me here. The driver appears to understand, because he doesn't press me for an answer.

The rush of traffic outside the car window streams by as we transition from city streets to the freeway.

Nearly twenty minutes later, Zeb breaks the silence. His view shifts between his side mirror and the rearview mirror.

"Tan sedan." He elbows the man beside him, Alec, getting his attention. "Five cars back. It's made our last four turns."

"How long?" Alec uses the passenger side mirror to check out the suspicious car.

"Been a few minutes," Zeb says.

"Agree. Looks suspicious."

A knot of fear bunches in my gut. A tail? How did Artemus Gonzales' men find me? Hank Stafford's last words ring through my head. *There's a leak.* With his lifeblood bleeding out while I held him in my arms, my former handler and protector, gave me the number to a Guardian HRS hotline.

Artemus Gonzales is a filthy rich, middle-aged political power monger in Nicaragua. He's more than a wealthy businessman. He's connected to powerful men, like the President and the Minister of the Interior of Nicaragua. He's also heavily vested in the cartels, but I didn't think he had the resources to track me down this quickly.

How did he do it?

"Hold on." The driver calls out a warning.

The others brace as we veer off the freeway. Sandwiched between Rafe and Hayes, I barely move. Zeb takes an offramp, slamming me against Rafe as we zoom around the cloverleaf at speeds far over the posted speed limit.

We take the first offramp, pass under the freeway, and take the next on-ramp heading north, directly opposite the direction of our previous travel. I think we're headed back the way we came, but Zeb continues to the next offramp, and then the next. We take all four offramps at high speed and wind up back on the freeway, headed along our previous direction of travel.

"Did they follow?" Zeb scans the rearview mirror.

"Don't see them." Alec stares at the passenger mirror, looking back.

"If they're in front of us, that's where they'll stay. Meanwhile, might I suggest changing our current rendezvous with Chase?" Zeb calls whoever he was speaking to earlier and reports what happened.

I blow out a breath and close my eyes. The rapid beating of my heart slows with yet another narrow escape. I wish I could say I was getting accustomed to living life in constant fear, but there's no getting used to this.

After a few miles, we take another offramp and arrive at a small, unassuming hotel off the beaten path.

We pull around to the side and park next to a tricked out Jeep with a lift, a wench on the bumper, and a carrier strapped to the top. A mountain of a man, easily over six and a half feet tall, climbs out of the vehicle. With broad shoulders, tree trunk legs, wavy brown hair, and a face chiseled out of granite, the man is both beautifully stunning and uniquely terrifying.

The black tee-shirt he wears struggles to contain all his muscles, and well-worn blue jeans draw my eyes where they shouldn't go. His black, steel-toed boots scream *Don't mess with me*, and he looks mean enough to kick ass without breaking a sweat. He surveys the deserted parking lot before heading toward our vehicle.

"You have her?" His deep, modulated voice sends chills down my spine.

"We do." Zeb doesn't exit the vehicle.

"Thanks for the assist." He opens the door to the backseat. Rafe climbs out, and the man extends his hand, speaking quietly to me. "It's nice to meet you. Name's Chase, Chase Lawson. If you'll come with me, we can get going."

His touch sears my skin, sending an electrical charge zinging through my body. Every cell in my body screams to run away, yet I find myself inexplicably drawn to this man. He's intimidating and fierce, but dangerous to me for reasons that have nothing to do with protecting me.

THE ADVENTURE CONTINUES...

Intrigued? Now that you know a little more about Cara, the woman Bravo Team picked up at the airport, grab your copy of this thrilling romantic suspense today.

Another nonstop romantic adventure, Cara's Protector is best read before Rescuing Barbi, the final book in the Bravo Team series.

Until next time...

Ellie

ELLZ BELLZ

ELLIE'S FACEBOOK READER GROUP

If you are interested in joining the ELLZ BELLZ, Ellie's Facebook reader group, we'd love to have you.

Join Ellie's ELLZ BELLZ.
The ELLZ BELLZ Facebook Reader Group

Sign up for Ellie's Newsletter.
Elliemasters.com/newslettersignup

Cara's Protector

Rescuing Barbi

Military Romance

Guardian Personal Protection Specialists

Sybil's Protector

Lyra's Protector

The One I Want Series

(Small Town, Military Heroes)

By Jet & Ellie Masters

EACH BOOK IN THIS SERIES CAN BE READ AS A STANDALONE AND IS ABOUT A DIFFERENT COUPLE WITH AN HEA.

Saving Abby

Saving Ariel

Saving Brie

Saving Cate

Saving Dani

Saving Jen

Rockstar Romance

The Angel Fire Rock Romance Series

EACH BOOK IN THIS SERIES CAN BE READ AS A STANDALONE AND IS ABOUT A DIFFERENT COUPLE WITH AN HEA. IT IS RECOMMENDED THEY ARE READ IN ORDER.

Ashes to New (prequel)

Heart's Insanity (book 1)

Heart's Desire (book 2)

Heart's Collide (book 3)

Hearts Divided (book 4)

Hearts Entwined (book5)

Forest's FALL (book 6)

Hearts The Last Beat (book7)

Contemporary Romance

Firestorm

(Kristy Bromberg's Everyday Heroes World)

Billionaire Romance
Billionaire Boys Club

Hawke

Richard

Brody

Contemporary Romance

Cocky Captain

(Vi Keeland & Penelope Ward's Cocky Hero World)

Romantic Suspense

Each book is a standalone novel.

The Starling

~AND~

Science Fiction

Ellie Masters writing as L.A. Warren

Vendel Rising: a Science Fiction Serialized Novel

About the Author

Ellie Masters is a USA Today Bestselling author and Amazon Top 15 Author who writes Angsty, Steamy, Heart-Stopping, Pulse-Pounding, Can't-Stop-Reading Romantic Suspense. In addition, she's a wife, military mom, doctor, and retired Colonel. She writes romantic suspense filled with all your sexy, swoon-worthy alpha men. Her writing will tug at your heartstrings and leave your heart racing.

Born in the South, raised under the Hawaiian sun, Ellie has traveled the globe while in service to her country. The love of her life, her amazing husband, is her number one fan and biggest supporter. And yes! He's read every word she's written.

She has lived all over the United States—east, west, north, south and central—but grew up under the Hawaiian sun. She's also been privileged to have lived overseas, experiencing other cultures and making lifelong friends.

Now, Ellie is proud to call herself a Southern transplant, learning to say y'all and "bless her heart" with the best of them.

Ellie's favorite way to spend an evening is curled up on a couch, laptop in place, watching a fire, drinking a good wine, and bringing forth all the characters from her mind to the page and hopefully into the hearts of her readers.

FOR MORE INFORMATION
elliemasters.com

facebook.com/elliemastersromance

x.com/Ellie__Masters

instagram.com/ellie_masters

bookbub.com/authors/ellie-masters

goodreads.com/Ellie_Masters

Connect with Ellie Masters

Website:
elliemasters.com
Amazon Author Page:
elliemasters.com/amazon
Facebook:
elliemasters.com/Facebook
Goodreads:
elliemasters.com/Goodreads
Instagram:
elliemasters.com/Instagram

Final Thoughts

I hope you enjoyed this book as much as I enjoyed writing it. If you enjoyed reading this story, please consider leaving a review on Amazon and Goodreads, and please let other people know. A sentence is all it takes. Friend recommendations are the strongest catalyst for readers' purchase decisions! And I'd love to be able to continue bringing the characters and stories from My-Mind-to-the-Page.

Second, call or e-mail a friend and tell them about this book. If you really want them to read it, gift it to them. If you prefer digital friends, please use the "Recommend" feature of Goodreads to spread the word.

Or visit my blog https://elliemasters.com, where you can find out more about my writing process and personal life.

Come visit The EDGE: Dark Discussions where we'll have a chance to talk about my works, their creation, and maybe what the future has in store for my writing.

Facebook Reader Group: Ellz Bellz

Thank you so much for your support!

Love,

Ellie

Dedication

This book is dedicated to you, my reader. Thank you for spending a few hours of your time with me. I wouldn't be able to write without you to cheer me on. Your wonderful words, your support, and your willingness to join me on this journey is a gift beyond measure.

Whether this is the first book of mine you've read, or if you've been with me since the very beginning, thank you for believing in me as I bring these characters 'from my mind to the page and into your hearts.'

Love,
Ellie

THE END

www.ingramcontent.com/pod-product-compliance
Lightning Source LLC
Chambersburg PA
CBHW021239190726
48289CB00005B/1399